The wizard ~~....... ...., ...~~
and bone...

They had come for him, the redclad soldiers, and they had died. They had fallen to the sting of his daggers and the fire he cast from the demon rings that burnt his own flesh with their power. He had thought that the burns might be healed, that he might live to treat them.

That was before the sword bit into his lungs.

Now he waited, his long red hair lank with sweat, his skin frost-pale, his breath coming in gasps. Waited for the next onslaught.

He heard a sound behind him, and turned quickly. The captain of his household guard, cradling a squirming bundle, was running towards him.

"My Lord Zancharthus," he panted as he drew near, "I have your son."

"Leave Khymir," the wizard said thickly. "Take him south. Raise him to avenge me..." He pointed to the rings, which had fallen from his fingers. "Take them with you. Give them to him when he reaches manhood... only he can use them..."

Distant footsteps echoed through the door.

"Go!" Zancharthus cried.

ZORACHUS

MARK E. ROGERS

ACE FANTASY BOOKS
NEW YORK

To Kate, who lived through it all.

This book is an Ace Fantasy
original edition, and has never
been previously published.

ZORACHUS

An Ace Fantasy Book/published by arrangement with
the author

PRINTING HISTORY
Ace Fantasy edition/December 1986

ISBN: 0-441-95971-7

Ace Fantasy Books are published by The Berkley Publishing Group,
200 Madison Avenue, New York, New York 10016.
PRINTED IN THE UNITED STATES OF AMERICA

"That evil is deadliest which contains most share of good."
—Sibi Gayaan Bayazid
City of the Damned
Book IV, Chapter 4

prologue

GRIPPING THE WOUND in his side, bright scarlet blood leaking through his scorched fingers, the wizard paused beside the great stone seat at the head of the banquet table. His long red hair was lank with sweat, his skin frost-pale; his breath came in gasps. But as he turned to face his foes, he bared his teeth in a fierce grin, and his eyes glinted defiance.

Soldiers of the Cohort Ravener, twenty men in horned helms and red-lacquered scale-mail, were coming towards him, their curved two-handed swords still dripping with the blood of his guards and servants. Their unhurried advance bespoke their confidence; they were certain he could not withstand their numbers, that he had used up too much power.

"We're going to give Ordog your head, high priest!" one cried.

The wizard coughed out a gout of blood and laughed. "Maybe," he answered. "But haven't you wondered . . . why he didn't come for it himself?"

Halting and ragged as his voice was, it still carried enough menace to stop them in their tracks. More than one sword trembled.

His grin widened.

"At him!" a redclad shouted, and they charged, some rushing along the sides of the table, others leaping onto the top, scale-mail rattling, booted feet clattering on marble and wood.

The wizard laughed again, bounded up on the table and, like a black dragon unfolding its pinions, swept his cloak open. In a blaze of burnished metal, a swarm of tiny knives hissed from the cape's lining, each seeking a different target —some shooting straight at the foremost redclads, the rest swerving to strike the ones behind, all driving home with tremendous force, punching through armor. Screams rang out; dead and dying men collapsed on the tabletop, dropping on either side of the long trestle.

Not a single redclad remained on his feet.

Coughing, the wizard crumpled to his knees. He knew

1

more would be coming; he would have to use the demon-rings again. He looked at his soot-crusted fingers. The rings had seared them cruelly; he had switched them from finger to finger, but had discharged so many blasts that all the digits were burned. When he had removed the rings, he had thought the burns might be healed, that he might live to treat them. That was before the sword bit into his lungs.

He took the rings out once more and put them on, his scorched nerves sending angry charges of agony into his brain. But he was long-schooled in the discipline of ignoring pain; gritting his teeth, he slowly rose.

A hail of footbeats echoed through the door. He spat, blew sweat and blood from his mustache. Tightening his concentration, he readied himself to meet the next onslaught.

The footbeats grew louder and a second group of redclads poured into the hall, a scale-mailed wave rushing toward the table.

He extended his hands. The rings, each set with a single white gem, glittered wickedly.

A redclad sprang for the tabletop. Two bolts of blue-white lightning, crackling from the ring-jewels, converged in him while he was still in midair; as if struck by a giant hammer, he hurtled backwards head over heels, trailing steam and flying mail-scales, a huge hole gaping in his chest.

The others rushed along the table to left and right; the wizard dealt bolts one at a time, jolting them off their feet with fists of white-hot energy, vapor mushrooming from their riven bodies.

But with each discharge the rings grew hotter; with every blast a puff of blue smoke burst from under the circlets. The stench of charred flesh assailed the wizard's nostrils. He struggled ferociously to hold the pain at bay, to maintain his concentration . . .

Through bleared eyes he saw the remaining redclads waver. A few ran. For a moment it looked as though they all would.

But the moment passed; most of them rallied. He took a grim satisfaction in their courage—the Cohort was his handiwork. He had recruited well.

Firebolts took the brave ones. None got within five yards of him. And as the last struck the floor, the wizard's ring fingers dropped away, bones burned through. The rings rolled from the table.

Trembling, he climbed down to retrieve them. But he heard a door shut, and turned quickly. The captain of his household guard, cradling a squirming bundle, was running towards him, having entered through one of the secret passages that opened on the banquet hall.

"My Lord Zancharthus," he panted as he drew near, "I have your son."

Zancharthus opened his mouth to reply, and began coughing furiously. It was a long time before he spat out enough blood to speak.

"Leave Khymir," he said thickly. "Take him south. Raise him to avenge me . . . you'll be well rewarded. . . ." He pointed to the rings. "Take them with you. Give them to him when he reaches manhood . . . only he can use them. . . ."

Laying the child down, the captain went for the rings. He had no difficulty handling them; only the inner surfaces had been heated by the blasts. Placing the rings in a pouch hanging from his neck, he took up Zancharthus's son again.

More footbeats echoed through the door. Distant now, but approaching rapidly.

"Go!" Zancharthus said.

The captain bore the child to a second secret panel and disappeared.

Zancharthus considered his choices. He was determined to drag down with him as many of his enemies as he could. But not merely for revenge; the more redclads that were occupied with him, the fewer there would be to intercept the captain and his precious burden.

How to deal with them? The rings were gone. The Influences had shifted against him denying him many spells, and he had exhausted most of his native power—but not all.

Assuming a sorcerous stance, he muttered a formula. Half the redclads killed by the cloak-knives began to stir, jerking as the blades within worked their way outward. Emerging swiftly, the knives rose into the air, drawing into a cluster and hanging suspended, pointing toward the door, awaiting a mental command.

The third group of redclads appeared in the doorway. Wiser than the others, they had brought crossbows.

Zancharthus sent five blades streaking forward. Men clutched at faces or chests, crossbows dropping to the floor; the front rank crumpled.

The other redclads retreated shouting, several loosing

quarrels even as they disappeared. Steel points rammed into Zancharthus's left arm and right thigh. He howled and staggered, and as he fought for balance two redclads leaped back into view and took aim. He resumed his stance an instant before they loosed; knives pierced them, but their quarrels were already humming towards him. One sliced his cheek, whipping his head to one side. The second caught him full in the stomach, a numbing impact, and he felt his tunic and cloak tug at his shoulders as the bolt, passing clean through his body, ripped out of his back, rattling loudly over the floor behind him. Deadening coldness spread from his midsection down into his thighs, and his legs began to buckle; his whole body cried out for surrender.

But that was unthinkable. He forced himself instead to think of what they had done to his wife, his daughters, what they would do to his son if they caught him. . . .

"Come on!" he cried, straightening to his full height. "I'm not done yet!"

Six redclads rose to the challenge, fanning out as they rushed in. His last knives felled three before the survivors sent their quarrels thumping home.

He toppled.

The redclads watched him quiver, then become still. "It's over!" they bayed triumphantly.

Whooping, those outside rushed into the hall, congratulating and slapping them on the back. Their company would be fabulously rewarded; Thagranichus Ordog, their new master and Zancharthus's successor as High Priest of Tchernobog, had made his name through lavish gifts. Mother Khymir, the richest city in the world, would be at their feet. They had slain the mighty Mancdaman Zancharthus.

Or so they thought.

With a screech of protruding quarrel points against marble, he twisted, then raised himself from the floor; the redclads watched awestruck as he yanked two bolts from his body.

"What's the matter?" he asked hoarsely. "Bite off more than you can chew?"

With that they recovered their wits, and the arbalests still loaded came up; bowstring after bowstring twanged. With each impact, Zancharthus hurtled backwards, finally crashing against the wall, nailed to the wooden panels, head sagging forward on his chest.

The redclads moved nearer, watching him warily, ready to re-prime their crossbows at the least sign of life. But there was not even a hint of breath. At length they heaved laughter and grinned at each other, relaxing.

"Now," one said, "that present for Ordog."

Handing his arbalest to another man, he drew out his shortsword and strode forward. Cocking the blade back, he jerked Zancharthus's head up by the hair, and—

Loosed a tremendous shriek. Zancharthus's eyes were wide open, furiously alive, and he was even then rocking forward from the wall, wrenching out the quarrels that pinned him, hands still gripping the bolts he had pulled from his own flesh; the wizard's arms flailed round and the quarrels punched through the redclad's helmet on either side. Grimacing, the man dropped the shortsword and reached up at the shafts, just touching them; then his hands fell limply to his sides, and a final breath hissed through his clenched teeth.

Zancharthus knocked him over with a contemptuous kick.

The rest gaped at the bolt-riddled figure rearing up over their comrade's body; muttering curses and prayers, they backed away in dread. Zancharthus shambled after them, tugging with both hands at a bolt embedded in his chest.

"Hold your ground!" the redclad commander bawled to his men, barely mastering himself. "Prime your bows!"

They continued to retreat.

"Hold, damn you! Prime and shoot!"

They swore and shook their heads. Hurling his bow aside, drawing his sword, the commander had to slash one down before they obeyed.

Zancharthus drew closer, still tugging on the bolt. It came free with a splash of blood; he brandished it like a dagger.

Quarrels slid into grooves and the redclads took aim. Zancharthus kept coming, straight towards the gleaming points, blood-shiny free hand clawing the air.

"Kill him!" the commander cried.

The bows twanged again. Three whistling flights pounded into Zancharthus, knocked him right, then left, then stretched him out beside the table, dead.

But the redclads took no chances this time. Keeping their distance, they emptied every quarrel they had into his body. Only then did they dare take his head.

chapter

1

As was his privilege, the young redbeard rose from the carved granite seat known as the Chopping Block, scratched his head, stretched, and began to pace, speaking all the while. Behind their great stone table, the white-robed Masters listened closely, struggling to remind themselves that they were his judges, not his students.

Back and forth he strode, moving with a grace that belied his size. Well over six feet tall, he was bearlike in build, broad-shouldered, broad-hipped, massive and powerful, clad all in grey. His face was broad, with blue-grey eyes under heavy brows, and there was a small scar on his left cheek where an arrow, nearly spent, had struck him and lodged in bone. His hair was long, of a slightly browner red than his beard; it gleamed richly in the clear desert sunlight pouring in through the window.

His name was Mancdaman Zorachus. Thirty-three years old and already a Sharajnaghi Adept of the Sixth Level, he was in the process of trying for the Seventh. The first test, the Trial of the Intellect, was going well; he had shown a deep knowledge of Sharajnaghi doctrine, and for his original contribution had given a proof of the dependence of free will on God's existence. Now he was defending that proof. The Masters pressed him hard, but he demolished their counterarguments one after another.

Finally, there came a lull in the debate. White-bearded Ghaznavi looked round at the other Masters.

"Here we are," he said, "the assembled Seventh-Level Adepts of the Comahi Irakhoum, and this upstart's stopped us cold. Do any of you have any more questions for him?"

"Let's have the proof again," said *Sibi* Faschim. He had asked Zorachus to repeat it twice before, and had led the attack with great ferocity and skill. Unlike his colleagues, who were brown-skinned Kadjafim, he was a black from the southern kingdom of Numalia, the so-called "Land of Philosophers." Numalians were known for their hard-nosed rationalism, and he was no exception; he was widely thought to be the sharpest logician in the Order.

Zorachus nodded. He did not mind Faschim's request; in spite of the onslaughts he had endured he felt quite fresh.

"Free will," he began, still pacing, "is the power to act and think in accordance with the truth or to ignore it. It is therefore dependent on the ability of the mind to perceive truth—in short, upon reason.

"Now, reason is not a reflex. A rational conclusion is not a spasm triggered by irrational causes, for rationality cannot be an extension of irrationality. Hence, the source from which human minds come must itself be rational, must itself be a mind; we must accept the notion that minds have their origin, directly or indirectly, in God. Since reason is dependent on God, and free will is dependent on reason, free will is dependent on God."

Faschim pondered this awhile; then he leaned forward, stabbed the air with his hand (a gesture that always preceded his arguments) and said: "Another problem has occurred to me. I'm not sure the dependence of free will on reason has been shown. Consider this: A man from a heathen land believes he has a moral responsibility to sacrifice his firstborn child to a certain god. Now as we would all agree, he is mistaken in this. However, if he chooses to ignore what he considers to be the truth, and not sacrifice his child, he is demonstrating free will. But he never had the opportunity to act freely in accordance with the truth, for he had no knowledge of it; the action of his will was not dependent on rationality."

Zorachus shook his head. "I disagree," he replied. "For rationality is not limited to the perception of mortal truth. A heathen who thinks he has an obligation to sacrifice his firstborn is certainly mistaken. But if, because he believes that proposition, he then sacrifices his child, he is being rational; and he is ignoring what he sees as the truth if he doesn't. It takes a certain amount of understanding for a man to realize that a mortal precept applies in each individual case; he has reached his conclusion through a valid, if not a sound, syllogism. It also takes reason for the heathen to realize that the physical action of sacrificing his firstborn constitutes the desired moral action; and conversely, that by not taking the child to the altar and not plunging the knife in, he is not doing sacrifice, and is therefore acting, as he would think, immorally. Thus any action of the will is to some extent dependent on rationality—though it may indeed be rationality of a very elementary sort."

Faschim opened his mouth to speak, began the stabbing gesture—and stopped. "You're quite right of course," he said.

For the first time during the Trial, Zorachus showed his wide foolish grin. Even though he had all his teeth, there were large spaces between them, and the grin always dispelled his characteristic air of sagacity. Stopping in front of the Chopping Block, he folded his arms on his chest.

"Are there any more questions?" Ghaznavi asked again. There were none.

He eyed Zorachus. "Well then. The Council finds no objection to your proof; it appears both sound and orthodox, worthy to be entered into the body of Sharajnaghi doctrine, to be taught and defended. You've passed the First Trial, Zorachus. The Second awaits you."

The Masters rose from the table. But as they began to leave the chamber, their long white robes rustling, Ghaznavi paused, looked back, and said: "That was an extraordinary performance just now."

"Thank you, *Sibi,*" Zorachus replied, no longer grinning, showing his appreciation of the compliment with a slight quick bow of the head. Already he was banishing the distracting joy of victory, putting all thought of the First Trial from his mind. Complete concentration would be needed in the Second—the Trial of Will.

Ghaznavi turned once more and left. After a time, Zorachus followed, keeping well behind the Masters as they passed down the long stone corridor that led to the gymnasium.

Shouts and laughter echoed up ahead. the voices hushed respectfully moments after the Masters entered the gymnasium, but then the din resumed, louder than before.

Zorachus went in. The great chamber was well lit; a huge crystalline oculis in the ceiling admitted the sun, and the walls were painted a bright, reflective white. Dozens of greyclad lower-level adepts were gathered around the sparring-pit, some standing, others sitting on benches. The Masters were off to one side, conferring; they too were shouting, trying to hear each other in the overall racket. Zorachus caught Ghaznavi's leathery old bellow quite clearly.

Some of the greyclads spotted Zorachus as he headed for his armoring chamber, and a cheer of encouragement went up from the group. Feeling a mixture of embarrassment and elation, as well a some slight annoyance that his concentration was being disturbed, he entered the chamber and shut the door.

A small devotional bar lay to the right, beneath a plaque blazoned with the white flame that was the chief Sharajnaghi symbol of God. Zorachus knelt at the bar, bowing his head. He prayed for half an hour.

Finishing, he removed his oxhide sandals and rose, stripping down to his breechclout. After donning a leather jerkin and trews, he slipped into a knee-length quilted gambeson with elbow-length sleeves. A steel byrny went over the padding, mail of the finest riveted mesh, the strongest that the best Sharajnaghi smiths could contrive. He put on heelless knee-high boots studded with iron and plates of boiled leather, then girt his swordbelt about him and drew the shortsword from its sharkskin scabbard to inspect the blade. Its edges and point had been completely ground off. He turned the weapon hilt-floorward and sprang its pommel-catch. The hilt was long and hollow and contained three feet of chain, fine-linked but strong. One end of the chain was attached to the sword's crescent guard, the other to the pommel. In a typical Sharajnaghi shortsword the pommel would have been made of studded iron, but this was leather-covered cork. When he sprang the catch, the pommel dropped floorward, swinging pendulum-like at the end of its clinking tether. Zorachus smiled. He had never lost his keen appreciation of the Sharajnaghi hidden mace.

Satisfied that the weapon was ready, he carefully put the chain back in the hilt, fixed the pommel once more, and resheathed the blade. From a table he took up his helmet. It was spired, but otherwise without ornament; a camail fringed it, and a wire cage long enough to protect both face and throat was attached to the rim in front. The cage would have been little use in real combat; Zorachus usually fought without it, finding it a distraction. But it was adequate against blunted edges and points, and its use was mandatory in trials. He donned the helm, fastened the chin straps, and put steel vambraces on his forearms. Slipping his hands into heavy, padded gloves, he made one last genuflection before the white flame and went back out into the gymnasium.

Another cheer, this time thunderous, greeted him as he made for the pit. Perhaps a hundred more greyclads had joined the crowd, most of whom had no chance of getting close enough to the pit to see the trial. But this was a major event; no one under the age of forty had ever before tried for the Seventh Level, and it was considered a tremendous privilege merely to be close to history in the making.

The crowd parted to let Zorachus through; even so, he took many friendly buffets before descending the steps.

Reaching the bottom, he went to the center of the pit. The sparring mats were gone now. The hard-packed earth floor was bare. A black doorway yawned in each of the pit's four walls.

He looked up at the tier on which the Masters were assembled. Before it, at the edge of the pit, was a small platform on which stood *Sibi* Dauud, a tall, thin Master with close-cropped white hair and a wispy grey beard. His eyes met Zorachus's, and he raised his hands. The spectators quieted, and in a great voice he cried:

"'The body is a rebellious machine, the most persistent opponent of the will. Yet over it the will must have sovereignty, and the means by which this is achieved shall be the martial arts; a stern regimen shall reduce the flesh to the slavery which is its proper place. And only those who can prove their supremacy in these arts shall be admitted to the Seventh Level.' So wrote *Sibi* Washallah Irakhoum. Are you prepared to prove, Mancdaman Zorachus, that your body is a mere extension of your mind?"

"I am," Zorachus replied.

"May God grant you show your true mettle," Dauud said lowering his hands. He stepped down from the platform; the greyclads opened a path for him and he strode to the stairs, descending into the pit. It was his task to oversee the trial, to judge the deadliness of the blows dealt, and to stop the combat at the first sign of serious injury. He halted several yards from Zorachus. Ten long seconds passed.

"Begin!" he shouted.

Zorachus heard the door behind him open and a roll of footbeats. He wheeled and drew. His opponent, bearing a long padded club, was clad, like him, in full Sharajnaghi armor; he was also much taller than Zorachus, though less powerfully built.

He closed, club arcing down at Zorachus's helmet, a blur of speed. Zorachus dodged and jabbed his sword into the man's mailed side. The armor withstood the blunted point, but the sheer force of the thrust hurled the fellow clean off his feet and he landed with a grunt. There was no need for a ruling from Dauud. The victim crawled away on hands and knees.

He had almost reached the door he was making for when a second attacker, carrying a shield and a padded axe, leaped out, bounding over him. The newcomer was on Zorachus in an instant, feinting with his shield, then hacking at Zorachus's neck. Zorachus ducked and the axe looped down at his legs. He jumped over the blow and in midair launched a thrust at his opponent's face. The shield shot upwards to block the stab—too late. Face cage deeply dented, the man rocked backwards to the ground.

Immediately, a third man rushed in from the right brandishing an oaken, two-handed sword. Zorachus disarmed him with a lightning kick, and lunged. The other man leaped back and lashed out with a kick of his own, and Zorachus's sword flew from his hand. The combatants stared at each other for a breathless moment, then dashed for the longsword. Zorachus's opponent reached it first, but Zorachus tackled him in the next instant and once again the sword flew through the air. Scrambling free, Zorachus charged after it, his opponent hard behind; but when they were almost to the sword, Zorachus spun and dealt him a savage kick to the head. The man cartwheeled to the ground. Zorachus had the sword a second later, but heard the man gasp "quarter," and paid him no further heed. Retrieving his shortsword, he dropped the two-handed weapon. The rules of the trial forbade him to use two weapons at once, and he preferred stabbing to slashing.

His opponents were under no such constraint, however; the longsword had barely struck the ground when a fourth attacker entered the pit armed with a small padded axe and a cork-headed mace-and-chain. Zorachus stood his ground as the man pelted toward him. The mace head came lashing; Zorachus blocked it with an armored forearm. The chain wrapped around his vambrace, and he yanked his arm back, wrenching the mace truncheon from the man's hand. The axe whirled down; Zorachus parried with his sword and jabbed his steel into the wires warding the fellow's throat. The man staggered, gasped, and wobbled off.

As Zorachus untangled the mace chain from his arm, the

last attacker appeared carrying a shortsword. This one did not rush to the encounter; he moved slowly, cautiously. He was short, and even with the armor it could be seen that he was spare of build. But there was whipcorded sinew in every step he took, and he moved with crisp precision. His face was unrecognizable behind his helmet-cage, but Zorachus knew that stride well: this was Raschid Kestrel, his greatest friend, and reputedly the deadliest fighter among the non-Masters.

The two circled each other warily. Raschid feinted at Zorachus's chest. Zorachus lifted his left arm to block; Raschid jerked his sword back and snapped a kick into Zorachus's shin. Zorachus grunted with pain but did not retreat, and parried a lunge with a powerful sweep of his blade. The block seemed to throw Raschid off balance, and Zorachus succeeded in stabbing his sword arm. Raschid howled and leaped back, switched sword hands, and put his "wounded" arm behind him. Zorachus charged and Raschid, who was equally good with either hand, landed a slash across Zorachus's left bicep. Zorachus did not think it a crippling stroke, but Dauud disagreed; Zorachus put his left arm back.

The fight continued. Zorachus and Raschid leaped over singing strokes, blocked thrusts with scissor kicks, slashed and parried and lunged. Sword clashed on sword, and the pit resounded with the ring of struck metal, with cries and the stamping of feet. Second by second, the fight's fury intensified; swifter and swifter went the pace, and Zorachus felt the blood running like joyous fire in his veins. Like two incredible war machines, he and Raschid pitched back and forth, their blades seeming to leap from place to place without going the distance between. Dauud dodged and circled the opponents, displaying hardly less agility than they, eyes gleaming in admiration of their prowess.

Zorachus parried a swipe at his throat; his blade chipped. He lashed out at Raschid and their swords met with a terrific clang, and Zorachus's broke off at the hilt; out of the corner of his eye, he saw the blade flash as it hurtled through the air. Backpedaling, he reversed his grip on the hilt, tried to spring the latch on the pommel-mace, found it jammed—Raschid had struck the pommel a glancing blow earlier in the fight. And Zorachus had only one hand to work the latch. . . .

Raschid charged after him. Zorachus twisted aside from a glinting thrust, blocked another with his vambrace. Raschid landed a solid kick in Zorachus's midriff, almost doubling him over; coughing, nearly retching, he felt Raschid's sword connect with his leg and went down on one knee. Raschid lunged; Zorachus hurled himself onto his back, avoiding the stab. Raschid tried to hack at Zorachus's good leg, but Zorachus managed to kick the blade aside. In desperation, he hooked the pommel latch behind the edge of his helmet-cage and pulled; the latch opened, even as he rolled aside from another of Raschid's strokes.

He got up on one knee. Raschid bounded at him, shrieking, swordpoint speeding straight at Zorachus's face. Zorachus deflected it with his vambrace at the last instant. The sword rang as it glanced upward, screeched and skidded over the top of Zorachus's helmet. Zorachus flailed the mace, striking Raschid square in the helmet-cage. It bounced off harmlessly, but was a killing blow nonetheless.

Dauud signaled that the trial was over. The spectators, who had remained silent up until that point, erupted into cheers and applause. Realizing he was beaten, Raschid spun several times, "dying" as spectacularly as possible, collapsing at last in a grotesque heap.

Zorachus went over to him. Raschid leaped up and took off his helmet, grinning at his conqueror. Sweat trickled down his swarthy face, dripped from his dark mustache and beard.

"You're mighty proud of yourself, aren't you?" he panted. The words were drowned out by the thunder from the audience, but Zorachus lipread. He nodded jokingly, removed his helm and wiped his brow. His lungs burned, his stomach ached, his heart hammered against his ribs—but his mind floated on the verge of euphoria.

Dauud climbed back up the stairs and went to the platform. He raised his hands once more. The spectators were slower in quieting this time.

"You've passed the Second Trial, Mancdaman Zorachus," he cried. "May God grant you fare as well in the Third and last." Turning, he left with his white-robed peers.

Zorachus went up from the pit and strode towards his armoring chamber through a churning sea of greyclads, each pouring out congratulations. He laughed and smiled, but his thoughts were distant; once again he had thrust the joy of victory from his mind, his triumph in the pit already irrelevant. Entering the chamber, he closed the door and, as the noise outside died, stripped back down to his breechclout, transfixed by the knowledge that the last and ultimate trial was

before him. Terror and agony would engulf him, perhaps even
death; intellect and will would both be pushed to their utmost
limits.

He rested for a time, then prayed beneath the sign of the
flame. Finally, he slipped back into his regular garb and left
the chamber. Out of the gymnasium and through twisting corridors he went, then down a flight of well-worn, torchlit steps.

At the bottom, he entered the crypt where generations of
Sharajnaghi Masters were buried. The air was cool, but not
damp; it seemed oddly fresh, and there was even a hint of
some sweet fragrance.

The Masters had been laid in sealed niches, and beside
each vault stood a statue of the buried man, life-sized,
wrought with tremendous skill. All held burning tapers; stone
faces flickered in the golden light, some grim and ascetic,
others well-fed and robust. There were warrior faces, saintly
faces, countenances that proclaimed "I am a scholar," others
that seemed to say "I am a jester." It was a gloriously varied
company and one that was hard to ignore; Zorachus found his
concentration slipping as he passed through, but somehow that
did not disturb him. He felt presences watching over him,
reassuring him; even as his concentration wavered, his confidence grew.

He came to a second torchlit stair and descended a long
way. Deep beneath the earth, he reached a small door marked
with the sign of the flame.

"Open, please," he said.

An unseen warden swung the door back.

"Thank you, Antascar," Zorachus said, and went through,
striding into darkness.

"Good luck," hissed a voice behind him. It did not sound at
all human—but that was entirely appropriate.

Far in the sunken distance, Zorachus saw a blot of green
luminosity and made toward it down a gentle slope. After
what seemed an eternity, he drew near. The emerald glow
played over a great flat circle surrounded by stone pillars chiseled from the living rock. The radiance seemed to come from
above, but its source was invisible, if indeed there was a
source at all.

The pillars were thirty feet tall and spaced five feet apart.
In each gap stood a hooded figure, a Seventh Level Adept. No
others were present. The Third Trial was no mere athletic
contest to be gaped at by spectators, but a dark and terrible

business. Things often got out of hand. . . .

Zorachus arrived at the ring. The Master before him
stepped aside to let him pass and sang out a few words in an
arcane tongue. Zorachus went a short distance into the circle
and halted; the Masters turned, facing inwards, and two advanced from the side opposite Zorachus, planting themselves
fifty feet away from him, slipping their hoods back. He recognized Ghaznavi and a younger man named Khuroum. Khuroum cried:

"'The intellect and will of each candidate for the Seventh
Level must be great; but they will not avail if they are not in
perfect harmony. Indeed, such harmony is the single most important characteristic of a Master.' So wrote *Sibi* Washallah
Irakhoum. Are you prepared to prove, Mancdaman Zorachus,
that your will and intellect are so united that one is the com-
pletion of the other?"

"I am," Zorachus replied.

"Then let the wizard's duel begin!"

Echoes ran and fled.

Khuroum and Ghaznavi entered Dragon Stances.

Zorachus did likewise—and immediately attacked.

Twin cataracts of bloody light poured from his fists. Snaking and crackling, they sought his opponents.

Just in time, Ghaznavi and Khuroum raised their defensive
shields, force-screens that emanated from their palms; the
cataract-bolts rebounded into the stone. Viewed through the
overlapping barriers, the two Masters writhed like phantoms
in a mirage.

Zorachus conjured his own bucklers, waiting. Ghaznavi
and Khuroum stood rock-still for an agonizingly long time.
Were they hoping he would attack again? Or were they simply
force-letting, draining off repellent energy through their
shields? If they drained enough, they could start in with binding magic, spells and conjurings. But he could play that game
too. . . .

Suddenly dropping their righthand shields, the two
launched a keening barrage of yellow flame-needles, which
shattered on Zorachus's defenses with small scintillant flashes.
The attack intensified swiftly. Shocks began to penetrate,
lancing up through Zorachus's arms. One of his shields dissipated; he poured more power into the other.

Khuroum's strikes stopped. At first, Zorachus thought he
had been unable to maintain that mode of attack.

He realized his mistake when the blue cloud gushed from Khuroum's mouth. Crossing the ring in a heartbeat's space, it hurdled Zorachus's shield and engulfed him.

He kept enough wits to hold his breath, but his concentration broke; his shield blinked from existence and Ghaznavi's flame-needles shrieked in through the cloud. A storm of yellow-green light broke about Zorachus's brow, and his head snapped back as if he had been clubbed.

But the needles had a more terrifying effect. The smoke thickened as they passed through, grew cold, then wet; in seconds he was immersed in a great bubble of water. It conformed to his every move, denying him escape, and through it sang the current of Ghaznavi's strikes, excruciatingly magnified. Zorachus's mind reeled.

But he did not accept defeat.

With a tremendous effort of will, he shut out all distractions, plucking a freezing spell from his memory. Between maintaining his shields and his first strikes, he had done enough force-letting; slipping a trembling hand over his mouth, he articulated the words of the formula.

Just as Ghaznavi launched a new sheaf of flame-needles, the water hardened into a man-shaped azure statue. There was a terrific blast of splintered ice as the needles struck, and Zorachus's prison shattered. Drawing breath once more, he laughed.

After a stunned pause, Ghaznavi resumed his attacks. Zorachus raised a shield against him and turned his attention to Khuroum. The latter had spent much energy maintaining the bubble and was shifting into a Chimera Stance, one shield up.

Zorachus uttered a spell. At once, the floor beneath Khuroum revolved, spinning him round, turning his shield away from Zorachus, exposing his back. Zorachus struck him between the shoulders with a cataract bolt, and Khuroum sailed forward, landing in a heap.

Zorachus turned to Ghaznavi. His new shield was giving way under the old man's onslaught; a countermeasure was necessary. He sent power surging into his left hand and immediately his flesh was lit from within. He closed his eyes, and from his palm leaped a brilliant burst of white light.

The flame-needles stopped. Looking at Ghaznavi once more, he saw the old man pawing at his eyes, momentarily blinded. Zorachus prepared to finish him.

Ghaznavi cried out in a harsh, arcane tongue. At the shout, a creature like a giant squid materialized, hovering in the air between the combatants. Its curtain of tentacles lifted and, where its squid's beak should have been, there was a miserific parody of a human face, eyes glistening with lunacy, mouth wide open, filled with chisel-like teeth.

Tentacles darted, the monster drifted towards Zorachus, and from between the distended jaws came a long, pink, chancred tongue, whipping and questing. Zorachus conjured a second shield and held both at arm's length; swinging them side to side, he managed to bat tongue and tentacles away.

The creature came closer. Arms circled past the shields, snaring Zorachus, binding him with rubbery flesh at knee and hip and chest, pinning one arm. His shields vanished; he felt a tingling charge dispelling his repelling energies. The tongue slathered his face with slime and the tentacles reeled him towards the mouth, which gaped ever wider; the tongue withdrew behind the fences of vermin-clotted teeth and foul breath spewed over him, breath like the gust from a bloated, rotten stomach ripped by a hook.

Shouting a formula, he swept his free hand in a sorcerous pass. The tentacles gripping him were instantly racked by elemental pain. They shook with fierce spasms, squeezing his ribs almost to cracking. Then the coils loosened, and he slipped out and dropped to the floor.

Looking up, he saw the monster's lunatic expression had not changed, betrayed no agony; but the squid-like body drifted back, tentacles dragging over stone, the ones that had held him twitching and jerking.

Zorachus assumed a Griffin Stance and sped through a binding spell. As he did so, the monster swept in once more, perhaps guessing the pain-rune could only be worked once, tentacles slithering to seize him again. But Zorachus took control of the heaviest and sent it coiling with tremendous force around the creature's conelike upper body.

The monster stopped short. Its other tentacles whipped upwards to pull the crushing arm away, but the effort was useless. Normally, Zorachus could not have exerted such control, but the Influences were with him today, greatly strengthening his binding powers; his proxy grip grew tighter and tighter.

At last the creature's expression changed, becoming more mindless, more lunatic; the eyes popped wider and wider, bulging out between distended lids, growing rapidly blood-shot. Their tormented veins began to burst, spewing out little jets of inky filth.

The crushing tentacle pressed ever deeper into yielding flesh. In one last desperate effort, the creature let fall the other arms and went after Zorachus again. But by now it was near death and he eluded its clumsy sweeps with ease.

Bit by bit, the squid-like body drifted floorwards. Its arms went slack. Some great bag of fluids burst inside the cone; black slush poured from the hideous mouth. And, as abruptly as it had appeared, the monster vanished.

Zorachus and Ghaznavi faced each other once more.

Ghaznavi was visibly weakened, swaying on his feet; the shield he raised now was but a dim convection. It had cost him dearly to bring the monster from its own dimension and maintain it, second after second, in this world.

Zorachus never trifled with a shield of his own. Striking power seethed in his arms; his repelling energies had been restored the instant the creature released him. A human thunderhead, the power within him kept building, building. He now had more strength than at the beginning of the trial; the trial itself had freed his goetic genius to an extent he had never known before.

Ghaznavi struck out at him. An orange nimbus looped around Zorachus's shoulders, seeped into him. His flesh and eyes glowed, and thread-thin lightning crackled in his hair; his bones hummed with pain. But the attack was not enough.

As the glow faded, he entered a Basilisk Stance. Two white bolts sprang from his fists, shattered Ghaznavi's shield in a spray of sparks, and knocked the old man to his knees.

Zorachus debated whether he should blast him again, just to make sure. But Ghaznavi answered the question for him by rising and trying to reenter his stance.

Zorachus loosed two more strikes. Ghaznavi toppled, stunned.

The trial was over. All around the circle, the watchers dropped the shields they had conjured against the possibility of stray bolts.

Zorachus walked forward to his stricken opponents, helped Khuroum up, then the swiftly reviving Ghaznavi. As the other Masters gathered round, Ghaznavi stared at him in stark amazement.

"You beat us both," he said slowly. "The most we expected

was that you'd hold your own."

"Well, I tried to give my all, *Sibi*," Zorachus replied.

"For my part," Khuroum gasped, "I wish you'd been more lax. My back's one huge ache. And my pride's hurt beyond cure, I think. The very idea we could be so manhandled by a mere Sixth Leveler. . . ." His voice trailed off.

"Take comfort," Ghaznavi said. "Zorachus can hardly be considered a Sixth Leveler anymore, can he?" He looked at Zorachus and smiled. "Go to your chamber, Young Master. I'll send word when all is ready."

Zorachus nodded, beaming, and strode out from among his white-robed mentors. Leaving the dueling circle, he went back up toward the door, which put out a faint white light like a far-off beacon.

Young Master: the words echoed in his mind. Now at last he allowed himself to savor the joy of victory, to bask in his own elation.

After what seemed a surprisingly short walk, he arrived at the door. He did not realize he had run much of the distance.

"You won, eh?" whispered a disembodied voice.

"How did you know, Antascar?" Zorachus asked, breathing hard. "Could you see the Trial from here?"

"No. It's your aura. Pity you can't see it. Such colors. . . ."

"Well, we've all got our talents. And being human can be very pleasant."

Antascar gave a reedy laugh. "I know."

Zorachus was taken slightly aback. "You were human once?"

"For a while. Just after I was a rhinoceros—or was it a water buffalo? Anyway, I cut quite a swath among the young ladies in Fyrkaz. But that's another story. I suppose I should let you out, shouldn't I?"

"Please."

The door opened.

"Thank you," Zorachus said going out.

"Congratulations," Antascar said after him.

Zorachus waved over his shoulder. Taking the steps three at a time, he soon reached the crypt.

"As you probably know, I did it," he told the statues there as he half-marched, half-jogged along. "And if any of you helped, thanks. I'll try not to disappoint you."

He came to the second stairway and started up. At the top he began to sing "The Battle of Ghoramzaar," a stirring ballad

about the exploits of the first Sharajnaghim. As he headed for
his room, his voice got louder and louder, becoming a thundering bellow. He paused in his song only to shout greetings
to comrades, who collected behind him shouting questions.
Blissfully unresponsive, he continued singing. They did not
mind, especially since it was obvious how the trial had come
out, and they had a fine time using their semantic training to
phrase their questions as many ways as possible.

Coming to his door he turned to face them at last, still
singing. But shortly Raschid shouldered his way out of the
crowd, carrying a naked (and very sharp) shortsword; thrusting it at Zorachus's throat, he halted the point a fraction of an
inch from his flesh.

Zorachus's song died. The crowd became deathly silent.
Raschid's harsh, drill master's voice broke the stillness:

"Civil questions demand civil answers. Speak, jackal!"

Zorachus replied with a swift forearm block, brushing the
point aside; resuming the song where he had left off, he punc-
tuated a particularly heroic phrase by planting a kiss on Raschid's forehead. The crowd whooped, and Zorachus dashed
into his room and bolted his door.

He offered up a long and exultant prayer of thanksgiving,
then undressed and washed at a wallside basin. For a time he
strode back and forth, humming; afterwards he stretched himself out on the bed, reliving the trials in his mind, finally
falling into contented sleep.

There was a knock at the door. He woke instantly.

"It's time, Zorachus," called a voice from outside.

"Coming," Zorachus cried. He leaped from the bed, threw
on fresh garments, combed his hair, and bustled from the
room. Trailed by Ghaznavi's messenger, he managed to com-
pose himself on the way to the mighty dome that formed the
heart of Qanar-Sharaj, the Order's home.

A lush green smell filled his nostrils as he passed under the
arch. All along the pillars and pendentives of the dome's in-
terior, as high and higher than the huge round windows, grew
thick vines of ivy and flowering plants, an encircling sea of
emerald leaves shuddering in the cross breezes, dotted with
color, sending green skeins out across the mouths of the
smaller domes. Shafts of light slanted down from the western
windows, one falling on a huge dais-borne altar in the center
of the chamber. Upon the altar, plants had also been encour-

aged to grow and, while the green had been cleared away in spots for the placing of relics and vessels, the stone was covered with leaves, tendrils, and shoots. Mounted on a tall pedestal, a white-silver flame symbol reared up from the midst of the greenery, and it seemed as though the plants strove to touch it, curling up the pedestal in mysterious devotion.

A great assembly, most of the inhabitants of Qanar-Sharaj, stood before the dais. Three Masters were mounted on the stone platform: Ghaznavi, Faschim, and Dauud. They wore no vestments other than their robes, but nothing could have added to the splendor of those garments, which were worn only on days of ordination. Their stabbing whiteness made the trappings of the other Masters seem dingy by comparison.

As Zorachus approached, Ghaznavi lifted his right hand in benediction of the Order as a whole, then lifted his left to bless the initiate. At the second gesture, a lane opened in the throng and Zorachus passed through, stepping up onto the dais, halting between Faschim and Dauud. They laid hands on his shoulders and he knelt, head bowed. Presently, Ghaznavi, Grand Master of the Order, began to speak:

"In ancient times there was a wizard, Washallah Irakhoum; and he dwelt in a black castle in the mountains of Thangura, and practiced deadly arts of intellect and will; and in supplication of demon-gods, he shed the blood of children on an altar darkly stained.

"But one day his acolytes brought him a captive boy, and as the victim was sacrificed a vision came to Washallah Irakhoum. He saw the Majesty of God Almighty, Maker of Heaven and Earth, who so loved all things that he brought them into being; and the boy's blood sang, and the wizard heard, in words sweet yet terrible, the doom that the Maker had put upon him. And when the vision left him and the voice ceased, he looked upon the altar once more and saw the boy was gone, and that the sacrificial knife was clean, as though it had never tasted blood.

"From that day on he was a chastened man, accepting the Maker's decree. He burned his grimoires bound in human skin and destroyed the altar darkly stained; and the spirit went out of him and into his acolytes, and they became the first servants of the Order he founded, that was ordained by God.

"The Order flourished and did much to heal the wounds of this fallen world and prevent new wounds from being dealt; and soon outsiders began to call its adherents the Sharaj-

naghim, the Bringers of Light. The Seventh Level of this
Order was made up of Great Masters; and the Masters ruled
the Sharajnaghim through the grace of the Maker.

"Today, in this holy place, a new Master joins the old. In
the Trials of Intellect and Will, and both combined, he has
been found worthy. All honor under God, and the Grand Master, is his. Lift your eyes, Zorachus."

Zorachus looked up at Ghaznavi. The old man's face was
solemn but his eyes gleamed with sacramental joy. Ghaznavi
continued: "Do you swear to uphold the high office of a Sharajnaghi Master, to lead the Order and preserve its sanctity, to
use your great powers in the service of life, to obey the will of
God in all things, to follow His great dance?"

Listening to the words, Zorachus sensed a great weight
pressing on him, as if the hand of God had sought out his
shoulders. Yet he felt neither suffocated nor enslaved, but as a
woman might, accepting the body of her true lover, pressed
down with his weight, but rejoicing in his unsurpassable near-
ness.

"I do so swear," he replied.

Ghaznavi smiled and placed a palm across Zorachus's
forehead. A pulse of gentle energy passed into the initiate,
bathing his soul with warmth.

Ghaznavi bade him rise. Faschim and Dauud went to the
altar and removed from the reliquary the robe that had served
initiate Masters for a thousand years. It was brighter even than
the robes the three celebrants wore, and there were instants
when one could see in it not only the fabulous unity of whiteness, but also the colors of which its whiteness was composed, a sight maddening but for its beauty.

They put the robe on Zorachus and, with them, he turned
to face the congregation.

"His place is now upon the Seventh Level," Ghaznavi said.
"He is *Sibi* Mancdaman Zorachus, and to him is due the obe-
dience of all Sharajnaghim who are not Masters."

Zorachus looked out over the faces before him, rejoicing in
each one; and the smell of leaves and flowers delighted his
senses.

chapter

2

THE NEXT DAY, Ghaznavi summoned Zorachus to his study. The room was small and comfortable, equipped with a formidable if compact library; the walls were lined, floor to ceiling, with huge leatherbound tomes, iron-hasped, filled with doctrine and arcane lore. Ghaznavi's desk was by the window, and whenever he grew tired of work he could look out from his third-floor vantage over a half-mile of greenery bordered by red dunes, the Western Ocean rolling beyond. Sea breezes wafted in through the window, stirring the edge of weighted papers on his desk, making the potted flowers nod and sway.

Scattered amid the flowerpots and papers and paperweights were a dozen or so figurines. Several of them, strange reptilian shapes with horns and spikes and frills, had been cast in iron by the Order's chief smith at Ghaznavi's direction; Ghaznavi had wanted them for a lecture in which he expounded the theory that Thorgon Karrelssa had once been populated by such creatures. Among his evidence was a collection of petrified bones, which he said had belonged to these beasts. Needless to say, nobody believed him, and that episode had been one of the great disasters of his life. And though he still kept the reptilian figures at his desk (the bones were gathering dust in a storage room), he was no longer interested in them. Out of his whole menagerie, his present favorites were a crystal centaur and a manticore carved in amber, poised to strike with its scorpion tail. As Zorachus settled himself, Ghaznavi reached around, took up the manticore and toyed with it.

"I think this one helps my arthritis," the old man said. "The dealer said it would."

Zorachus smiled. "How much silver did he squeeze out of you?" he asked, with a familiarity he and Ghaznavi had long shared. Ever since his mid-twenties, he had been treated as a near-equal by several of the Masters—in private.

23

"None of your business," Ghaznavi answered. "Sceptic."

Zorachus shrugged. "It would be simple enough to test it for healing properties—" He checked himself. "Excuse me. It's amber, isn't it?" For some undiscovered reason, amber was not susceptible to the name magic that underlay Sharaj-naghi experimental technique.

"Observant of you," Ghaznavi said smugly. "Do you remember the orphans who visited us?"

"From Karradesh?"

Ghaznavi nodded. "The one who claimed to be a wizard-natural said he saw an aura around the beast."

"He also said he could read minds, and we caught him cheating," Zorachus countered.

"True. But naturals often cheat when the faculty isn't running."

"Why don't you show the figure to Antascar?" Zorachus asked. "He can see auras, you know."

Ghaznavi harrumphed. "Too much of a bother."

"Well," Zorachus said after a short pause, deciding to humor him, "maybe it does help. Your hands must have been limber enough yesterday. The flame-needles were very nasty."

Ghaznavi smiled quietly. "Not bad for an old man, eh?" He pursed his lips and shook his head slightly. "But it didn't make much difference."

"You don't know how sorely you tried me."

Ghaznavi shook his head again. "I saw what was happening," he answered. "Do you have any idea of your real strength?"

"I'm not sure," Zorachus said. "There was a moment towards the end. . . ."

Ghaznavi stretched and said off-handedly: "You may be the greatest sorcerer who ever lived."

There was silence for the next few moments. Zorachus was both unnerved and embarrassed. He knew he was powerful, but he had never dreamed of such language being applied to him. He flushed, the arrow scar on his cheek going white.

"Other men have beaten two Masters at once," he said.

"True," Ghaznavi admitted. "But in every case I know of it was mostly luck. Not even Moujiz of the Black Anarites could claim otherwise. You, on the other hand, *outfought* Khuroum and me. You didn't even try to counter my demon with one of your own. I thought perhaps you wouldn't have remembered."

"You taught me too well. I recognized that dribbling cuttlefish even before it showed its face."

Ghaznavi laughed. "See what I mean? I marvel to think what you'll be like twenty years from now."

"Burnt out," Zorachus replied. He did not say it to get assurances to the contrary; it was a thing that often happened to sorcerous prodigies.

"Perhaps," Ghaznavi said. "But in the meantime we'll put your gifts to the best advantage. That's why I summoned you." He put the manticore back on the table. "What do you know about Khymir?"

Surprise and dismay filled Zorachus's eyes. "Why do you ask?"

"For good reason," Ghaznavi replied.

"Of course. I'm sorry—I just wasn't expecting. . . ."

"What do you know about Khymir?" Ghaznavi asked again, watching him closely.

"The Order's been my only family. . . ."

"I know. But answer the question."

Zorachus nodded. "Khymir's a city lying far to the north."

"What do you know about its people?"

"That they're great sinners," Zorachus said, voice tinged with shame.

"They're steeped in vice and blood," Ghaznavi said. "They openly worship Tchernobog, the Black God; and he fosters them as an argument against organic life, working through an order of wizard-priests. What do you know about that order?"

Zorachus downcast his eyes. "That my father was once its chief."

"Mancdaman Zancharthus," Ghaznavi said. "Moujiz's equal, or so it's said. One can see how you came by your talents. Do you remember him at all?"

Zorachus shook his head. "I remember nothing about Khymir. I've always thought of myself as a Kadjafi—even though my name's so outlandish."

"We wanted to shield you from the facts, but you had to know that much."

"I know." Zorachus had no trouble imagining the hideous namespells that could have been worked on him in his ignorance. Slowly he looked up at Ghaznavi. "Why did you open the wound?"

"An envoy from the High Priest of Tchernobog has arrived," Ghaznavi answered. "He wants to see you very badly."

Zorachus knitted his brow. "Why?"

"To persuade you to return to Khymir and claim your inheritance."

"What inheritance?"

"Your father was a fantastically wealthy man."

"Before he was overthrown and killed."

"The power's changed hands again. A man named Ghorchalanchor Kletus is now High Priest."

Zorachus tossed his hands up. "But why does he want to give me such wealth? Surely he could find good enough uses for it himself."

"If so, why did he make the offer? It would seem he wants to link himself to the Mancdaman name. Your father was extremely popular and you're the sole heir."

"How in God's name did they find out where I was?" Zorachus asked bitterly.

"They've known all along," Ghaznavi said. "Haven't you heard how you wound up in Sharajnaghi hands?"

"I know one of my father's retainers fled to Thangura and put me under the Order's protection. But I never pressed too deeply into the facts. I hate being reminded of my lineage. Taking the slightest interest in it always seemed like a kind of betrayal."

"Understandable," Ghaznavi said. "As it is, though, you don't have things quite straight. The retainer put you under Faschim's *personal* protection. I doubt he knew anything about the Order. Faschim met him in Thangura. The man came staggering out of a back alley, bleeding badly, holding you in his arms. The footpads who stabbed him saw him hand you over to Faschim; they'd been hired by an ambassador sent by your father's successor. Realizing they were up against a Sharajnaghi, they hung back, but they must have told the ambassador you were with us."

"What happened to the retainer?"

"He died, but not before gasping out his story. He wanted you to avenge him when you reached manhood, and thought Faschim would raise you with a roaring desire to go back to Khymir and overthrow the usurpers. He made it clear you'd be a very profitable commodity."

"Did the ambassador make any attempts to get at me?"

Ghaznavi nodded. "Several teams of assassins were sent. We dealt with them, but the attempts didn't stop until we persuaded the Khanate to step in."

"I'm grateful," Zorachus said. "But you still haven't told me why you brought up this whole matter. Do you think I'd have the slightest interest in my 'inheritance'?" At the last word, his voice thickened with disgust.

"No," Ghaznavi answered. "But you do have a duty to the Order."

"We need gold from devil worshippers?"

"To thwart certain of their plans, yes. Though the Mancdaman name will be even more useful, I think. I want you to return with the envoy."

"To Khymir?"

"Yes. How's your Old Malochian?" Khymir was once a colony of Malochan, and an archaic form of Malochian was still spoken there, though it was used elsewhere only by scholars and wizards.

"Fluent," Zorachus replied. "But what do you want me to do? Convert everyone there?" He laughed.

Ghaznavi laughed too, but sadly. "That would thwart the Black Priests neatly enough. I wish to God there was some chance of it."

"What *do* you have in mind then?"

"Containment. Forcing the priests to make do with what they've got."

"I don't follow you."

"I'll explain," Ghaznavi answered. "As you know, Tchernobog has a terrible hunger. And the Priests, by offering up Khymirian criminals and paupers, and preying off the Kragehul barbarians surrounding Khymir, have been able to keep it satisfied—so far. But it's been growing since Khymir was founded; indeed, since Tchernobog and his followers fell from heaven. And soon the Priests will no longer be able to spill enough blood, at least with their present hunting grounds. That leaves them two options. They could choose not to satisfy Tchernobog, but that would be the end of them. If they lost the sorcerous aid he grants, they'd be finished by their enemies in the city. On the other hand, they could try to feed him, but they'd need a much wider hunting ground than they now have. It seems Thagranichus Ordog, the man who overthrew your father, was deposed for failing to make the second choice. From what I could gather from the Khanate's intelligence reports, he was losing confidence, growing afraid of overextending himself. His successor, Kletus, is a much tougher sort. I've reason to think he's planning a campaign of

conquest the like of which the world has never seen—the
Influences will be magnifying black sorceries for the next two
decades and an order like the Black Priesthood could take
awesome advantage. Who could stand against such an onslaught? Not the Kragehul. They're brave fighters, but it
would be hopeless."

"And you don't think it would stop with them?" Zorachus
asked.

Ghaznavi shook his head. "The lands south of the Utgards
are full of potential victims. And most of them are far less
able than the barbarians to defend themselves. The Khymirians will need them after they've exhausted their supply of
Kragehul. Tchernobog's hunger grows by leaps and, like any
pampered hunger, the more it gets, the more it craves."

"But how exactly am I going to stop all this?" Zorachus
asked.

Ghaznavi's face wrinkled in a cunning smile. "A plan entered my mind this morning as I listened to the envoy. I was
surprised and delighted by his proposal; we've long been
keeping track of events in Khymir, hoping the Priests would
give us an opening. Now they've come right to our doorstep
to do so.

"As I said before, Kletus wants to ally himself with the
Mancdaman name. He'll almost certainly take you into his
confidence. If he is indeed planning an invasion, you must
expose and publicly repudiate the scheme. That would throw
him off balance, maybe even topple the Priesthood. The Khymirian Merchant's Guild has long opposed the Priests, though
there's an uneasy truce in effect; the Guildsmen are very powerful themselves, and keep magicians of their own. They don't
need sacrifices, and the sources of their wealth are so great
and secure that they wouldn't want any part of the invasion.
You could point out how Kletus would have to recruit thousands of mercenaries for his great campaign—victories won
by sorcery still have to be consolidated by troops. But those
troops would also give Kletus the strength to crush the Guild
once and for all. Needless to say, the Guildsmen would be
mightily aroused; and with you on their side, their chances of
overthrowing the Priests would be good. Your name—not to
mention your magic—would bolster them enormously. Your
father tried to reform the Priesthood, you see, make it less
tyrannical. Kletus probably wants your support to reassure his
foes, keep them off guard; but the son of Mancdaman Zan-

charthus would be, if anything, an even more obvious asset to the Guild."

"Your plan *sounds* very clever," Zorachus said. "But has it occurred to you that I might not live long enough to achieve anything at all? Kletus's offer might be bait. He might think I'm a potential rival. That might be why he wants me back—to kill me at his leisure."

"Maybe," Ghaznavi said. "But I think it's more likely that he'd try to wring every last ounce of benefit from you before moving in for the kill."

Zorachus shifted in his seat. "That's supposed to comfort me? Surely he'll want me dead the minute I turn on him."

"In which case you'll defend yourself. And after those exhibitions yesterday, I think you'll manage. Especially with the Guild on your side. Of course, you'll be in the gravest danger. . . ."

"And not just physically," Zorachus broke in. "The real threat's against my soul, isn't it? The whole purpose of Khymir is to make converts for Tchernobog—you said it yourself."

"That's why I'm not going to command you to go," Ghaznavi answered. "I wouldn't blame you if you didn't touch the mission."

"You did, however, make a point of mentioning my duty to the Order."

"A man also has a duty to himself. If you think the threat's too great, stay here. If not. . . ."

"But *you* think I'm up to it, don't you?"

"The *Comahi Irakhoum*'s the greatest of the White Orders, and you're its greatest son, the strongest human soul I've ever met."

Again Zorachus was deeply embarrassed. "I wish I had as much faith in Mancdaman Zorachus as you do."

"I know you're not perfect."

Zorachus leaned forward. "*Angels* have fallen with less provocation than I'll get in Khymir."

"Yes, and one of them is behind the Khymirian threat," Ghaznavi answered, unfazed. "Which renders the mission all the more urgent."

Zorachus leaned back, folding his arms on his chest. "I know. But I can't help feeling uneasy about Kletus's assumption that I'd even consider allying myself with him. Maybe he knows something about me that you don't."

Ghaznavi smiled. "I doubt his spies could be *that* good.
But undoubtedly he *thinks* he knows all about you. Indeed, he
probably thinks he knows all about everyone. Khymirians,
particularly the Black Priests, believe all men are motivated
by the same drives they are. When they look at our order they
see it's powerful, able to defeat other orders again and again;
they see we have influence on the Khanate, and that we've
found ways to get the local population to supply most of our
basic needs. *Therefore*, the Priests think, *the Sharajnaghim
are sane—they are the same as us.* They can't understand an
order like ours. The very fact that they think they could enlist
your aid proves it."

"But given that," Zorachus said, "Won't they think I'll be
trying to subvert them? Trying to extend Sharajnaghi influence?"

"The envoy seems to take it for granted. He didn't think it
necessary to speak only to you. He was happy to give me the
message. However much the Priests fear us, they think the
benefits of having you outweigh the risks."

"Does that mean I could bring someone with me? Raschid
perhaps, just for companionship? Seeing as how they already
suspect—"

"No. It would be better to reduce the suspicions they already have. We want them to take you into their confidence as
soon as possible—the farther Kletus's plan is from fruition,
the better. And so you should pretend you're making a clean
break from the Order. Having Raschid with you would make
that much more difficult."

"They wouldn't have to know he's a Sharajnaghi. He could
pose as a servant, or—"

"They probably know we don't keep servants or slaves,
though God knows what they think our motives must be. And
it's not as if you could simply pick Raschid up on your way to
the harbor. Believe me, the less complicated we make things
seem, the better. And the best way to do that is to send you
alone." Ghaznavi paused. "Will you accept the mission?"

Zorachus sighed. "Seems I'm the only man for the job,
doesn't it?" He stared blankly through the window. "My vows
seemed so beautiful yesterday."

Ghaznavi laughed sympathetically. "And now, suddenly,
you have to take them seriously and they appear a lot less
seductive. I know the feeling."

"Do the other Masters know about your plan yet?" Zorachus asked, shifting his gaze back to the old man.

"No. I'll summon the council shortly."

"What about the envoy? Is it wise to keep him waiting?"

"I told him you'd be indisposed, for a while at least. He said he'd be back in three days."

"If he only knew what we have in mind. . . ." Zorachus's voice trailed off.

"I don't imagine he'd approve. But considering what his master seems to be planning, I don't think we have an alternative."

"You know," Zorachus said, "the Guildsmen will want my aid when the fighting starts. They'll want me to kill for them."

"*If* the fighting starts," Ghaznavi said. "My information might be wrong."

Zorachus hardly heard him. "I won't be able to conceal how powerful I am. Not when Kletus attacks."

Ghaznavi shrugged. "Use the Code. You know when killing's lawful. The Guildsmen will just have to go along with you. You'll be too valuable to them in other ways. Of course, before Kletus confides in you, you'll have to be more careful about revealing your scruples. A certain amount of lip service to our ideals would be allowable, I suppose; you were, after all, brought up as a Sharajnaghi, and I expect the Priests will take that into account. But anything more than lip service would be dangerous—especially if you didn't conceal your motives."

"Why? Don't the priests regard our scruples as mere subterfuge?"

"I'm sure. But if you act consistently in accordance with our moral teachings, and Kletus can't detect any other kind of behavior, he'll likely conclude you're insane. Or worse yet, that you're plotting in some way he can't fathom. Either way, he might keep his distance. Luckily, though, unless your temporary alliance with him provokes some kind of hostilities from the Guild, the question of killing for *him*—rather than for the Guild—shouldn't arise." Ghaznavi paused, as though he had just thought of something. "And while we're on the subject of bloodshed. . . ." Producing a brass key, he unlocked a drawer in his desk, took out a small leather bag, and threw it to Zorachus. "Another part of your inheritance."

Zorachus untied the pouch and upended it. Two rings fell out into his palm. The circlets were of some unfamiliar grey metal with a single, dazzling blue-white gem set in each; the jewels' glare made his eyes hurt. He winced and looked at Ghaznavi.

"They're gorgeous," he said. "Bit hard on the eyes, though."

"They're not for looking. They contain demons. Flame demons. Put them on and stand up."

They both rose.

"Look out the window," the old man said. "See the out-cropping off to the left?"

Zorachus nodded. A lone chimney of stone rose above the vegetation.

"Extend your fists, concentrate on it briefly, and will the demons to destroy it."

"Simple as that?"

"Simple as that."

Zorachus obeyed. Lightning leaped from the rings, striking the outcropping, shattering it, sending stone fragments hurtling through the air.

"My fingers are cooking!" Zorachus gasped, slipping the circlets from his hands and dropping them on his chair. "Is there a spell I can put on the rings so they won't heat up?"

But Ghaznavi was distracted. Bending over the desk, he eyed some of his potted flowers. Two blossoms were smoking.

"Damn," he said. "You've singed my nasturtiums." He straightened and turned. "What did you say?"

Zorachus repeated himself.

"There's already a spell on the outside of the circlets," Ghaznavi said. "Protects your other fingers, even as it allows the heat to dissipate. But the inside has to be in perfect contact with your skin. A spell would interfere. Don't worry, though. The demons won't generate so much heat when you're dealing with people."

"How are the bolts against force-shields?"

"Not very good."

"What's their range?"

"Not much better than the distance to the outcropping; their power fades sharply after that. Something else you should know: You can use the rings when you're traveling over water. The demons aren't affected."

"Not even by the ocean?"

"No."

"You said the rings were part of my inheritance," Zorachus

said. "Did the envoy give them to you?"

"No. Your father's man gave them to Faschim. He said they were Mancdaman family heirlooms. They bear inscriptions saying the demons will only serve a sorcerer of the Mancdaman line. That's not exactly true; Faschim found a spell to bind the demons for short periods. We learned much about them. Fascinating creatures, but incredibly deadly. We decided to withhold the rings until you became a Master."

"Can the demons be lawfully used?" Zorachus asked.

"Would I give you the rings if they couldn't?" Ghaznavi asked, irritated.

"Pardon me. I was only trying to make sure. You and Faschim have been known to get so wrapped up in experiments that certain key facts slip by you. . . ."

"The demons are almost completely malevolent," Ghaznavi gritted. "It's as legitimate for a Sharajnaghi to enslave them as to perform an exorcism."

"I'm familiar with the First Justification," Zorachus said. "It was one of the first things you taught me, remember?"

Ghaznavi's expression softened. "You were so young. . . ." He laughed. "You're so young *now!*"

"It won't last." Zorachus picked up the rings, found they had cooled considerably, and started to put them on again.

"Don't wear them," Ghaznavi said. "Not unless it's necessary. Keep them in the pouch. The circlets begin to eat through flesh after a quarter of an hour or so. Some property of the metal."

Zorachus put the rings back in the pouch, tightened the drawstring, and slipped the thong around his neck. "Will there be time for me to get something to eat before the council?"

"I expect so. But if you meet any of your lower-level cronies, don't mention my plan. There's always the chance we've been infiltrated. It would be better if we passed you off as a renegade, for reasons I've already mentioned."

Zorachus's face twisted with dismay. "You mean it'll be necessary for most of the Order to think I'm a traitor?"

"I'm afraid so. But the news doesn't have to get out till you've already left—we can spare you that much discomfort, at least."

"How can you possibly hope to pull it off? After all, I've just been ordained, and. . . ."

"There are precedents. Nadim Shawarra abandoned the Order one week after being ordained a Master. For a slave girl. I remember it clearly. She wasn't even that pretty."

"But—"

"There'll be no problems. Lower-levellers usually believe Masters. And if we have evidence, they'll have no choice. Certain secret writings of yours might be found. I could conjure up a diary in your handwriting, in which you express all kinds of doubts."

"I see," Zorachus said dejectedly.

"It must be done," Ghaznavi told him.

Zorachus looked pleadingly at him. "Could I at least tell Raschid? He's my best friend. I don't want him thinking I'm an apostate."

"The council would have to vote on it," Ghaznavi answered, his face very hard. "And I for one would vote against it."

"If I asked him not to tell anyone else, he wouldn't."

Ghaznavi was silent.

"I trust him completely," Zorachus went on.

"So do I," Ghaznavi said. "But. . . ."

"Well, if you agree he's trustworthy, you've got no case."

Ghaznavi eyed him for a few moments. "Does it mean that much to you?"

Zorachus nodded.

"All right," Ghaznavi said, and wagged a finger at him. "But I can't guarantee what the other Masters will think."

Zorachus smiled.

chapter

3

THREE DAYS LATER Zorachus went to one of Qanar-Sharaj's many gardens. Awaiting him were three men.

Two were broad shouldered, similar to Zorachus in build, wearing black leather scale-mail and carrying triangular crimson-lacquered shields blazoned with the sign of a black hand; on their heads were round steel helms with cheekguards and nasals, and long straight swords in shagreen scabbards hung at their belts. Their eyes were shadowed under their helmet rims and their lips were thin.

The third man was short and sagged with middle age, though Zorachus guessed he had once been well proportioned. His face was still handsome by most standards, framed by long brown hair and a well-trimmed beard. Yet, to Zorachus's mind, it was quite unpleasant—a satyr's face, almost mindlessly sensual. The frank lewdness of the milky blue eyes was startling. The man wore a black silk blouse embroidered with coiling ruby-red firedrakes, and his black brocade cloak, traced about the borders by swirls of platinum thread, was clasped at his right shoulder by a brooch in the shape of a black hand. His trews were scarlet, stuffed into knee-high boots crafted of some dark blue reptilian hide, and at his hip was a sword much like those of his armored companions but much more ornate, its pommel and crosspiece of damascened iron, grip tightly wound with electrum wires. He smelled heavily of perfume, so much so that the scent of the nearby flowers was utterly smothered. The perfume was unpleasantly familiar, but Zorachus could not quite place it.

"Mancdaman Zorachus?" the man asked.

Zorachus nodded.

"I'm Brachus Lir Tchernaar," the other said bowing, "Emissary of His Anointed Steward Ghorchalanchor Kletus, the

High Priest of Tchernobog and Lord of Khymir. Have you heard my Lord's proposal?"

"Yes," Zorachus replied. "I accept."

Suddenly he realized what Tchernaar's perfume was: a blend of aloes and myrrh. Burial spices.

"My Master will be delighted," Tchernaar said. "And Mother Khymir will be at your feet."

Zorachus forced a smile. He hoped it looked genuine. "That should take the sting out of losing my friends here."

"Losing them? Not just leaving them?"

"Let's just say I'm not going to be well remembered when they realize I've struck out on my own."

"Unfortunate," Tchernaar said. "But you'll make new friends. There are many handsome men and boys in Khymir. You'll have your pick." He spoke without the slightest trace of unctuousness; there was nothing of the procurer in his voice. He could have been talking about food.

There was a long pause.

"When do we leave?" Zorachus asked at last.

"As soon as you're ready," Tchernaar answered. "I've a ship at Thangura. Three ships, to be exact."

"Three?"

"Two for escort. You're valuable cargo, my Lord, and the voyage north is dangerous. We have to pass along the Muspel coast, and Muspellheim's populated by barbarians called the Kragehul; they hate Khymirians and prey on our shipping— those who won't accept tribute, that is. And even the ones that do, attack from time to time. To make matters worse, the coast itself is a pirate's paradise—thousands of fjords and offshore islands. We might need some of your magic—you Sharajnaghim are formidible wizards, I've heard."

"I'm no longer a Sharajnaghi, I'm afraid," Zorachus answered. "And even Sharajnaghim can't do much magic at sea." He wanted to keep his possession of the demon-rings secret as long as possible. The less Kletus found out about his capabilities, the better.

"Pity," Tchernaar said.

There was another pause. Zorachus noticed one of the envoy's men playing with a beetle that had apparently lighted on him. The guard overturned his hand and righted it again, allowing the insect to scuttle all the way round. Then he brushed it off and stamped on it, grinding his foot powerfully, pointlessly, against the stone walk.

"Well," Zorachus said, looking back at Tchernaar, "I've something to attend to now, but I could be ready shortly."

"In an hour, perhaps? We could catch the afternoon tide."

Zorachus nodded. "That's the hottest part of the day, though."

"We don't mind if you don't. We Khymirians aren't much bothered by heat. Do you have any baggage you need help with?"

"No."

"Do you have a horse?"

Zorachus shook his head.

"No matter," Tchernaar said. "I've brought one for you."

"Very good."

"All right then. We'll wait for you at the south gate."

"One last thing," Zorachus said. "If anyone asks you *why* you're waiting, say you're merely expecting a *message* from me. It might spare some unpleasantness."

"Certainly."

"In an hour, then."

Leaving the garden, Zorachus went to his chamber. Closing the door, he leaned against it for a time, looking fondly at the room and its contents. Then he crossed wearily to his bed and sank down on it, one arm behind his head. Already low, his spirits sank steadily.

He knew he must leave Qanar-Sharaj. It was his duty to the Order. But that did not comfort him. And everything in the chamber seemed to be conspiring to make leaving harder. The mattress, which had always been hard and lumpy, had somehow become preternaturally comfortable; the paint on the walls had turned a shade of white hardly less wondrous than that of the robe he had donned at his ordination. He began to treasure even the cracks in the ceiling, and that cobweb dangling in the corner seemed like a gift from God. . . .

He thought about Tchernaar and Khymir. The city's evil was legendary—but no legend, he was sure. *Impossible to exaggerate*, Faschim had said during the council. The words still rang in Zorachus's mind. He wondered: What depravities would he be confronted with? What atrocities? Utterly isolated, could he keep his sanity? Ghaznavi had perfect faith in him. So did the other Masters. But was it justified? Despite everything they had said, Zorachus's doubts remained, and ultimately his faith in Ghaznavi's judgement had weighed more heavily than his own estimate of himself. Ghaznavi was a wise man, full of experience; he had often placed full confidence in Zorachus when Zorachus himself had recommended against it, and every time that confidence had been vindicated. Yet Zorachus kept coming back and back to the question: Could anyone truly know his heart of hearts better than he did?

Dejection became apprehension. He knelt beside the bed and prayed. But he had hardly begun when there was a knock at the door.

"Come in," he called, rising.

Raschid entered. He eyed Zorachus's face, reading his mood.

"Let me guess," he said. "You're all choked up about going."

"Also about *where* I'm going," Zorachus said.

"When do you leave?"

"Less than an hour."

Raschid laughed. "Don't take it so hard."

Zorachus's eyes widened with amazement. "How can you say that?"

Raschid laughed again, as if it were perfectly obvious. "You get to visit Khymir, the wonder of the northern world. Think of its history—"

"I *am* thinking of its history," Zorachus broke in.

Raschid went on as if he had not heard him, striding about the room: "You'll travel the very streets where so many colorful characters have walked. You'll see Banipal Khezach, the fabled Black Tower, exchange points of view with people of different religious backgrounds . . . think of how stimulating it'll be!"

"It's a shame the envoy's seen me already," Zorachus answered. "We could send *you* with him."

"There aren't many of us who'll get a chance like yours," Raschid answered flippantly, leaning against a wall.

"What do you mean?" Zorachus demanded. "I could very well find myself with half the wizards and soldiers in Khymir after my blood."

Raschid shrugged.

"And I'm not too pleased about having to plunge myself nose-deep into a tarpit of vice."

Raschid grinned and folded his arms on his chest. "You'll appreciate Qanar-Sharaj that much more when you return."

"What in God's name is the matter with you?" Zorachus

exploded. "You didn't seem to think this was all so funny the other day."

"You weren't wallowing in your own sweet misery then."

"No? I would've had cause enough. How would you like to be surrounded by Khymirians? By hateful men when hate's forbidden?"

At that a squint of annoyance replaced the patient good humor in Raschid's eyes. "I don't suppose I'd like it very much. But there's something that seems even worse to me right now. How would you like it if your best friend decided to spend his last hour with you—rather, his last less-than-an-hour—chewing your ear off with self-pity?" He headed for the door.

"Wait!" Zorachus cried. Raschid knew how to communicate scorn in absolutely withering fashion, a skill acquired in several years of drilling cringing recruits. And, while Zorachus had not cringed, much of the whining mood had been cleansed from his mind.

Raschid turned and sneered: "The tragedy queen commands." He curtsied.

"You know," Zorachus laughed, "you have a gaping void where your sympathy should be."

Raschid grinned once more. "You noticed, eh? Of course, it's not as if you inspired any, sniveling that way."

"Watch your tongue. I'm a Master now. And I might point out that I wasn't sniveling at you very long."

"It seemed like hours, *Sibi,*" Raschid answered, delivering the last word with a great dose of sarcasm.

"As a matter of fact, it seemed like you were chewing *my* ear off most of the way. All that nonsense about Khymir."

"*I* thought it was funny."

"I suppose it was. But that only made it more infuriating."

"Sorry. I was only trying to take you out of yourself."

Zorachus continued: "And I really wonder how you'd like it if you had this mission."

Raschid sat on a stool. "You know, ever since you told me about it, I've been wondering about exactly that."

"Reached any conclusions?"

"I think I'd be pleased."

Shaking his head in disbelief, Zorachus sat on the edge of his bed. "Why?"

"Any number of reasons. Because I'd been judged worthy of such a task. Because I had a chance to do something really important. Because I'd be confronted by such evil that I'd have no doubt of goodness. Or God."

"The last seems pretty dubious to me," Zorachus said sourly. "My faith isn't weak enough to need that kind of support—especially if it means exposing myself to such temptation."

Raschid looked at him sidelong. "You really meant that nonsense about hating the Khymirians? You, the man who nurses Black Anarites back to health and then has the patience to convert them? I don't think you're capable of hating anyone."

"If what I've heard about the Khymirians is true," Zorachus said, "the Black Anarites are saints in comparison. The Khymirians have been under the Enemy's shadow for a far longer time. I can easily imagine them provoking me."

"To do what?"

"Abuse my powers."

Raschid shook his head smugly, unwilling to entertain the possibility. "I'll tell you this, dear friend. That won't be your problem at all. It'll be making sure you use enough power when the time comes. If there's anything that *really* hinders a Sharajnaghi, it's all that sweet reasonableness."

"You're dead wrong," Zorachus replied.

"Well, maybe. But here's another thing for you to consider. The very fact that you're so worried means you've got nothing to worry about. I know perfectly well you'll be your usual even-tempered self during the troubles ahead. And you know it too. Otherwise you wouldn't have agreed to go."

Zorachus was silent for a few moments. "I have agreed, haven't I?"

Raschid nodded cheerfully. "You know," he said, "once you leave, everyone's going to be trying to figure you out. Except the Masters and me." He chuckled. "Now, Jaffar of course will think he's got you pegged. And he'll be wrong as always. . . ."

Zorachus laughed grimly. "But he'll get more of an audience than usual. After all, what better evidence for him than an apostate Sharajnaghi?"

"Sharajnaghi *Master*," Raschid put in.

"I can hear him even now," Zorachus went on, "preaching about the infinite corruptibility of all men, demonstrating that the commandment against judging others stems not from imperfect human knowledge, but from the fact that everyone's a swine, and swine can't judge other swine. . . ."

"And so on till nausea sets in."

"I wish the Council had declared Total Depravity heterodox
a long time ago," Zorachus said with a sigh. "After all, I don't
want to score points for Jaffar—even if they're only temporary." He paused. "Let's talk about something else."

"Such as?"

"How are you coming with that new kick?"

"Not so well. Can't get my leg up fast enough."

"If anyone can manage it, it's going to be you."

"I don't know."

"It's just a matter of time. . . ."

In the end, Raschid was compelled to agree, and they
passed on to a highly technical discussion of the moves they
had used in the Second Trial.

Presently, Zorachus eyed his water clock. It ran on the flow
that filled his basin; the design was his invention, and the
whole Order had adopted it.

"I'd better be going," he said.

They rose and went to embrace each other, but Raschid
stopped dead, staring at something on the floor. Zorachus
looked too. A large centipede was crawling slowly along.
Raschid lifted his foot to crush it.

"Don't," Zorachus said, recalling the Khymirian and the
beetle. "That kind's not dangerous."

"Yes, but you know how I hate the sight of them. One bit
my mother, once."

"I know. But this one's not hurting anyone."

"And you're going to massacre all those Khymirians?"
Raschid asked wryly. "Mercy incarnate, that's what you are."

"Right."

They hugged. And all at once Raschid was weeping bitterly.

"Now look who's feeling sorry for himself," he said, and
stormed out cursing.

Zorachus wept too, but quickly brought himself under control. Taking off his sandals and white robe, he folded the latter
and laid it reverently on the bed. Then he donned trousers and
a tunic, both grey, the typical garb of lower-level Sharajnaghim, and girt on a swordbelt. After putting on a pair of
brown boots, he got his sack and slung it over his shoulder. In
it were his mailshirt and padding, helmet (with the cage re-

moved) vambraces, armored gloves and boots, and two changes of clothes identical to those he now wore. There was also a set of woolen cold weather garments, for while Khymir was known to be unnaturally hot all year round, the northern clime surrounding it was brisk at the best of times.

He gave his room one last, lingering look. Then he went out and made his way to the gate. The lower-level adepts he met seemed surprised to see him without his Master's robes, and some spoke to him, but he answered them with silence. The gatewardens, both of whom he knew quite well, asked him where he was going; he passed them by without so much as a glance.

Tchernaar and his men were outside, waiting in the overhanging shadow of the gatehouse. The envoy was mounted on a black horse, one of the guards on another. But the guard got down as Zorachus approached—the Sharajnaghi guessed he had climbed up only to keep the gatewards from wondering who the horse was for. Zorachus allowed the man to take his bag and fasten it to the saddle; having been raised without servants of any kind, it irked him to accept such aid, but it was a minor enough matter for him to let it pass. He mounted up.

"Zorachus!" one of the gatewards cried. "*Sibi* Zorachus!"

Ignoring him, Zorachus put up the sunhood attached to his tunic; Tchernaar donned a Kadjafi headdress, and his men did likewise, wearing theirs over their helmets.

"Where are you going, *Sibi?*" the gateward called.

Zorachus and the others set off.

"*Sibi* Zorachus!"

Zorachus did not look back.

It was breathtakingly hot on the road. Convections rose shimmering from the baking red clay surface. Tall date palms lined either side, but they gave little shade. A few birds sang in the palm fronds, but their chirping came only in short gasps, as if they were all but choked by the heat.

As his horse clopped along, Zorachus spied something writhing in the road's red dust—a large scorpion with sunstroke was stinging itself to death.

Suddenly dread seized the Sharajnaghi; somehow he knew the scorpion was an evil omen. He felt a powerful urge to leap off the horse and tear back to the safety of Qanar-Sharaj. . . .

Yet he remained in the saddle. He could practically hear

Ghaznavi: *You saw a scorpion stinging itself? That's why you came back?*

He steadied himself. He had no reason to trust his own premonitions. He had never gotten anything but false alarms. Bit by bit, the dread left him.

They rode on.

Thangura was a mighty, fortified city, with tall red sandstone walls; Zorachus and his companions reached it just as the heat eased and people were beginning to venture from their houses. Welcome breezes swept through the narrow streets, which soon grew crowded.

Zorachus's party threaded a path to the harbor. Hemmed on the west by castellated breakwaters, it was wide and horseshoe shaped. Two towers flanked its mouth, a giant chain stretching between them.

Striding through the newly revived bustle of the port, Tchernaar's men led the way, making for a narrow pier set off from the others, which lunged far out into the harbor. Three long, black ships were moored to it, moderate of draft, their bows tall and curved, bearing hands carved in black wood instead of figureheads. Each vessel had a single tall black mast, and their poopdecks were ringed with loopholed castles.

"Our fleet," Tchernaar said. "We'll be on the ship at the end, the *Zancharthus.*"

Zorachus noticed a man fishing on the nearest of the three. Making a catch, the angler took it from his hook, sliced its tail off, and tossed the maimed, flopping creature back into the water. He started to rebait his hook, looked up and stopped.

"Lord Tchernaar's coming!" he cried in Khymirian. Word spread to the other ships as Zorachus and his companions went out along the pier; men flocked to the rails. Most were Khymirians, large and red-haired, bearing a strong resemblance to Zorachus. The rest were swarthy Kadjafim and sandy-haired Tarchans.

"Lord Tchernaar!" one fellow called. "Is that *him?* Is that Lord Mancdaman?"

"Yes!" Tchernaar replied. Cheers broke out. Men started to pour down the gangways, but their officers called them back.

Zorachus's party reached the *Zancharthus*'s plank. He and Tchernaar dismounted and went aboard, the guards bringing up the rear with the horses. A noisy crowd of sailors and men-at-arms hemmed in Zorachus and the envoy near the rail.

"Make way for the Captain!" came a bull-throated bellow. "Make way!"

The throng quieted and a lane opened. A short, fat man approached Zorachus. He wore a white linen shirt and an embroidered blue vest, baggy trousers and boots with upturned toes; his skin was brown, his pate bald and shiny, his huge hooked nose archetypically Kadjafi.

Tchernaar nodded towards Zorachus. "This is Lord Mancdaman," he said. "Lord Mancdaman, Captain Klazmouran."

The Captain bowed. "Welcome aboard, My Lord."

"I want to leave as soon as possible," Tchernaar said.

Klazmouran nodded, and collared a sailor. "Tell the other captains to make ready." As the man made off, the Captain shouted: "The rest of you dogs know what to do! Don't stand around gaping. *Bogra!*"

The crowd began to disperse, but a barefoot Kadjafi youth ran up beside Klazmouran. The Captain pointed to Zorachus.

"Bogra, show our honored guest to my—rather his— quarters," he said. "Here's the key. And take his bag."

Zorachus was even then swinging it down from his horse. He doubted the slim adolescent would be able to handle the weight of the armor, but let him have it anyway—only to take it back after a few paces as Bogra buckled under the load.

The youth led him under the poop to a finely carved hardwood door, which he unlocked; taking the key, Zorachus dismissed him and entered.

The cabin was spacious and luxuriously furnished. Along one bulkhead stood a large bed, with many silken pillows strewn across its wine-purple cover; opposite were an ornate table and bench. An empty chart rack stood on one side of the table, a massive ivory-inlaid wardrobe on the other. All the furniture was bolted to the floor. From the panelled ceiling hung several fine gold lamps; two portholes stood open in the stern bulkhead.

Zorachus opened the wardrobe, minded to stow his bag. Inside, he found a full rack of clothes. At first he thought Klazmouran had forgotten his garments, then he realized they were for him. They were packed very close together, but even so he could make out at least ten different designs. There were a half-dozen garments of varying lengths cut in each style— lacking his measurements, whoever made them had compensated in the only way possible.

He took out a silk robe in which serpentine motifs of purple, crimson, and deep blue were fantastically intertwined. The workmanship was astonishing, and he considered putting the robe on; it was the longest of the six in that pattern and he guessed it would fit. But his sterner self prevailed; he was not about to acquire a taste for such decadent fineries, and he saw he might easily do exactly that. He hung the garment back up, shut the wardrobe, and shoved his bag under the bed.

Footsteps approached, and he turned as Tchernaar came in looking very upset. The funeral smell of his perfume filled the cabin; he had just given himself a fresh sprinkling.

"Is something wrong?" Zorachus asked.

Tchernaar tossed his hands up. "Indeed there is, My Lord. We brought some slaves for you from Khymir, two women and a boy. We were going to surprise you. But they escaped last night, Klazmouran doesn't know how, and . . ."

"Don't concern yourself."

Tchernaar looked amazed. "You're not angry?"

"It's not as if I was expecting them. And I've been celibate all my life. I think I can hold out."

"Well, that's nice for you, My Lord," Tchernaar sulked. "But those whores took *my* bedmate with them."

"Did you come here just to tell me all this?"

Tchernaar shook his head. "I thought I'd see how you liked your quarters."

"Very much, thank you."

Tchernaar's face seemed to brighten a bit. "Finest cabin on the ship. I slept here myself on the voyage down."

"I thought this was Klazmouran's cabin."

"It was. I persuaded him to give it up, and now I'm surrendering it to you. Have you looked in the wardrobe?"

Zorachus nodded.

"What do you think?"

"I only looked closely at one of the robes, but the workmanship was magnificent."

"We had a team of Malochians on the job. Our Khymirian clothiers have been falling off lately and we wanted you to have the best."

"Very kind of you," Zorachus said, smiling. "But I'll wear my own clothes."

Tchernaar nodded towards the wardrobe. "Those *are* yours."

Zorachus caught himself. "Of course. But fine silks don't

make very practical shipwear."

"Practical enough. It doesn't matter if you ruin them. We've got more for you down in the hold."

"I don't want to make a habit of wastefulness," Zorachus answered firmly. "Especially with my own property."

"But—"

"Is it wise to use things not in accordance with their purposes? To destroy them without good reason? Does an intelligent man chop wood with a sword when he has an axe?"

Tchernaar shrugged. "I suppose not. Still—"

"Would you excuse me for a while?" Zorachus broke in. "I'd like to sleep a bit. It's been a trying day for me, leaving home and all. . . ." His voice trailed off.

"I understand, my Lord," Tchernaar said, and left, closing the door behind him. But the funeral smell lingered, sweet and cloying.

Zorachus sat on the bed. He did not need sleep, but Tchernaar made him acutely uncomfortable.

Trying to take his mind off his situation, he thought about the proof he had presented in the First Trial. He suddenly realized there was a hole in it, or something like a hole—perhaps. He set about trying to devise a way around the problem. In the end, he succeeded to his satisfaction. And by then, the voyage had begun.

chapter

4

FOR THE FIRST few days, he considered spending the trip locked in his cabin. It was a grim prospect, but perhaps less so than spending much time outside.

First, there was Tchernaar. Whenever Zorachus went on deck, the envoy was always around, even in the dark hours of the morning; the Sharajnaghi wondered if he ever slept. Finding Zorachus, Tchernaar would attempt conversation. Sometimes Zorachus humored him, trying to ignore the Khymirian's frequent advances. Sometimes Zorachus would say he wanted to be alone and Tchernaar would leave, but come back shortly on some pretext. Sometimes Zorachus said nothing at all and Tchernaar would go on with a monologue, and if that died out, he would still stand there, lingering silently. And when Zorachus went back to his cabin, Tchernaar would follow all the way to his door.

Yet Tchernaar did not disturb him nearly as much as the men kissing or fondling or even buggering each other. Zorachus would avert his eyes, or keep them fixed on sea or shoreline, but even then he would still hear obscene commands, simperings, moans, passionate slobberings. Some of this behavior was plainly for his benefit, and Tchernaar had hinted several times that Zorachus and he should join in.

But despite all this, Zorachus found he could not keep entirely to his cabin. Spacious and pleasant as it was, he still felt too confined—and the long voyage had just begun. Finally, he decided he could force himself to ignore the others whenever necessary, and practiced spending more and more time on deck. He came to feel comfortable enough.

Up the coast the convoy pressed, day after day. Hundreds of miles of desert slipped by to starboard.

The ships hugged the coast tightly—even when much time could have been saved by cutting across the larger bays. Zorachus asked Klazmouran why.

47

"There are *things* in the deeper water, my Lord," the Captain replied. "Surely you've heard of sea serpents—or worse."

"Yes," Zorachus answered. "But I've seen ships that weren't keeping so close to the shoreline. Are their captains reckless?"

Klazmouran shook his head. "Those weren't Khymirian ships."

"The monsters single out Khymirians?"

"Strange, isn't it? But true. If we ventured out much farther than we are now, we'd be gobbled down. Luckily, the beasts don't like the shallows. They come in once in a while though, and that's more than enough."

"Why are they so particular about their victims?"

"I've no idea," Klazmouran said. He laughed wearily. "Why is anything the way it is, my Lord? It's just the way things are, and we have to live with it."

"You don't have to," Zorachus replied. "Couldn't you get a command on a Kadjafi or Tarchan vessel?"

"Wouldn't consider it," Klazmouran said. "There are too many benefits to serving the Black Priesthood. Particularly to a man of my tastes."

"I see," Zorachus said. He did not carry the exchange further.

The convoy pushed ever northward, past the seaward end of the Andohar mountains and along the level Tarchan coast. The weather began to get chilly, at least to Zorachus's mind. He was used to the perpetual heat of the Kadjafi lands, and warm days by northern standards seemed almost raw to him; even on the brightest days, the sun looked positively watery.

About halfway up the Tarchan coast, the towns began to show earthworks and stockades; timber watchtowers loomed amid thatched roofs. The Kragehul sometimes raided this far south.

The convoy's men at arms, Khymirian marines, started wearing their helmets and black scale-mail, and kept their triangular shields close at hand. Zorachus took likewise to his armor, and thought often of the demon-rings. Tchernaar went about in a spired helm and ring-mail; Klazmouran spurned armor, but most of the sailors wore whatever protection they could.

The country to starboard continued flat for a long distance, then rose in arid, bladelike ridges, running east to west, which sometimes thrust out into the ocean. Before long, the ridges piled together to form the buttressed fastness of the Utgard Mountains. The Utgards were high and grim indeed; serrate snowpeaks stabbed up through layers of cloud, their spires bitter sharp. The lower slopes were dark with thick forest.

It got genuinely cold, though this was a balmy spring for that northern clime; there was snow, but not much. Zorachus broke out his cold-weather clothes, wearing them under his armor.

The convoy wove in and out between dozens of small islands. There were many places where it could have been ambushed, but the chief danger was a meeting with pirates heading south; the waters west of the Utgards were the territory of Kragehul who accepted Khymirian tribute, but who made no attempt to stop attacks on Khymirians by northern corsairs simply passing through.

The convoy's luck held. It encountered only single Kragehul ships and there was no challenge from them—save a single arrow from a long galley speeding by under oar. The shot amazed Zorachus; it had been against a strong, sleet-filled wind, and the distance between the ships was not small. Even so, the shaft took a sailor on the *Zancharthus* through the ear and pinned his head to the mast.

But the man was not killed outright. Screaming, he snapped the arrow and ran a few paces before a marine tripped him, grinning. He got up again; another man tripped him. This time he stayed on the deck, moaning, trying to pull the rest of the shaft from his head.

"Finish him!" Klazmouran ordered.

Marines gathered round, drew their swords, and obliged happily, laughing and joking as they hacked at him. A severed finger landed near Zorachus.

"Throw him overboard!" Klazmouran cried.

Grumbling, annoyed at their amusement being cut short, they gathered the dead man up and complied. Zorachus nudged the finger over the side with his foot, hardly believing what he had seen.

Tchernaar came up to him. "That Klazmouran," he said. "Just can't stand the men having any real fun."

One grey afternoon, three Kragehul ships were seen approaching from the southwest. Their bright yellow sails indi-

cated they were pirate craft from Drekjar, an island several
hundred miles off the coast. The Drekjar Kragehul attacked
Khymirians without hesitation.

The Khymirian vessels were traveling in file, the *Zancharthus* in the middle; with horn blasts, Klazmouran signaled
the other ships to close in. The basic Khymirian naval tactic
was to grapple vessels together, forming a floating fortress.

Both escorts sprouted oars. The one behind sped to catch
up, but the other only widened its lead, its captain obviously
hoping the other two ships would satisfy the Kragehul.

He had not reckoned on the reef, however. Hardly had he
embarked on that treacherous course when his ship ran
aground, mast snapping off, black sail fluttering forward.

Sizing up the situation, Klazmouran decided not to link up
with the escort behind; better far to sacrifice it. He guessed at
least one of the Kragehul would fasten on it, with another
going after the grounded ship. The third might keep coming,
but he thought it more likely it would join one of the others for
easier pickings. He ordered his sweeps unshipped, and the
Zancharthus picked up speed. He gave a wide berth to the
stranded escort, avoiding the reef; he smirked as he eyed the
men scurrying in panicked confusion on her deck.

After a time the other escort was attacked, grappled from
either side. The remaining Kragehul vessel continued forward,
making for the stranded ship. The reef proved no obstacle to
her shallow hull as she glided toward her prey, archers loosing
swarms of arrows.

Locked in his cabin during all this, Zorachus lay serenely
on his bed, deep in a trance. Suffering from a splitting headache, he had lowered himself into that state some time before
the Kragehul were sighted. Rousing himself several hours
after the *Zancharthus* made good its escape, he was dumb-
founded to learn what had happened.

Leaving the Utgards behind, skirting the Muspellheim
Peninsula, the ship passed the vast swamp called Fengarth;
northward, the country grew mountainous again, and great
fjords extended inland between treeclad slopes ridged with
white.

As the distance to Khymir narrowed, the *Zancharthus* traveled more and more by night, sheltering by day in small bays
on uninhabited outer islands. Most of the northern Kragehul

refused to deal with Khymirians; living closer to the city, they
knew them too well.

One morning, as Klazmouran steered in towards a hiding
place, a hulk was sighted, floating bows-up. A closer look
showed the prow bore a carven black hand.

Suddenly a cloud of dark smoke boiled up from the western side of the island Klazmouran was making for. Was another Khymirian ship burning there? Klazmouran changed
course, rounding the island on the eastern side.

It was a dangerous predicament. There was no real shelter
for twenty or more leagues, but there was no help for it; they
had to risk running north under the sun, by sail and sweep.

Zorachus, who had been awake most of the night, decided
not to go back to his cabin, too apprehensive to want sleep.
Leaning on the port rail, he watched the island slipping by,
half-listening to Tchernaar, who stood next to him complain-
ing that their present plight was somehow Klazmouran's fault.
At last Zorachus suggested he should take his complaints to
the Captain; Tchernaar hustled off to do precisely that.

Not long after, a swarm of gulls circling over a patch of
water drew Zorachus's attention. Presently, to his astonishment, a whale surfaced beneath them and lay blowing among
the whitecaps for a while. The birds skimmed down, and
seemed to be picking things off the vast beast—little clinging
animals, or so Zorachus guessed. Astonishment had become
sheer delight; he had never seen a whale before, and he stared
at it wide-eyed and open-mouthed, childlike in his wonder.

The leviathan submerged. The birds circled for a moment
longer, then flew over the ship. Zorachus hurried to the starboard rail hoping they would show him where the whale
would breach again.

They did. The whale rose spouting under them—but
quickly went down once more. Zorachus muttered a curse in
disappointment.

Then he noticed the water boiling not far from where the
beast had disappeared; huge bubbles rose and burst, domes of
trapped air yards across; spray and foam leaped thirty feet
above the churning sea. A tremendous rumbling swelled beneath the surface, and as it reached its crescendo a titanic
scaly arch lifted from the seething deep like a portent of
doomsday, the head and neck of a colossal serpent, the serpent
of serpents; the rear half of the whale's body dangled from the
fang-studded jaws, flukes trailing foam. The serpent flipped

its head back and the whale was *gone;* there was not even a bulge in the reptile's neck as its victim went down. Awe-struck, Zorachus felt as though he was contemplating the very idea of *monster* in the mind of God, revealed in all its power and terror and glory.

The serpent turned. Loop after loop of scaly body appeared in the foam. Leisurely, the creature swam toward the *Zan-charthus*.

The marines and sailors, who were already frightened half out of their wits, now went mad; many rushed below deck, while others cowered against the starboard rail—Tchernaar and Klazmouran among them. The ship veered, no one at the wheel.

Slowly, Zorachus took out the demon-rings and put them on. He doubted he could kill the serpent or drive it off, even with such terrible weapons, but they were the best he had. He prayed.

The monster came closer and closer, showing a wake like a wind-driven iceberg's, but its pace remained unhurried. It did not seem to be moving to the attack. Zorachus resolved not to strike until it made a hostile move.

It came in range of the demon-rings, swimming for a while parallel to the ship. Its gaze remained fixed; Zorachus had the uncanny feeling that the huge green eyes were staring directly at him.

The serpent moved slowly inward once more. Zorachus readied himself. He let the monster get very close. It occurred to him that it might go into ship-swamping throes of agony if he managed to wound it, but he knew he would have to take the risk.

He heard Tchernaar shouting, then pounding footbeats. The envoy came up beside him, voice raw with desperation: "Isn't there *anything* you can do? Are you sure there's no spell?"

"Get away!" Zorachus snapped.

"We'll die if you don't do something! This is no time for keeping secrets! You Sharajnaghim must have worked some-thing out. . . ." He began to sob. "Please do something, any-thing. . . ."

"Get away!" Zorachus cried.

Tchernaar plucked at him. "You *have* to—"

Zorachus struck him. Tchernaar toppled to the deck, stunned.

Some fifty feet away, head arched downwards, the serpent was once again swimming parallel to the ship. Its dripping underside was hung with long strands of kelp; bright red crabs the size of dogs clambered in the hanging gardens, and pink shrimp a yard long squirmed among the dangling leaves.

Zorachus studied the serpent's face. The eyes still seemed to be fixed on him, deep and calm and very wise. He wondered if their wisdom was only an illusion, if the serpent was really nothing but an unreasoning brute.

I reason, said a voice in his mind.

With a shock, Zorachus realized the voice was the serpent's.

"Are you going to attack?" he asked aloud.

No, the serpent replied. *I will spare the ship for your sake. I merely wanted to see you.*

"Why?"

Because you are the one. And now is the best time.

Zorachus did not know what the serpent meant, but an exquisite thrill of fear ran down his spine.

"Who are you, my Lord?" he asked.

"I am Zathlan," the serpent answered, and disappeared gently beneath the waves.

Groaning, shaking his head, Tchernaar got to his feet. "You know, Lord Mancdaman," he said, "I thought I heard you *talking* to that thing."

"I didn't realize I was speaking aloud," Zorachus replied. "His mind and mine were in contact."

"Has he gone?"

"Yes."

The envoy leaned over the rail, looking down into the water. "He's not lurking under the ship somewhere?"

"I don't think so," Zorachus replied.

"What did he say to you? Why didn't he attack?"

"It was all very strange. I didn't understand him. I don't know why he spared the ship." Zorachus paused. "I'm sorry I struck you, but you were distracting me."

"From what?" Tchernaar asked, leaning back, a suspicious glint in his eye. "Could it be you know some spell after all?"

Zorachus shook his head, ready with an answer: "The serpent was already speaking to me."

"I see."

They turned. The sailors and marines abovedeck were still cowering against the far rail, apparently expecting the serpent

to rise any second and destroy them. Klazmouran had not
budged. Tchernaar went across the deck, crying, "The
danger's past!"

Ill at ease, Zorachus stared westward, pondering the things
Zathlan had said. He took the demon-rings off and returned
them to their pouch.

The *Zancharthus* reached the second hiding place without
further incident. Zorachus went to his cabin and fell asleep.

When he woke, it was night, and the ship was moving
again. He had had some kind of evil dream, but could remember little of it, save that Zathlan was in it and was in great
pain that Zorachus knew he had somehow caused.

After having some of the food and drink that he kept in his
cabin, the Sharajnaghi went back on deck. Tchernaar found
him almost immediately and began to regale him, as he had
several times before, with descriptions of the Mancdaman inheritance. Trying to take his mind off the encounter with
Zathlan, and the dream, Zorachus paid closer attention than
usual.

After a while, Tchernaar paused. Then he said: "You know,
my Lord, Providence has been very good to you."

"You believe in Providence?" Zorachus asked, surprised.

Tchernaar laughed, teeth gleaming in the light of a nearby
lamp. "Not really. You know how you find yourself mouthing
old sayings and worn-out words when you don't have anything to say?"

"I suppose."

"We Khymirians used to believe in it," Tchernaar went on.
"But we've put such nonsense behind us. We believe in the
Powers, of course. *They've* been kind to you. But not out of
some kind of benevolent forethought. They make chaos, not
order. They're nothing but chaos themselves, and we're handiwork—little bits of squawking confusion."

Zorachus's curiosity was piqued. He had never heard phi-
losophy from Tchernaar before.

"If I live long enough in Khymir," he said, "will I come to
believe that? About the Powers—and myself?"

Tchernaar laughed again. "As if you don't already."

Zorachus had expected such an answer. "Well, what if I
didn't?"

"Then Mother Khymir would certainly convince you. The

truth about things is very clear there. Clearer than anywhere else."

"You know," Zorachus said slowly, "it's hard for me to imagine that I'd be able to enjoy my wealth, or anything else, if I thought I was nothing more than a little bit of squawking confusion."

"Come now, my Lord," Tchernaar said. "What do you think enjoyment is? Distraction."

"Would you believe me if I told you I was brought up to think differently?" Zorachus asked. "To think that true pleasures deepen one's knowledge of reality? That they feed the mind rather than stifle it?"

"I would not believe it," Tchernaar answered. "But if I decided to take such an idea seriously, I'd ask first what you meant by 'true pleasures.'"

"Ones that don't destroy—that aren't only pain disguised."

"But everything's a disguise," Tchernaar countered. "And if one's tastes run to pain, what of that? Pleasure's simply a matter of preference."

"What if some preferences rob the mind of reason? Without reason, man's only a beast."

"Man *is* only a beast," Tchernaar said. "The one that lays human dung."

There was a pause.

"Tell me,' the envoy said presently, "About the arguments you were just making. . . ."

"What of them?"

"I've heard that members of your Order regularly trot out such nonsense as if they believed it. Why the pretense? Anyone could see through it, you know."

"I'm not in the Order anymore."

"Of course not, my Lord. But that doesn't answer my question."

"Well, perhaps the answer lies in the fact that not everyone sees through that 'nonsense.' As long as that's true, it has its uses."

Tchernaar shrugged. "If indeed people can be taken in by it. . . . But they'd have to be very stupid."

"It's unwise to leave even stupid people out of your calculations," Zorachus answered. "It's also good to learn which people *are* stupid."

Tchernaar laughed. "Is that why you were arguing with me?"

"Well, to be honest, I did want to see how you'd react. I've had few Khymirians to study until recently. But you only confirmed my expectations."

"I see," Tchernaar said. He was silent for a few moments, then laughed again. "You know, my Lord, I just had an amusing thought. Can you imagine a man in your position going to Khymir, a man who really believed in that Sharajnaghi sham doctrine? How frustrated he'd be! It would probably drive him right out of his mind."

"If he really believed it," Zorachus said casually, "why would he go to Khymir?"

"He wouldn't, of course. But it's just splendid to think of him biting his lips when some delectable piece of meat wiggled by, just begging to be buggered or sliced. Can you imagine it?"

"I think so."

"Aren't you glad you're the sensible sort? There's nothing to keep you from appreciating Khymir's fine points. She offers total freedom to a man with enough power and will."

"So I've heard," Zorachus said. "That's why I chose as I did. However. . . ."

"What, my Lord?"

"You must forgive me, but sometimes I wonder if I'm deluded—if any freedom could be so complete. Nothing's forbidden?"

Tchernaar shook his head. "Not to a man of your rank."

"I could rape?"

"Yes."

"Kill?"

"Provided you made sufficient reparations. And you'll have the money. When I spoke of *slicing*, I meant precisely that."

"I could do *anything* to anyone I took a fancy to?"

"If they weren't of your rank. And if they were, you could always ask. There are some who'll submit to anything."

"Would they eat dung if I told them to?"

"Yours? Some would, I think." Tchernaar smiled.

"They wouldn't be looked down upon?"

"Certainly not. Most of us have tried it. Experimentation is essential in Khymir. There are so many diversions—take some of the creatures our wizards have bred. Remember me mentioning my bedmate?"

"The one the prostitutes escaped with?"

Tchernaar nodded. "She was a hybrid. Just the right combination of human and beast. I imagine she fetched those whores a good price. I miss her very badly. She struggled so deliciously. I had to keep her chained so tight." He sighed. "Domination's a tremendous thrill. I hope you experience it soon." He giggled. "Of course, you could come to my cabin and try it right now."

"Tchernaar," Zorachus said, struggling to restrain his disgust, "When are you going to realize that I want nothing to do with your body?"

"I realized a long time ago," Tchernaar said cheerfully. "But there's always the chance you'll change your mind."

"I think not."

"Well, even if that's true, my Lord, I don't mind. Humiliation can be very stimulating."

"God in heaven," Zorachus said under his breath, almost unconsciously.

"What was that, my Lord?"

"Never mind," Zorachus replied, deciding to return to his cabin.

But at that moment there came a cry from up near the bow, and he and Tchernaar went to see what was going on, as did many others.

One of the cooks had been fishing with a large pole and had snagged something very heavy; two sailors had had to help him haul his catch up onto the deck—a dead Khymirian marine, the fishhook lodged in his belt. The corpse's face and throat were badly slashed, and one hand still clutched a tuft of blond hair.

"Kragehul hair, I'll warrant," said the cook. The corpse had not been in the water long; the crabs had just started in on the pale flesh.

"His ship must've been taken somewhere near," said another man.

Klazmouran came up, having left the wheel to Karim, the first mate. "Get rid of the damn thing," he said. "There's no point gaping at it." He stalked off. The corpse went back over the side.

"I wonder how many of us will be joining him before this voyage ends?" a marine asked.

"I wish the wind would pick up," a sailor said. It had been falling off for some time. "Last thing we need is to be becalmed."

As if to realize the man's worst fears, the breeze picked that moment to die out completely. The sail flapped, going slack. His comrades burned glares at him.

"Had to open your mouth, eh?" one snarled.

"Maybe it'll start up again," Zorachus said.

"Not for a good long while, my Lord," a veteran sailor answered grimly. "When the wind stops off Muspellheim, it stops for hours."

Men cursed and prayed. Klazmouran ordered the oars unshipped, and the *Zancharthus* crawled northward. Zorachus remained on deck. Tchernaar kept close by, alternating between horror stories about the Kragehul and fearful, knuckle-chewing silence.

The wind returned at first light. Canvas billowed and the ship plowed the waves with renewed speed. But it continued under oar; the nearest refuge was still three hours away.

The sun rose in an oyster-colored sky, painting the clouds with fire. The *Zancharthus* swept on.

And two red sails appeared astern.

Tchernaar vanished belowdeck. Klazmouran ordered more speed from his sweepsmen, but there was no hope of losing the Kragehul. They were gaining too swiftly. Nor was there a way to beach the ship and flee on foot; the coast was too rugged.

Zorachus pondered the situation. Using the rings, he guessed he could cripple or even sink both Kragehul vessels. But bolts powerful enough to do it would heat the rings fearfully. Finding a bucket, he filled it with drinking water from a cask and went onto the castle. Klazmouran was up there, bellowing orders at the ship's bowmen who crouched at the castle's loopholes.

The Kragehul ships drew nearer, oars beating, sails taut. Their topstrakes were painted bright red; black dragons coiled on the long yellow flags fluttering from the masts, and gold-decked dragonheads were carved on the prows. Bright-helmed warriors strained at the oars; others sent arrows whistling once the *Zancharthus* came in range. Aimed at the Khymirian castle, most of the shafts stuck in the bulkhead, but a few streaked in through the loopholes and black-clad bowmen slumped. The other Khymirian archers tried to return fire against the wind; their shots fell short, striking the water in spurts of foam. But, as the distance narrowed, they began to pick off some of the Kragehul. Several pirates toppled into the brine.

Pulling a dead man away from a loophole, Zorachus eyed the Kragehul ships; they were now in range of the rings. He took the rings out and put them on, extending his arms through the loophole.

Lightning blazed forth, striking the mast of the starboard dragonhead. Oaken fragments flew, peppering holes in the square red sail. Kragehul clutched at splinter-riddled bodies and two fell overboard; the mast toppled backwards, draping the canvas over oar-stand, sweepsmen, and stern-post. The galley began to fall back.

Scorched fingers trembling, Zorachus turned to the water-bucket just as Klazmouran, an arrow in his throat, crumpled and knocked it over. Water splashed across the boards. Zorachus tried to cool the rings as it ran out the scuppers, but in vain. Blowing on the rings, he turned back to the loophole.

The other Kragehul ship was still closing; even after what had happened to the first dragonhead, its oarsmen had not stinted. And before Zorachus could loose more bolts, one of its archers put an arrow into the Sharajnaghi's left shoulder.

Gasping, Zorachus snapped the shaft and twisted away from the loophole, battling a tide of blackness welling up in his brain. Gritting his teeth, he fought to remain conscious, calling on deep reserves of will and training.

The blackness subsided. His shoulder throbbed, but he knew he could ignore the pain.

He crouched before the loophole once more, extended his hands and concentrated. Firebolts crackled from the rings, struck the second ship's mast and shivered it to kindling. The upper part of the tree toppled over the side, sail and rigging fouling the long sweeps to starboard. The dragonhead fell back.

Zorachus smiled. The *Zancharthus* was out of danger. Exaltation drowned the pain in his fingers and shoulder.

Then he saw the burning streaks hurtle across the widening but still too narrow gap between the ships. Fire arrows.

He watched them pass overhead, turned to see them strike the sail. In half a minute the canvas was consumed.

He looked back at the Kragehul ships, still blowing on the rings. The men on the first dragonhead had managed to hurl the sail and broken mast overboard, and those on the second were disentangling their oars. On both vessels, the unmanned sweeps had acted as brakes, and the dragonheads were now well behind the *Zancharthus*, which was still coasting forward. But soon both were pressing north again, slower than before, yet fast enough. Zorachus was amazed by the pirates' bravery. He guessed they had never seen, and had probably never heard of, such magic as he had used against them. Yet they were not dismayed. He was deeply saddened that he would have to send most of them, perhaps all of them, to their deaths.

"Blast them again, Lord Mancdaman!" a marine cried.

"Not till they're back in range," Zorachus answered. Pain flared in his shoulder; he could feel blood spreading warmly through his gambeson.

"You'll send 'em under?"

Zorachus nodded.

"Praise the Powers!" the marine shouted. "War magic at sea!"

The dragonheads closed in once more. Arrow after arrow thudded into the *Zancharthus*'s castle, killing or wounding many of the remaining Khymirian archers. A shaft narrowly missed Zorachus's head.

The dragonheads came in range. Zorachus extended his hands, but an instant before he willed the demon-rings to strike, there was a burst of pain from the arrow wound, and his concentration wavered; the dragon prow of the starboard ship exploded, but nowhere near the waterline.

The twinge in his shoulder subsided, but pain shrieked marrow-deep in his fingers at the heat from the rings. His concentration was even worse when he struck again; the bolts fell far short of the mangled Kragehul bow.

He paused for a few moments, focused his mind as powerfully as he could, and launched two more bolts. The pirate's bow disintegrated; a wave poured down the hull, and the ship sank in seconds. Cased in mail, most of the crew went with it, but a few managed to save themselves by clinging to sea chests or rowing benches.

The other dragonhead neared the *Zancharthus*. Zorachus knew he had to cool the rings if he was to use them again; the pain was simply too great. Half crouching, he rushed to the front of the castle and bounded down the steps. Dashing to the water cask, he tossed the lid aside and plunged his hands in; steam rose in wisps. He whipped his hands back and forth through the water. The pain in his fingers lessened and he pulled his dripping hands out.

It was then that he saw the dragon prow slide up along the port side, polished amber eyes glittering wickedly, jaws set with interlocking rakes of killer whale teeth; oars shipped, the Kragehul vessel skimmed forward on momentum, crunching through Khymirian sweeps. Arrows and casting axes decimated the sailors and marines along the *Zancharthus*'s rail. Grappling hooks followed. The two hulls clashed with a terrific jolt and the Kragehul leaped aboard in a flourish of steel —byrnied blond giants hacking furiously at their foes, warding off Khymirian strokes with huge wooden round-shields.

Zorachus saw the melee was too wild for him to use the rings and drew his sword. Despite the burns on his hands, despite the pain, he could grip it well enough.

"Oh my God," he said, summoning his strength, "deliver me." Then he roared and charged into the fight.

Blood-spattered chaos awaited him, the din of combat ripped the air, mad shouts and screeches of agony, the crunch of triangular shields splitting under axe blows, the clang and slither of steel on steel. A Kragehul appeared before him— Zorachus stabbed him in the side. As the man sagged, eyes bulging, jaw working soundlessly, another pirate rushed up, sword gleaming. Zorachus ducked a powerful slash and cut off the man's swordhand. The Kragehul turned rime-white and stumbled backward. A third charged in from the left; Zorachus wheeled to meet him, stepped forward, and opened his throat before he could launch a stroke. Face registering awful surprise, the man staggered, then lashed out with his sword in a final desperate bid for vengeance. Zorachus dodged the stroke with ease. Sword and roundshield dropped from the Kragehul's hands and he fell onto all fours. A dead Tarchan sailor flopped down across his back, and the Kragehul collapsed. Howling in triumph, the Tarchan's slayer, a huge yellow-bearded pirate, turned to look for new prey; his eyes locked with Zorachus's and he grinned fiercely, apparently not even seeing Zorachus's point shooting toward his face. The thrust passed between his jaws, up into his brain; the Kragehul was a corpse before the grin could drop from his lips.

The fight raged on. Steel glittered everywhere. Weapons shattered; sword shards spun through the air. A spear passed under Zorachus's arm, and a thrown seax knife clanged off the Sharajnaghi's helmet. In front of him, four butchered Khymir-

ians went down, almost at once; three barbarians stormed over
them. Zorachus got in under the foremost's two-handed axe
and stabbed him, leaped back, sidestepped the second man's
mighty downward stroke, and bounded over the blow the third
man aimed at his legs. But no sooner had his feet touched the
deck when he sprang back up, and the third man took his
shortsword through the cheek. Zorachus atop him, the man
rocked backward dead, the Sharajnaghi struggling to pull free
his sword. Roaring, the second man whirled and bounded forward, axe singing down; releasing his sword hilt, Zorachus
threw himself out of the axe's way, and the weapon sank deep
into the dead man's ribcage, sticking tight. Zorachus slammed
his vambrace against the axeman's kneecap, shattering bone.
The Kragehul howled, loosed the axe helve and clutched his
knee. Zorachus punched him in the side of the throat and the
Kragehul fell in a heap, helmet rolling free, blond locks spilling forward over his head.

Zorachus rose, breathing hard. He was no longer in the
thick of the fight, but could see things were going badly for
his allies. They were simply no match for the Kragehul.

He craved rest—a few moments at least. He was growing
dizzy from blood loss, and the arrow wound and the burns
were sheer torment. But with a powerful tug he freed his
sword and goaded himself towards the nearest knot of slaughter.

Kragehul after Kragehul went down before him. Rallying a
handful of marines, he charged headlong to the rescue of a
group of sailors pinned against the starboard rail; he himself
killed half the Kragehul assailing them. Wherever the fray was
sharpest, he went; all over the ship Khymirians took heart.

The tide turned. The Kragehul had been outnumbered from
the start, but now, thanks to Zorachus, they were being over-
whelmed. Blade piercing barbarian flesh again and again, he
strewed the deck with corpses, his allies following eagerly in
his wake, hacking, slicing. One group of Kragehul after another was annihilated.

The carnage hastened towards its close. Stubbornly courageous, most of the remaining pirates went down fighting on
the *Zancharthus,* but the rest slipped back onto the dragonhead and tried to cut the grapnel lines, only to abandon their
efforts as marines swarmed aboard. The Kragehul formed a
small, doomed shield wall up near the bow.

Zorachus did not join in that final butchery. He had done

all that was necessary. He wiped and sheathed his sword, barely able to slide the blade back into the scabbard. His head spun; he had lost much blood. His gambeson was soaked. Eyes half closed, ears ringing, he leaned on the port rail. Pain gnawed at his fingers. It occurred to him that he should take the rings off before they ate further into his burns, but all he did was stare stupidly at them through slitted lids.

He half noticed that the din of combat had stopped. The Khymirians were laughing and shouting. But above their racket he heard a voice bellowing in what he guessed was the Kragehul tongue; almost unconsciously he snapped his eyes wide open and looked toward the bow of the Kragehul ship. A large crowd of marines milled there.

All at once, a giant Kragehul rushed naked out of the throng, crisscrossed wounds dripping blood. Several marines bolted in pursuit, seized him, and forced him down over a rowing bench. One took off his armor, unbuckled his belt, and let his trousers drop.

Zorachus straightened, gripping the rail with both hands, nails digging into the oak, mind echoing with a single maddening thought: *You saved these vermin?*

His fury mounted till he could contain it no longer. Trembling in every member, eyes distended, arrow scar flaming red on his cheek, he screamed, seeing the other deck as through a fever dream, details impossibly distinct; every bead of sweat stood out clearly on the rapist's forehead as he looked up, and every strand of his hair glistened with its own greasy sheen. The men holding the Kragehul looked up too, as well as those who had come up behind the rapist waiting for their turn, and the moist whiteness of their eyes, the redness of their dripping tongues, and the fulsome pink of their sweaty, blood-speckled faces seemed to vibrate in Zorachus's mind; the whole world reverberated with his shriek.

He thought of turning the rings on them, blasting them to rags for the sheer pleasure of it—and recoiled instantly from the idea, shocked by the murderousness of his own emotions. Never before had he experienced such hatred, let alone actual bloodlust. Nothing had prepared him for the sheer *terror* of it. It was like coming face to face with a demon . . .

A tremendous spasm of pain swept out from his shoulder wound. His hand shot up towards the arrow stump. Then the shimmering world exploded in sparks.

chapter

5

He woke in his bed, feverish, bathed in perspiration, his blanket damp with it: an evil taste was in his mouth. Vicious aches badgered him, running from his fingers to his elbows, and down from his wounded shoulder along the left side of his chest. He stank of infected, seared, and sweaty flesh.

He looked at a porthole. It was dark outside.

He sat up, the bed creaking beneath him. There came a sharp breath from outside his cabin, and he turned his head, a marine entered.

"I see you're awake, my Lord," he said.

"I see you are, too," Zorachus said groggily, and pulled the blanket aside. His armor and padding had been removed: he was clad in a finely embroidered knee-length, white linen shirt.

He looked at his hands. His burned fingers were rudely bandaged, the dressings stained with dark ointment.

"Where are my rings?" he asked.

"In the table, my Lord," the marine replied. "Righthand drawer."

Zorachus sniffed his fingers. The smell was grievous, but not as bad as what was coming from his shoulder. Above the arrow wound his shirt was blotted with glistening umber. He yanked the garment open, popping buttons. The arrow stump had been removed, the wound dressed even more greasily than his fingers. Whoever had tended him apparently swore by unguents: the Sharajnaghi wondered if there might be some perverse unguent cult in Khymir. He ripped the bandage off. The revealed skin was black where a cauterizing torch had been applied—far too long.

"My Lord," the marine groaned, "now look what you've done. Karim'll have to put another dressing on. . . ."

Zorachus spat a laugh and started taking the bandages off

his fingers. The marine grabbed him.

"It's for your own good, my Lord."

"Let me go," Zorachus said.

"No."

"Let me go," Zorachus repeated, simmering.

"Not till you agree to stop tampering with your bandages. Karim and Lord Tchernaar'll have my hide."

"Well then, I'll give you an excuse." Racked with pain and fever though he was, Zorachus was still several times stronger than the marine, he freed himself with ease.

But the marine would not give up and tried to lay hands on him once more. Zorachus struck him in the face. The marine shot back across the room and tumbled out into the hall.

"Tell Karim and Tchernaar I can heal myself," Zorachus called after him, grimacing. The hand he had used launched a horrendous protest: its burned digits seemed to be threatening to secede.

The marine rose, pawed at his mouth, and vanished from sight. Moments later Zorachus heard him speaking to someone in the corridor; the word "delirious" was all the Sharajnaghi caught. Tchernaar and Karim came in shortly, the marine in tow. Zorachus had his fingers uncovered by then.

"What's all this, Lord Mancdaman?" Tchernaar asked.

"I'm not delirious, if that's what you're wondering," Zorachus answered. "I *am* running a fever, but my head's clear; I smell my wounds very distinctly."

"I did my best," Karim said. "But I'm no doctor."

"I'll treat myself from now on," Zorachus said.

"How?" Tchernaar asked.

"A healing spell," Zorachus replied. "It's one of the few Sharajnaghi magics that can be worked at sea."

"That, and sinking ships," Tchernaar said. "I understand you blew one of those dragonheads clean out of the water."

"Not quite."

"I wish I'd been abovedeck to see it. But tell me, my Lord: why did you keep such powers secret?"

"A wise man never displays his strongest weapons—unless he has to." Feeling dizzy, the Sharajnaghi lay back down. He guessed he would not be clear witted for long, and knew he should begin the healing spell as soon as possible. "I'd like to be left alone now. Would you see I'm not disturbed for the next twenty-four hours?"

Tchernaar turned to the marine. "You heard him. Pass it on to the next man on duty."

The marine nodded. Still fingering his split lip, he shot a peeved glance at Zorachus.

"Well then," Tchernaar said, "we'll be off."

"Would you close the door on the way out?" Zorachus asked.

Tchernaar nodded, leaving with the others.

Zorachus took one last look at his seared fingers, folded his arms on his chest, and closed his eyes. Concentration was difficult, but he attained the necessary level, then uttered a spell which took three minutes to complete—a formula that, it was written, had been revealed to Washallah Irakhoum by the angel Shuriel himself. Finishing, Zorachus dropped off into a deep trance.

Twenty-four hours later, alert and refreshed, his pains and fever gone, he reassumed physical perceptions. He still reeked of sweat, but the other stenches had vanished.

Sitting on the edge of the bed, he took a deep breath, rose, and stripped off his shirt. His once-wounded shoulder was coated with a dark gelatinous substance, the residue of dead flesh. His fingers were likewise gummed. He wiped them and his shoulder off with the shirt, then washed as well as he could, using strong soap and seawater from a barrel.

While he was drying himself, he realized how hungry he was. Getting out bread and cheese, and wine in a skin bottle, he ate steadily for twenty minutes, wrapped in his blanket.

Finishing, he decided to get dressed and go outside. His gear had been laid out on the bench, the cloth goods cleaned, the arrow hole in the byrny repaired; the new links, browned iron, stood out clearly against the grey steel.

Chain mail, he thought. *Ugh.* He felt too good to want to bother with the weight; the trance had left him in a slightly euphoric state. His better judgement protested, but he decided to dispense with his armor for the first time in several weeks.

Once he had his clothes on, he took the demon-rings from the table drawer, put them in their pouch, and went on deck.

The moon was up, bright and full. He looked at the mast. A new sail had been set.

He went up to the poopdeck where Karim was at the wheel.

"Good evening, Lord Mancdaman," the new captain said.

"Good evening," Zorachus answered, striding over to the port rail. He looked at the silverlit coast, watching the mouth of a fjord slide past. The air was cool but pleasant, the sea calm. The only sounds were an occasional flap of the sail and the gentle rush of the water. He was perfectly content to remain at the rail for a long while, gazing at the coast and the mild waves. He knew the ship must be very close to Khymir, and he wanted to enjoy as much tranquility as possible before his true ordeal began. He prayed that Tchernaar would not appear, at least for a few hours.

God obliged.

The moon set. The night grew old, and the breeze stiffened. A fringe of yellow light appeared behind the eastern peaks. The glow grew steadily, and finally the sun lifted over the mountains.

Karim did not run the ship toward cover; there were no good hiding places nearby and the distance to Khymir was short. He steered northwestward around a jagged cape, the northern tip of the great island the *Zancharthus* had been skirting for two hundred miles. The ship pushed out across a broad expanse of open water. The walls of Muspellheim were blue in the distance, but a long stretch of coast was obscured by a towering line of thunderheads. The ship made straight towards those titanic clouds.

"Aren't there monsters in these waters?" Zorachus asked Karim. "We're so far from the coast. . . ." Zathlan had spared the ship, but the Sharajnaghi had no reason to think other leviathans would do likewise.

Karim shook his head. "Too many reefs. The beasts can manage in narrows and shallows, but they prefer not to."

The ship skimmed onward, the black hand on its prow still pointing toward the clouds. Zorachus gazed at them. They seethed visibly, full of movement. But they did not, as far as he could tell, drift on the wind.

Midway through the morning, Tchernaar appeared on the castle and came up to him.

"You're looking fit, my Lord," the envoy said appreciatively. "I see your hands are healed."

Zorachus nodded.

"We should reach Khymir sometime early this afternoon, I think," Tchernaar said. "The Great Mother lies beyond those thunderheads up ahead—or rather, inside them. They hem her in, a perpetual barrier. And in the center it's always warm—

even by Kadjafi standards, I think."

"The clouds keep the cold out?"

Tchernaar shook his head. "The spell does it. It was laid down a thousand years ago, by the first Adepts of Tcherno-bog. Five weeks of constant blood offerings were needed."

"Then why the thunderheads?" Zorachus asked. "Such angry-looking clouds."

"Aren't they? Always roiling and threatening. They're the reaction to the spell. And to Khymir. There are powerful pres-ences in Muspellheim, you see, spirits of stone, sea, and air. They hate Khymir, hate all her comfortable, incongruous heat. You'll feel it when we pass under the clouds; it'll be all around you, boiling, probing rage."

"Do these presences ever gobble up ships?"

"They've been known to," Tchernaar replied. "Sometimes the seas are mountainous beneath the clouds, and ships are struck by lightning and vanish without a trace. But when the situation gets too unruly, our wizards massacre some of the neighboring Kragehul with sendings. That usually quiets things."

"You take reprisals against the weather?"

"It works," Tchernaar said. He scanned Zorachus's face. "If you're worried about our passage, relax. There was a fine slaughter of the barbarians shortly before we left Khymir. Things should be reasonably calm. Respectful, I might say."

The ship sailed ever nearer the clouds. For all their men-ace, Zorachus thought them gorgeous: tremendous billows of thick vapor, huger than the hugest mountains, shimmering white above, darkening to blue, then deep purple beneath. The water below was steeped in shadow, but every few seconds the darkness was torn by forked lightning.

The sea grew choppier with each passing mile, lashed by swelling crosswinds. The *Zancharthus*'s progress became more difficult, and the hull heaved violently. At Karim's order, sailors strung heavy-weather lines on both decks. Tchernaar got nauseous and went below, but Zorachus re-mained on the poop; going to the castle's forward bulkhead, he gripped it with one hand and a heavy-weather line with the other. The ship's motion did not bother him; he rather enjoyed the jouncing ride.

After much tacking, the *Zancharthus* eventually reached the thunder-racked western fringe of the clouds, and there Zorachus saw a vista which surpassed his wildest notions of grandeur. The clouds rose like a wall above him, layer after purple-shadowed layer, and as the ship entered the darkness beneath, he looked skyward along that vapory expanse like a man standing at the base of a cliff. For all he knew, it might have risen ten miles, and he could see all the way to the mushrooming heights, which rolled out mightily against the blue vault of heaven.

Then the vision was gone; the ship sailed on into lightning-fraught gloom. When the bolts streaked down, everything on deck stood out in vivid relief, and stark shadows fled across the boards. Zorachus's ears were nearly split by the blasting thunder. A hundred yards in, torrential rain pelted the vessel, and he was soaked to the skin as he eyed the brief flashing vistas of cloud and tormented sea.

He waited to feel the hostility Tchernaar had described, and after a while his mind began to hum with sensation; the hatred *was* there, a seething nimbus of it playing about the ship. The farther in the *Zancharthus* went, the more intense the nimbus grew.

Suddenly, somehow, he knew the lightning itself was becoming charged with hate; the Presences were not so respectful after all. Damp as they were, the Sharajnaghi's shorthairs began to lift, and his scalp crawled as with the pricks of tiny needles. Noticing a crimson glow playing weirdly about the masthead, he kneeled, still clutching bulkhead and rope, and looked out through the castle gate.

Seconds later the black sky split open in a bloody flash; a red bolt slashed down, struck the masthead and forked to the deck beneath, blasting two sailors to bits.

Most of the men on deck scrambled below, leaving too few to tack the sail. The crosswinds changed; the ship was driven back.

But the Presences had taken some satisfaction in the killings, enough for the moment—feeling the anger in the clouds recede, Zorachus stood back up. The men below deck felt it too and soon returned to resume tacking. The ship continued on its tortuous course. The storm's violence lessened. The *Zancharthus* began to make better progress.

Zorachus looked past the plunging prow. A bar of light gleamed through the rain, between the churning cloud-ceiling and the waves. The ship closed on it gradually, emerging at last from the dark and rain and wind.

Steamy warmth settled over Zorachus's wet flesh, a cloying hothouse exhalation. He suddenly felt as if he were entombed in the womb of a gigantic dead animal, rotting and cooking in the sun.

The ship heaved no longer. Sail slack, it coasted out into a wide greenish expanse of tepid-looking water. The sea was impossibly, unnaturally calm. It almost seemed as though the heavy air were pressing it flat, smothering it with a damp, warm pillow. The glazed water was storm-bounded to north, west, and south. Thunderclaps reached Zorachus's ears, but they were stifled, muffled, the thick enchantment hovering over the place holding even them in sway.

To the east was a line of vegetation-matted cliffs, and in their midst rose a great mountain, the tallest Zorachus had ever seen. But there was no snow on it, even on the topmost ridges. Three thousand feet up its sheer seaward face, on a shelf that looked as though a giant blade had planed it from the stone, lay Mother Khymir.

Nothing had prepared him for the sight of her; her opulence was proverbial, but the reality of it was beyond his wildest imaginings. Thangura, city of the Great Khan, was small and rude by comparison. Behind the Great Mother's massive walls of dark blue stone, rose hundreds of purple, silver, and golden domes, needle-like turquoise minarets, and adamantine arches —all of breathtaking size. Titanic equestrian statues and figures of monstrous creatures reared up on the peaks of black pyramids. Immense aqueducts spanned the city from the encircling mountains. A vast blank-eyed stone face stared seaward, smiling cruelly, flanked by two black hands set on pillars. Ziggurat-like structures, with what appeared to be ruined temples on their crowns, thrust skyward.

But mightiest of all was the sky-raking black tower lunging up out of the city's heart; Zorachus hardly believed his eyes. It loomed incredibly stark against the slopes behind. The other buildings could not counterbalance its awesome severity. The surrounding precincts seemed a mere sprawl in comparison.

Zorachus felt a strong pang of foreboding. The tower had the look of a weapon, of a sword or spear poised to disembowel the heavens; it was a colossal blasphemy, rendered still more terrible by its domination of the city at its feet. Khymir might well have been the Great Mother, a vast supine pillow of flesh. But at her center rose a mocking masculine power, a mad force battening on a multitude of human lives. The Sharajnaghi did not need to be told that the tower

was Banipal Khezach, the temple of Tchernobog the Black
Lord, the archangel who fell because he opposed the creation
of organic life. Zorachus wondered if the Khymirians knew
what they had in their midst, if they realized that their every
wallow in blood and mire was but a vindication of the Black
Lord's ultimate purpose—to cure creation of the Organic
Plague.

Karim called to a sailor on the main deck, sending him
down with orders for the sweepsmen. Shortly, the long oars
were clacking in their ports.

The Captain steered directly for a chasm in the cliff face,
which cut off the southern approach to Khymir. The *Zancharthus* drew slowly near the cleft.

Two Khymirian warships waited ahead on either side of the
opening, a barrier-chain strung between them. As the *Zancharthus* approached, the chain was lowered and she passed
through.

It was low tide and huge runnels stood revealed in the stone
to left and right; in the ages before the waters were magically
stilled, powerful waves had undercut the chasm's sides. Mast
shipped, a large vessel could have passed easily beneath the
curving overhangs. The grooves were matted with seaweed;
dark strands dangled down.

Strange sea birds, gorgeously varicolored, soared and
swooped between the chasm's frowning walls, their cries
echoing and reechoing a perpetual chorale. A marine shot one
that dipped too close to the ship; the dart went clear through
the creature, which jerked in midair but somehow continued
flying. Flapping towards the northern wall, it smashed into it
and hung there, head caught in a crevice. The other birds
flocked round; one by one, they swept down on their still-
twitching fellow, pecked and tore, and flew off with gaudy
feathers clenched in their beaks.

The ship pressed deeper into the channel. Looking up,
Zorachus saw a long bridge spanning the gap. It was a brilliant feat of engineering; he had no idea of how it had been
accomplished, and he knew a good deal about bridge building.
But he was not surprised. Not after seeing Banipal Khezach.

Presently, Karim ordered the ship's lamps lit and steered to
port. A gigantic cave mouth yawned in the northern wall; the
Zancharthus passed inside.

After some distance, the ship rounded a bend. A broad disc
of green twilight slipped into view and the *Zancharthus* en-

tered an immense domed cavern a mile or more across. Its
ceiling was an unearthly star chart of green-glowing lights,
five hundred feet high at the peak.

The cavern's far wall was girt with an enormous semicircular ledge, upon which many warehouses had been built and
from which led many stone quays. Moored to the quays were
hundreds of ships of all classes, and a smaller number were
anchored in the harbor. Thousands of lamps and torches burned
upon their decks, prows, and rigging, so that the vessels looked
like luminous fish in the depths of a dimly green-lit sea.

The *Zancharthus* crossed the harbor slowly. Karim ordered
the oars withdrawn and steered for a quay on the right, where
space was reserved for the Priesthood's warships. The vessel
coasted alongside and was soon moored.

Tchernaar came up on the castle wearing purple silks and a
bright yellow-green cape.

"When do we leave?" Zorachus asked.

"We could go now," Tchernaar said. "Wouldn't be able to
ride, however." Because the tide was so low, the *Zancharthus*
was too far down for the horses to be unloaded even with the
ship's winches. Iron-runged ladders set in the side of the quay
were the only way up.

"I don't mind."

"Shall I have your clothes sent to your house?"

"I can carry my own bag."

"One of my men can manage that. But I was referring to
the clothes in your wardrobe."

"Oh, of course. By all means, send them."

"I suppose you can't wait to start wearing them. But I
expect they'll seem rather tawdry compared to what you'll be
wearing tomorrow night."

"Tomorrow night?" Zorachus asked.

"Lord Kletus will almost certainly be holding a banquet to
celebrate your arrival. You'll be presented to the lords and
ladies of Khymir, and it's important that you come clothed in
special gifts from Kletus, to show your respect for him. He'll
send tailors around beforehand, and they'll make sure you're
dressed as spectacularly as possible."

"Fine."

They went down from the castle, Zorachus going to his
cabin to get his bag and change out of his cold-weather garb.
When he came back out, Tchernaar was shouting to someone
in the hold, giving instructions regarding his horse and posses-

sions. When he was finished, the envoy summoned up a half-dozen marines.

"Ready, Lord Mancdaman?" he asked.

Zorachus nodded. The group climbed one of the quayside ladders and made their way to the crowded waterfront. Passing between two torch-flanked warehouses, they came out close to the cave's curving wall. Cut through the wall was a wide ramp-tunnel; traffic to and from the ships traveled that path.

But there was another way up. A shaft had been bored in the cave's ceiling, and from it hung two huge hawsers, one attached to the top of a great steel cage, the other running via pulleys into a gigantic pit nearby. The pit was guarded by soldiers with bows and spears, and a strong reek of excrement and sweat rose from it. As Zorachus's party made for the cage, the Sharajnaghi got close enough to the pit's edge to glimpse a battalion of filthy slaves chained naked to the spokes of a hoisting machine; most were Kragehul, or so he guessed from their looks. Armored overseers with whips and swords stood about them.

Zorachus and his escort reached the cage. The keeper opened the gate and they filed in. Zorachus winced to think of the labor they were going to cause the slaves in the pit.

The keeper entered the cage, shut the door with a clang, and whistled to the pit guards. They signaled the overseers and the crack of whips split the air, followed by brutish grunts of pain. The cage began to rise.

Talking and joking with the keeper, the marines clustered toward the back. Zorachus and Tchernaar remained near the gate.

"Lord Kletus keeps this lift for his servants," Tchernaar explained, face red in the light of a hanging taper. "It's quite handy."

"Must be horrible taking cargo up that ramp," Zorachus said.

"People and animals are always dropping dead. Fouls the traffic something awful. It's good we don't have to depend on foreign food. The traffic would be five times as heavy and perfectly impossible."

Zorachus's eyebrows arched with surprise. "I would've thought most of your food was imported. Do you have farms? The land looked so rugged around the city. . . ."

"Far too rugged for farming," Tchernaar agreed. "But even

if it weren't, all that dirt-grubbing's such a bother. So's fishing, for that matter. Luckily, the founding fathers gave us food as well as warmth—plants conjured from another dimension. They need little sunlight and only a bit of soil. Large numbers can be raised indoors, in the smallest rooms, and the fruit can be prepared many ways."

"Sounds like the ideal crop," Zorachus said.

"No, there are drawbacks. Three, to be exact. To start with, the fruit's versatile, but pretty bland by itself. Nourishing, but unfit for the discriminating palate. We need spices. That's why we trade so heavily with the southern countries."

"Isn't it possible to find alien spices?" Zorachus had a broad knowledge of military magic and many scientific forms; but he had never studied the agricultural kind.

"In theory, yes," Tchernaar answered. "But most alien plants don't flourish on our plane. The right types, if indeed they exist, have eluded us. Some of the Guild wizards are still looking, I believe. If they ever succeed, we won't have to deal with those southern pirates. We'll be completely self-sufficient—like a maid with a mirror, as the saying goes."

"What do you pay for the spices?"

"Gold. There are rich lodes in the mountains, the fountainhead of our wealth. But we have other sources, too. Booty from our wars with the Kragehul, slaves, amber, resins. Our wizards also supply wealthy southerners with bedmates. The Emir of Frykaz got one recently. Part cuttlefish. Charming beast."

"Do you ever trade those food plants?" Zorachus asked. "There'd be quite a market. Famine would become a thing of the past. . . ."

"And then the market would dry up, wouldn't it?" Tchernaar laughed. "But the plants won't grow outside Khymir. There's something about the atmosphere here. The ambience of the place, if you will. That's their second drawback."

"You mentioned a third."

Tchernaar nodded. "They need human blood," he said matter-of-factly. Casual discussion of the most loathsome things seemed to be a typical Khymirian trait, as far as Zorachus could tell.

"Why is that a problem?" the Sharajnaghi asked after a while, having raised silent thanks that the *Zancharthus* had reprovisioned in Thangura. "Do you think there's something sacred about human blood?"

Tchernaar harrumphed. "It's costly stuff, that's all. The blood slaves in the upper-class households could be put to much better use. And among the poor, parents have to give their firstborn to the plants. Can you imagine sacrificing something so delicious?"

"No," Zorachus said. After a pause, he asked: "Why do the plants need *human* blood? Won't some other sort do?"

"Yes, but only if it's from rational animals, creatures that can think. And there's no point in chasing through alien dimensions after them. Not when we've got a healthy supply of people. And it's not as though we go through a lot of slaves; they aren't killed. We just graft shoots into two of the victim's major veins. Blood flows through the plants and their sap flows through the slave. Plants and victim become parts of each other, and the bodies begin to produce extraordinary amounts of blood. One human can serve a roomful of growths. The plants are all connected."

"And what happens to the slave's mind?" Zorachus asked.

Tchernaar laughed. "It *vegetates,* as you might expect. After the first few weeks, the slaves lose the power of speech, and soon they don't react to anything at all. They just hang on the stakes, staring off into space. Some don't even blink and their eyes get frightfully thick with dust, like grey cataracts." He paused and seemed to slip into a reverie; Zorachus guessed he had nothing more to say.

Just as well, the Sharajnaghi thought.

But Tchernaar was not finished.

"When I was young," he went on, "I used to go into the garden and look at the bodies. We had a large garden, so we needed more slaves than usual.

"I was sixteen when a young girl was installed. She was Kragehul, golden-haired, about my age. She already had very nice breasts—we hang the victims up nude, of course.

"I visited her often. She was wide awake for a long while, longer than most garden slaves. Unfortunately, she was too far up on the pole for me to enter her, and that was a genuine torment to me—I was still fond of plain womanflesh back then. She excited me greatly, trussed up there the way she was. But I had a fine time with her feet and legs—that is, until her nerves went dead and she didn't react anymore. I used to burn her. My parents didn't want me to waste a drop of that precious blood, so I just raised a lovely crop of blisters. And each morning when I came back, they were gone; the plant sap healed them from within, very quickly, so I could start all over again each time, playing with fresh new skin. . . ."

By now Zorachus had heard far more than enough, but he knew from experience that whatever he did—short of violence—Tchernaar would find some pretext to finish his story sometime during the next hour. There was no stifling the envoy when he waxed autobiographical.

"I often think of her," Tchernaar said. "My first love, as the Southrons would say." He sighed. "I tried to find out how she felt about me. I begged her to tell me. But I never got anything but curses and shrieks. She never admitted the truth to me or herself. She never realized she was just playing a game."

"Game?" Zorachus asked. "Do you think she liked being burned?"

Tchernaar never blinked. "Of course she liked it," he answered, as if it were the most obvious thing in the world. "I've already told you how she cursed me. That was one of the best indications."

"I would've taken the curses for curses. Simply because *you* enjoy pain. . . ." Zorachus's voice trailed off.

Tchernaar smiled patiently. "In some ways you're very naive, my Lord. There are two kinds of people in the world: honest and dishonest, those who acknowledge their desires and those who deny them. And the dishonest ones are always most aroused by the very things they pretend to find most repulsive. I've seen this in many countries—particularly in your Kadjafi lands, if I might be so bold. Most Kadjafim, the stupid hypocritical majority, are always condemning us Khymirians, calling us degenerates because we roger our mothers and fathers and sons. But they burn to do the same. Moralizing about our pleasures gives them an excuse to dwell on them at length. And then they scuttle into their rooms and stroke themselves behind locked doors, or pretend that their wives are their daughters or their sons."

"You sound so sure," Zorachus said. "How many Kadjafi minds have you read?"

"We Khymirians see through things." Tchernaar said. "We live authentically, so we recognize sham when we see it. Except for that, all human beings are like us. There isn't a virgin that ever lived who didn't dream of being raped by a horse, or having another girl's mouth between her legs. Our virgins differ from the others only in that they're more honest, and so they don't remain virgins long. Believe me, that girl in the garden enjoyed it. She would've enjoyed anything I might have done to her, even if she thought she didn't. Deep down, the pleasure must've been there."

"Once again, are you a mind reader?"

"I know myself. Self-knowledge is the key. From that you can learn everything about human beings. We're all made of the same stuff. How often must I repeat it? I knew what she felt because I'd felt it myself. I'd seen that the most dominant people, the proudest, most dominant *men* enjoyed humiliation and pain, just as I did."

The envoy began running a palm up and down a steel bar in front of him. "We had a retainer. His name was Drathazcar. He said I was the prettiest thing he'd ever seen, but I spurned his advances. My father was very old and hadn't instructed me in the Arts of Manhood; I was still uninitiated. And uninterested—even though Drathazcar was very handsome.

"One night he got tired of my rejections and came into my chamber. He held a knife to my throat and told me he'd kill me if I cried out. I submitted. At first, I hated the pain. But then I came to enjoy it—to enjoy it *intensely*. And, as he lay atop me panting, I told him so. He said he'd known I'd enjoy it all along.

"He came to my room every night after that. Once he let me see how I'd enjoy mounting him and holding the knife to *his* throat. I was amazed; he seemed so dominant. But my amazement didn't keep me from taking him. He asked me to cut him slightly. I did so, several times—and then, on a whim, I sliced deep into his throat, opened him ear to ear. He bucked beneath me most satisfactorily, and as the red streams gushed over the pillows and covers I thought I'd never surpass the pleasure I felt that night.

"But even as I rolled free, he turned his head weakly towards me. There was nothing on his face but fulfillment. Not emotion, not intelligence, nothing but gratification. His whole being was drowned in pleasure. His eyes were glazed, completely mindless. They might have been the eyes of an idiot.

"I realized then how feeble *my* pleasure had been; what's more, I saw how basic his desire for pain must have been. I'd long known, of course, that my parents and older brothers and friends had such needs; I'd learned I was like them. But now I'd seen how *strong* the desire was, even in a powerful man like Drathazcar. I realized how truly, universally human it must be. The appetite for feeling pain was every bit as basic as the need to inflict it. I had both in every measure, as far as I could tell; so did everyone else. Everyone was like me.

"I sat up late into the night with Drathazcar's corpse, paddling my fingers in his blood, licking them clean, thinking about life more deeply than I ever thought before. I analyzed what I knew, saw that all human motives derived from the twin desires. I was delighted. For the first time I had a real sense of community with the rest of the human race.

"My discoveries were still fresh in my mind when the girl was strung up. I felt a matchless sense of adventure as I courted her. I never let her seeming lack of enthusiasm discourage me. I knew that all the cursing and writhing and spitting was only a front. I knew she needed to feel sweet helplessness, to embrace mindless pain. I served her until she couldn't accept my aid any longer. But never a word of gratitude did I get from her."

Zorachus saw a tear well up in the envoy's eye and spill down his cheek. Tchernaar no longer looked satyrlike, but more like a sad infant, aged horribly beyond its years. Despite his revulsion Zorachus was filled with pity as he realized that Tchernaar had indeed been an infant once; the Sharajnaghi shuddered to think of the parts of the baby that might remain, trapped and slowly suffocating, the only parts of Tchernaar yet alive, the only regions where the sinner had not become his sin. Was there any way they might still be reached?

"It depresses me to think of her," Tchernaar continued after a time. "She reminds me of my youth, and I'm getting old. I don't enjoy things as much anymore and I'm beginning to sag. I've got arthritis now, and wrinkles. I don't think my life will be very nice if it lasts much longer. I think it will be horrible. To be tormented by memories of desire and have nothing to wake up to but increasing debilitation. . . . I'm forty-three, Zorachus, *forty-three!* I used to be as potent as a stallion, but now. . . ."

"When you were younger," Zorachus said slowly, "did it never occur to you that decay would begin long before your death? That the pattern you imposed on your life would only make the end that much more hideous?" He guessed what Tchernaar's answer would be like, but simple charity had forced him to speak, to try and raise such questions, perhaps for the first time, in Tchernaar's mind. He doubted Tchernaar

would fathom his true intentions; more than likely the envoy
would think he was simply trying to mock him.

Tchernaar gave a fleshless, cackling laugh. "What are you
saying, my Lord? That I should've made my life wretched and
pleasureless throughout, so that I'd feel more comfortable
when the blood dried in my veins?"

"I've nothing against pleasure," Zorachus replied. "But
perhaps there are kinds of pleasure, very deep kinds, that
don't fade with age, that you never bothered to investigate."

Tchernaar shook his head adamantly. "Nothing worthwhile
could have escaped me."

"You're sure?"

Tchernaar nodded. "It would be splendid if I were wrong,
of course. Certainly I want more than I can get from life. But
there simply isn't any more."

Zorachus laughed. "Have you experienced everything in
the world? Have you had the guidance of every human sage?
Have you traveled through all the dimensions, explored the
Higher Planes? Is it inconceivable to you that there are joys
that surpass the giving and receiving of pain and humiliation?"

Tchernaar smiled bitterly. "I know perfectly well what's
available in those Higher Planes of yours, and it's very much
the same sort of thing we have here. How could one place be
so totally different from another? Friction may be supplied by
an alien slit, but it's still friction. The blood may be a different
color, the screams of pain perfectly uncanny; but one tires of
such things just the same. *There is nothing more than what we
have.* The universe is meaningless chaos. It signifies nothing
more than the gurgle of vomit in a drunken beggar's throat.
Our only refuge is pleasure, and that can't last. But it becomes
that much more vital for us to hurl ourselves into our senses,
to escape the truth. We must let our sense enslave our minds.
We must be devoured, just as Drathazcar was. We must sam-
ple all distractions, drink from every cesspool, leave no sanc-
tuary undefiled. And when we reach the limits of our capacity
to delude ourselves, there's only one alternative. . . ."

The envoy gulped, nodded to himself, and went on. "You
know, Drathazcar's face still haunts me. Even more than the
girl's. There could be few things more exquisite than what he
felt." He laughed. "Pardon me, my Lord. There *is* a pleasure I
haven't sampled yet. But I will soon. I *must* do it soon. The
old grow insensitive. They slide too gradually to their
deaths. . . ." His eyes took on a shimmering delirium. "I'll

seize my chance while I can still savor it. It'll be even better than a slit throat. I'll surpass Drathazcar . . . Lord Kletus gave me a present. A jar full of worms. I'll use them at the banquet." He giggled.

"What do you mean?"

"You'll see. You'll be there to watch my face. You'll see." Tchernaar glanced up through the latticed ceiling. "Why, we're almost to the top." He began to hum a little tune. ‑

Zorachus looked away from him, wondering if God Himself could touch such a soul. The Sharajnaghi's mind boggled at the miracle it would take.

chapter

6

SHORTLY, THE CAGE came up in a broad stone hall. Narrow windows admitted knifelike shafts of sunlight, racks of mailshirts and polished weapons lined the walls. A marine stood guard at each door.

The cagekeeper went to the gate and threw it open. Zorachus and Tchernaar strode through, followed by their troops. Tchernaar drew the Sharajnaghi aside by a table where a clerk was working. The clerk looked up, but before he could speak a great commotion began. The doorwards had guessed who Zorachus was and were calling other men to come and see; perhaps a score of blackclads came pouring toward Zorachus's party. Tchernaar was nonplussed to learn that word of his mission had filtered down to the lower ranks, but he recovered sufficiently to say that Zorachus was not Zorachus at all—Lord Mancdaman, it seemed, had decided to remain on the ship.

"This is merely his retainer," the envoy explained.

Disappointed, the crowd receded. Tchernaar was pleased; the word of Zorachus's arrival would have spread swiftly and he did not like the idea of a mob dogging the party through the streets of Khymir.

The envoy turned back to the clerk, pointing to Zorachus. "Lord Mancdaman's retainer is of Khymirian blood, but was raised in the south."

"Very good," the clerk said, looking at the Sharajnaghi. "Within two weeks you must attend a demonstration in New Execution Square." He droned on in a bored voice, which clearly indicated he had recited the words many times. "There you'll see what becomes of those who plot against the Black Priesthood. . . ."

"It's an exhibition by swordsmen of the Cohort Ravener," Tchernaar broke in. "The Cohort is the Priesthood's elite guard."

"All newcomers are required to attend," the clerk went on, "under penalty of death. Give me your hand."

Zorachus extended it and the clerk pressed it with a stamplike device. The Sharajnaghi examined his hand, but could see no mark.

"You're now the proud bearer of an invisible—and permanent—brand," Tchernaar said. "Only specially trained agents of the Priesthood can see it. It tells when you were stamped. When you go to the demonstration, you'll be given another brand. If you went more than two weeks without the second one, you'd be assassinated by the first agent that noticed."

"There's an exhibition every third day," the clerk said. "One should be starting within the hour."

Tchernaar nodded. The group passed from the hall. On the way to the street, the envoy had to explain to various guards three times that Zorachus was not Zorachus. Finally, Tchernaar put his hood up; if people did not recognize him, they would not guess who Zorachus was, either.

Leaving the armory, the group pressed northward. Zorachus was amazed by the number of stone buildings he saw; everything seemed to be masonwork. Minor gods were supplicated in temples every bit as huge as many dedicated to major deities in Thangura.

The streets were thronged with people, churning floods of them; gaudily dressed Khymirians, turbaned Kadjafi sailors, Tarchan merchants in austere homespun, Urguz and Mirkut wanderers in handsome, tooled-leather vests and trews. This was Khymir's Foreign Quarter; a hundred tongues merged in a steady yapping babble, interwoven with shouts and laughter. Musical instruments twanged and rattled from streetside inns. Animals bleated and lowed in mangers and butcher shops. The smells were thick and cloying; the Khymirian burial-spice perfume would have been nauseating if unalloyed, but luckily it had to compete with the perfumes favored by the various nationalities, as well as raw sewage running in the gutters, animal manure, decaying offal, and rank, human sweat.

Amid all that, Zorachus caught the pungent scent of Kadjafi goat's-milk cheese, and instantly was acutely aware that he had not eaten since rising from his trance. Finding the stall where the cheese was being sold, he had Tchernaar buy him a

hunk of it, some bread and a bottle of wine. The company
proceeded. Zorachus polished the meal off in minutes as he
walked along.

While he was eating he had paid virtually no attention to
his surroundings; hunger always made him single-minded. But
now he began to feel a deepening claustrophobia, as if he
were crawling through a narrowing tunnel. Indeed, the streets
were narrowing, and growing more heavily packed; the
frowning stone piles on either side developed ledges and balconies that leaned out against the sky and blotted the way in
shadow. The facades grew more and more ornate, more and
more precarious, some kissing fulsomely above the passersby;
catwalks and bridges arched between opposing windows and
roofs. Sticky fluids dripped down, and stalactites of unknown
substances depended from the overhangs. Stinking, bloated
insects hovered in the thick air.

Zorachus noticed that the myrrh-aloes scent had grown
considerably. They were now well out of the Foreign Quarter,
and while there were still many foreigners on the streets, they
were far outnumbered by the Khymirians. There was less
racket; indeed, there were often short lulls in the street pande-
monium, like pauses between breaths, and then the shuffle
and squelch of feet in offal-choked alleyways could be heard,
and low moanings from the leaning windows; the very houses
seemed to be whispering to each other, and the stinking insects droned. Squalid images assaulted the Sharajnaghi's eyes
—old women hunched over a small fire, cooking skinned rats;
tubercular children with painted faces peering out of dark
doorways, licking their lips at passersby; squinting cripples
with festering, fly-ridden bodies, leering up from dollies or
stumping along on crutches. Realizing he was still holding the
empty wine bottle, Zorachus tossed it onto a mass of offal
bulging out of a hole in a crumbling, mold-splotched wall.
The bottle started a small avalanche of garbage; among other
things, a bare, blackened rotting human foot was revealed.

The company entered an area with many shops. Pornographic statues writhed along window ledges, flanked by
wooden phalli. Mummified crocodiles and cockatrices could
be seen hanging from the ceilings of apothecaries' nooks. In
one such shop, Zorachus saw a huge pot belching plumes of
yellow smoke, and a wizened little man pulling some sort of
pale hide out of it with a pair of tongs. Part of the skin
drooped over the tongs, swaying and dripping; empty eye

holes stared blankly, and a mouth sagged open in a silent steaming howl. The wizened man looked critically at the sacklike human face and lowered the hide back into the cauldron.

The company turned right down an unusually crowded street. Its sides were lined with brothels. Though the group had already passed a dozen or so, none had been as large or ornate as these. Each house catered to a different clientele, and before them were stages squirming with live demonstrations. Every permutation of the sex act was on display, and most of the stages revolved so that no one might be deprived a glimpse of pumping genitals.

After the apothecary's cauldron, Zorachus thought the demonstrations a relative improvement; but there was stronger fare up ahead. Hot brands sizzled pinioned flesh, and wheels popped arms from sockets; one lavish house, its facade painted to look as if it were splattered with fresh blood, even sported a gruesome echo of Tchernaar's tale—a swarthy, hook-nosed man atop a black woman, both their faces idiotically slack, both driving small knives slowly and repeatedly into each other's flesh.

Shortly, they reached New Execution Square. But as they entered they had to pass a cordon of marines, and Zorachus's hand was stamped a second time. Unless they were Khymirians, people were not allowed to leave once they were inside; all the exits were blocked with troops.

The square was two hundred yards on a side. To the north, it was bordered by a crumbling stone wall some forty feet tall, part of an abandoned, partially collapsed temple. A semicircular platform bulged out from the wall's center, but otherwise the barrier was featureless. A crowd of perhaps a thousand had gathered before the stage, and more were arriving all the time. Zorachus's group headed for the throng.

"Do you see those fellows tied to those stakes on the platform?" Tchernaar asked Zorachus.

After the gloom of the streets, Zorachus's eyes were not used to the hazy sunshine. He squinted, making out ten men.

"What exactly is going to happen to them?" Zorachus asked.

Tchernaar smiled knowingly. "Something drastic."

"If this exhibition's for newcomers," Zorachus said, "why's it held so far from the Foreign Quarter?"

"My Masters have more on their minds than making life easy for foreigners."

"What do you mean?"

"Well, the Merchant's Guild pretty much controls the southern part of the city. But the Guildsmen publicly acknowledge the authority of the Priesthood—as long as they're granted certain favors, and a good deal of autonomy. They were disturbed when foreign patronage of the brothels in this area dropped off recently; they wanted more traffic flowing through. The demonstrations used to be held near the armory, but the Priests agreed to move them to this square, as a favor to the Guild."

The group reached the outskirts of the crowd and pressed through to the front, the blackclads shouldering a path. A cordon of marines kept the throng well back from the platform.

Zorachus looked at the men tied to the stakes. All were naked and had received cruel and recent beatings. Six of the men were blond Kragehul giants; the remaining four were redhaired, with brandmarks shaped like black hands on their foreheads.

Now and then children in the crowd would pry up cobblestones and hurl them at the captives; fully one-third of the throng was made up of noisy Khymirian youngsters. The others were mostly adult foreigners.

"All these children," Zorachus said, "and so few Khymirian adults. Why?"

Tchernaar laughed. "No matter how spectacular something is, it gets tiresome if you see it too many times. When these cubs reach their teens, they'll be bored with this. Just as I was."

Soon after, Zorachus noticed the children quieting, the adults following suit. Once the crowd was silent, he heard a sound like the rush of a sword slashing the air. It seemed there was only one blade, but the sound was muffled, distant—too far off for him to be hearing the rush of a single edge. It came from the east, growing louder all the time, and presently the crowd pulled back from the wall on the cordon's eastern side; Zorachus saw something glittering over their heads. The rushing grew still louder, and shortly a file of tall men in red-lacquered scales appeared, marching between the crowd fringe and the wall, the marines in the cordon letting them pass. The

redclads wore crimson helms with cheekguards and neck
plates, and short curving horns on the sides; their scale-shirts
reached to their knees, and had elbow-length shoulder guards
of steel-studded leather. The redclads made no clatter with
their strides; their only sound was the sword rush as they performed a five-stroke drill again and again. With both hands
they whirled their curving, long-hilted blades, slashing verti-
cally right, then left, then horizontally in three ferocious
blows, swords shining like wheels of fire, spinning at terrific
speed.

The rhythm of those strokes never faltering, they reached
the platform steps, marched to the top, and lined up before the
prisoners. One of the Kragehul grinned with smashed lips and
shouted a few lines that sounded like verse. The other Kragehul laughed. The men with the branded foreheads began to
scream, offering bribes, begging mercy. As if in answer, the
redclads tripled their gleaming strokes. The Kragehul who had
shouted spat at the swordsman before him. Zorachus could not
see if he hit his mark.

Abruptly, the swords stopped short in midair, the redclads'
arms going rigid as iron.

The Kragehul prisoners eyed the blades calmly, smiling;
the others continued to scream, the foam of terror bursting
from their lips, faces writhing under the shadows of the
swords. For ten long seconds the blades hung motionless.

Then the redclads loosed a thunderous cry and stepped forward, weapons singing down, severing the captives' left arms
at the shoulders, flashing back, shearing off the victims right
arms, looping up and severing the heads, sweeping down and
cutting the torsos through just above the shortribs, sweeping
down again and slicing through the legs at mid-thigh. The drill
was completed in less than a second; the victims simply
seemed to burst apart in tremendous splashes of blood.

The redclads stepped back, swords motionless once more.

The crowd gasped, finally reacting. There was scattered
applause, mostly from the younger children.

Dripping with gore, the redclads waited another ten seconds. Resuming their drill, they turned, going down the steps,
rounding the stage to the west. The crowd quickly opened a
path along the wall.

Zorachus pondered what he had seen. Much as he had been
revolted by the slaughter, he was extremely impressed by the
way it had been carried out. He had never seen anyone but

Sharajnaghim use horizontal strokes so devastatingly.

"Now don't tell me you didn't appreciate that, Lord Manc-daman," Tchernaar said. "You being such a fine swordsman and all."

"Is the whole Cohort that good?" Zorachus asked.

"Not really. That was a special squad. Still, I've heard it said—by people who would know—that the redclads are the finest swordsmen in Thorgon Karrelssa. But after hearing about your deeds on the ship, I wonder if the Sharaj-naghim. . . ."

"If I were you," Zorachus broke in, "I'd try to avoid hasty generalizations."

Tchernaar smiled, thinking it a joke.

The crowd was dispersing. "Let's be off," the envoy said, and the company headed east.

"We could've used some of those men during the sea fight," Zorachus said.

"True," Tchernaar answered. "But they never leave the city. It's part of a tithe agreement between the Priesthood and the Guild. The Guildsmen pay for part of the redclads' up-keep—in exchange for a promise that they won't be used in 'foreign adventures.' Under the wording of the agreement, my trip to fetch you would've been considered an 'adventure,' and the Guildsmen wouldn't have waived the clause—not if a potential power like you was going to be brought under the Priesthood's wing. In fact, they weren't even informed of my mission, though I expect they know now. Kletus must've let the news slip out to create a sense of expectation. . . . In any case, it was thought the convoy would be enough to bring you back safely."

Zorachus wiped sweat from his brow. "Are there many Khymirians in the Cohort?"

"Why do you ask?"

"I was simply wondering."

"Nine out of ten are foreigners," Tchernaar said. "The Great Mother bears few real warriors these days."

Zorachus had suspected as much.

They left the square and eventually turned north on a wide boulevard flanked by palatial homes. A quarter-mile or so ahead, the mansions gave way to colossal black pillars, and at the end of the pillared stretch rose Banipal Khezach, a moun-tain unto itself, bastion upon bastion, culminating in the ti-tanic, sky-raking black spike.

"You're taking me to the tower?" Zorachus asked.

Tchernaar shook his head. "To your palace. The last house on the right." It was a monstrous mass of blood-colored stone, standing head and shoulders over the buildings nearby.

"I'm surprised it's not closer to the tower," Zorachus said.

"Why? Because your father was High Priest?"

Zorachus nodded.

"Zancharthus was unusual, as High Priests go," Tchernaar explained. "The strictures were a good deal slacker then, but even so it was strange for a husband and father to enter the Priesthood. In any case, he had to set up house outside the temple grounds. Ordog gave the palace to one of his lieutenants after your father was killed."

After a time the company reached the palace's outer gate. The gatewards crossed their halberds, but they recognized Tchernaar when he pulled his hood back and they raised the weapons. Looking at Zorachus, they guessed his identity but said nothing, dumbstruck. Zorachus's party went through. But they went only a few yards before the Sharajnaghi halted, staring at the palace.

For all its height, it seemed squat and oppressive. The first story was marked by a line of heavy, bulging columns, the upper stories by fluted pilasters; there were many balconies and tall windows, and scrollwork abounded. Carven nudes entwined next to rearing monsters, all of them wrapped in stone tendrils and about to be buried under avalanches of red-marble fruit.

"Quite a sight, eh?" Tchernaar asked.

Zorachus nodded blankly and looked back down, feeling a bit of a headache. They started forward again.

The walkway bisected a garden of gaudy, waxen-looking flowers. The blossoms gave off a thick scent similar to myrrh and aloes; Tchernaar's perfume was utterly lost in it. Attracted by the smell, bloated, buzzing insects lit on the flowers and crawled inside, vanishing under heavy petals. Zorachus never saw any of them come back out.

He and the others reached the palace's massive stone steps and went up to the doors. The brazen valves were taller than three tall men, the knockers so heavy that Tchernaar needed both hands to lift one. He banged once. A postern opened.

"Lord Tchernaar," said a guard within, "Is that *him?*"

Tchernaar laughed. "What do you think?" he said. The guards let them through. The envoy leaned close to the man who had spoken, and said: "Fetch Louchan. Tell him I've brought Lord Mancdaman."

The guard, wide-eyed, looked Zorachus over one last time and dashed off shouting. His cries brought a racket from all parts of the house, and servants and men-at-arms began to pour from the doorways, emptying into the chamber whispering and pointing. Finally, a tall, bald man appeared with the guard Tchernaar had sent off.

"Lord Mancdaman," Tchernaar said, "This is Kirmar Louchan, Head Steward of your household."

Louchan bowed deeply. "My Lord," he said, and directed one of his people to take Zorachus's bag from the marine who had been carrying it.

"The rest, of course, are your household staff," Tchernaar went on. "Guards, chattel, and hired help, yours to use as you please." He flashed the Sharajnaghi a lewd grin. "And so, my Lord, my mission's done. I must report to the tower. But I'll see you tomorrow night, I expect—for the last time, if my Master permits." He bowed. "Your Lordship." Then he left, the marines with him.

Zorachus eyed Louchan. The Steward was clad in purple robes and seemed to be a young man, but his skin was jaundiced, as if from age. His eyes were pale green, almost yellow; the left seemed to be a trifle crossed and had a catlike slit-pupil. Zorachus realized it must be made of glass, and noticed a thread-thin scar running from forehead to chin, bisecting the eyesocket.

"What may I do for you, my Lord?" Louchan asked.

Zorachus thought a bit. "Well, to begin with," he said, "you can tell me how this household is fed."

"We have certain plants . . ."

"Take me to them," Zorachus broke in.

"Right now?"

"Right now."

Louchan shrugged and turned, signaled two guards forward. "The rest of you, back to work!" The crowd scattered. "Follow me, my Lord."

Flanked by the guards, the Sharajnaghi walked behind him. They traveled wide, lushly decorated halls; the house was furnished with much erotic art, and Zorachus could not help noticing that the figure work was brilliant, even if it was arranged in the most luridly pornographic fashion imaginable.

But after a time the corridors grew narrow and austere; the

group had entered an area of workshops and storerooms. Louchan stopped before an iron-braced door.

"We have to keep the room closed up tight," he said, fishing out the proper key. "Otherwise, there's a good deal of
pilfering. You'd think we never fed the help...." The lock
snicked and he opened the door. He and Zorachus went in, the
guards remaining outside.

The garden chamber was very large, and dimly lit by several murkily tinted crystal skylights. The air was humid, even
for Khymir, and curiously odor-free—but it did have a
strange, rusty *taste*. *Like blood,* Zorachus thought.

The floor was dirt, and at regular intervals large circular
clumps of pale creepers bulged up out of it, thick as a man's
wrist at their bases, finger-thin toward the tips. They were
leafless, but covered with small domes that twitched and
shimmered.

Cradled in the middle of each clump, like eggs in a nest,
were a dozen or more bulbous fruit, glowing faintly, bloodily;
from the center of each fruit cluster rose several transparent,
yellow-glowing tubular growths filled with pulsing, plasma-
like fluid. The tube-growths snaked up poles set in the earth
nearby, into the naked human bodies pinioned near the tops,
entering the major veins of forearms and thighs.

Sickened, Zorachus squinted through the twilight at the
victims. Most of their faces were vacuous, but the eyes of a
blond man and woman near the front burned down at him.
The man was huge, muscled like a war horse, handsome but
for a broken nose. The woman was long-limbed and broad-
hipped, with large breasts; her face was round, pretty, and
snub-nosed, framed by a tangled mane.

"Why were those two put up there?" Zorachus asked. "The
blond pair in front?"

"The man was a gladiator," Louchan said. "He was un-
lucky enough to kill the best fighter from the stable that eventually bought out his master. His new owner never forgot it,
and when he heard we needed blood slaves, he turned this one
over to us."

"And the woman?"

"She was with him when he was first captured. His original
master kept them together to pacify him; the two of them
simply refused to get used to Khymirian ways. She was also a
convenient hostage if her mate didn't show enough enthusiasm in the arena. The second owner gave her to us to twist the

knife—you should've seen him when we strung them up. He was so pleased that his heart just gave out. He collapsed right where you're standing, as a matter of fact. Then it was their turn to laugh."

"They're Kragehul?"

"Yes."

"Do they understand Khymirian?"

"Very well."

"What would happen to them if they were separated from the plants?"

"They'd do well enough—with their wounds tended."

"What abut the other victims?"

"They'd die. Their spirits have fled."

"I see," Zorachus replied, knowing what he must do. He was the master of the house; the plants were his possessions, the victims his property. If he allowed the horror in this room to continue, he would be responsible. According to the Code, a Sharajnaghi could witness crimes and not intervene, provided he had a strong reason. But he could not stand aside where he had absolute control.

"I want every plant in this chamber rooted up and burned," he said.

At the words, Louchan's mouth dropped open.

Zorachus went on: "Allow the mindless bodies to die unmutilated. Have them buried whole. As for those two Kragehul, see that they get the finest care. When would they be ready to walk?"

"Tomorrow morning, I expect. But—"

"Bring them to my chamber then."

Face pinched, Louchan nodded.

"What's wrong?" Zorachus asked.

"Why have the garden torn up, my Lord?"

"Because it's dangerous."

Louchan cocked his head forward, squinting with his real eye. "Dangerous, my Lord?"

"About five years ago," Zorachus began, "a member of the wizard's order I belonged to ran tests on plants that had fed on human blood or flesh. He learned that such growths absorb spiritual residues from the corpses. On battlefields, or in other places where there's been much killing, the plants absorb the hatreds of the dead, become wells of pure rage, quite, capable of harming people. It can be shown that fatal and near-fatal accidents happen with distressing frequency to people living near such plants. Now the victims in this room were strung up without their consent, weren't they?"

"All but two, as far as I know. But. . . ."

"Surely you realize the implications. They must have been filled with rage. I've no intention of letting their residues jeopardize me or my servants."

Louchan rubbed his bald pate. "We Khymirians have been using these plants for years, Lord Mancdaman, and we've never had any trouble."

"Hmm." Zorachus said. "Well, perhaps they're an exception. I'll investigate. But until the matter's settled, I want to be on the safe side."

Louchan sighed. "And you want all the bodies buried *whole?*"

Zorachus nodded.

"Why? Some of the guards could have a splendid time with them. It would keep their morale up."

"When the plants are destroyed," Zorachus answered, "the hatreds they've absorbed will rejoin the spirits of the victims. The spirits will curse this house if the bodies are abused."

"I see," Louchan said heavily.

Zorachus smiled, pleased with his inventions. They were actually quite plausible, conflicting with nothing he knew about the spiritual realm; he had, in fact, heard similar notions seriously proposed.

"You know, Lord Mancdaman," Louchan said, "once the garden's gone, this household will be very expensive to feed. We'll have to use imported food, and . . ."

"I'm a vastly wealthy man, aren't I?" Zorachus asked.

"Your strongroom overflows."

"Well then," Zorachus said cheerfully, "there's no problem at all. Buy as much imported food as you need. Dispose of whatever blood-fruit you have around the house—anything made from blood-fruit as well. Get rid of it today. And I don't mean by feeding it to the staff."

"What about dinner?" Louchan demanded.

"I won't be having any tonight, I think. As for the staff, make theirs from whatever foreign food you have around. If there isn't enough, go out and get more."

Louchan nodded, muttering under his breath, sweat dripping from his nose.

Zorachus's eyes drifted to the Kragehul. He smiled at them; the fury of their glares doubled in reply. He could tell what they were thinking, what they believed his motives for saving them must be. He appreciated their anger; indeed, he welcomed it. Non-Khymirians! Two people who had actually managed to avoid being absorbed! True, the man had been a gladiator, a professional killer. But he had also had no choice. It would be a fine thing to talk to them. *You've been isolated too long,* Zorachus told himself. And the man might prove useful. Even before learning about his past, Zorachus had noted that he had the look of a formidible fighter—bodyguard material.

Louchan saw Zorachus studying them. "How do you want them dressed tomorrow?" he asked. "We have large wardrobes. Any whim can be accommodated."

"Just dress them. Nothing fancy or strange."

"Very well, my Lord."

"Now show me to my room."

They turned and made for the door, but before they reached it, Louchan tripped and fell violently. His glass eye rolled out. Snatching it up, he wiped it off, and Zorachus helped him to his feet.

"What did I tell you about those plants?" Zorachus asked. "Bad residues."

Louchan said nothing, replacing his eye.

They went back out into the hall and the guards flanked Zorachus once more. Louchan closed up the room, then led the way to the second floor.

When they came to the door of Zorachus's chamber, Louchan unlocked it, swung it wide, and gave the key to Zorachus.

"Bring my breakfast at the ninth hour," Zorachus told him. "Bread and cheese and butter. Also some strong wine. Bring the Kragehul at the same time. See there's enough for the three of us." He went inside. "Make sure I'm not disturbed tonight," he said over his shoulder, and shut the door.

Paying no attention to the room's sumptuously obscene decorations, he went to the bed, took off his swordbelt, and lay down. He was completely exhausted, drained by what he had seen that day; yet his insides still seethed with frustration. He had put a halt to the horror in the garden, but there had been so much else he had been powerless to stop . . . for the thousandth time he wondered if he could fulfill his mission without snapping. His mind returned to that delirious instant back on the ship, when he had thought of ripping into his allies with the demon-rings. How much greater would the temptation be when allies became mortal enemies? Confronted by one atrocity after another, would he find it irresistibly easy to respond with atrocities of his own?

Worn out as he was, he was a long time falling asleep.

chapter

7

UPON WAKING THE following morning, Zorachus changed into fresh clothes and went out onto the balcony, which overlooked a park full of short, waxen-leaved trees. Flesh-colored blossoms nodded on the boughs, even though there was no breeze; here and there a fountain gushed, sending up ponderous foamless surges that looked more like white oil than water. Two gigantic bronze statues towered above the treetops, facing each other—one a grimacing male nude poised to hurl a spear, the other a woman in flowing robes, baring her breast to receive the impact.

Thunder rolled off westward, muffled but menacing. Zorachus surveyed the clouds, noticing a purple-shadowed cavern yawning in one of them, flickering with red lightning. Four smaller holes widened slowly above, like eyes and nostrils over a gaping mouth. Zorachus knew the resemblance to a face was not accidental. The Presences were at work, he was sure of it, threatening the city they hated. For a time, the face stared hungrily towards Khymir; then the cloud's shape shifted, becoming a huge menacing fist. Gradually the fist sprouted spikes, changing into a gauntlet, which melted in turn into a dragon-headed ship. Many of the other clouds had taken on the appearance of weapons, hammers and axes and bladed mauls, tinted red as though the vapors themselves were dyed with blood; a greenish serpent shape reared up, reminding Zorachus briefly, ominously, of Zathlan, before it became a charging warrior. An opening appeared, very dark, shaped like the black hand figureheads of Khymirian ships; it was soon smothered by a billowing avalanche of white.

Watching the thunderheads, Zorachus felt like a soldier on the battlement of a besieged fortress, looking out over a churning sea of enemy troops. A wall of magic held the spirits of earth and sky and water at bay for now. But he read the warning in the clouds, heard it in the thunder: *Our day will come.*

Eventually, the strange shapes vanished from the clouds. Yet even then the thunderheads lost little of their threatening look.

Zorachus went back into his room and was about to lie down again, when there came a knock from the hall. Girding on his swordbelt, he went and opened the door.

Louchan entered, followed by a black slave with a folding table, and another with a tray of bread and cheese and butter. A tall red wine bottle reared up in the midst of the piled food. The slaves retired after setting the tray up, and Louchan signaled. Looking surly, the Kragehul garden slaves marched in, household guards at their backs with drawn swords.

"Everything satisfactory, Lord Mancdaman?" Louchan asked.

Zorachus nodded. "You can go. The guards too."

They looked to Louchan; his face had lengthened with dismay. "I think it would be better if they stayed, my Lord," the steward said. "The doorwards might not be enough. Those slaves are dangerous."

"So am I," Zorachus replied. "I don't think I'll have any trouble."

Louchan gestured helplessly. "But. . . ."

"Obey me."

The steward nodded and headed out with the guards. Zorachus went to the table and took a piece of bread.

"Are you hungry?" he asked the Kragehul.

They said nothing, eyes full of suspicion.

"As you can see, there's more than enough here for the three of us."

Their silence continued. He smeared cheese on the bread with the tray spoon and took a bite.

"It's very good," he said.

Still no response. He shrugged. Bread in one hand, wine bottle in the other, he backed over to a chair and sat down.

The Kragehul man looked at the table and said something to the woman in their native tongue. They stepped up to the table, grabbed some small loaves, and started slowly towards Zorachus.

Zorachus eyed them calmly. They came closer and closer.

"Are you going to eat that bread or throw it at me?" he asked.

They glanced at each other as if he had discovered their hidden intention; then the man shouted and they hurled the loaves. It was a foolish-looking gesture, but the bread was heavy and hard; Zorachus leaped sideways from the chair, and the missiles struck the chair's back with substantial thumps.

The Kragehul charged, the man holding a small knife that Zorachus had not noticed on the tray. The Sharajnaghi put the wine bottle on the chair and, still holding his cheese-smeared bread, drew his sword with his free hand.

The man reached him before the woman and lunged with the knife. Zorachus slapped it out of his hand with the flat of his sword and dodged the woman's flying tackle. Arms flailing, fingers outstretched, golden mane streaming, she sailed past him shrieking. Her mate went for the knife. Zorachus kicked him in the head, sending him sprawling across the floor.

A doorward poked his head in.

"Everything's under control!" Zorachus told him.

A moment later he heard a snarl and footbeats. Taking a bite of bread, he dropped to one knee, bending forward. The woman hurtled over him, landing hard.

The guard shouted and rushed in, sword drawn. Zorachus bounded up and sped past the woman, tossing the bread aside, sheathing his blade. Grabbing the guard's hauberk, he hurled him mightily at the second doorward, who was hard behind. Dropping their swords, the two rolled backwards in a tangle of arms and legs. The Sharajnaghi ran after them, and hardly had they regained their feet when he flung one through the door, then the other.

"Damn it all!" he cried, "I told you everything's under control! Don't come in here again unless I call for you! That's a direct order!" He shut the door.

Turning, he saw that both Kragehul had recovered and were charging once more. He drew his blade again. The man grabbed up one of the fallen swords, hardly pausing in his headlong rush; roaring, he brought it down at Zorachus's head. The Sharajnaghi dodged, then dodged again as the woman dashed in, jabbing with the second sword. Knocking her senseless with a blow to the jaw, he pivoted to meet her companion blade for blade. The man was a splendid fighter, only a trifle slower than Zorachus; his strength was terrific. Before, Zorachus had disarmed him easily because of the unequal lengths of their weapons, but now, with the shorter blade, he was having a difficult time. Back and forth they swept, feet clattering over the marble floor, steel clanging.

Finally, Zorachus knocked one of the Kragehul's legs out from under with a lightning kick. The man fell heavily on his back. Leaping forward, Zorachus stamped the sword from the Kragehul's fist, kicked it aside, and placed his point at the fellow's throat.

"No more tricks," he growled. "I'll spare you if you let me."

The Kragehul could not speak for a while, his wind knocked out. "What do you want with us?" he gasped after a time.

"First off," Zorachus said, "swear on your honor that neither you nor your woman will try to escape, or attack me or my servants." He did not know if the man took his own honor seriously, but he was fairly sure that any reluctance to swear, or attempt at trick wording would show that the Kragehul would consider himself bound.

"I won't attack you or your servants," the man said. "And I won't try to escape."

"Not good enough. You didn't mention your woman, and . . ."

"She's my *wife,* you pig!" the Kragehul broke in.

Pleased that the man thought the distinction so important, Zorachus went on: "You didn't swear on your honor, either."

"I swear on my honor."

"Don't try to fool me," Zorachus snapped. "Give me the whole oath."

The Kragehul's face was purplish with rage. He looked as though he would spit bile at any moment. Zorachus pricked his neck, almost drawing blood.

"Come on," he grated.

The Kragehul's face grew darker and darker, and he closed his eyes.

"Kill me," he said.

Zorachus saw his mistake. The Kragehul obviously thought that all manner of horrors were in store for him and his wife, and the oath, if taken, would leave them unable to resist. Zorachus pulled the sword point back somewhat, ready at an instant's warning to yank it well away from the man's throat; there was too good a chance that the fellow would attempt suicide by jerking upwards.

"Remember your wife," Zorachus said. "If you force me to

kill you, it'll go a lot harder on her." That was true, of course, but not in the way he knew the Kragehul would take it. "And consider this: You really don't know what I have in mind. I might not be interested in your bodies at all. For all you know, I might sleep only with old men and carp."

The Kragehul opened his eyes. He hesitated a few seconds more, then swore the oath. Satisfied with the wording, Zorachus was aware that he might still be trying to fool him. He had known all along that the barbarian's reluctance might be pure sham. But he took the chance, withdrawing his sword. The Kragehul rubbed his throat.

Zorachus got the man's blade and pulled the woman's from her unconscious grip. Returning to the door, he opened it and handed the brands back to the guards, who looked at him sheepishly.

"Quarrel's over," he announced cheerfully, and closed the door again, going to the table. Sheathing his sword, he took up another piece of bread and smeared cheese on it.

The Kragehul man was over by his wife now, kneeling beside her. She was coming to. He took one of her hands and stroked it.

"She'll be wide awake soon," Zorachus said after a swallow of bread. "I only tapped her." Taking another bite, he asked between chews: "How are your wounds holding up? The ones where the plants were attached?"

The man examined his bandages and looked at the ones on his wife, pushing her shift up to look at the dressing on her thigh.

"Any blood?" Zorachus asked.

The man shook his head. "Catgut works wonders."

"Even so, you're lucky you didn't spring a leak while we were fighting. An open thigh can drain a man in minutes—though I expect you know that from your gladiator days."

The Kragehul eyed him narrowly. "Why are you so interested in our health, you Khymirian dog?"

The epithet stung. "I wasn't raised in Khymir," Zorachus replied. "I'm a Khymirian by blood only. Do you know anything about me?"

"I heard one of the gardeners talking about you. Your father was High Priest of the Black God. Mancdaman Zancharthus. He slaughtered thousands of Kragehul with his own hands."

"Well, to begin with," Zorachus said, "I'm not my father.

Though I'd think that would be obvious." He finished his last two bites of bread.

The woman was fully conscious by then. She sat up. Her husband spoke to her in Kragehul. Her face pinched with shock and amazement; Zorachus guessed she had been told about the oath.

The man continued talking—explaining the mitigating circumstances, no doubt. Presently, his wife looked fiercely at Zorachus.

"What are you going to do with us?" she demanded.

The Sharajnaghi laughed. "What do you think?"

"That you want to bed us. Why else have us brought to your chamber?"

"You couldn't be more . . ." Zorachus stopped suddenly, realizing the room might be penetrated with listening holes, and that even now some spy of Kletus's might be eavesdropping; the High Priest had, after all, provided the household staff. Zorachus did want to be on guard while talking to the Kragehul. Aching to reveal himself, to speak without having to conceal his detestation of everything Khymirian, he decided to shift the scene of conversation.

"Come out onto the balcony," he said, and picked up the tray. "We'll talk there." He went outside and put the tray down. It was some time before the Kragehul joined him. As they came up, he snapped his fingers and said, "The wine." Going back, he returned with the bottle.

"What are your names?" he asked.

"Halfdan Skarp-Hedinsson," the man replied. "My wife's name is Asa."

"Mine's Mancdaman Zorachus, as you already know; but I like real introductions. When were you strung up in the garden?"

"A week ago," Asa said.

"Louchan said you two were very loyal to each other," Zorachus said. "That you wouldn't give in to Khymirian ways."

Asa nodded. "And we won't give in to you."

"How exactly would you go about resisting me?"

"We could kill ourselves," Asa said. "Halfdan swore nothing about that."

"But he did swear that you wouldn't try to escape. And suicide would be an escape of a sort."

"I don't know about that," Halfdan said.

"Well, in that case, it wouldn't be too easy," Zorachus went on. "True, it's a good drop from this balcony, but I could probably keep you from jumping—one of you at least. But, luckily, I don't think that situation's going to arise. You *will* wait until you're sure of my intentions, won't you?"

"We *are* sure of your intentions," Halfdan snapped.

"No you're not. You wouldn't have let me spare you. Believe me, I don't want to rape either of you. Or seduce you, for that matter."

"Why else would you have us taken down?"

"Because it sickened me to see those plants feeding on you."

Halfdan spat a laugh. "You expect us to believe that?"

"Yes. How much do you know about the Kadjafim?"

"I've been to Fyrkaz."

"Do the Kadjafim grow crops that drink human blood?"

"Not as far as I know."

"Do you think they'd approve of such plants?"

"Probably not," the Kragehul admitted.

"Well, then," Zorachus continued, "I was brought up by Kadjafim. Their customs are my customs. When I say those plants sicken me, I speak the truth."

Halfdan rumbled deep in his throat.

"If it weren't true, why would I have had *all* the bodies taken down?"

"For the reason you gave Louchan," Asa said.

It was a good point. Zorachus paused. He thought for a while, but could come up with no better response than the truth. "That was all nonsense I made up to cover my real motives," he said.

"Why did you have to cover up your real motives?" Halfdan asked sarcastically.

Zorachus blinked, scratched his head. He had wanted the Kragehuls' company so much he had not anticipated any of the problems.

"Well?" Halfdan demanded.

Zorachus uncorked the wine and took a pull, then sat down beside the food tray.

"What do you want with us, you bastard?" Halfdan growled down at him.

"Would you believe me if I said I simply wanted to talk to you?" Zorachus asked.

"Do you think we're idiots?" Asa snarled.

Zorachus looked up at them. In spite of his frustration, in spite of the hatred in their eyes, he still wanted their conversation. He greatly admired their fierce loyalty to each other and their resistance to Khymir; he suddenly wished he could have not only their conversation but their friendship. He would need friends in the days ahead, people who would remind him that there was a world of sanity outside Khymir.

Having gotten no answer to her question, Asa had started haranguing Halfdan in Kragehul. Zorachus waited till she was done, then asked:

"Would you agree to become my bodyguard, Halfdan?"

"Why would you want a Kragehul bodyguard?" Halfdan demanded.

"I don't trust Khymirians. Also they seem to be poor fighters, too bent on preserving their own hides. Those are faults you don't have. And you're an expert with a sword."

"You beat me," Halfdan sulked.

"That doesn't mean I've no use for you. There's just so much one man can handle."

"But why should I agree to serve *you?*" Halfdan gritted, fists knotting at his sides. "I hate Khymirians. They turn my stomach."

"I understand. I've seen so many loathsome things since I've been among them . . . I'm a Sharajnaghi, Halfdan, and I've faced evil before, but. . . ."

"Sharajnaghi?" Asa asked.

"It means *Bringer of Light,*" Zorachus explained. "The Sharajnaghim are members of the *Comahi Irakhoum,* a holy order of wizards."

"*You're* a holy man?" Halfdan asked incredulously.

"Well, I'm a member of the order."

"Why'd you come to Khymir?"

"I can't tell you."

"Then why should we believe you about anything?" Asa asked. "It doesn't make sense for a holy man to come to Khymir. Not unless Khymir had something he wanted. In which case he wouldn't be *too* holy, would he?"

"He came to get his inheritance," Halfdan put in. "Louchan said he would." He grinned down at Zorachus. "You like gold too much, holy man."

"Do you like gold?" Zorachus asked.

"Of course. But I don't pretend not to. I don't try to seem better than I am."

"I don't imagine you do," Zorachus answered. "But that's beside the point. Will you become my bodyguard?"

"Do I have any choice?"

Zorachus nodded. "If you refuse, I'll free you both and you can leave Khymir."

"I'll refuse," Halfdan assured him.

"However," Zorachus continued, "If you stay, you'll be freed just the same. And when I no longer need your services, you'll leave this city an extremely rich man. I'll pay you fantastically well. Money means nothing to me."

Halfdan jeered. "If that were true, you wouldn't have come here in the first place."

"If it weren't true, would I have ordered the garden ripped up? That was a very expensive command."

Halfdan grumbled something under his breath.

"Why would I offer you so much for your sword arm, if I were so greedy?"

"How should I know?"

"Just think. If you leave now, you'll go as a penniless freeman. If you help me, you'll leave with more gold than you could carry in a wagon."

"You're insane," Halfdan said with great conviction.

"I'm nothing of the sort. I think you'll discover that for yourself—if you give me a chance."

"I'll give you nothing. You're trying to trick me."

Zorachus shook his head. "I don't have to trick you. I don't even have to bribe you, though I've tried my best. You owe me much. You and Asa both. I saved you from the plants, and I could have killed you when you attacked me. I won't force you to repay those debts, but I ask you to. If you insist on leaving, I'll let you go. But I don't think you will." He did not know if the Kragehul would feel themselves obligated, but the gamble paid off. Halfdan's face darkened once more, and he and Asa launched into a furious conversation in Kragehul. Finally, he looked back down at Zorachus and grated:

"I'll become your bodyguard."

"Very good," Zorachus said.

"Can Asa stay with me?"

"Of course. You two can have the room next to mine. Whenever I don't need your services, you can keep each other company." He took another pull of wine, and offered the bottle to Halfdan. "Take a drink—to seal our agreement."

Looking sullen, Halfdan hesitated before taking the bottle

—then downed several gulps.

"Good stuff," he said sourly, wiping his lips.

Zorachus nodded. He knew the vintage. "Thanguran, thirty years old. We Sharajnaghim use it on High Feast Days."

Halfdan handed the bottle to Asa. She sipped it delicately. Her drinking style came as a surprise to Zorachus; dressed in a shapeless grey shift of coarse fabric, blonde mane unbound, she looked too barbaric to be capable of anything so ladylike.

"It's no good drinking on an empty stomach," Zorachus said. "Have some food. There's plenty, and one shouldn't let things go to waste."

"You sound like my mother," Asa said.

"She sounds like a very intelligent woman," Zorachus replied. He patted the tessellated pave. "Take the weight off your feet."

They sat down across from him. Halfdan was the first to start eating. Asa watched him for a few moments, almost as if she expected him to spit the food back out; then she followed his example. Both ate with tremendous vigor, Halfdan almost savagely, Asa with a quiet grace that utterly belied the amount of food she was packing away. Zorachus also did his share. The wine bottle went round and round, and the food pile shrank. Finally, tray and bottle were empty, and the well-stuffed trio reclined on the checkered stone. Resting on one elbow, Zorachus eyed his new confederates.

"How did you like that?" he asked.

"Well enough," Halfdan said. "But don't think we're off guard because we're stuffed."

"I wouldn't think anything of the sort," Zorachus replied. "But—" There was a knock at the door inside. "What now?" he wondered aloud as he rose.

"Do you want me to come with you?" Halfdan asked.

"You are my bodyguard," Zorachus replied, and went to answer the door. Halfdan got there first and opened it. Louchan entered, arms tucked inside his hanging sleeves, yellow forehead beaded with sweat.

"Well?" Zorachus asked.

"News of your arrival has spread all over the city, my Lord," Louchan said. "A crowd of beggars has gathered outside, hoping for charity."

"How could anyone hope for charity in Khymir?"

Louchan shrugged. "It's the same as anywhere else, my Lord. It's not given willingly, but it's given. Aren't beggars organized in the southlands? Don't they pester their victims until they wring money out of them?"

Zorachus ignored the question. "How big is the crowd?"

"There must be five thousand of the wretches out there. They've been gathering since dawn."

"Why didn't you inform me earlier?"

"The crowd remained small for a long time, and afterward I feared to intrude. You *did* want to be alone with your guests. I thought of sending a messenger to the tower, to fetch enough troops to drive the scum off; but then I thought you might want to go out and make some kind of gesture. The Priests must think so too, otherwise they would've acted on their own. Word must've reached them. . . ."

"Is the crowd very quiet? I was just out on the balcony and I heard nothing."

"It's almost as if they want to make a good impression. Your father was so well respected. But I expect they'll change their tactics if they don't get a response soon. What are you going to do, my Lord?"

"I certainly don't want to offend anyone unnecessarily," Zorachus answered. "I'll go and speak to them."

"You needn't. With your permission, I'll supervise an appropriate dole. . . ."

Zorachus shook his head. "I'd better go out." He nodded towards Halfdan. "This is my new bodyguard, by the way. Give him and Asa the room next to mine. See to it that he's armored to his satisfaction before the afternoon's out. He'll be coming with me tonight."

"Where?" Halfdan asked.

"A banquet. At Banipal Khezach."

The Kragehul grunted.

"Another thing about him," Zorachus told Louchan. "He's to be freed."

"Me too," Asa broke in, having just come up.

"Her too," Zorachus said. "And while you're procuring *their* papers, get enough for the rest of my chattel."

"You want to free *all* your slaves, my Lord?" Louchan asked, incredulous.

"Yes. Slaves always hate their masters. They're untrustworthy as long as you own them. But once they're freed, they're grateful."

"Grateful, My Lord? Most of them will just up and leave immediately."

"So? Hire replacements. I want this to be a happy household, Louchan." The Sharajnaghi tossed off a laugh. "But in the meantime, we'd best see to the beggars."

They went into the hall, where the group was rounded out by several guards Louchan had brought.

"You can talk to the mob from the outer wall," Louchan told Zorachus as they walked along. "That would be safe enough."

Going downstairs, they passed outside and went up inside one of the small towers near the gate. Zorachus looked out over the throng of beggars. Squatting on the cobbles, they were a pitiable lot, many of them horrendously deformed. Some seemed to be little more than shapeless bundles of rags and all were sewer-filthy; thirty feet above them, he could smell nothing but the stench of unwashed and diseased bodies.

He looked north and south along the street. Groups of mounted redclads waited on the outskirts of the crowd.

A murmur went up from the back of the throng: he had been noticed. Outstretching his arms, he cried in a great voice: "Hear me! I am Mancdaman Zorachus!"

Scabby, grime-crusted faces lifted. Those beggars who could, leaped to their feet, and there was a storm of shouts. He made no attempt to stifle the uproar; it was a long time before the mob quieted.

"I'm a stranger in this . . . *remarkable* city, the city of my birth," he continued. "As yet, I have few friends here. But I'd like to change that; and to secure the goodwill of Khymir's less fortunate, I'll buy the largest granary in the city and there will be a daily dole of Tarchan wheat."

The beggars thundered approval. He turned to see Louchan's reaction. The steward was clearly appalled, rubbing his pate frantically with both hands, eyes closed in disbelief. Zorachus could not help but laugh. Nor could he help noticing how well his maneuvers were keeping Kletus's hireling off balance.

He looked at Halfdan and Asa. They too were thunderstruck; he had evidently proven his contempt for money.

He returned his gaze to the beggars. They were ecstatic, flailing their bandaged paws, blessing and thanking him. He was pleased. A few more grand gestures, and he guessed he would have the allegiance of large segments of the Khymirian mob. But he was also glad he could feed so many people.

He waited once more for the racket to die down. "When

the grain runs out," he cried, "I'll buy more and grant other kinds of dole. No one will go hungry in Khymir if I can help it."

There was another wild demonstration. But some in the crowd were not satisfied.

"Food's all right, my Lord," bellowed one bullish voice. "But man doesn't live on bread alone!"

"What else do you want?" Zorachus asked. "Medicine, lodging . . ."

"Entertainment!" the beggar answered. "Open the whore-houses! Give us children with pretty backsides and fresh faces to slice! Let the arenas swim with blood!"

The others roared enthusiasm, and at once the pity Zorachus had felt for the crowd deserted him. Until then he had seen the beggars as fellow human beings, wretches trapped and decaying in the Great Mother's mazy, incubating womb. Now he saw only twisted monstrosities, filth-caked demons, beings delighting in evil, their outer hideousness a mere re-flection of the hideousness within. And as he stared at them from on high, he had a chilling thought: *This is what it's like to be God, to see men as they really are.*

Instantly, the blasphemy of the idea brought him up short. *But you're not God, are you? So how would you know?*

Wiping sweat from his face, trembling slightly, he silently begged God's forgiveness. Then, remembering his audience, he raised his hands. The crowd quieted.

"As yet," he shouted, "I'm ignorant of most Khymirian pleasures, but doubtless I won't remain so for long. And once I've learned, I'll see that you share the diversions that I myself enjoy. You'll be denied only those that your rank doesn't enti-tle you to. Fair enough?"

The crowd clamored the affirmative. In the lull that fol-lowed, he cried:

"And so I take my leave of you, truly hoping I've won your affection. You're the people of my blood, and I pray my return to Khymir will usher in a new era of improvements!"

The crowd roared a final time. He and his escort went down from the tower. As they headed towards the front steps, Louchan pushed up beside him.

"A *whole* granary, my Lord?" he demanded, bellowing to make himself heard over the racket behind the wall.

"The biggest in the city," Zorachus answered. "I can afford it, can't I?"

"Yes, but. . . ."

"Start in on it this afternoon. Meet any price. That should speed things up."

"Yes, my Lord."

"Have you seen to the garden?"

"The plants are being torn up even now."

"What about the new food supply?"

"I'm making good progress."

"Excellent." Zorachus said nothing for a moment. "When you've got the time, make sure to take care of those manumission papers."

"Yes, my Lord."

Zorachus headed up the stairs with the Kragehul and the guards. Louchan remained below; sitting on the lowest step, he buried his face in his hands.

chapter

8

KLETUS'S TAILORS CAME just before the twelfth hour, accompanied by a train of slaves bearing bales of fabric and large pattern books. Zorachus told them to clothe him as they thought best and they set to work, outfitting him in a splendidly embroidered tunic of wine-purple silk with a broad, python-skin belt, and black leather pants, miserably hot, embossed with floral designs; on his feet went low boots, crafted of the scaly blue hide of some unearthly reptile, and round his shoulders was draped a red-lined, emerald-dotted, cloth-of-gold mantle.

Once they were done (and their work took up the better part of the afternoon) he dismissed them and sent for Louchan and the Kragehul. The steward arrived first, looking exhausted and carrying a sheaf of manumission papers. There were thirty slaves in the household and he had hired several scribes to draw up the documents. Seated at his desk, the Sharajnaghi signed each paper with a quill pen, asking Louchan about his errands all the while.

He finished Halfdan's and Asa's as they came in, Asa hanging on her husband's arm, golden hair shining. Zorachus's gaze went to her; pure pleasure filled him. For the first time, he saw she was not merely pretty, but beautiful. It was a dauntless, deceptive sort of beauty, peasant beauty, nothing refined about it. But that only made it more exhilarating to see.

She was still clad in the simple shift she had worn that morning, but Halfdan was now sumptuously attired. He had on a knee-length shirt of silvered chain-mail; a gold-hilted Kragehul longsword hung from his belt; and around his neck he wore a heavy silver medallion. His conical helm was of brightly burnished steel. As he and his wife reached Zorachus, the Sharajnaghi handed them their freedom.

y?" Halfdan asked, squinting

operty," Zorachus replied.
ned at him, then ran her eyes
feasting on the words—even
er upside down. Halfdan was
achus straight in the eye and

er in the stack and rose. "You
d. "Make sure the papers are

"I will, my Lord, ___ ___ard answered heavily. He took up the sheaf and left.

"Let's go out on the balcony," Zorachus said. This time the Kragehul followed promptly.

"That's a fine byrny, Halfdan," the Sharajnaghi said as they came out into the sunlight.

Halfdan looked down proudly at the silver-glinting links. "It's from Serkland—that is, your precious Kadjafi lands."

"I recognized the workmanship."

"I've got a shield too, but I left it in my room."

"Why the medallion?" Zorachus asked, pointing to it.

"You said I could be armored any way I chose. I've heard that silver wards off some kinds of evil. That's why I wanted a silvered byrny as well. There are many wizards in this city, and they're even more rotten than the other Khymirians."

"So I've heard. But I've also heard that silver is useful only in rare situations. It affects only a few kinds of demons."

Halfdan grunted. "Well, it's best to be on the safe side."

"True."

"I see you're all dressed up, yourself," Halfdan said.

"You noticed, eh?" Zorachus asked.

"You look like something I saw in a fever once."

Zorachus laughed. "I like the tunic well enough, but as for the rest. . . ."

"Can I have a garden, Master?" Asa broke in, looking hopefully at him.

Halfdan frowned. "Don't interrupt him. And remember, he's not your master anymore."

"You can both call me Zorachus," Zorachus said. "And yes, Asa, you can certainly have a garden."

She smiled. "I'll talk to the mason about it. He can wall a

space in on our balcony and I'll have it filled with dirt."

"Hush," Halfdan said. "What makes you think Zorachus wants to hear your womanish prattle?"

"Haven't you ever wanted to hear womanish prattle?" Zorachus asked.

"Now and then. But there's a time and a place for everything. And when two men are talking, that's not the time."

Zorachus sighed. "I'm sorry, but I just spent a long voyage surrounded by men with nothing on their minds except torture and fondling each other, and it's good to hear a woman talking about gardens."

Halfdan mumbled something.

"I'll plant herbs and tomatoes," Asa said.

"What are tomatoes?" Zorachus asked.

"A kind of berry, I think. Not sweet, but delicious anyway. I bought some seeds in the market while Halfdan was being outfitted."

"Well, my blessing's upon them, for what it's worth. I'm already looking forward to the harvest."

There was a pause.

"You're a strange one," Halfdan said presently. "But I think we've got you figured out."

"Think so?"

"It was that business with the wheat that put us on to you," Halfdan continued. "Wheat's very expensive in Khymir. We decided you didn't come here for the money."

"Why then?"

"To take over the city," Asa said. "You're using the wheat to buy support from the rabble. But you'd better watch out."

"Why?"

"Remember those wizards I spoke of?" Halfdan asked. "You'll run up against them sooner or later."

"I'll deal with them," Zorachus said.

"With the Black Priests of Tchernobog?" Halfdan asked sarcastically.

Zorachus nodded. "I'm a Sharajnaghi Adept of the Seventh Level. And we Sharajnaghim are the greatest wizards in Thorgon Karrelssa."

"I don't know," Halfdan said, eyeing him critically. "You don't look like much of a wizard to me."

"What should wizards look like?"

"Well, the *powerful* ones are a lot older than you."

"What do you mean by powerful?"

Halfdan thought a bit and lifted his hands. *"Powerful,* you know."

"Like being able to transform things?"

"Like being able to *lift* them. That's the kind of power I'd like. Save me a lot of work."

"I see," Zorachus said, considering binding spells. He settled on one he could use without first sluicing off some of his repelling energies; the Influences were right. Assuming a Griffin Stance, he uttered a formula, and before Halfdan knew it, he was floating three feet off the pave.

"Put him down!" Asa shouted, stamping her foot.

"Would you like to take a little spin out over the park?" Zorachus asked Halfdan, who was gaping like a fish.

"No!" Halfdan cried.

Zorachus shrugged and lowered him. "How was that?."

"You made your point," Halfdan answered quickly.

Zorachus dropped stance and smiled.

Halfdan folded his arms on his chest. "If you *do* take over, how will you treat my people?"

"I won't make war on them."

"That's good. You might be lying, of course. But you seem to be a just man; and seeming's all you can ever know about anyone, isn't it? If you can keep my people from being attacked, I'll be honored to serve you."

"I'll promise you this," Zorachus said. "If my work here succeeds, the Kragehul will escape a great evil."

Not long afterward, word came that a palanquin and escort from Kletus had arrived.

"Well, Halfdan," Zorachus said, "we're off to Banipal Khezach."

"And what am I supposed to do in the meantime?" Asa demanded.

"Surely you don't want to come with us," Zorachus said. "It's going to be loathsome."

"I don't want to be alone."

"Stay in our room and keep the door locked," Halfdan said.

"We won't stay any longer than we have to," Zorachus assured her. He turned to Halfdan. "Go down to the stables and get yourself a horse. Meet me around front."

They left the room, Zorachus going down to the front gate.

A palanquin awaited him, attended by six muscular slaves and an armored overseer on horseback; an escort of redclads lounged against the wall.

"I'm Mancdaman Zorachus," the Sharajnaghi announced. The redclads snapped to attention.

"His Anointed Steward sends his greetings," one said, bowing.

The overseer motioned towards the palanquin. "For you, my Lord." He took out his whip, eyeing the slaves' broad backs.

"Wait a moment," Zorachus said. "I've a man coming."

The overseer nodded and rested the whip across his mailed thighs.

Zorachus stooped and lay down in the palanquin. It was heavily padded, voluptuously comfortable, The struts were richly carved.

He looked up at the canopy. Beautifully painted in all-but-luminous colors, a naked fleshy woman and a greenish lamia arched over him, locked fiercely in each other's arms, bosom to bosom, the lamia biting the woman's neck. Small trickles of blood crawled over the white flesh.

Zorachus felt a surge of heat in his loins. His eyes fixed on the merging breasts; he found that detail intensely erotic—it was the first time he had been aroused by anything in Khymir. Even while watching the bordello exhibitions, he had managed to keep their obscenity uppermost in mind. But in this painting, skill cancelled out obscenity; it was a wrench to tear his gaze away. He stared down at his hands. His palms glistened with sweat, much more than Khymir's heat could normally milk from them.

After what seemed an eternity, he heard hooves and leaned out of the palanquin. Halfdan rode near.

"All set, my Lord," he called.

Zorachus gave a silent nod and signaled the overseer, whose whip hissed and cracked as the Sharajnaghi settled back.

"Hola, dogs!" the man cried. "Grab those poles!"

The slaves rushed to obey. The company started down the avenue of pillars towards Banipal Khezach.

Zorachus watched the columns slipping past for a while, but soon felt the urge to look back up at the canopy. It was all he could do to resist it, and he almost succumbed before something caught his attention on a strut beside him—an oval, carven face, leering knowingly at him with lecherous, slitted eyes. The mouth hung open, twin tongues issuing from it, more heavily varnished than the rest of the face, seeming to glisten with yellowish saliva. One extended sideways, and a little globule of varnish hung from the tip. The other lolled down over the lower lip. Its tip curled, just a bit, and in the curl two tiny figures entwined. Despite his disgust, Zorachus looked closer. Intricately carved, a woman and a lamia embraced there, bosom to bosom, the lamia biting the woman's neck.

He looked away, and then, almost unconsciously, looked upwards; instantly he noticed (and wondered how he could not have noticed before) that the woman in the painting also had two tongues, one extending into the shadows on the far side of her face, the other hanging lewdly over her lower lip; and where the second tongue curled, there was a small, oval, twin-tongued face leering down at him.

Feeling as though he were under some kind of direct spiritual assault, almost as if he was in the presence of the very degenerate who had invented these diseased images, he snapped his eyes shut and did not open them again until the palanquin came to a halt twenty minutes later. He got out as soon as it was set down.

Above him loomed the lower bastion of Banipal Khezach. Its ebon blocks had a dull red sheen in the late afternoon sun, and the doors of the huge southern entrance were open. Between the iron valves stood a line of redclads.

Halfdan dismounted, entrusted the horse to the overseer, and went with Zorachus to the threshold. The escort troops remained behind.

As the pair neared the redclads at the entrance, a bizarre figure appeared behind the swordsmen and stumbled out into the light: Tchernaar. He held a half-drained chalcedony wine cup, and was clad only in a studded leather harness that let his naked genitals dangle; he was plainly afflicted with some scrofulous venereal disease.

"Lord Mancdaman!" he cried, coming up close and trying to embrace him; Zorachus stepped back in disgust. Tchernaar followed, plucking at him, and Halfdan struck the envoy in the mouth. Tchernaar staggered and fell on his knees, blood dribbling over his chin.

Eager to be rid of him, Zorachus forgot momentarily that Tchernaar was probably intended as a guide, and he and Half-

dan strode forward. The redclads let them pass and they found
themselves in a cavernous hallway, where they halted after a
few moments, not knowing where to go, looking at their surroundings. The walls gave off a disastrous grey glow. They
were carved into swirling bas-reliefs of life-size coupling
bodies, every curve and depression of flesh brilliantly delin-
eated. But for all their realism and beautifully rendered action,
the figures looked strangely lifeless. Zorachus guessed it was
a trick of the light; everything seemed carved out of dead ash.

Suddenly he realized that his skin, which had been filmed
with sweat ever since he entered Khymir, was now dry; his
mouth and lips felt slightly parched. And, though he felt the
heat as keenly as before, he had an eerie impression that there
was no real warmth inside Banipal Khezach, that what he felt
was something cold and ashen masquerading as heat. . . .

Uncertain footsteps came from behind. He looked over his
shoulder and there was Tchernaar, swaying, grinning, pointing
to a small, frosted-glass bottle hanging around his neck; it
appeared full of some kind of squirming life.

"Worms," he giggled, drooling blood.

Zorachus turned again, but Tchernaar plucked at his arm
and said, "Follow me, my Lord," and staggered down the
hall. They followed a good distance along the corridor, then
into a broad side passage, its black walls bare save for
torches, and came to a steel, redclad-flanked door. Tchernaar
tripped a lever and the barrier slid back; they went through,
the door closing noiselessly behind them.

It was dark inside, the only light coming from a few reddish gems glowing on the ceiling. Zorachus could barely make
out the sides of a small, squat chamber.

"What now?" he asked. But before Tchernaar could reply,
there was a lurch of upward motion.

"Private lift," Tchernaar mumbled. "My Master's own.
Only way up to his chambers. Makes it hard on the assassins.
Won't work if you don't think the right name." He belched.
"There's a demon beneath us, you see. Part of one, anyway.
Ordog brought it over. The rest of the body's in another di-
mension. The arm pushes up through the shaft, pumping up
and down. . . ."

The elevator halted and the door opened; they stepped into
a narrow corridor, passed between two more redclads at its
end, and crossed into a large chamber whose floor and ceiling
belled to form a concave lens. Zorachus knew the purpose of

this architectural peculiarity; the room was designed to dissipate magical energies. Any wizard entering it would be instantly bereft of sorcerous powers, and completely at the
mercy of the ten Cohort Ravener swordsmen warding the far
door.

The trio traversed the sloping floor, Tchernaar with some
difficulty, reaching their destination at last—the banquet room
of Kletus's quarters. Lit by white orbs on pedestals, the vast,
windowless hall stretched before them, walls and pillars and
vaulted ceiling tricked out in gold-trimmed jade veneer.

The room was full of people—men and women in gaudy
dress, soldiers in various liveries, and black-robed figures
Zorachus guessed were Priests of Tchernobog. The air
hummed with laughter and conversation. Ring-clotted fingers
picked dainties from slave-borne trays, and electrum goblets
gleamed against rouged lips. Some people lounged on the
couches and pillows that had been arranged in a great circle in
the middle of the room; others walked about. Mouths met
hungrily and bodies rubbed against bodies. Hands palped and
searched beneath sumptuous garments.

A bald steward, forehead deeply branded with the Black
Hand, met Zorachus and his companions as they started across
the room. He smiled broadly when he learned who had arrived; turning, he pounded the floor with his ebony staff. The
room resounded with the strokes and all eyes turned to the
newcomers.

"Lord Mancdaman Zorachus!" he announced.

The banqueters converged swiftly, and out of their numbers
came a huge man, a full head taller than Zorachus, clad all in
black. He looked about fifty years old, with close-cropped
grey hair and keen, vigorous blue eyes. His jaw was slablike,
his brow massive and willful; his face radiated such dignity
and confidence that Zorachus doubted he could be Khymirian.
It was the countenance of an awesomely self-contained man,
the near-perfect expression of inner density—courageous,
ruthless, sheerly despotic.

"His Anointed Steward, Ghorchalanchor Kletus," the staff-
bearer said. "High Priest of Tchernobog, the Black Lord."

Kletus bowed to Zorachus. "Welcome to my house, the
house of my Master."

Zorachus bowed in turn. Kletus scrutinized the Sharajnaghi, sizing him up. Zorachus had the uncanny feeling that

the High Priest did not miss a fold of his tunic or jewel of his mantle.

"My tailors did their work well," Kletus said.

"I don't know how to thank you," Zorachus replied.

Kletus smiled and pointed to Halfdan. "Who's that?"

"Halfdan Skarp-Hedinsson, my bodyguard," Zorachus said.

"Expecting trouble?"

Zorachus shook his head. "I prefer to be on the safe side. Have I offended you? If so, I apologize."

"It's all right. Some of my other guests brought retainers too. After all, they're not on their home ground. But I hope all these precautions prove unnecessary. It would be such a shame if anything marred your evening." He took Zorachus's arm; it was immediately apparent that the High Priest was a tremendously strong man. "But before the banquet begins in earnest, I'll introduce you to the others." Followed by Halfdan, they waded into the crowd.

"Lady Mournir Clethusancta," Kletus said, indicating a tall, dark woman apparently in her late twenties. She was extremely beautiful in a starved sort of way, with finely chiseled features and high cheekbones. Her eyes were an unearthly violet-blue, and her hair, black and lustrous, flowed down over her shoulders in thick, perfumed curls. She was clad in a green silk dress that bared her hard, flat belly and lifted her small, naked breasts. Next to her was a voluptuous, identically dressed blonde, and Clethusancta had her hand inside the other's garment, stroking her loins. Her arm moved with sinuous serpentine grace; it seemed to have no joints. Both women were completely expressionless.

Zorachus found himself staring at Clethusancta's hand beneath the silk. For the second time that evening he was aroused; once again he was deeply disturbed. He tried not to look, but his eyes kept wandering back. He hardly listened as Kletus went on with an anecdote about a poet who had killed himself over Clethusancta; it was only when the High Priest mentioned that she was a member of the Merchants' Guild that Zorachus began to pay attention—here was a prospective ally. The Sharajnaghi did not like the idea of having to deal with her. Merely looking at her, even in the most businesslike atmosphere, would bring back unnerving memories; he was relieved when Kletus, after introducing him to her unimportant companion, moved on to someone else.

"Kourgon Zarathonzar," the High Priest announced, singling out a young, dark-haired man, broad shouldered, magnificently built, clad in priestly robes. "He's one of my chief acolytes, a very powerful mage for one so young."

"For one so young?" Zarathonzar said, as though it was an insult.

Kletus laughed. "He'd be a powerful wizard at any age," he acknowledged, and nudged Zorachus. "Tchernaar tells me you're quite a wizard yourself. Something about sinking a Kragehul ship?"

Zorachus nodded, then thought immediately of his Kragehul bodyguard; looking back at Halfdan, he found the barbarian's face considerably soured.

"It was self defense," the Sharajnaghi explained.

Halfdan's expression did not soften, but he shrugged. Zorachus turned.

"Why apologize to *him?*" Zarathonzar asked.

"I prefer to keep his goodwill," Zorachus replied.

"He's a Kragehul then?" Zarathonzar sniffed the air. "I should've known. The stench is unmistakable."

Halfdan rumbled to himself.

"Does his belly hurt?" Zarathonzar asked.

Zorachus made no answer.

"How did you sink the ship?" Kletus asked him quickly. "I'm amazed you could muster such force at sea. You wouldn't have the Mancdaman rings, would you?"

Zorachus nodded; there was no point in trying to deceive him.

"So they weren't lost after all," Kletus said.

Zarathonzar sneered at Zorachus. "The Mancdaman rings, eh?" He spat a laugh. "So the demons did all the work. From what Tchernaar said, we all thought you must be quite a power. You're something of a disappointment."

"Enough of that," Kletus said. "Lord Mancdaman's our guest. And besides, the rings can't be wielded effectively by a weakling—or so I've heard."

"I'm sure," Zarathonzar answered.

Zorachus eyed him. A study in will and arrogance, the young priest's face had many echoes of Kletus's. But where Kletus seemed a chinkless cliff of strength, Zarathonzar revealed a serious weakness; his eyes were wild, possibly hysterical. He looked like the sort of man Zorachus always preferred to meet in battle—one controlled by his blood.

Kletus, displeased with his acolyte, turned from him to introduce Zorachus to several other people. Two were members of the Merchant's Guild, Clethusancta's close allies, apparently. One was named Marmaros Maranchthus, the other, Klissandrian Porchos; both were fat, middle-aged men of average height, richly dressed, with many jeweled rings sparkling on their fingers. They were polite to Zorachus, asking him about political conditions in the southlands, and his voyage. But with Kletus they were frigid, barely smiling when he attempted to joke, avoiding eye contact with him. Zorachus was pleased to note their obvious animosity towards the High Priest.

Presently, Kletus moved on to a huge black man in Cohort Ravener livery, who stood nearby with his horned helm tucked under one arm. His features were heavy and immobile; they seemed cast in steel. His eyes were dead black, like holes bored into a tomb.

"Cetewayo Thulusu," Kletus said. "Captain of the Cohort Ravener, and the greatest swordsman in Khymir. Armor's like paper to him."

"I'm honored to meet you, Lord Mancdaman," the black said slowly, bowing, his voice extremely resonant.

"I saw some of your men in action yesterday," the Sharajnaghi said. "A very impressive display."

Thulusu's face remained impassive. "As it's intended to be, my Lord. I'll relay your compliments to the troops."

At that moment, a midget in priestly robes came up beside the Captain. The contrast in size was comical and amazing. Kletus introduced the newcomer as Oulchar Lysthragon, another of the Chief Acolytes.

"Do you know what they say about me, Lord Mancdaman?" Lysthragon asked, looking at no one in particular and playing with a small silken purse at his hip.

"What?"

"Can't you guess?"

"No."

"You're sure?"

"Quite."

"Should I give you a clue?"

"Certainly," Zorachus said, annoyed and uncomfortable, wanting to get the conversation over quickly.

"They say it behind my back."

Zorachus pondered this. "They say that you like to tell strangers what's said about you behind your back."

Lysthragon shook his head. "They say I'm *short*," he answered, and grinned. Up until then, his face had been soft and childlike. But as he showed his teeth, which were yellow and pointed, wrinkles began to spread, great furrowed nets of them, out from the corners of his mouth and from under his eyes, and he took on the look of a wizened monkey; Zorachus could only guess how old he was.

"Forty-five," the midget said, throwing his head back and laughing. His eyes, however, remained fixed on Zorachus. Very carefully, he slid both index fingers into his nostrils. "Do you know how pig vomit tastes?" he asked. "I do."

Kletus hustled Zorachus away, launching into a new round of introductions. Midway through, he finally let go of Zorachus's arm, produced a large wallet of meat, and began popping the chunks into his mouth—talking all the while. The sinister dignity of his appearance dropped away; even though the introductions somehow continued to flow, his mouth bulged grotesquely and he made loud, gulping sounds. He finished the wallet in an astonishingly short time. Tucking it away, he produced another, much larger than the first, and resumed eating. Finishing that, he took out a third, then a fourth, and by the time he emptied the fifth, he had introduced most of the guests.

Zorachus managed to forget nearly all of their names, but was roused to attention at the end; before him stood a stunning, red-haired woman, six feet tall and black-robed. Her face was pale, her eyes large and heavy-lidded; to Zorachus's mind, she looked very near perfection.

"Lady Tchersachor Sathaswentha," Kletus announced. The woman smiled invitingly at the Sharajnaghi and bowed her head. Zorachus smiled back in spite of himself and bowed, then turned to Kletus.

"She wears the robes of your order," he observed. "I'm surprised that you admit women."

"We don't," Kletus answered, "if they're only women."

Zorachus looked back at Sathaswentha. A black-robed man stood in her place, red-bearded, pale-skinned.

"Lord Tchersachor Sathaswenthar," Kletus said. "Yet another of my Chief Acolytes."

Zorachus studied Sathaswenthar's face. The full lips were much less red, the eyelashes shorter, the ruddy hair cropped, and, of course, there was the beard. But the features were the same.

"Very convincing illusion," Zorachus said. Caught off balance, he did not suspect it was anything more. "Which one is the real you?"

"This one," Sathaswenthar said, tapping his chest. "But it wasn't an illusion. The breasts were real. My hips were round and wide. You're a man who appreciates womanflesh. I could tell by the way you looked at me. Perhaps—"

"Not yet," Kletus broke in. "There'll be time for that later," He signaled the steward and cried to the guests: "Dinner will be served shortly. Take your places."

He led Zorachus over to one of the couches. Unlike the others, which were wooden, it was cast of iron, though well-padded. They sat down; the couch groaned beneath them. Zorachus did not see how their weight could make the iron give voice, but before he could ask Kletus about it, the High Priest said:

"You really should take Sathaswenthar up on his offer. *His* knowledge of male needs makes *her* a very good mount."

"I don't doubt it," Zorachus said.

The words had barely left his mouth when Sathaswenthar sat on the couch next to theirs and, before his eyes, turned voluptuously female. Sathaswentha's tongue, moist and pointed, snaked out and glossed her upper lip. Zorachus smiled and looked unhurriedly away.

Slaves came by with appetizers and goblets of wine. Zorachus drank heartily and ate shrimp, bread, and cheese. Kletus also drank, but remained aloof from the food until the viands were brought—then started in with a vengeance. Zorachus began on the meat at the same time, but Kletus rapidly outstripped him, even though the Sharajnaghi had a strong appetite; the High Priest ate with both hands, shoveling huge fistfuls of flesh down his gullet. Occasionally, he paused to breathe or drink, but soon resumed his attack on the meat. He ate until his sweat, defying the dryness of the air, poured down his face, and the veins of his forehead stood out like cords; his nose ran in torrents, his jaws champed and champed, and his teeth grew fouler and fouler with hanging threads and tissues, spiderwebs of sinew into which new handfuls were greedily stuffed. Bits of meat escaping his teeth ran over his lower lip in thick streams of saliva. He finished nine-tenths of a yard-wide, high-piled platter, magnanimously

granted Zorachus the rest (even though Zorachus's appetite
had deserted him) and called for another; quickly devouring its
contents, he called for a third, eating ever more quickly, ever
more grimly. Again and again his beslimed, blood-caked
hands dived into the piled flesh. He ignored all other courses,
the pastries and pies and heaped bowls of delicacies; his
hunger remained fixed on the meat.

For another hour he continued his incredible, single-
minded gluttony. Then, skin purple and blotched, eyes rolling
back in their sockets, he sagged and smiled, working at his
clotted teeth with a fine gold pick, wiping the foulness from
his face with a silk napkin. His robes were completely soaked
with perspiration and clung to his body; Zorachus was as-
tounded to see that the High Priest's stomach was not the least
bit bloated—even though the Sharajnaghi guessed he had
eaten well over a hundred pounds of meat.

The other feasters had long since glutted themselves and
lounged like replete pythons, conversing wearily with each
other, lazily fondling each others' buttocks and breasts and
genitals.

Kletus clapped his hands. Sweat flew from his sodden
sleeves, dousing Zorachus.

Two huge, nude men, powerfully muscled and heavily
scarred, marched into the center of the ring formed by the
pillows and couches, hands behind their backs. One was
black-bearded and bald, the other clean-shaven, with long
yellow hair. They looked to Kletus.

He nodded. They brought thier hands around and folded
them on their chests. Both wore steel gauntlets with half-inch
spikes jutting from the knuckles.

Bowing to Kletus, they squared off. Their ponderous
movements roused the feasters; the fondling hands moved
faster, animated with expectant excitement.

The two men closed and the onlookers screamed wildly as
the gauntlets flashed, spikes hammering into flesh, both
punches connecting. Blood streamed down the blond man's
cheek, poured from holes in the other's chest.

The boxers backpedalled, closed again. The bald one
blocked a punch and smashed a ferocious blow into his opponent's right shoulder. The blond man retreated, shrieking. The
bald one followed eagerly, arms windmilling. His foe planted
his feet, absorbed two horrific blows to the arms, and began to
land strokes of his own. The boxers traded punch after punch,

gauntlets slapping and thudding against quivering flesh. The floor was soon splattered with blood.

Zorachus felt an almost desperate urge to intervene, to put a stop to the carnage; but he suppressed it, watching helplessly as the fighters bludgeoned and ripped each other. He could not even safely look away—he dared not reveal how this sport sickened him. Any hint of squeamishness might brand him a weakling, an undesirable ally, to a man like Kletus. And out of the corner of his eye he saw the High Priest glancing at him every few seconds.

The combat seemed to go on forever. Both men lost an eye and reduced each other's faces to pulped meat; shoulders and pectoral muscles hung in tatters. And still the terrible gauntlets swung.

Please God, Zorachus thought. *Put an end to it . . .*

The bald man slipped on a patch of blood-greased stone; the other, totally blind after the last exchange, lashed out in desperation, spinning completely about as he failed to connect. The bald man raised himself on one arm and rammed a fist into his antagonist's stomach, and the blond man fell with a scream. The bald one crawled forward once more, struck him in the stomach again. His victim jerked up into a sitting position—and caught a brace of steelshod knuckles square in the forehead. Bone gave, and he flopped backwards, dead.

His conqueror stood up wobbling. To the sound of rabid applause, he extended a gauntlet towards Kletus, smiling hideously with what was left of his mouth.

Kletus gave a laugh like stones rattling down a scree, and signaled Oulchar Lysthragon.

"Pay him," he cried.

The midget grinned, face wrinkling hideously as he rose and took the purse from his belt. The boxer turned to him.

Lysthragon hurled the purse. As it flew, its drawstring came somehow undone and the purse's mouth yawned open, a swiftly widening black cavity—in seconds the flying hole was yards wide.

Dumbstruck, the boxer retreated clumsily, tripping over the blond man's corpse. The hole dropped over them both and, for an instant, the spectators glimpsed a large, silken sheet settling flat against the floor. Then it shrank and bunched up, and where the bald man and his victim had sprawled there was only a small purse.

The applause had stopped while the purse did its work;

delicious awe had silenced the audience. Now the clapping
resumed, this time for Lysthragon. He bowed and sat back
down, sending a slave to retrieve the purse.

"Do you always deal with the winners that way?" Zorachus
asked Kletus as the applause slacked off.

Kletus shook his head. "We prepared that little surprise in
your honor. Of course, once the news gets round, we'll have a
hard time hiring boxers. I hope you realize the sacrifice we
made for you."

Out in the middle of the ring, slaves with mops and buckets
were cleansing the blood from the floor. When they finished,
Kletus motioned to his steward. Shortly, a small, brown-
skinned woman, raven-tressed and exquisitely formed, strode
out into the circle, clad only in gold breastplates and a jeweled
kirtle. Lithe and muscular, she posed seductively, oiled skin
glistening.

"Beautiful, isn't she?" Kletus asked. "One of you will have
her tonight."

Over on the right, Clethusancta shoved her blonde companion from her lap. "Your terms?" she cried, rising.

Kletus did not answer. "Anyone else interested in her?"

Several noblemen shouted the affirmative.

"How interested?"

They shouted extravagant bids of gold and jewels, striving
to outdo each other—and Clethusancta, who had quickly
joined in. But Kletus shook his head.

"I don't want your riches," he said. "I want a demonstration of skill."

At his words, two redclads marched up to the girl, deposited their swords on either side of her and marched off.

"How many of you would be willing to foot the Dance of
Steel for her?" Kletus asked.

"I'm game!" Clethusancta replied.

Her former mistress, having overcome the first shock of
rejection, rose from the floor, grabbing desperately at the
merchant queen.

"Please, my Lady," she implored. "Take pity on me . . ."

Clethusancta had long nails, thickly lacquered with a metallic polish that made them steel-hard; eyes fixed on the
swarthy slavegirl, she raked the blonde's face. Pawing at her
torn flesh, the blonde tottered back, shrieking.

Clethusancta looked at her at last, smiling coldly. The
blonde snarled, whipping a dagger from her belt.

Instantly, Clethusancta sprang like a great hunting cat, knocked the blade from the blonde's grasp, and ripped her throat out with both hands. The blonde crumpled, to scattered applause.

Picking up a napkin, Clethusancta daintily wiped her fingers, having somehow avoided most of the jetting blood. She returned her gaze to the slave girl, who smiled in appreciation.

"You'll have your chance, Clethusancta," Kletus cried, and turned back to the noblemen. "But what of you? Will any of you meet her, blade for blade?"

Only one accepted the challenge, a man named Balorg Tchaldusaar. He stepped out into the ring and, with a quick movement, threw off his robes to reveal a lean, sinewy body. Naked but for loincloth and sandals, he advanced to the swords and picked one up.

Across from him, Clethusancta slipped out of her dress and shoes; nude and barefoot, she went to the other sword with long graceful strides, muscles shimmering under her skin. She picked the blade up, then kissed the swarthy girl full on the lips and slid a hand into her kirtle.

At the sight of her taking such liberties with the prize, Tchaldusaar cursed and swept the slave aside. His blade flashed at Clethusancta, who parried the stroke and launched one of her own, flicking a shallow slash across his chest. He screamed, retreating a step; Clethusancta laughed at him. Again he closed in a whirl of steel. Three times their blades met, ringing. But in the lull that followed, Kletus stood up towering from his iron couch, arms outspread, voice filling the hall like a thunderclap:

"Enough! Whoever looses the next stroke, dies that instant!"

A shadow fell on Tchaldusaar and Clethusancta, and the swarthy girl cried out and ran from the circle. Above the combatants a mass of dark cloud had appeared, dim red light pulsing inside it. Clutching what might have been an alien arbalest, a vaguely human shape, with eyes like live coals, was silhouetted against the glow.

"The umpire," Kletus said. "And a strict one."

Tchaldusaar and Clethusancta lowered their swords.

"That's better," Kletus said mockingly. "We don't want mere butchery, you know. The boxers were quite enough. It's time for something aesthetic. Assume your stances."

They raised their weapons again, bodies arching and tightening, sinews standing out like wires. Every contrast of male and female musculature was revealed.

Kletus clapped his hands. Invisible musicians began to play; with unearthly pipes, strings, and drums, they performed an orgiastic melody. Clethusancta and Tchaldusaar whirled in time, gyring gracefully, swords whistling. Their blades met in a shower of sparks and sprang back, the screech of stricken metal one more clash of percussion in the demonic music.

"They must keep the rhythm," Kletus told Zorachus. "The first to miss a step, or strike out of time, will be killed by the umpire. That usually happens before a fatal wound's dealt." He cried out suddenly as Tchaldusaar gashed Clethusancta's right thigh. "For a second there I thought I'd spoken too soon..."

"Do all Khymirian's know the dance?" Zorachus asked.

"No. Only the children of wealthy families, and not many of them, these days. It used to be one of the marks of real breeding, but the young don't want to be bothered anymore. They care so little for grace...." Kletus cried out again; Tchaldusaar had scored a glancing blow on Clethusancta's shoulder. "Those two out there are among the few that still know it. I guessed they wouldn't be able to resist the girl—or the chance to kill each other legally. There's an old grudge between them."

Zorachus found this combat less horrible to watch than the first; It even held a certain fascination for him. The dance involved great speed and agility, and Clethusancta, who was beginning to assert herself, was a marvel to behold. Even the blood streaking her skin could not detract from her beauty. Indeed, the trickles and droplets only seemed to enhance the muscles they touched, the limbs they rilled from, glittering ruby-red....

Stop it, he told himself, appalled that such an idea could enter his head. Struggling to free his mind from the dance's spell, he forced himself to concentrate on the thought of steel tearing flesh, of human bodies, God's own images, being shredded into so much bloody refuse.

The dance itself began to aid him. The participants still moved swiftly, but they were less graceful now, clearly straining to maintain their paces, pain evident in every step. Wounds swelled or sagged open hideously, revealing the ripped tissues within. The dance was showing its true face.

Clethusancta had gained the upper hand. She had been slashed several times, but none of the wounds was serious— Tchaldusaar had taken a deep slice across the ribs that was pouring out blood at a tremendous rate. Finally, after a savage exchange in which Clethusancta split his nose, he fumbled his paces, and the demon umpire loosed its bolt. The missile penetrated Tchaldusaar's chest and came out his lower back, spending itself as it struck the floor, skidding lazily to a halt. Wobbling, he continued upright, but let his guard drop; Clethusancta stabbed him in the throat and he toppled backwards. To wild applause, she straddled his still-jerking legs and started to strip off his loincloth. But Kletus leaped to his feet and, banishing the umpire and the invisible musicians with a violent gesture, called her to a halt.

"You won't mutilate him in my hall!" he cried.

"Why not?" Clethusancta demanded, sword still poised.

"The girl's prize enough."

"I'll have his *meat!*" Clethusancta shrieked.

"I'll kill you on the spot," Kletus replied.

At that, Clethusancta's fellow merchants began to murmur.

"Let her take it!" Klissandrian Porchos shouted.

"Tchaldusaar has no more use for it!" added Marmaros Maranchthus.

"*I* rule here!" Kletus roared. "And that slut won't use this banquet to glut her hatred of my sex!"

Clethusancta trembled with rage. "I'm a force to be reckoned with! I won't be denied!"

Kletus boomed a scornful laugh. "Really? I'm High Priest of the Black Lord, sow. Defy me, and I'll brush you from existence. Your power lies in gold. Mine stems from Tchernobog himself. Against me, you cannot stand."

"Kill me" Clethusancta answered, "and you'll have to kill the whole Guild. Attack the Guild, and the city will explode in your face. We grant the dole. We make life possible. You take it away. You prey on the poor, drag their sons and daughters off to be sacrificed. You're throne's not so secure. We can hurt you, Kletus. So let me have my trophy."

He stared at her venomously; his left hand rose, and Zorachus was sure he was going to enter a stance. Clethusancta and the other merchants flinching back, apparently thought so too.

Then a change came over the High Priest, and he shrugged and let his hand fall.

"Perhaps we can compromise," he said wearily. "What will you give me for my permission?"

Clethusancta smiled, victorious. Even with her face splashed with blood, she was still ravishingly beautiful; she thought a moment and beckoned to the slave girl, who ran over eagerly.

"We'll make love here," the merchant queen announced. "For all to watch. We'll give your guests a performance like they've never seen. Think of your fame as a banquet master then!"

"Very well," Kletus replied.

Immediately, she started to cut into Tchaldusaar. But once again Kletus stopped her.

"Afterwards," he said.

Clethusancta nodded. "This *is* your hall." She laid the sword down; kneeling, she stripped the slave girl and stretched languorously back beside Tchaldusaar. The girl settled atop her and began to lick the blood from her skin.

Watching them, Zorachus felt that terrible heat in his loins again, but was soon distracted; Kletus leaned forward and looked past the Sharajnaghi, made several quick hand gestures, then settled back.

Zorachus guessed the signals had been to Sathaswentha; after a time he looked casually over at her, and noticed immediately that she had arranged herself in one of the few sitting stances; small shields, almost invisible, were dissipating and reforming about her hands. She was force-letting.

Noticing Zorachus's attention, she smiled as if they were sharing a little joke.

Zorachus returned his gaze to the entertainment. It was not long before he heard Sathaswentha whispering a spell.

Out on the floor, the girl was sucking on Clethusancta's small breasts, the merchant queen heaving luxuriously beneath her, stroking her back, caressing her legs with naked feet.

Sathaswentha completed her spell.

The slave girl's head lifted. Clethusancta tried in vain to force it down again. Puzzlement twisted her face—then terror.

Scales of chitin were sprouting on the girl's forehead and cheeks; her eyes bulged into faceted greenish globes, twitching antennae thrusting out above. Her whole head metamorphosed into a wasplike horror, mouth a vertical slit, bordered by clashing mandibles.

Clethusancta screamed and struggled, but the girl held her fast, pinning her arms to the floor. The terrible mouth descended on the merchant queen's left breast, mandibles sawing and flashing like the blades of some gruesome reaping machine.

Chuckling, Sathaswentha undid the spell on the girl once Clethusancta was dead. The slave's face jerked up out of the hole in Clethusancta's ribcage and she tried to scream, but all that came out was a torrent of crimson vomit.

Sathaswentha rose and assumed what looked like a Dragon Stance, crying an incantation. Twin purplish beams shot from her hands, striking the girl and Clethusancta, who shrank and withered, puckering like leaves cast onto a fire. When Sathaswentha halted the bolts, not even ash remained. She sat down to widespread clapping.

But some in the audience were not so pleased. Faces livid, Clethusancta's Guild allies were on their feet, glaring at Kletus and Sathaswentha.

"Murderers!" Porchos cried, voice full of rage and amazement.

"What do you care if one of my slaves dies?" Kletus asked.

Startled by the joke, Porchos hesitated, then shouted with renewed fury: "Are you mad? Jesting at a time like this?"

Kletus shrugged. "Clethusancta defied and threatened me in my own house. I had every right to have her killed—and you know it."

"You should have spared her all the same," Maranchthus said. "It would've been better all around."

Kletus smiled freezingly. "Are you threatening me?"

"I'm merely stating facts."

"State another such fact, and you'll be carried from this hall in pieces."

Porchos and Maranchthus whispered to each other and, bowing curtly to the High Priest, started for the door together with their followers, the other Guildsmen and their relatives not far behind. Kletus detailed a priest to command the demon-lift for them.

"They're such fools," he told Zorachus. "Also inconsiderate, putting such a damper on your feast. I don't think they respect you."

"I can live without their respect," Zorachus replied. "I am, however, a bit amazed by their disrespect for you."

Kletus studied his face. "As I said, they're fools."

"Their threats carry no weight?"

"I didn't say that," Kletus replied, watching the slaves dragging Tchaldusaar's corpse away. "The people support them strongly. They have thousands of troops and hundreds of wizards. But the Priesthood's stronger than the Guild. We control the Cohort Ravener, the navy, the marines. And we're the most powerful mages in Khymir—blades in the hands of Tchernobog."

"Then why don't you just crush the Guild?"

"It's useful. The Guildsmen handle matters that would sully us—trade, paltry things like that."

"I see," Zorachus said. "I thought it might be because Tchernobog wasn't powerful enough."

Kletus's reaction was unexpected. Zorachus anticipated anger, but the High Priest only smiled.

"He has more than enough power. He's the most powerful being in the universe."

"But I've heard that another being created him," Zorachus said.

Kletus laughed. "You mean that senile flatulence your Sharajnaghi mentors pretend to worship? He didn't create the Black Lord. Tchernobog is what he's willed himself to be, self-existent, the eternal principle of pure spirit. At most, the Sharajnaghi God is only one of his avatars—the aspect which best reveals his humor, I think. Which would explain why the Sharajnaghim are such masters of farce."

"Still, you must admit they're effective."

Kletus nodded. "Though sometimes I wonder if they're operating in my universe."

Zorachus wanted to answer: *They're not—they're in the real one*. He thought of Qanar-Sharaj, and sweet memories stabbed him to the marrow; his first meeting with Raschid, Ghaznavi congratulating him on the water-clock he had invented, the ordination. . . .

Tchernaar came up beside Kletus. He seemed to have sobered a bit; he was less wobbly, though he shivered with excitement.

"My Lord," he said, "I'm ready." He tapped the bottle hanging from his neck. "I can't wait any longer." The words came slurred, partially from the wine, partially because his upper lip was badly swollen where Halfdan had struck him.

Kletus smiled. "You've been a faithful servant. I won't keep you any longer. This is as good a time as any."

Tchernaar slipped the bottle off and proffered it to Kletus. "Will you pour them over me?"

Kletus shook his head. "There's no need. When you're out in the ring, lay the bottle on its side and uncork it. I'll tell you what to do after that."

Tchernaar nodded gratefully, kissed Kletus's hand, and entered the circle. Kletus took up a napkin and wiped the spot where Tchernaar had pressed his lips.

Reaching the center, Tchernaar turned around and around, making sure he had everyone's attention. Satisfied, he stopped and cried:

"My friends, these are my last moments among you. The time has come for me to die—and die well." He held up the bottle. "There are worms in this, brought from another plane by His Anointed Steward. I'm going to let them feed on me, but I'll feel no pain; their saliva's a powerful drug. My Lord tells me it brings incredible ecstasy. . . ." Tittering, he began to fondle himself. Barely managing a last "Good-bye," he threw off his harness, laid the bottle on its side, and uncorked it, retreating.

It started to grow. Soon it was a foot long, then a yard, its frosted sides becoming transparent. A squirming knot of huge worms could be seen inside, also growing, maggot-shaped but black as oil.

Tchernaar sank to his knees, staring raptly at them. "Thank you, Lord Kletus," he said repeatedly, rocking to and fro in anticipation.

And all the while Kletus, having assumed a sitting stance, was force-letting just as Sathaswentha had done.

Presently, the bottle and worms stopped growing.

"Crawl in," Kletus told Tchernaar. Tchernaar looked at him and gave a pathetic, swollen-lipped parody of a smile.

"Go on," the High Priest urged.

Tchernaar looked back at the bottle. Out of its mouth came the liquid, slithering sounds of the worms oozing ceaselessly over each other. As yet, the clotted mass had not moved from the back of the vessel.

"You'll *love* it," Kletus said.

Tchernaar hesitated a few more seconds. Then, like a pale, shaven dog, he scrambled into the opening. The worms crawled forward, and he dived among them, embracing the pulpy bodies.

Kletus rose. Assuming a stance unfamiliar to Zorachus, he

raced through a formula; with invisible strands of will, he lifted the cork, which had also grown, and impelled it tightly into the bottle's mouth, muffling Tchernaar's first cries.

They were not cries of ecstasy. The envoy was struggling violently with the battening worms, which obscured half his body. The bottle rolled back and forth, and from time to time there was a glimpse of his shrieking face.

"I lied about the worms," Kletus cried, laughing. "They cause pain, as you can see. Incredibly intense. I don't imagine it would be possible for anyone to enjoy it."

The audience roared with delight.

He sat back down. The couch groaned loudly, as if under the weight of several tons.

"What did Tchernaar do to deserve that?" Zorachus asked, shouting to be heard over the laughter.

"He asked me to suggest a pleasant way to die," Kletus answered.

"But he was your man. You said he was your faithful servant. . . ."

"I'd be willing to say it again. The fact is that I want him to continue serving me—right up until his soul oozes its contemptible little way from his mouth. He pleases me best by dying in the most agonizing fashion imaginable. It's as simple as that."

"As simple as that."

"Worried I might deal the same way with you?" Kletus asked, studying Zorachus's face. "You could probably defend yourself. But more importantly, we're partners. I don't kill anyone I need. I'm not a frivolous man."

At those last words, Zorachus nearly burst out laughing, but as his eyes wandered back to the bottle, his grim amusement died. Tchernaar, still bucking under the vermiform blanket, had turned around and was trying to push the cork from the bottle. The audience shouted and stamped, offering mock encouragement, and they jeered in disappointment as he dropped back from the stopper, apparently exhausted. But as the worms chewed deeper, he seemed to get his second wind and launched himself forward with a terrific effort; the cork fell from the bottle mouth and he poked his head through. His eyes widened as they found Kletus.

"I'll kill you!" he cried. Somehow, agony had dredged a spark of manhood from within him; groaning, wheezing, he began to pull himself from the hole. The audience cried out in cruel approval. Half his body slid out onto the floor. He crawled still farther, trailing worms. He was nearly clear of the bottle mouth—then he stopped.

Zorachus thought he was dead. Several worms were embedded deep in the envoy's ribcage, and the Sharajnaghi guessed one had found his heart.

But he was wrong.

Tchernaar's expression changed. It went blank, then became a mask of delirious pleasure. Little ragged giggles came out of him. He twisted slowly, languidly, like a man atop an invisible succubus. He lifted himself once more on his hands and knees. Gradually he backed into the bottle, rejecting the world outside, withdrawing into his self-contained universe of abominable rapture. Like a man losing himself in a vast, comfortable bed, he lay down, placidly accepting the worms' gnawing services.

Kletus roared an oath; the unbelievable had happened. Jumping up, he resumed his stance and flipped the bottle upright. Tchernaar and the worms slid down into the bottom. Rumbling an incantation, Kletus revoked the spell by which bottle and worms had grown, and they shrank to their previous size; the crimson liquid that had been Tchernaar gushed out through the bottle's mouth, geysering up and up, almost splashing the ceiling before collapsing upon itself.

With a gesture Kletus vaporized all but a few drops. A dozen small dark shapes also remained, tumbling amid the red beads; striking the floor, the worms crawled back towards the bottle, leaving small trails of blood.

Kletus sat back down; again the couch gave voice. He turned to Zorachus. Already he seemed to have regained most of his composure.

"Have you taken a fancy to anyone here?" he asked. "Besides your bodyguard, that is?"

Halfdan began growling something in Kragehul.

"Be still," Zorachus said. Halfdan obeyed.

"He has a vicious temper," Kletus said.

"You insulted him," Zorachus replied. "He's a Kragehul, remember? I don't sleep with him. He's merely a bodyguard."

"I meant no harm. I was just making a little joke. Tchernaar told me you don't like manflesh." He looked at Halfdan. "However, it would be wise for this strawhead to remember he's already given me sufficient cause to blot him out." He returned his gaze to Zorachus. "Now then. Did you see anyone you liked? There's going to be an hour's lull until the next round of entertainment. You'll have to pass the time somehow."

"I really have my pick?"

"Absolutely. You're the guest of honor and may not be refused."

"Very good. Is there someplace we can talk?"

"There will be plenty of time for talk later. In the meantime there's Sathaswentha, or . . ."

Zorachus shook his head. "I'm the guest of honor. Don't refuse me."

Kletus laughed. "Very well. We can go to my garden."

"A blood-fruit garden?"

Kletus laughed again. "Nothing so prosaic. Come with me."

chapter

9

THE HIGH PRIEST led the way to a small, iron door.

"Wait here," Zorachus told Halfdan.

Kletus unlocked the door and opened it.

"After you," he told Zorachus, and the Sharajnaghi went in. Kletus followed, closing the door behind him.

"Did you say something?" he asked.

"No," Zorachus answered, but he lied; he had uttered the beginning of a Kadjafi curse, softly, almost unconsciously, the instant he saw what the room contained. Even after the banquet, he could still be shocked.

Most of the dirt floor before him was carpeted with what appeared to be nude men bathed in a sourceless white light, completely motionless, intertwined in a bewildering variety of sexual positions.

All were exact duplicates of Ghorchalanchor Kletus.

Mirrors covered the chamber's walls and ceiling, multiplying the High Priest's images a thousandfold. Tremendous vistas composed of nothing but his reflections stretched into infinity like demonic theophanies.

"The bodies are grown from a kind of fungus I breed specially to my purposes," Kletus said. "They have the exact feel and warmth of human flesh, but they're much tougher. You couldn't crush them with a boulder." He strode over to one of them, which lay on its belly. "See that cord? There, at the base of its spine? That's the connection between the body and the main growths down in the soil. It's long enough to allow considerable freedom of movement." At his words, the duplicate rose up on all fours, crawled about, and stopped still. "All of them are completely subject to my will. I can make them assume any position I want."

"Why do they all look like you?" Zorachus asked, straining to keep his voice free of the loathing he felt.

135

Kletus laughed. "You might say I needed a place where I could be alone with myself—an erotic necessity until my need for the erotic vanishes altogether. You see, I learned quite a while ago that nothing in the external world could satisfy my basic desires—except where the external provided an extension of myself, or became an extension of my will. It seems to be the same for everyone; hence, that inevitable progression from heterosexual to homosexual partners, and in some cases, to masturbation in a room full of mirrors."

"You believe no one can love another?"

Kletus nodded matter-of-factly. "Even when someone develops an attachment, he desires only those qualities that he himself shares. Even when he makes love to his partner, he loves only himself."

Zorachus decided to immerse himself in conversation as deeply as possible; it would make it that much easier to blot out his surroundings. "Let me see if I'm understanding you correctly," he said. "Let's suppose a man and woman are engaged in furious sexual intercourse. You'd say he takes no pleasure in the fact that she has female genitals, correct?"

"Yes."

"But if that's true, what exactly is he enjoying?"

"The fact that she's pressed beneath him, conforming to his will," Kletus replied. "He may think that he's enjoying her body, but he actually takes pleasure only in those aspects of her that have become extensions of himself."

Zorachus smiled thinly. "How does your theory hold for a man who prefers to have the woman on top?"

"That's a much more complex situation, of course," Kletus replied very seriously. "But his pleasure would stem from the basic human need to inflict humiliation. In order to most fully appreciate our success in inflicting humiliation, we must humiliate ourselves. When the woman's on top, it's a sign of dominance, but not dominance *she* exercises. It's the man who's actually holding himself in subjection, humiliator and victim both."

"Is that what you feel when a woman's on top?" Zorachus asked, astonished by the weird consistency of Kletus's notions.

"I no longer make love to women," Kletus answered haughtily, apparently annoyed by the mere suggestion. "Female flesh doesn't arouse me." He waved a hand over the motionless replicas. "Are *they* female?"

"Please don't take offense," Zorachus answered. "I was merely trying to find out how much first-hand experience you've had. Of such feelings, that is."

"When I still found women attractive, I didn't think overly much," Kletus replied. "I didn't analyze my desires. But now I'm able to put things in their proper perspective."

"Did you decide—consciously decide—that you disliked women because they were different from you?"

Kletus shook his head. "It was very gradual. More evolution than decision. I simply found myself spending more and more time with men. But now I know why my preference for male flesh won out. Women are reminders of ambiguities that I don't appreciate. The only pleasure I take from women these days is watching them being tortured. Or killed. I did feel some excitement when Clethusancta killed the blonde. And I very much enjoyed watching her and that slave die."

"Did you also enjoy watching those boxers pound each other apart? That was male flesh."

Kletus nodded. "Something I've also discarded my taste for—my *sexual* taste. Most male flesh, that is. I will of course step in when some bitch is going to inflict some insult upon it—I couldn't let Clethusancta carve up Tchaldusaar, for example. But for the most part I remain preoccupied with myself. I don't even roger these facsimiles anymore. Not that looking at them no longer arouses me; but I use them only for inspiration. I'd rather think of them as pictures in my mind, anyway. It excites me greatly to watch them couple, transformed into my fantasies even as I imagine them. It excites me even more to destroy them in various ways. Their very toughness, a reflection of my own power, makes it quite a challenge. I exult in my own creations even as I annihilate them. . . ." He paused, chuckling. "They look so much like me, and they're animated solely by my will! It's so easy to think of myself as one of them, almost to incarnate myself, as it were, to imagine my own feelings as I sacrifice myself to myself . . . I tell you, when I'm in this room, I'm so *sufficient*. . . ."

"I'm surprised you ever come out at all," Zorachus said drily, concealing his awe at the sheer depth of Kletus's self-absorption.

"I want to expand my universe," the High Priest answered. "Even here I can't forget the unnerving fact that there's an outside world. But when the world's my own sweet portrait. . . ."

"Just where will I fit into this 'portrait' of yours?" Zorachus asked.

Kletus laughed soothingly. "You'll be well provided for."

"In return for what? Becoming an extension of your will?"

"In effect, yes. Except that you've already given yourself to me. By coming to Khymir at my summons, you became one of the fingers of my hand."

The High Priest's brazenness was so astounding that Zorachus simply had to smile.

Kletus smiled too. "You find my arrogance amusing?" he asked.

"No. It's just that I've never met anyone quite so— *straightforward* as you."

"I can afford to be straightforward. I'm the center of my universe, and my universe will eventually be all center. I can see no point in allowing you illusions about our relationship."

"I hope you don't think I'll become more docile."

"I think you'll become more *pragmatic*," Kletus said with a fatherly smile. "After all, you do want to take full advantage of your situation. If you'll remember, I said we were partners a while ago. . . ."

Zorachus nodded. "That's why I wanted to speak to you. But all this talk about becoming a finger on your hand—that doesn't sound like partnership. That sounds like slavery."

"Of course," Kletus answered. *"Everyone's* my slave, even if they don't realize it. I didn't say it was an equal partnership. I know you must find that galling; all men hate those who command them, and that's as it should be. But you should take everything into consideration. All my fingers are pampered. There's a place for you in the Priesthood. A high one."

Zorachus was silent a few moments. "I'm not sure I want to join your order."

Kletus smiled with good-natured dubiousness. "Come now! What else could you want? To stay in your palace and glut your senses? I don't think you're that sort. Not many men would want to talk business when they had a chance to lie with Sathaswentha. And believe me, I find that tremendously admirable. You already have enough restraint to prevent your will from clouding, and at a very early age. I'm nearly twice as old as you and still haven't overcome my need for the erotic. I was brought up in typical Khymirian fashion. For all the good points of our child rearing, we've never laid enough emphasis on will. Consequently, I acquired a strong addiction to sex. I was taught to confuse desire for pleasure with desire for external things—a confusion all that wallowing in flesh only aggravated. I'm only now transcending it. But I will say I'm transcending it with a vengeance. Already there are few kinds of flesh I don't despise, and I'm quickly whittling the number down."

"That appetite for meat will simply disappear?" Zorachus asked, remembering the High Priest clearing platter after platter.

"I've no appetite for meat," Kletus replied. "I've an appetite for *eating* meat, if you see the distinction. I find the idea of it turning into *me* very satisfying. Either it becomes me, or it becomes dung. Not that it was ever much more than dung to begin with."

"That's an article of faith in your order, isn't it? That flesh is vile?"

Kletus laughed. "Our order has no articles of faith. You don't even have to believe in Tchernobog, just so long as you observe certain religious formalities. Take your father, for example. He turned into a complete atheist after becoming High Priest. Very reform minded. That's why he was so popular. He only got into trouble when he tried to turn the Priesthood into a mere secular government.

"Now, as for flesh, it's worshipped as well as damned. The grossest sensuality and the struggle towards purification go on side by side. The former's merely more visible. Practically all the lower-level adepts are sensualists. But if they want to advance, a belief in the ultimate importance of spirit is very useful. Full initiates have usually recognized flesh for what it is. Lysthragon and Sathaswenthar both share my views, for example."

Zorachus was puzzled. "Sathaswenthar? Then why would he transform himself into a woman and seduce men?"

"Because he enjoys mocking the sexual act, especially the heterosexual act: it begets flesh. But it's also a kind of spiritual exercise. All that slime makes it very easy to keep the body's true nature ever in mind. And by enjoying men the way women do, he reminds himself what pigs women are."

"What about Zarathonzar? Isn't he a Chief Acolyte?"

"By virtue of his talents. We need him. But he's not a full initiate. He has much to learn, but we're teaching him. Already he despises women and has begun to butcher the young boys he presently favors. More promising still, he's taken to spending more and more time alone with his mirrors. Soon he'll be a perfect servant of the Black God."

"The Black God," Zorachus mused. "Your Lord and Master."

Kletus looked at him sidelong. "Why say it that way?"

"I'm just wondering where *he* fits into your universe. I should think yours would merely be part of his."

Kletus was unperturbed by the question. "His goals and mine are, to all intents and purposes, the same. I think of him the same way I think of myself."

"It sounds very cozy," Zorachus said, admiring the High Priest's rationalization in spite of himself. "But what exactly are these common goals of yours?"

"To expand our influence, of course. Even now we're planning a great enterprise, one in which you'll play a very important part. . . ." Kletus smiled conspiratorially.

"What do you have in mind?" Zorachus asked, knowing that the revelation of Kletus's true intentions was at hand, wanting desperately to discover that Ghaznavi had been wrong, that the mission to Khymir had been unnecessary all along, that the nightmare was over instead of only beginning. . . .

"The conquest of Muspellheim," Kletus said, each word falling like a hammer blow against the frail glass of Zorachus's hopes. "Tchernobog wants victims. I want meat. The Kragehul will satisfy us both."

"You eat *human* meat?" Zorachus asked, appalled yet not surprised.

"Certainly. What could be better than turning *people* into myself?"

Then Zorachus remembered what he had eaten at the banquet. "Is that what you served me?" he asked quietly, feeling a surge of nausea, but maintaining his composure.

"It was beef on the platters," Kletus answered. "The only manflesh was in my wallets. I wouldn't serve it to someone without asking. It *is* an acquired taste. And why waste it?"

Zorachus was relieved, though much of his queasiness remained. "Why attack Muspellheim?" he asked. "Can't you make do with the slaves you already have?"

"I could, for a while. But my needs, like the Dark Lord's, are growing. Soon, quite literally, they'll know no bounds."

Zorachus was dumbstruck. He knew the High Priest was talking about thousands of bodies, hundreds of thousands. He did not doubt Kletus's intention to devour them all, and he knew Kletus had acquired some means of doing precisely that. The orgy of flesh eating at the banquet was but a mild foretaste of the orgy to come.

"And you need my aid?" Zorachus asked.

Kletus nodded. "You'll be invaluable."

"How?"

"By throwing my Khymirian opponents off balance. As you must have guessed, the city's divided into two camps. The first's made up of the Priesthood and most of the nobles, the second of the Merchant Guildsmen and their followers. The Guildsmen will certainly spurn cooperation in the invasion. They get everything they need through trade, and they dislike foreign adventuring—they've been burned at it. But they'll also be unwilling to leave such an undertaking solely in priestly hands. We'll have to levy much more than our present tithes to hire the necessary numbers of Southron mercenaries, and since Khymir will serve for quite some time as a staging area, the mercenaries themselves will tilt the balance of power overwhelmingly in our favor. To prevent that, the Guildsmen will fight ferociously.

"But you'll weaken them. The city eagerly awaited your arrival. The Mancdaman name is illustrious. It brings immediate memories of better times whenever it's uttered. You've already shown that such times might be returning; I heard how you secured many allies this morning. People will listen to you when you support the invasion. They'll be reassured when you tell them that the Priesthood isn't going to use its new regiments inside the city. After all, wasn't your father the famous reformer Mancdaman Zancharthus? And didn't he try to make the Priesthood less oppressive? Much of the mob, which would normally back the Guild, will turn to the Priesthood."

"You're sure of that?" Zorachus asked.

"Perfectly," Kletus replied. "A little voice told me." He laughed.

"When do you want me to join your order?"

"As soon as possible, naturally. It would be splendid if I could make an announcement tonight."

Zorachus raised a hand. "As I said, I'm not sure. . . ."

"And I suppose you don't know if you want to back the invasion, either."

Zorachus nodded. "I need some time to think. Will you give me a day?"

"I'd prefer not," Kletus said smiling, but with a hint of menace in his voice.

Zorachus was unfazed. "Don't pressure me."

Kletus's eyes bore down on him.

"What are you worried about?" Zorachus asked. "Aren't you already sure I'll join you? Would you have told me your plan otherwise?"

"No," the High Priest admitted. "I'm sure." But the threat in his voice remained.

"All right, then. Do you mind if I don't rejoin the banquet? As I said, I need to think."

"Do as you wish."

"I'll go back to my palace, then. Will you see me out?"

Kletus shook his head. "Have my steward help you with the lift." Behind him, the replicas began to writhe; his left hand wandered under his robes, and returned with a meat wallet.

"You'll have my decision tomorrow," Zorachus said. "Farewell."

Leaving the chamber, he was overjoyed suddenly at the simple sight of Halfdan's bluff, ruddy face, like a thirst-racked wanderer stumbling across water in a desert; it was a tremendous comfort to see someone who was no part of Kletus's universe. Even the city outside would seem like a place of primal innocence compared to Kletus's garden.

Passing back through the banquet chamber, they found the steward; two minutes later they reached the great South Gate. The steward called for Zorachus's palanquin and escort, but the Sharajnaghi, seeing the palanquin again, remembered the canopy painting and the twin-tongued face, and decided he would rather walk. Feeling safe enough, he also dismissed the guards, since he wanted to talk to Halfdan alone.

The Kragehul's horse had been brought to him by the overseer. Halfdan, leading it by the reins, set off with Zorachus.

"Did you feel the air in there?" Zorachus asked quietly.

Halfdan nodded. "Like Death Himself had sucked all the life from it. I never thought I'd find this Khymirian damp so pleasant." He paused. "What did you and Kletus talk about?"

Zorachus told him. Halfdan swore when he learned of the invasion, but was delighted with Zorachus's plan to throw in with the Guild.

"You're a slippery one, aren't you?" he said. "A real shape-changer."

chapter

10

THE NEXT MORNING, Zorachus asked Louchan where Klissandrian Porchos lived.

"Lord Kletus wants me to talk to him," he explained. "There was some trouble at the banquet and he thought I might be able to smooth things over..."

He got directions and set out with Halfdan through the steaming streets, hiding his face with a hood to avoid being mobbed. Porchos's palace was on the southeast side of Khymir; the trip took well over an hour. The Guildsman seemed delighted by the visit.

"We're not disturbing you?" Zorachus asked.

"Certainly not," Porchos replied. "You came at just the right time. I'm sufficiently recuperated...." he chuckled.

"From what?"

"Some love-play."

"I see."

"Broke in a little Tarchan girl. Tiny wisp of a thing, five years old...." Porchos smiled and seemed lost in reverie.

Zorachus's eyes wandered, taking in the details of his sumptuous surroundings. His attention was swiftly drawn to a gold dragon statue set in a niche, a perfect example of motion captured in an inanimate object, an astounding depiction of frenzied energy. He read aloud the name engraved on the base: "Lazarak."

That roused Porchos and he turned to look at the figure.

"Lazarak of the Golden Mail," he said. "A name revered in Khymirian history. He was a a great general."

"A dragon?" Zorachus asked.

Turning once more, Porchos shook his head. "He became one after his burial."

"I've never heard of such a thing," Zorachus said. "Is it just a legend?"

"Nothing of the sort, although no one knows for certain

why it happened. Some say the Black Lord transformed him for some unguessable reason. Others say he was enchanted by a power from the very stones. That seems more likely to me. The catacombs under this city are eerie places; strange forces well up from the center of the earth. The lowest levels merge into tunnels made by the Shreeth—dwarfish creatures, incredibly strong and ferocious. I've heard they worship a stone idol set in a lake of molten lava."

Zorachus was still staring at the statue of Lazarak. "Is he still alive?"

Porchos nodded. "And completely mad. He's trapped in the catacombs—the tunnels are too narrow for him to escape. Now and again he tries to smash his way out, hurling himself against the walls of his prison, widening his chamber, breaking into other vaults. But mostly he sleeps and dreams of revenge."

"On whom?"

"The Black Priests. He grew too powerful, you see, and they had him murdered—which is why I don't think their god was responsible for his transformation. Obviously, Tchernobog had no use for him to begin with. . . . In any case, one of their agents drove a spear through the gilded scale-mail he always wore. The spear hole can still be seen; his mail became his new skin when he changed, and there's a fiery wound in his chest.

"But so much for Khymirian lore. Come on: I've a place where we can talk more privately."

He led Zorachus and Halfdan to a large room in the center of the house.

"It's perfectly soundproofed," the merchant said, sitting in a large padded chair. "I had one of my wizards do the work. He designed the blocks specially. It was all very expensive, but a man should have a place where he can speak without being overheard. Sit down, sit down."

Zorachus settled across from him and Halfdan planted himself behind the Sharajnaghi's chair. Zorachus had thought it unwise to leave Halfdan outside; they were, after all, in enemy territory. There was always the chance that Porchos might seize a chance to eliminate Kletus's prized new ally. But the merchant did not seem to mind Halfdan's presence.

"Formidable looking bodyguard you've got there," he observed appreciatively.

"That's how a bodyguard *should* look," Zorachus said. "I'm surprised you don't travel with any. Those men last night were all Maranchthus's, weren't they?"

"How did you guess?"

"Their hands only went to their hilts when someone went near *him*."

Porchos laughed. "His traveling army. He's always telling me I should have one. He doesn't put as much faith in my mages as I do." He plucked at his multicolored robe. "This is my bodyguard."

"Armor?"

"Hardly. I'll show you how it works. Have your man take a slash at me."

"Are you quite sure . . ."

"It will be all right."

Zorachus shrugged. "Go ahead, Halfdan."

"You must be joking," Halfdan protested.

"Use the flat if you're worried," Porchos said.

Halfdan grunted and drew his sword. Advancing round Zorachus's chair, he swung at Porchos half-heartedly.

Instantly, one of Porchos's sleeves lengthened and lashed upwards, enwrapping the sword blade, wrenching it from Halfdan's hand. As the Kragehul cried out in amazement, Porchos's other sleeve shot out, wrapped around Halfdan's neck, and whipped back again. Halfdan cursed and retreated. Both sleeves shortened to their previous lengths.

"The robe's a living creature," Porchos explained. "From another dimension, of course. I've many such garments. At the slightest hint of danger, the robe disarms the attacker and extrudes needles full of poison. If I'd willed it, that second blow would have been fatal."

Rubbing his throat, Halfdan picked his sword back up and resumed his post.

"Maranchthus is skeptical?" Zorachus asked. "Haven't you ever given him a demonstration?"

"Of course," Porchos answered. "But he still thinks it's only a worthless trick. He lectured me for half an hour after we left the banquet. Said what happened to Clethusancta would happen to me. She never traveled with a guard of any sort."

"Would it have made any difference if she had?"

"I doubt it. Maranchthus likes to hear himself talk. Kletus

wouldn't have been fazed if she'd had a whole squad of suicide troops in the hall."

"Then why didn't you try to persuade Clethusancta to back down?"

"She wouldn't have. But I thought Kletus might, to avoid marring your evening. That's why I didn't expect his treachery. I should have realized. He knows his own power so well."

"It's a shame he has so much," Zorachus said.

Porchos eyed him silently.

"I'd like him so much better if he had none at all," Zorachus went on.

Porchos folded his hands before his face. "Harsh words from one of his own partners."

"I'm not his partner. He may think I'm one of the fingers on his hand, but I'm not going to let him rule me. It's as simple as that."

"Is it? I thought perhaps you might have made some sort of discovery. . . ."

"Other than the fact that he's a domineering madman?"

"Yes. About his connection to your father."

"What was that?"

"They were very close, at first. Zancharthus took Kletus under his wing, fostered his rise in the Priesthood. But some say Kletus betrayed him. That he was the man who prodded Thagranichus Ordog to usurp the High Priesthood."

"I know nothing about that," Zorachus said, wondering if there was anything to it. Having no memory of his father, he told himself that it mattered little, even if it were true. Perhaps he even owed Kletus a debt of gratitude; he would have been raised a Khymirian if his father had not been killed.

"I see," Porchos said. "I thought it unlikely myself. I expect that if Kletus had actually been involved, we would have known for certain by now. In any case, your independence from him is admirable. Does he know about it?"

"He will, as of this afternoon. I'm going to denounce him. And his Priesthood. And his plan to invade Muspellheim."

Porchos lowered his hands, skin paling. "To do *what?*"

Zorachus told him Kletus's scheme.

"But why bring this information to me?" Porchos asked.

"When he realizes I've turned on him, he'll turn on me. There's only one power I can ally myself with: the Guild."

Porchos smiled and thought a bit, pursing his lips. "Your name *would* be very useful to us. Now more than ever. We suspected Kletus had some plot in mind, but we never guessed it could be so grandiose. When was he going to put it into effect?"

"He didn't say. But he was anxious to get my decision, loath to grant me even one day. I expect my denunciation will set him back very badly."

"Perhaps even undo his plan altogether," Porchos added.

"Will the Guild support me, then?"

"*I'd* like to support you," Porchos assured him. "That doesn't mean my colleagues will, though. I could do nothing if they overruled me."

"What's the chance of that?"

Porchos laughed. "Not much, when the stakes are this high. But one can't be absolutely sure. People are unpredictable. They seem perfectly solid on the surface, but underneath? Great shifting quagmires, no more real than anything else. Which is to say, not real at all."

"Nothing is real?"

"*I* don't think so. Not this moment, at any rate. Riding those little girls often seems real enough. But the rest. . . ." He laughed. "Ah well, I don't suppose I'd have it any different. Wouldn't it be dreadful if things *were* real? What a thought. Gives one the shivers."

"It doesn't bother me," Zorachus answered. *Thank God,* he thought.

Porchos's face twisted with incredulity. "No?"

Zorachus shook his head.

"Surely it's just a passing thing."

"No."

Porchos shrugged.

"When will you contact the other Guildsmen?" Zorachus asked.

Porchos rose. "I'll send for them straightaway." He rubbed his hands together. "If only I could see the look on Kletus's face when he finds out what you've done."

The main altar room of Tchernobog was located at the top of Banipal Khezach, but there were many smaller chapels in the temple. In one of these, a dark chamber on the first floor, blackly barrel-vaulted and lined with squat pillars, Kletus and

Sathaswenthar were administering one of their order's many charities.

The room was packed with beggars and dolly riding cripples waving hunks of meat and plucked chickens in their scab-crusted hands. Their voices clamored hideously, and their stench competed mightily with the sickly sweet incense burning on the altar of the Black Hand.

Kletus pointed to two of the mendicants. One had a withered arm and the other, leaning on a crutch, a paralyzed leg; their toothless maws gaped as they shrieked their delight. Buffeted and cursed by their fellows, they came forward, proffering their gifts of meat. Kletus took up the flesh and turned to the blazing oblation dish, lowering the offerings slowly into the devouring flames. As he did so, Sathaswenthar silenced the crowd and intoned a prayer to Tchernobog, his words echoing hollowly through the hall:

> *"Black Father,*
> *Master of the spiritual world,*
> *Power is thy name.*
> *Your will endures,*
> *Your black grip holds,*
> *Your reign will last eternally.*
> *Relish the destruction of these fleshly abominations,*
> *And grant us your favor,*
> *So that we might deal with others*
> *As they would deal with us.*
> *Lead us not into discomfort,*
> *And deliver us from disease;*
> *For thine is the cleansing force,*
> *Almighty against all things seen and touched,*
> *That can succor us from the corruptions of the flesh."*

As the prayer closed, Kletus turned, strode to the chosen beggars, and laid his hands upon their matted heads.

"Fight well, my sons," he said. "Tchernobog's blessing and a sack of gold to the victor."

The beggars stepped back from the dais, the other mendicants screaming encouragement, oddsmakers among them taking bets. The contest promised to be fairly even; the man with the withered arm was more mobile, but the cripple, who could balance on his right leg, had his crutch for a weapon.

They squared off, eyeing each other grimly. A long time passed. Neither made a move. Suspense became boredom for the spectators.

"Come on, my sons," Kletus prodded threateningly.

The cripple hopped forward, swinging his crutch at his opponent. The latter laughed and leaped out of range—only to lose his footing and fall backward, knocking his wind out against the hard stone floor. The cripple advanced with surprising speed; stunned, the fallen man sprawled helpless as the crutch rose again and again, cracking his ribs and finally his skull. The other mendicants roared, some with pleasure, some, having bet on the wrong man, with dismay.

Panting, the victor turned to Kletus. Once he received his reward, there would be more beggars chosen, more offerings, more fights.

But before the beggar could hobble up to the altar, Kourgon Zarathonzar, dragging a struggling man, thrust his way out of the crowd and hurled the cripple from his path. The crowd rumbled to see their peer treated so; they did not have much use for each other, but disrespect for one was disrespect for them all.

Zarathonzar was undaunted by their displeasure. Still clutching his captive he turned, assumed a one-handed Chimera Stance, and launched several keening greenish bolts into the crowd. A dozen beggars fell with broken bones, but even they picked themselves up and joined the mad dash for the door, the victor of the contest stumping along furiously at the rear.

"That was unwise," Kletus told Zarathonzar calmly as the racket died. "Bad politics."

"Politics be hanged!" Zarathonzar shouted, hauling his captive to his feet. The man wore a green messenger's tunic, and had been badly beaten about the face. "This fool was spreading *them!*"

"Spreading what?"

Zarathonzar plucked a sheet of crumpled vellum from his belt. Kletus strode forward, took it and read. His eyes widened in angry amazement as he realized his plans had been revealed: he loosed a thunderous cry when he saw Zorachus's signature.

Zarathonzar jerked the messenger by the tunic and pointed vehemently at his bloodied face. "He was in Kralorg Square.

He'd posted several of the damn bills and was reading another to the rabble."

"My Lord High Priest," the messenger wailed. "I was only doing my job. Porchos hired me, but. . . ."

"Porchos!" Zarathonzar screeched, as if no more hateful name could be uttered. *"Porchos!"* An earsplitting torrent of unintelligible syllables poured from his mouth; clutching the messenger's throat with his left hand, he lifted him up off the floor at arm's length, shaking him as a child might shake a rattle. Suddenly, his right hand flew upward in a blur, catching the messenger hard under the nose, jamming his nasal bones into his brain and killing him instantly. Zarathonzar tossed his flopping corpse away as if it were so much refuse.

Kletus, meanwhile, had gotten a grip on himself. Watching Zarathonzar rage always heightened his appreciation of level-headedness.

"If I were you," the High Priest said, handing the denunciation to Sathaswenthar, "I'd try not to lose my mind every time something angered me. A violent temper's a serious weakness."

"You're no one to talk," Zarathonzar jeered. "How calm were you with Clethusancta? And what was that cry just now?"

"I didn't lose control last night," Kletus answered. "And as for that cry, it was the only sound I made. Have you ever heard me break into gibberish? My mind's not so easily overturned. . . ."

"Spare me," Zarathonzar snarled.

Kletus nodded, and smiled the smile he always wore when he was making a mental note to pay someone back for an affront. "There *are* more important matters to attend to," he said, "Killing Mancdaman Zorachus, for example."

chapter

11

ZORACHUS AND HALFDAN returned to the Mancdaman palace
even as the denunciation, having been reproduced hundreds of
times by means of a copying spell, was being published. With
them came a large company of Guild troops in browned mail,
bearing kite-shaped shields. Having been told to obey Zorachus in everything, the household troops stood idly by as the
new retainers took over.

Some time later, Louchan appeared. He had been off on an
errand, but was not surprised to see his underlings packing, or
the Guild troops—he had read the denunciation. Meeting
Zorachus, he grinned wickedly.

"Good luck, Lord Mancdaman," he said, clearly hoping
Zorachus would get nothing of the sort.

"And good luck to you, Louchan," Zorachus said, trying to
mean it. "I hope your new master's easier to deal with than I
was."

Louchan bowed. "Thank you, my Lord," he said, and
made off.

Eventually, the old household gathered near the main stairway, heavily guarded by the Guild troops. Each member received a year's pay from Zorachus. Then they were herded
out.

As night approached, another contingent of Guild troops
arrived, accompanied by a group of servants drawn from the
vast labor force the Guild commanded. Many food-tasters and
food-watchers were included to safeguard Zorachus's meals.
There was also a mason, as the Sharajnaghi had requested; he
did not want the building of Asa's tomato garden delayed by
the change of staff.

The newcomers were led by Louchan's replacement, a
flabby little Tarchan named Alandax Sharthas, whose main
qualification was that he had been lieutenant steward of the
palace when it belonged to Kordus Kragon, one of Thagrani-

chus Ordog's Chief Acolytes. Besides that, he had an extremely commanding personality, surprisingly so, in light of his appearance; servants and soldiers jumped when he spoke. He also had a seeming lack of Khymirian attitudes, apparent even in small snatches of his conversation, and was always ending orders with phrases like "hop to it, you degenerate!" During one brief lull in the evening's activity (there was much moving in and rearranging to be done), Zorachus, wondering why the Tarchan had remained in Khymir after being freed, asked him if he liked the city.

"I suppose I hate it, my Lord," Sharthas replied, shaking his head like a sad old hound. His commanding mien had vanished; he was speaking to the master of the house. "Khymir will be the death of me. But I can't leave."

"Why?"

Sharthas gave a watery smile and wiped sweat from his brow. "I won't burden you with the details."

"I don't mind," Zorachus said.

The steward's face reddened; he seemed to be thinking of some excuse not to continue the conversation. Noticing several guards moving weapons into the wrong room, he roared directions at them and they stopped by the threshold, looking confused.

"Really, my Lord," Sharthas said, "I should attend to business. It'll take a long time to get your house in order."

"Of course," Zorachus replied. "But once things are squared away, you should come up to my room for a bit. Halfdan and Asa will be there. We can all have some wine."

Sharthas smiled uncomfortably. "That's very kind of you. But to be frank, I really don't want to share your bed. I know that sounds insubordinate, but I wasn't brought up in Khymir and I have different . . . how do you say it . . . *preferences*."

Zorachus laughed. "I wasn't brought up in Khymir, either. All we want to do is talk. Get acquainted. There won't be any groping, my word on it."

Sharthas was hesitant. "Well. . . . I suppose I *could* get enough work done. . . . But I'm sure it wouldn't be till midnight, at least."

"We'll see you then," Zorachus answered. Sharthas hurried off to deal with the guards, his meekness dropping away.

The night bustled on. Echoing shouts frequently made it sound as if Sharthas were in several places at once; there were few matters that did not receive his loud, competent attention.

But after a time the activity began to slacken. Zorachus and the two Kragehul went to relax on his balcony, with a bottle of some lesser Tarchan vintage.

The Khymirian night oppressed them at first. Closer, denser than usual, the humid air hung heavy in their lungs. Gloom swarmed about the small circle of light from their lamp.

They passed the wine around. It took a while to hearten them, but gradually their spirits rose. The darkness seemed to recede a bit; the night seemed less thick.

Asa told of the problems she had had with the new mason. He was a foreigner of some sort who did not understand Khymirian very well, and her efforts to explain to him her garden plan seemed quite hilarious in retrospect—although she had been very frustrated at the time. He apparently thought the word *tomato* meant *wax tadpole,* and had spent a lot of time trying to demonstrate to her that she would not be able to raise such creatures (or mold them) in the structure he had outlined. Almost until the end, her every attempt to enlighten the fellow had gone horribly wrong, and by the time she finished telling Halfdan and Zorachus about her endeavors, they were stretched out on the polished stones, sides near splitting.

Recovering, Zorachus said: "Reminds me of this merchant I met in Thangura once. . . . " and went on to describe how the fellow had been part of a trade mission to an eastern land; woefully ignorant of the language, he had many misadventures, finally accepting some malicious advice on what to say to the monarch at an audience that had been arranged. When the time came and he stood before the throne, he said proudly: "Your majesty, I hope your wife becomes a big whore in my country." The hall filled with gasps, but the king, who hated his wife, only smiled and said: "That will be fine, but she'll have to send the money back here."

Halfdan came up with one of his own, a long and somewhat melancholy tale about a Tarchan man visiting Muspellheim whose name sound very much like "Pig, spit on me," in Kragehul. Needless to say, whenever he introduced himself, he found himself covered with spittle and surrounded by furious Kragehul. He blundered into four swordfights before he finally found out what was happening, but by then it was too late; one arm hacked off at the shoulder, he said to his opponent as he sagged down, dying, "Hell, it isn't even my real name."

"God," Zorachus laughed, "what's so funny about that?"

Halfdan and Asa continued with anecdotes about their relatives. For the first time, Zorachus heard of Asa's infamous cousin Gerd, who was so ugly her parents made her sit at the door of their hall to scare off evil spirits; Halfdan told about his uncle's attempt to convince his wife that he couldn't possibly have visited Torgunn the swineherd's daughter because a sorcerer had turned him into a prawn, and his uncle's frantic attempts to line up a roster of witnesses. Zorachus responded with a story about a Sharajnaghi who *had* actually been turned accidentally into a prawn. And just as accidentally eaten, by the Great Khan himself.

"That is definitely *not* funny," Asa said.

"I never said it was," Zorachus said.

"Then tell Halfdan to stop laughing."

"He's *your* husband," Zorachus said and started to chuckle. "Actually, now that I think about it, though. . . ."

Soon all three of them were roaring again. It was a long time before they settled down, and a long lull followed. Tired of laughing, they did not mind the hush. A wonderful hour had passed, filled with high good humor. They lay quietly on the balcony, contented.

But contentment passed. The dark seemed to creep inward once more. Little by little, feeding on their silence, the night's oppression came on them again.

Zorachus remembered how hot it was, became aware of how much he was sweating; his hair clung to his head, his clothes to his skin. But he resolved to ignore the heat and the lung-smothering humidity, refused to be pinioned by the steaming stillness. He drove himself to speak, even though the words themselves had no great urgency—any would do to push aside the damp, warm pillow stifling them.

"I invited Sharthas up," he said. "I'm surprised he isn't here yet."

"That fleshy little loudmouth?" Halfdan demanded, sitting up, roused by his own contempt.

"Did he shout at you?" Zorachus asked.

"No. But I don't like him."

"He was nice to me," Asa said.

"He knows we're high in Zorachus's favor," Halfdan answered. "If Zorachus wasn't the Master. . . ."

"Then Sharthas wouldn't be here, either," Asa said.

Checked, Halfdan grunted, "Why *did* you ask him up?" he asked Zorachus.

"For some talk," the Sharajnaghi replied. "He isn't a Khymirian, you know."

Halfdan jeered. "Tarchans aren't much better."

Asa nudged him. "Don't be silly. That Tarchan noble your father held hostage wasn't a bad sort."

"He gave my father a damned hard clout when he tried to escape," Halfdan shot back.

Asa frowned. "What would you expect? He wanted to keep his wife and children from having to pay all that ransom. That's really very reasonable. Besides, he taught you how to play chess." She looked at Zorachus earnestly. "Halfdan's a very good chess player, you know."

"I am that," Halfdan said sullenly.

"And you owe it all to him," Asa answered. "A Tarchan."

"This Sharthas never did me any favors," Halfdan grumbled.

"Well, he helped *me* find the mason."

"He's ugly. And he's probably a Guild spy."

"I expect we've enough of them now," Zorachus said. "But better Guild spies than Kletus's. Now that the Guild's publicly allied with us, we don't have to be *quite* so shy about showing how un-Khymirian we are. . . ."

"Asa and I have never been shy about that," Halfdan broke in.

"Well, *I* had to be careful. If Kletus had thought I was insane, he might never have revealed his scheme. But the Guild's bound to me. They can't withdraw their support, no matter how crazy I seem. Of course, I still don't want them to know my real plans, so we'd better stay clear of them when Sharthas is around."

"Right," Asa said firmly.

There was a knock on the inside door.

"That must be him," Zorachus said, and went to answer it. Returning with Sharthas, he sat, motioning the steward to do likewise. Sharthas complied hesitantly.

"You look a bit taut," Zorachus said. "Have some wine. It'll loosen you up."

Sharthas plucked at the sagging flesh under his chin. "Actually, my Lord, I could do with a bit *less* slack," he answered. "But as you're the master here. . . ." Taking the bottle, he downed several gulps.

"Save some for us!" Halfdan cried.

"There's plenty left," Sharthas answered apologetically. Halfdan took the bottle away from him, hefting its contents.

"Maybe," he rumbled.

"The wine reminds me of home," Sharthas said wistfully. "Blessed Tarchan. All that sweet ignorance. . . ."

"How did you wind up in Khymir?" Asa asked.

"I lived in a little village at the mouth of the Arkflight," Sharthas began. "Kragehul swept in one day and carried me and my brothers off . . ."

"And you still haven't forgiven us for it, have you?" Halfdan broke in.

"I was quite upset at the time," Sharthas said. "But I don't think much about it now. As a matter of fact, I suppose I was treated rather well. From what I could gather, we were the best booty they could find. It had been a dismal raid and they wanted to save what little they had. They were going to sell us as thralls. But they never got the chance.

"Halfway up the Muspel coast, they ran into the Khymirian fleet. They fought fiercely but were heavily outnumbered. The ship I was on caught fire, my brothers were killed, as were most of the crew. The Khymirians took me off, but tossed me in the brig—decided they'd sell me themselves, along with the surviving pirates. It was then that I started to see just how easy I'd had it with the Kragehul. The Khymirians acted like . . . well, Khymirians; at the time I found it hard to believe their cruelty. It frequently slipped their minds that they wanted us alive—they tortured several of the Kragehul to death, and I got my share, too. But as you can see, I managed to survive, and was sold as scullery help into the household of Kordus Kragon. Eventually, I worked my way up to lieutenant steward."

"How did you gain your freedom?" Zorachus asked.

"In a dice game. Kragon was a great one for gambling. He'd gamble with anyone for anything. One night, when he was alone and drunk, he invited me into his room. 'Come on, Sharthas, you hangdog,' he said taking out his dice, 'I'll play you for your clothes—and you can play me for your freedom.' He won time after time. Never seemed bothered that he was winning things that were already his. Finally I was down to my left shoe—and then he lost. Next afternoon, in the throes of a terrible headache, he signed my manumission. Somehow he remembered our deal. It surprised me greatly. He'd been so drunk."

"I'm surprised he paid up," Zorachus said. "I wouldn't have expected a Khymirian to be so conscientious."

"It was the way he was," Sharthas said. "He could sit down and eat live babies, but he never cheated at gambling and always paid his debts. I'll never understand Khymirians. Most of us . . . rather, most of *them*, are wicked or insane, and the rest are both."

"Yet you stay among them," Halfdan said suspiciously.

The Tarchan nodded guiltily.

Halfdan barked a laugh. "Gorm's Hammer! If I had my freedom, I'd be out of this city before you could blink."

"But you do," Zorachus said.

Halfdan harrumphed and pointed to Sharthas. "If I were *him*, and I had my freedom, I'd leave."

"Why *do* you stay, Sharthas?" Asa asked.

Sharthas looked pained. "I'd really rather not talk about it."

"Do you have a woman here?"

Sharthas remained silent.

"If it was a woman, he'd tell us," Halfdan jeered. "It's probably a boy—if it's human at all."

"It's a woman," Sharthas replied quickly.

"Couldn't you take her with you?" Asa asked.

"She's not mine."

"Is she married?"

Sharthas downcast his eyes. "She's a slave. In a brothel."

"Khymirian?"

"No, she's black."

"Can't you buy her?"

Sharthas shook his head. "Even if I had the money, her master wouldn't sell. She's much too popular. God, she's beautiful." Pausing, he smiled slightly. "And expensive. My poor purse. I try to visit her every week or so."

"Like a sheep to the slaughter," Halfdan said. "Don't you have any backbone, man? Forget her and leave this sty. She's just a woman."

"Just a woman!" Asa cried. "And what am I?"

"Nothing more."

"Do you know anything you'd like better?"

"A woman with a bit more respect."

Asa laughed harshly. "You mean the kind who'd respect you more each time you insulted her?"

"I didn't say that. And I didn't insult you. I insulted *women*. As a race. I don't see why you should take it personally."

"I don't see why you should talk that way at all, belittling me and my mother."

Halfdan's jaw dropped. "Your mother. I never..."

"And as for poor Sharthas..." Tears welled up in Asa's eyes and she laid a comforting hand on the Tarchan's knee. "I understand how he feels. It must be terrible."

"What's your woman's name?" Zorachus asked Sharthas.

"Chatonha," Sharthas replied.

"Barbaric," Halfdan sulked.

"I like it," Asa said stoutly.

"I bet she has a ring in her nose," Halfdan went on.

"She wouldn't have any such thing," Asa returned.

"Actually, she does," Sharthas said. "And it's rather fetching."

Asa's face clouded and she withdrew her hand. "If you say so." She was very disturbed to think that anyone would wear a nosering.

Guessing how she felt, Sharthas opened his mouth to make a further defense of the bauble—then closed it again, wearily resting his chin on his palm, eyes full of embarrassment.

Halfdan folded his hands behind his head and smiled smugly at Asa. She ignored him.

Delighted with the absurd note on which the conversation had faltered, Zorachus studied the three of them with great amusement, unable to empathize much with Sharthas's discomfort, Halfdan and Asa were obviously right about noserings.

Suddenly, warm, stinging sweat trickled into his eyes. He rubbed them, but the salty irritation remained. It was some time before his sight cleared.

He looked at the others again. Their expressions had changed, become apprehensive. He told himself it was the silence; their voices had held back the night's oppression, but now it had settled once more, black pressure squeezing perspiration-slick flesh.

Yet he quickly realized it was not just the silence and the turgid air. Something was about to happen. His mind hummed with sensation, as it had when he had passed beneath the

thunder barrier, a feeling that the atmosphere had taken on
some kind of charge. But where the charge he had felt under
the clouds was clean, righteous despite its violence, the force
he felt now was utterly foul, redolent of a spiritual corruption that had suppurated for ages.

And he had sensed it before, if only dimly; he was sure
of it. In the palanquin. Looking at the images of that twin-
tongued face.

But had they been mere images even then?

A titanic hissing came from the west, and bloody, hellish
light swept across the city, bathing the balcony. Zorachus and
his companions leaped to their feet. Asa clutched at Halfdan,
but he pushed her away and drew his sword, red light flashing
on the steel. Sharthas prayed. Zorachus stood tensely, silently,
arms at his sides.

A half-mile distant, a vast, leering, crimson-glowing face
hovered over Khymir; double-tongued, it was the face from
the palanquin.

"Mancdaman Zorachus!" the apparition thundered, form-
ing the syllables even though its tongues continued to loll and
crawl outside the mouth. What might have been a giant
woman and a lamia sheltered in the curl of the lower tongue.
"I am Morkûlg the Mask, herald and messenger of His
Anointed Steward Ghorchalanchor Kletus, High Priest of
Tchernobog and Lord of Khymir. You are challenged, as all
Kymir is witness, to meet His Anointed Servant, Kourgon
Zarathonzar, in a wizards' duel in Kralorg Square, tomorrow
at the fourth hour. And there will you surely die."

Morkûlg's leering eyes creased shut and his jaws began to
grind, fangs driving into the tongues; black blood spurted as
the tongues hitched gruesomely back into the mouth, and there
was a shriek as the points stabbed through the shapes that the
lower one held; then the tongues disappeared behind the
fangs. Chewing steadily, drooling dark streams, Morkûlg shot
backward through the night sky. In seconds he was nothing
more than a dwindling red star on the horizon, a point of light
that flared and vanished. But his words still echoed from the
mountainsides and over the rooftops, and as the reverberations
faded, an outcry of human voices rose from all parts of the
city.

"Sharthas," Zorachus said, "I want to talk to my council-
lors."

"Of course, my Lord," the steward replied in a trembling voice, withdrawing.

"Tell the guards we're not to be disturbed—unless there's a message from the Guild."

"Certainly," Sharthas called over his shoulder.

"Are you going to fight Zarathonzar?" Asa asked Zorachus once Sharthas had disappeared. "If they can control demons like that. . . ."

"It was only a phantasm," he replied. "More than an illusion, but not much more. I could conjure one as frightening if the need arose."

"But it looked so real. And I could *feel* it. . . ."

Zorachus nodded. "It was a real demon's image. And they gave us a taste of its presence to add to the horror. But it wasn't fully invoked. Don't worry. I needn't refuse the challenge."

"Maybe not the wizardly end of it," Halfdan said. "But there's sure to be some sort of treachery involved."

"I wouldn't be surprised, but I can't back down. Kletus wants me dead, or publicly cowed. Either way, he wins."

"Well," Halfdan said, "If you can beat Zarathonzar, the guards and I'll do our damnedest to protect you afterward. We'd have to leave enough men here to hold the palace, of course, but I'm sure we could get some more men from the Guild."

"Will you let me go with you?" Asa asked.

"To the *duel?*" Halfdan demanded.

"Yes."

"Out of the question."

"It'd be much too dangerous," Zorachus agreed. "However it goes, the square's likely to erupt into a riot. Halfdan and I might be killed."

"Then sharing your fate would be the only honorable thing," Asa said resolutely. "Halfdan's my husband, and you're my friend."

"You'd still be better off alive," Zorachus said.

"I'm coming with you," Asa insisted. "It's as simple as that."

"I'll lock you in your room," Halfdan snapped.

"You wouldn't dare!"

"Try me."

Asa folded her arms truculently on her chest. "All right

then. But I'll make your life hell if you *do* come back. And if you *don't,* I'll kill myself. So there's no point in not taking me."

"Would she kill herself, Halfdan?" Zorachus asked.

"She *can* be awfully contrary," Halfdan said.

"Hmm," Zorachus said. His first thought, pure philosopher's reflex, was that he should try to demonstrate the immorality of suicide to her. But she had the look of someone whose mind was set, and furthermore, he did not know how to begin arguing about that particular subject with a Kragehul barbarian. And even if he managed to talk her out of any thought of killing herself, there was always her other threat.

"Would she really make your life hell?" he asked Halfdan.

"As I said, she can be awfully. . ."

"Contrary," Asa broke in.

Halfdan shrugged and tried to look as if he had never opposed her accompanying them in the first place. "I'll let you come if Zorachus agrees."

Zorachus nodded his assent. "Well, she is *your* wife." He felt a twinge of jealousy; for an instant he doubted his wisdom in choosing celibacy. Could he have inspired such devotion in a woman?

Halfdan kissed Asa, gave her a hug that brought a gasp to her lips. "Yes, for good or ill, she's mine," he growled affectionately.

chapter

12

KRALORG SQUARE LAY east of Banipal Khezach. Once it had
been a kind of religious bazaar, where various cults had competed for worshippers but the cults had withered and their temples had fallen into scabrous disrepair. Defaced and weathered
idols stared down mournfully from facades covered with moss
and mold. What little traffic the square still saw was drawn by
the diseased whores who plied their trade in temple alleys and
alcoves.

But today "Dead God Place" (as the area was often jokingly called) was thronged; public wizards' duels were extravagant entertainments that came along once in a lifetime.
Spectators fought and elbowed each other for places. Some
were mounted on crates, wagons, or stools; others had slaves
to stand on, or had hired men for that purpose. Many people
had gone up onto the roofs or balconies of the temples. The
most reckless (or death-hungry) stood on the rim of the dueling circle, or even inside. Oddsmakers threaded their way
through the crowd, and pickpockets did splendid business.
Vendors hawked food and drink, as well as a drug that was
said to make violence more arousing to jaded onlookers.
Troops of beggars extorted charity from helpless victims.
Small groups of redclads were scattered throughout the crowd;
tall black hand standards stood, as if in benediction, over several of the units. A single, large contingent of Guild soldiers
waited on the western side of the square.

Zorachus and Zarathonzar arrived with their followers at
roughly the same time, shortly before the fourth hour. Eager
for the duel to begin, the crowd parted to let them pass—
though the priest and his men drew a storm of curses and
catcalls.

Stepping up to the edge of the dueling circle, Zorachus
scanned the enemy retinue. Zarathonzar was the only visible

priest. Apparently his colleagues thought it prudent to keep
out of the danger zone. He was well-protected nonetheless;
with him stood at least twenty Cohort Ravener swordsmen,
one a towering black—Thulusu.

A lock of damp hair fell before Zorachus's eyes, trailing
sweat across his forehead. He brushed it away cursing the
heat. His stomach was knotted with apprehension, not only for
himself, but Halfdan and Asa as well. He prayed for victory,
and for the priestly faction to forgo treachery; he implored
God not to let this square become the grave of his mission and
his friends.

The last few minutes passed sluggishly, but finally a sun-
dial on one of the temple facades indicated the fourth hour.

Zarathonzar swaggered into the dueling circle. The crowd
hushed.

"Mancdaman Zorachus!" he cried. "Come forth, dog!"

Zorachus turned and shook hands with Halfdan. "Good
luck," the Kragehul said and stepped back. Zorachus reached
for his ring pouch, but as he did so, Asa leaped up, hugged
him tightly, and kissed him on the cheek. His arms swept
round her, and for an aching moment he returned her embrace.
He had never held a woman before.

"Win, Zorachus," she begged. "Please win."

"Come forth, dog!" Zarathonzar shouted, the sound of his
voice incredibly hateful in Zorachus's ears. Stifling the anger
that spurted up in him, Zorachus let Asa go, smiling at her and
Halfdan. Then, still feeling the warmth of her lips on his
cheek, he turned and went out into the circle, veering off to
the side to reduce the chance of a stray bolt striking his followers.

Thirty feet from Zarathonzar he halted and unhurriedly entered a two-shielded Dragon Stance. Zarathonzar assumed
something like a Basilisk Stance, one shield up. The two
faced each other like iron statues, garments hanging motionless in the stagnant air.

Suddenly, Zorachus realized he had forgotten to put the
demon-rings on. He knew the oversight might prove fatal, but
he could not afford to take them from the pouch now. Blood
pounding in his throat, he squinted through the bright afternoon haze towards his foe. The wait went on fifteen, twenty
long seconds.

Zarathonzar's free hand whipped forward in a crimson

glare; a reddish spiral bolt, flinging off green sparks, struck Zorachus's shields in a dazzling blast, caromed skyward and dissipated. The impact jolted the Sharajnaghi, but not badly —it would have taken several such bolts to harm him even if his shields had been down.

Zarathonzar launched another and another, probing. Zorachus let his defenses look weaker than they were, and at the fourth impact, dropped his forward shield. Seeing that, Zarathonzar immediately discarded his protection, raising his hands for a swift double strike.

But as the priest's shield vanished, Zorachus launched a strike of his own—a staccato line of glittering blue crescents that hammered into Zarathonzar's stomach. The priest's robes exploded in black tatters and he hurtled back several feet. Yet, to Zorachus's amazement, he did not fall; indeed, Zarathonzar retained enough control to raise two shields. Half his muscular body laid bare, he drew himself erect, eyes burning.

Zorachus lashed out with cataract strikes. Zarathonzar withstood them with ease, watching his foe warily, obviously expecting another ruse.

Zorachus maintained his strikes for several more seconds, then shifted into a Binding Stance and shouted a summoning spell. He knew it would not work—he had not done enough forceletting.

Zarathonzar shifted stance too, began a counterspell. Zorachus had not expected him to have completed his forceletting so early in the duel, but it did not matter. Zorachus's feint had done its work.

Dropping his remaining shield, the Sharajnaghi launched two powerful greenish beams straight down into the ground. Bits of crushed cobblestones peppered his trouser legs as he shot into the air.

Too late, Zarathonzar grasped what was happening. Freeing one hand, he unleashed a savage, sun-bright bolt which passed between Zorachus's legs and slammed devastatingly into the crowd behind.

High above the smoking pavement, Zorachus thrust his arms up and sent two maximum crescent strikes over the top of Zarathonzar's remaining shield. Stunned, the priest catapulted backward to the cobbles, shield dissipated, hair burned down to the scalp, tattered robes blasted from his body. Thunderous cheers rose from the crowd.

Landing, Zorachus eyed Zarathonzar's prostrate form. He supposed he would have no more trouble with him—for the time being, at least.

If only I could finish him, Zorachus thought. *Put him out of the war once and for all*—

But that was out of the question. Sharajnaghim were forbidden to kill helpless enemies. He was disgusted with himself for having thought of it at all. And yet—Zarathonzar was a Priest of Tchernobog. A child murderer. A monstrously evil man. He deserved to die. They all deserved it. . . .

"Enough," Zorachus gritted, shaking his head. Turning, he headed back towards his retinue.

He had only gone a few paces when he heard the cheers give way to warnings; Halfdan and a dozen others were pointing to something behind him. He spun, hurling up both shields.

Incredibly, Zarathonzar was on his feet again, swaying as he entered a stance; two yard-long spears of furious energy, white and crackling, shot from his palms. Zorachus's shields held against them, but the bolts did not deflect or dissipate— hanging in midair, they grew sharper, brighter, thinner. Finally, no more bitter glaring threads, they pierced the shields. Zorachus had shifted an instant before and they missed his body, but one halted over his right arm, the other beneath it, pressing into his flesh, they expanded once more, somehow keeping their focus, tangible as oaken dowels. Before he could think of a counterspell, they lifted from the horizontal to vertical and his arm was savagely dislocated; flesh split wide and pain tore his mind in white-hot bursts. His shields deserted him and a long shriek came ripping from his throat. The adamantine spears tilted back and back. . . .

Then they were gone. Through agony-bleared eyes, he saw Zarathonzar teetering, pawing dizzily at his head. Zorachus's crescent strikes had taken their toll, the priest's astounding recovery notwithstanding.

Forcing his mind to function, Zorachus sized up his position. His right arm was useless for strikes, though he could still emanate a shield from the palm. Grabbing his dangling right hand, he tucked the fingers inside his belt, palm outwards. With a supreme effort he forced energy down through his shrieking tissues; a weak shield took shape.

Across from him, Zarathonzar managed to restore one of his shields, but it was no stronger than the Sharajnaghi's. Zor-

achus launched a yellow, left-hand strike, the most powerful at
his command, and Zarathonzar's buckler shattered. Zorachus
launched another, slamming the priest's chest. Zorathonzar's
skin purpled with a massive hemorrhage, yet even so his massive strength did not give out. However much his repelling
forces had been disrupted, his binding forces were another
matter. Clumsily, he assumed a one-handed binding stance,
and without even a spell ripped up the pavement before him,
forming a barrier of cobblestones.

Zorachus launched a bolt at the wall. It struck with a vicious crack and powdered stone spat from the cobbles. But the
barrier still stood and, even as the sound of impact echoed
from the surrounding temples, the wall rose and hurtled at
Zorachus with tremendous speed.

He blasted it again, widening the gouge he had made. Still
in one piece, the wall swept near.

He dodged. Momentum carried it outside the ring and into
the spectators. There was a sickening crunch and a chorus of
screams and shouts.

Zorachus hit Zarathonzar with two more bolts, stabbing
with cruel precision into the priest's hemorrhaged flesh. Zarathonzar went down on one knee—and was up again in an
instant.

Impossible, Zorachus thought, appalled by the priest's en-
durance. *How in God's name*. . . .

Cries from the crowd told him the wall was moving again;
he wheeled to see the careening mass almost upon him.
Dodging it, he remembered the rings and tugged at the pouch,
but found he could not undo it one-handed.

The wall started back at him, picking up speed. He
launched a bolt at it; it might as well have been aimed at the
sky. He opted for the first spell that leaped to mind muttering a
four-word formula, hoping he had exhausted enough of his
repelling energies, sensing he was just on the borderline. . . .

Most of the wall vanished. He had opened a dimensional
portal, a doorway to another plane, in its path. But a chunk
was sheared off and, trailing a streak of pulverized stone, it
kept coming, crashing into his feeble right-hand shield. Mere
stone would have penetrated; the shield was proof only against
magic. But magic held the chunk together and the missile
could not strike home. Even so, his stricken shoulder was
badly twisted by the impact and he rocked to the pavement,
screaming with pain, shield gone.

The wall fragment shot forward, halted over his face, then descended like the maul of an invisible giant. He rolled. Striking the pavement where his head had been a split instant before, it shattered.

He lifted himself on one elbow. Zarathonzar stood across from him, still in his binding stance, though barely upright. The gigantic bruise Zorachus had dealt him had darkened to black; his skin was pale white elsewhere. Zorachus guessed he was dying. But he also knew the priest might yet be able to drag him down.

The Sharajnaghi conjured another portal; it opened under Zarathonzar just as the priest bound one of the cobbles from the wall fragment and sent it glancing off Zorachus's chin. The Sharajnaghi was not badly hurt but his mind was jarred, his spell broken, and as Zarathonzar plunged into the portal it snapped shut about his waist, slicing him in half.

The priest looked downwards in agony and amazement, gesturing helplessly. Then his arms fell at his sides and his head sagged; chin on chest, he died, an upright nude torso resting forlornly on the pavement like a broken statue.

Zorachus got to his feet. His right hand slipped from his belt, and his dislocated arm hung limp at his side, sleeve soaked with blood. Warm, sticky moisture plastered his tunic to the side of his chest. He stared stupidly at the red drops falling from his right thumb.

It occurred to him that the crowd was strangely silent. Looking up, he noticed redclads spreading out from the eastern side of the dueling circle, forming a cordon two ranks deep before the crowd.

Turning, he stumbled toward his followers. Halfdan and several retainers rushed out from the shieldburg to join him.

"Where did all those redclads come from?" the Sharajnaghi asked as they hurried him away.

"They hid their numbers," Halfdan puffed. "Stayed in small groups till the duel began and everyone was distracted. Then they gathered around those standards."

They got Zorachus inside the shieldburg as the redclads closed in from the north and south. But the pincers halted before moving across the shieldburg's eastern flank; led by Thulusu, the men from Zarathonzar's retinue, much reinforced, were trotting over to fill the gap. When that was done, Zorachus's company would be completely surrounded; several

ranks of redclads had come up from the west, facing the
wedge-shaped enclave on two sides.

"Where are the Guild troops?" Zorachus asked Halfdan,
wincing at a throb from his shoulder.

The Kragehul pointed. Many of the soldiers were still
mounted on the wagons and stools they had climbed upon to
watch the duel. "The bastards haven't stirred an inch," Halfdan growled. "Maybe they were bought. And maybe they're
just cowards." He looked at the bloodstain slowly blackening
Zorachus's's grey tunic. "Will you be able to help us? We'll
need some magic to get us out of this. . . ."

"I don't know," Zorachus replied.

"Well, then, get into the middle of the wedge."

Zorachus complied weakly, supported by Asa.

Halfdan looked round at the retainers. Many of those
nearby had already turned anxiously towards him, faces grav-
en with fear. They knew what the redclads were capable of.

So did he. But he roared a laugh.

"All right then," he cried. "Since our friends in the main
body don't want to join us, we should go join them! Keep
your shields up! Hold your formation! Let's go!"

The wedge pushed against the redclads; the redclads gave
way, the crowd behind making room, shouting for them to let
Zorachus pass. A few rocks bounced off crimson scale-mail.

The wedge pressed on. It began to look as if the redclads
might let them through.

Then Thulusu's voice boomed out and the redclad ranks
stiffened, their huge, two-handed swords flashing free; Zorachus's men drew their brands in reply.

Halfdan returned to the eastern side of the wedge. Thulusu's men had filled the gap left by the shieldburg's brief
advance.

"What's the meaning of this?" Halfdan cried, taking a
place in the line and brandishing his sword at Thulusu. "Lord
Mancdaman defeated Zorathonzar in fair combat!"

"Indeed," Thulusu replied. "And it's only fitting that he
should receive my Lord Kletus's congratulations—face to
face. My men'll gladly serve as an honor guard."

"And what if he won't come?" Halfdan demanded.

Thulusu grinned down at him, teeth gleaming white. "Then
you'll all die," he said with high good humor.

Halfdan squinted at him for a few moments and then said

over his shoulder: "What do you think, Lord Mancdaman?"

It was some time before Zorachus answered. "I'm afraid I don't care a fig about Lord Kletus's congratulations," he called in a loud but trembling voice.

Halfdan turned back to Thulusu. "You heard him," he said apologetically, and with blinding speed slashed at the giant black's face.

Jumping backward, Thulusu barely saved himself; even so, the bridge of his nose was shorn through.

"Kill them!" he cried to his men. As they closed on all sides, blades crashing against the retainers' bucklers, he charged at Halfdan, roaring, hewing. The top of Halfdan's shield was reduced to splinters in seconds; the Kragehul had not managed to launch a single stroke when the buckler's grip was smashed from his hand. With a powerful descending sweep, Thulusu battered the Kragehul's sword down, and a second blow ripped Halfdan's byrny, slicing his gambeson, just missing his flesh.

Clapping both hands to his hilt, Halfdan tried to go on the offensive, but his first two strokes were effortlessly parried, and then Thulusu's steel came whistling repayment. Halfdan ducked; the blade caught the top of his helmet and shaved it away. The helm was strapped on tightly, and he felt as if his head had been batted clean off his shoulders; as things popped in his neck, cursing, grimacing, he saw Thulusu raising his sword for the final blow, and struck upwards as the sword descended. There was a spatter of red as his edge sheared off Thulusu's right hand at the wrist. Thulusu howled, his stump geysering blood as he retreated. Halfdan laughed fiercely.

But the redclads gave him no respite; one bounded to take Thulusu's place, striking furiously. Halfdan deflected the first stroke, leaped over the next, and hacked into the man's chest. So much blood boiled forth that Halfdan thought for a moment the red scale-mail was melting; but the man barely flinched, and bashed a great dent in Halfdan's helm, tearing the scalp beneath. Blood streaming down his brow, dripping past one eye, Halfdan grunted and lunged, driving his sword deep through the hole in the redclad's armor. The man shrieked and hurled himself back off the point, falling in a heap.

All at once Halfdan realized there were redclads on either side of him; the front line of the wedge had been broken. He slipped back through the second shieldwall, panting.

A dead retainer fell beside him. Halfdan took the shield from the corpse's arm and leaped back into the fight. He wounded two redclads and killed another, but the retainers flanking him were hewn down and he had to retreat once more.

The wedge shrank steadily. The terrible Cohort Ravener swords rose and fell, hammering, rending; the air was filled with the boom and crunch of them pounding the buckler-walls, and bits of rim and wood flew from the battered shields. If the redclads had not been too eager, hampering themselves with their own numbers, the fight would have ended quickly.

Even so, it promised to end soon enough. The retainers were no match for such foes, and the Guild troops showed no sign of coming to their aid. The other spectators hurled more and more stones at the redclads—but kept their distance.

Sick and weary, Zorachus leaned on Asa's shoulder, watching the carnage close in. Near them a redclad broke into the shieldburg, sword wheeling. Two retainers set on him, but he killed them both with a single stroke, then rushed at Zorachus and Asa.

Asa hurled a dagger. It struck his left eye pommel-first, and he yowled and dropped his sword. Leaving Zorachus tottering, Asa stooped, snatched up her weapon, and jabbed it hilt-deep in the redclad's throat. Mouth working soundlessly, he grabbed her wrist with both hands. She punched his injured eye with her free fist, and he let go and stumbled off, the knife still in his neck. Three retainers struck him down in a flurry of steel.

Asa gave a ringing yell, arms raised in triumph, red-gold mane streaming . . . then rushed back to Zorachus, lending him her shoulder once more.

"Showed the bastard, didn't I, Zorachus?" she cried. "Did you see?" Laughing, she called to Halfdan in the Kragehul tongue. He was close by, but if he heard he gave no sign as he hacked ferociously at the redclads hemming him, felling one after another, a tower of strength in a crumbling fortress.

Zorachus was seized by admiration for him and Asa. They were barbaric and bloodthirsty, but greathearted, unafraid, even joyous in the face of certain death; simply knowing that such souls existed sent a wave of sheer exhilaration coursing through him, driving back the weakness in his veins. His mind freed itself from pain and dizziness. Was there any way he could save them?

The rings.

He could wield one, for a while at least. He told Asa to open the pouch and took one out, sliding it up his finger with his teeth.

A retainer's severed hand bumped against his foot. Two redclads bounded in over the decapitated body, one after another.

Zorachus discharged the ring into the first. The bolt went clear through him, ripping into the man behind—they catapulted backward out of the wedge.

Zorachus raised his good hand, fist clenched, and sent four bolts crackling over his retainers' heads into the surrounding enemy. Horn-helmed heads and armored chests shattered. Melted byrny scales streaked like meteors. Pink steam billowed.

The redclads faltered in their attack, pulled back from the wedge. The retainers laughed and jeered at them, waving their notched swords and blade-chewed shields.

But it was not over yet. The redclad commanders rallied their men and again the long curving brands thundered into the battered shieldwall.

Zorachus answered with a fresh series of blasts. Scale-mailed bodies spun and crumpled. Mouths belched smoke and blood. Once more, the redclads retreated.

At that, the Guild captain finally ordered his men into the fight; ripping their swords free, they leaped down from their stools and wagons and shouldered a way through the spectators who stood in their path, joining furious battle with the redclads, felling many. And for a few moments they kept the advantage; Zorachus's magic had dismayed the redclads and their numbers were depleted, not only by the fighting, but also because many had gone with maimed Thulusu, bearing him through the crowd on the other side of the dueling circle, guarding him with a fence of steel.

Yet soon the redclads began to take a deadly toll, and the sound of their swords was like the chopping of cleavers in a butcher shop; the Guild troops wavered, their losses frightful, mounting almost every time a redclad's brand fell.

But Zorachus came to their aid, with Asa's help, he transferred the demon-ring to an unscorched finger and dealt out more firebolts, trying to avoid his allies, killing six redclads outright, blowing arms or legs off five more.

That was too much for the rest. They were brave men facing steel, but this fire magic was another matter; Still keeping their order, giving Zorachus's men a wide berth, they withdrew towards the dueling circle, which was still cordoned off by their comrades.

The Guild troops made no attempt to follow—though they killed the redclad wounded with relish.

The redclads pushed out across the circle. When they reached the far side, one of their officers sounded a horn blast and the cordon-troops backed towards their comrades.

Rumbling and jeering, the mob followed cautiously, hurling cobbles. As the last cordon-troops rejoined their fellows, the redclads were severely pelted and soon engulfed by the crowd. Closing ranks, they continued eastward from the square, hacking apart any who stayed in their path.

The Guild troops meanwhile had joined Zorachus's retainers, carrying loot stripped from friend and foe alike. The retainers grumbled, cursing them for not coming sooner into the fight, and another battle nearly broke out then and there; but the Guild captain and Halfdan prevented it. Smiling broadly, the captain came forward to meet Zorachus.

"Glad to see you're alive, Lord Mancdaman," he said.

"If he is, it's no thanks to you," Asa snapped, shifting under Zorachus's shoulder, grunting.

"Shh," Zorachus said, "After all, he did order his men in—eventually. I'm wondering, though, what his masters'll say when they learn what happened."

"I waited till I saw a *real* opening," the captain explained. He leaned close to Zorachus, and in a low voice said: "Those fools of mine would've *all* been slaughtered if you hadn't panicked the redclads. A crowd of bumbling cowards, that's all I've got to work with. Maranchthus is too much of a miser to hire *real* swordsmen, and. . . ."

"So you think your men are a bunch of bumblers and cowards?" Asa demanded, shouting with all the lungpower at her disposal, which was considerable. The captain's jaw sagged. Curses went up from his troops.

"Cowards?" cried one brown-mailed soldier, clutching a bleeding arm. *"We're* cowards? Who was it that told us to hold back?"

"Asa, not another word," Zorachus said. In spite of everything, he did not want to see the captain murdered on the spot. But his weakness had returned, and he delivered the command with little authority.

"He said Maranchthus won't spend enough money to hire decent troops," Asa crowed.

"Bitch," the captain snarled, and wheeled to face his men, minded to make some denial. The sight of their faces shattered that hope, he darted off to the side. A half-dozen soldiers rushed after him, swearing. More joined the chase.

"Was that necessary?" Zorachus asked Asa numbly.

A shriek erupted in the near distance, then was brutally cut off.

"I couldn't let him get away with it," she replied, wincing as more and more of Zorachus's weight fell on her.

"I'm sure the Guildsmen would've punished. . . ." His voice trailed off. Somehow, he could not bring himself to feel any pity for the man. He was too exhausted.

"Think you can make it back to the palace?" Halfdan asked. "You've lost a lot of blood."

Before Zorachus could answer, a wave of dizziness swept him. His legs seemed to go boneless and, in spite of Asa's support, he fell on his hands and knees. "Healing spell. . . ." he mumbled, and collapsed. The world upended in oblivion.

Wounds bandaged, Thulusu lay on a cot in his austere quarters brooding, waiting for Kletus. Finally, the High Priest arrived, with Lysthragon and Sathaswenthar. Thulusu started to sit up, but Kletus waved him back down.

"I grieve to have failed you, my Lord," the black said. The words were heartfelt; he was capable of deep devotion to a man he freely chose to acknowledge as his master, and Kletus was that man, embodying the only human qualities Thulusu valued—strength, ruthlessness, and will—to an almost superhuman degree. Thulusu had been shamed in the service of his iron-hard ideal, and though his voice was calm and his face impassive, his anguish was intense.

"Don't fret over it," Kletus answered, very businesslike. He had had full reports of the events in Kralorg Square from several sources. "The fault was mine. I didn't think Zorachus would still be able to cause much trouble after a bout with Zarathonzar."

"If I'd been there, I would've kept up the attack," Thulusu

said. "My troops would've obeyed me, but I let that bastard take my hand off. . . ."

Kletus smiled soothingly. "You're not made of steel. A fighter can't always be in top form."

"I lost control. I let him enrage me."

Kletus lifted his hands. "That's all in the past. You're one of my best servants and we'll have you back in action soon enough. I know of a demon who can forge you a hand that will be just as good as the old one."

"How do you feel?" Sathaswenthar asked Thulusu.

The black raised his bandaged stump. "Like gutting the man who did this to me."

"That's better," Kletus said. "Rage against him, not yourself. The self is sacred. I've willed it so." He paused. "However, the man you want—Zorachus's bodyguard, correct?—will probably be dead before you get a chance at him. We'll be avenging Zarathonzar and your great black paw very soon."

"What happened to Zarathonzar's corpse?" Thulusu asked. "It was still sitting in the square when I was borne off."

"The main force didn't have time for it," Kletus said ruefully. "Pity. The crowd tore it apart. The available half, that is. Carried his head about on a pole."

"He deserved better," Thulusu said. "He fought well."

"He fought at well as he could. But he was far overmatched."

"It seemed an even enough contest to me. I know Zorachus felled him quickly, but he came back. . . ."

"Yes, he came back," Kletus admitted. "But only because Zorachus spared him."

"*Spared* him?" Thulusu asked, puzzled.

"Why, I don't know."

"Maybe he thought Zarathonzar was already dead."

Kletus shook his head. "A wizard of Zorachus's caliber knows the difference between lethal and non-lethal strikes. He used stun-bolts. They're very powerful and produce some spectacular side effects. But they simply don't kill."

"But what makes you think he's such a powerful wizard? He could hardly stand when the duel was over. Zarathonzar almost had him."

"Because Zarathonzar took him by surprise. Zorachus thought he was out cold—and with very good reason. Yet even with the advantage of surprise, Zarathonzar still lost."

"But. . . ."

A twinge of impatience entered Kletus's expression. "You simply don't realize how difficult are the spells Zorachus used," he broke in. "According to my observers, he opened two dimensional portals all by himself—*two* in less than a minute. Quite a trick—especially when you consider that Zarathonzar had already torn one of his arms half off. I'm afraid we mustn't underestimate him. If the reports are correct, and I have no reason to think they're not, Zarathonzar fought the most powerful mage who's ever lived."

Thulusu was silent for a few moments, digesting this. "Then why didn't Zorachus kill him right off?"

"I don't know," Kletus answered, but the look in his eyes plainly showed that he had already given the matter some hard thought.

"It's almost as if. . . ." Lysthragon ended in a senile titter.

"As if what?" Kletus asked.

Lysthragon grinned his mindless monkey's grin. "As if he took all that Sharajnaghi nonsense seriously."

Kletus snorted at the very idea, knowing Lysthragon was simply indulging his taste for absurdity. But Thulusu asked:

"What nonsense is that?"

"Zorachus was once a Sharajnaghi," Sathaswenthar explained, "a member of a wizard's order called the *Comahi Irakhoum*. Publicly, Sharajnaghim always maintain that killing should be avoided unless it's absolutely necessary—that helpless foes should be spared, for example."

"But what could be more necessary than killing one's enemies? What difference does it make if they're helpless?"

"None, of course," Kletus replied. "As I'm sure Zorachus himself realizes. I can't imagine him, or anyone, sparing a foe because of the Sharajnaghi Code."

"Then why did he do it?" Thulusu pressed.

"Who can say? Perhaps he doesn't *like* killing, or thinks he doesn't. There are people who seem to be repulsed by the very idea."

"He certainly wasn't very enthused over the entertainment at the banquet," Sathaswenthar put in.

"Still," Kletus continued, "he can't be too squeamish. He wouldn't have chosen to set himself against us."

A slight smile touched Sathaswenthar's lips. "True enough."

"He's badly wounded," Kletus said. "If we conjure a sending, we might finish him tonight."

"What about the Guildsmen?"

"We'll deal with them soon enough. But Zorachus must be eliminated first. They're spiders. He's a serpent."

"You're frightened of him," Thulusu said, disturbed to detect apprehension in his idol.

Kletus nodded. "He's thirty-three years old and already wields a power greater than mine," he said with disarming candor. "In a very real sense, he's one of my nightmares come true. Why shouldn't I fear him?"

Thulusu pondered the High Priest's reply. It occurred to him that the man Kletus feared might be a more worthy master; but then he thought about Zorachus sparing Zarathonzar, and his lack of enthusiasm at the banquet. It *was* possible that Zorachus had no taste for blood, that he was a weakling at heart despite his prowess. . . .

Thulusu decided to put the matter aside for further consideration. In the meantime, Kletus was still the closest thing to perfection that he had certain knowledge of, and he watched with admiration as his lord brought out one of his meat wallets and took a huge mouthful of human flesh.

chapter
13

ZORACHUS WOKE. DULL pain gnawed deep in his shoulder and his burned fingers ached but it seemed to him that some measure of his strength had returned.

He heard a gentle whirring noise beside him. Asa was sitting next to the bed, playing raptly with a lever-operated wheel-toy, face lit with a childlike half-smile.

His eyes searched the room. It was not his chamber—this one was much bigger, almost cavernous, and there were no windows. The ceiling writhed with swirling ornaments, and the walls were knobbed and irregular. Larger-than-life statues of copulating bodies thrust up from the floor, obscene marble lumps, bright blood-red, as was almost everything else in the room. The chamber looked like the inside of a candlelit internal organ. The only details breaking the effect, even slightly, were several silver candlesticks on a grotesquely carved cabinet.

He looked back at Asa. She was still playing with the toy but noticed presently that he was awake.

"He's come round," she called to Halfdan, who stood outside talking with two guards. He came in, silver medallion gleaming on his chest.

"Why did you put me in this room?" Zorachus asked as he sat up. "It may be the ugliest place I've ever seen."

Before Halfdan could reply, Asa cut in: "We wanted to surprise you."

"Thanks," Zorachus said.

"We thought it safer than yours," Halfdan said. "No balconies or windows."

Zorachus nodded. His left hand, fingers swathed in linen strips, wandered over to his wounded shoulder. "Who tended me?"

"Porchos sent a surgeon," Asa said. "The best in Khymir,

from what I gathered. Kadjafi named Aliphar. He did the strangest things to you."

"Such as?"

"Well, to start with, he took a bit of your blood and made passes over it. Then he picked one of the slaves he'd brought with him, stuck a little tube into his arm, and ran the other end of it into yours. The slave made fists and his blood started pumping into your veins. Dr. Aliphar stitched you up, and before he finished, switched slaves, since the first one was looking a bit pale. Finally, he decided you'd had enough. That little bandage on your arm is where he pulled the tube out."

"It was incredible," Halfdan said.

"That's putting it mildly, from the sound of it," Zorachus said.

"He said he came up with the idea all by himself," Halfdan went on. "Asa and I were pretty leery about letting him use it on you, but decided to let him go ahead. Seems it worked. I wouldn't have expected you to wake for another couple of days—if at all. Your shoulder clotted up before we got half-way to the palace, but your clothes were already sodden."

"Did Aliphar sew you up too?" Zorachus asked, eyeing a shaved and threaded strip on Halfdan's scalp.

The Kragehul shook his head. "Shartas did the honors. He's no mean hand with a needle himself."

Zorachus was silent a few moments. "Did Porchos send any messages?"

"His congratulations, and a suggestion that we should stay quietly here. He also gave us reinforcements—a hundred and fifty troops, and several of his household wizards."

"Wizards," Zorachus said, almost to himself, pleasantly surprised. When he had asked the Guildsmen for a new household, they had turned down his request for mages, saying they feared to weaken their own defenses, but he had guessed they did not trust him enough to lend him such help.

"They'll stay until you've recovered," Halfdan said. "They're downstairs. Do you want to talk to them?"

Zorachus shook his head. "How's Sharthas managing? He must have his hands full with all those new troops."

"Yes, but he seems to thrive on it."

"What's been happening in the city?"

"Riots, full-scale battles," Halfdan answered joyfully. "All hell's broken loose."

Zorachus sighed heavily. "How's the Guild been faring?"

"Well in the south, badly in the north. Pretty much as you'd expect."

"There was a wizard's battle a half a mile from here," Asa said excitedly. "Some priests were trying to get back to the tower and Guild magicians attacked them. When it was over, a whole palace was lying in ruins and both groups had killed each other to a man."

"You've touched off a real blaze, Zorachus," Halfdan said. "Fate's working mightily through you."

"Let's just hope fate doesn't make him undo himself," Asa added. "Or us."

Zorachus laughed. "If I'm undone, it'll be because my own actions undid me. *I* chose to put myself into this situation."

"But fate makes your choices," Asa countered. "You act as you're destined to act."

"I don't think so," Zorachus answered. "I think human beings have something called free will."

"And what's that?" Halfdan asked.

"The power to make our own choices, decide our own destinies—at least partially."

"That's foolish," Halfdan answered. "Decide our own destinies? No man lives till nightfall whom fate dooms at dawning."

"Perhaps not. And if fate's preparing to drop a rock on my head, I'm in deep trouble, certainly. But the mere fact that fate's planning such a thing doesn't cause me to walk underneath. The choice isn't thrust on me from outside."

"Why would you think something like that?" Asa asked. Plainly the idea of such freedom was quite foreign to her.

"Because that's my experience."

"When you walk under falling rocks?" Halfdan asked, in all seriousness.

"No, when I make choices. As far as I can tell, I make them freely. But I also believe in free will because of problems that arise if you say people don't have it. Consider evil people, for example. If you say an evildoer's driven by fate to commit his crimes, then you're also saying he's no worse than a good man."

"Why is that?" Asa asked.

"Because a *good* man's also driven by fate to do *good* deeds. Neither man's responsible for his actions."

"That's true, but . . ." Asa's voice trailed off.

"If fate controls everything," Zorachus went on, "then you and Halfdan are no better than Khymirians. It's as simple as that."

"Simple as what?" Halfdan broke in. "How can you say we're as bad as they are?"

"Oh, I don't think you are," Zorachus replied.

"But if we say there's no free will," Asa said slowly, thinking it through, "then we have to admit we are, right?"

"Right. And if you insist on saying you're better than they are. . . ."

"Then we have to say that there's free will."

Zorachus nodded. "Pretty good, eh?"

Asa smiled briefly; she had never encountered philosophical argument before, even of such a rudimentary sort. But then she looked very stern and jabbed a forefinger at him. "Mind you, I'm not convinced, I'll have to think about this."

"By all means."

"No better than Khymirians, the very idea," Halfdan muttered. "And as for that business about fate and the rock, if fate knows exactly when to drop it, how can you say she didn't destine you to be under it? After all, She's fate. That's the kind of thing she does."

"Suppose I drop a rock on you," Zorachus answered. "Simply because I know when you'll be under it, does that mean I put you there?"

"No."

"Well, maybe fate just watches. And drops the rocks at the right time. The same way I would."

"But why would you want to drop a rock on me anyway?"

"Same reason as fate."

"Oh."

"You know," Zorachus said, "I'm awfully hungry. Would one of you go collar a servant, and—"

A shout from outside cut him short. A guard rushed in, sword drawn.

"We saw a face!" he cried, speeding towards the bed.

"What kind of face?" Halfdan demanded.

"Like the one in the sky last night, only small," the doorward said. "Two tongues."

Zorachus's stomach tightened; sure enough, he began to feel Morkûlg's presence. He grabbed for his ring-sack—only to find it was not around his neck.

"Where's the pouch?" he cried, swinging his legs over the side of the bed.

"We didn't take it off," Halfdan answered, unsheathing his blade.

"The last time I saw it," Asa said, "I was putting your ring back after the fighting stopped."

"You had it when we brought you here," Halfdan assured the Sharajnaghi. He bit his lip. "Wait a second . . . Aliphar's slaves were all over you for a second there."

"Thieving bastards," Asa spat.

The guard, meanwhile, was shifting his sword uneasily from hand to hand.

"Do you have any orders, Lord Mancdaman?" he asked.

Zorachus barely heard the question, he had been trying to estimate his power without the rings.

"What?" he asked.

"Do you have any orders, my Lord?"

The Sharajnaghi remembered that Porchos's mages were downstairs. "Fetch the Guild wizards. Hurry!"

The man turned and sprinted for the door. Zorachus watched him for a moment, looked away—and swept his eyes back, shouting with terror and surprise. On the man's surcoat, like a wide reddish stain, leered Morkûlg the Mask.

Hearing Zorachus, the soldier stopped and spun, trembling. "What's wrong?" he screamed.

"The face," Zorachus answered, rising. "It's on your back!"

The doorward turned round and round, looking over his shoulder, trying frantically, impossibly to see it. Each time he revolved, the apparition grew fainter.

"It's gone!" Zorachus called at last. But the words left his mouth in a white plume; all at once the room had gone arctic, marrow-biting. He could no longer feel any trace of Morkûlg's presence, but what other threat did the cold portend?

Hearing the cries, the second guard had entered and stood not far from the threshold. Without warning, the door slammed thunderously shut behind him. Whirling, he tried to open it.

"It's jammed!" he shrieked over his shoulder. "We're trapped in here! Help me!"

Halfdan and the first guard bolted over. They pushed and struggled, but the barrier did not yield.

"Don't waste your strength!" Zorachus shouted. "Get out of the way! Maybe I can blast it down!"

They moved aside. He entered a stance and loosed a fusillade of strikes. The door held.

"Come back over—" Before the Sharajnaghi could finish, the candles faltered and winked out. The room went totally black.

"Stay where you are!" he cried. "I'll conjure a demon to smash a way out!"

He uttered a spell but felt no power loss; something was interfering. He tried another spell. Still nothing.

"The magic's not working!" he shouted.

"Is there anything you can do?" Asa asked frantically, invisible in the darkness at his side.

"I don't know. . . ." He stopped, hearing a soft slithering in front of him.

"What's that?" Asa wailed.

"Maybe nothing at all," he answered. "Only a trick to frighten us."

"Can't you conjure a light?"

"Not in *this* darkness."

The slithering grew louder, and there was a series of short, venomous hisses, like serpentine laughter. Then came abrupt, utter silence.

"Zorachus!" Halfdan bellowed. "Should we come across now?"

"No!"

"*No!*" echoed a fleshless voice. "Don't try it yet!" Wild booming laughter filled the room, followed by sounds like a gigantic axe thumping into flesh.

"Halfdan!" Asa screamed. Zorachus heard her start forward. He reached about blindly, snagged her dress and yanked her back.

"I'm all right!" came Halfdan's voice. The laughter and the chopping sounds were already fading. Silence fell once more —only to be broken by one last horrific thud, directly in front of Zorachus and Asa. Warm thick fluid splashed over them.

"Blood!" Asa cried, flailing about. Zorachus's hand met hers and clasped it.

"Ignore it," he told her, certain now that the real threat had not yet appeared. "You faced the redclads. You can control your fear now."

"This is different. I can't *see*—"

"There's nothing out there. We're just being toyed with, mocked—for the time being." His voice rose to a roar. "Half-dan! Try it now!"

Footsteps clattered through the darkness.

"We're over here!" the Sharajnaghi called. "Follow the sound of my voice!"

That proved unnecessary. Light was provided—of a sort.

It spread from one corner of the room, a disastrous grey glow that leeched flesh as colorless as ash and blackened red marble, making the chamber seem one huge cavern of rotting tissue; dead and frigid, it was the only kind of light that could have appeared in that darkness, no threat to the nothingness of shadow, light that might have been kindled in the lowest circle of hell.

Its source was an oval sac seven feet long. Inside, a huddled figure, indistinct through the translucent membrane, immerged in some kind of fluid. The sac rocked gently back and forth, quivering.

"The toying's over," Zorachus told Asa.

The guards reached the bed, Halfdan some distance behind them; he had stopped the instant the glow appeared, staring at the sac.

"Halfdan, get over here!" Zorachus yelled.

"Whatever that thing inside is," Halfdan growled. "I'll stab it before it crawls out!"

"No!" Zorachus commanded.

But the Kragehul ran heedlessly over to the sac and thrust at it several times. The membrane would not give.

"Get away from it!" Zorachus roared.

Halfdan kept stabbing.

There came a low bubbling cry from inside the sac and the shape within moved; membrane bulged and ripped, and waxen embryonic fingers, armed with curving talons, thrust through, stinking amniotic fluid gushing about them, lit by their effulgence. The hand retreated for a moment, then tore the sac wide open. Colder than ice, a noisome wave drove Halfdan back.

The sending struggled and kicked in the swiftly draining sac, batting about savagely with its taloned hands, pantherish snarls erupting from its throat. The membrane was already partially shredded when Halfdan rose and splashed forward, hacking at a clawed foot. The blade sprang back notched, and the foot lashed out, dealing him a glancing blow that sent him somersaulting fifteen feet backwards.

The thing sat up, the sac slipping down over its shoulders. The glowing body rose dripping; nine feet tall, shaped like a sexless human fetus, the great discs of its eyes, still partially sheathed in their translucent lids, were a delicate, robin's egg blue.

Slowly it stepped out of the sac and made for Halfdan. The Kragehul got to his feet and half-staggered, half-ran to the bed.

"Remind me to do everything you tell me from now on," he told Zorachus.

"Everyone, listen!" Zorachus cried. "I might be able to open a portal. When I give the word, follow me!" He ran swiftly through the spell as the fetus approached—and once again felt no power loss. He guessed the demon's presence had been interfering with his binding magic from the first, even before the glowing horror had materialized.

"Scatter!" he cried.

They split up, the fetus reaching the bed moments later. Ripping off the massive headboard, it hefted it thoughtfully, then hurled it at Halfdan and Asa.

They dodged. The headboard struck a wall and shattered in a burst of splinters.

The Kragehul ran past the first guard, and for some reason the fetus turned its attention to him; dragging the mangled bed, rubbing an eye sleepily with its free hand, it wandered in his direction. He tried to dash away; it hurled the bed. Trailing a long whirl of silken sheets, the great mass whooshed through the air. A jagged spar caught the guard's leg, snapping bone. He flopped down screeching.

The demon thudded forward and flipped the bed aside. Across the room, Zorachus tried to distract it with bolts, but it seemed not to feel them. It snatched up the guard by the heel, spun him twice around its head, and smashed his skull against the ceiling. Then, dragging the corpse, it shambled off toward other prey—Halfdan and Asa again.

They were raising a din by the door, knocking and shouting, answering thumps and muffled cries from the hallway. "Get a battering ram!" they yelled, breath smoking in the cold.

As the fetus drew near, Halfdan heard it and looked back

just in time to see it lash out with the dead guard. He ducked, yanking Asa down with him; colliding ferociously with the door's reinforced oak, the body burst inside its mail, its whole surcoat going instantly black with blood, steam gusting from the cloth as hot gore met frigid air. Halfdan and Asa darted to the side.

The demon cast the corpse down, then scrutinized the door for a few seconds, as if wondering at the sounds coming from the other side. Then it turned.

Suddenly, a long, leathery whip wrapped around its neck, jerking it forward on its hands and knees. Zorachus had found a spell that worked; draining his half-restored strength to the dregs, he had summoned a knobbed monstrosity that looked like a sea anemone with legs. Standing back from the demon fetus, thin tentacles switching viciously through the air, it landed strokes that would have shredded steel, even as it tightened its grip on its opponent's neck.

Never flinching, the fetus rose effortlessly under the rain of lash blows; growling, it tore through the whip that bound it as if it had been a piece of grass, seized two more of the flailing appendages and yanked them from their sockets. Zorachus's demon fell back with a ululating cry.

Snatching up a sculpture, the fetus stamped forward and smashed it down on its foe. The whip demon crumpled and vanished. The sculpture hung in midair for a moment, then struck the floor and split in two.

The fetus looked about, spied the second guard cowering in a corner. Grabbing another sculpture, it rolled it over the floor at him. The guard started from the corner, then retreated before the rumbling marble juggernaut. With a mighty impact, the statue wedged itself between the corner walls, hemming him in. He tried to scramble over it; the demon closed in and plucked him out. Holding him suspended, oblivious to his curses and the jabs of his dagger, it yanked the sculpture free, lifted one end, shoved his head and shoulders under—and dropped three tons of marble on him. There was a loud crunch; the guard's heels drummed the floor and went still.

The fetus turned. Dazed by his sorcerous exertions, Zorachus was an easy target on his knees by the ruined bed. The demon thudded over to him and its huge glowing hands reached out.

"God, God. . . ." The Sharajnaghi mumbled, watching numbly as the taloned fingers opened to seize and mangle—

Then jerked back. The monster straightened, a titanic gasp blasting spittle from its mouth.

The Kragehul had fallen on it from behind, Halfdan with his sword, Asa with dagger and silver candlestick. Neither blade had any effect, but the candlestick burned and tore; Asa dealt two horrendous lacerations before realizing it.

"Silver!" she cried. "Silver wounds it!"

The demon pivoted bellowing and they fell back. Halfdan sheathed his sword, grabbed two candlesticks off a cabinet, and slung the silver medallion from around his neck.

Swaying, the demon remained where it was, as it reached to feel the gashes smoking on its back and thigh. It loosed roar after roar, but made no attempt to follow the Kragehul.

They watched it for a few moments, panting, lungs smarting with the cold.

"Come on!" Halfdan shouted at last, and they rushed forward. He flung a candlestick as he charged; the missile struck the demon's brow in a spatter of vapor, and the fetus reeled and clapped a hand to the wound.

"Want some more?" Halfdan cried. Swinging his medallion at the end of its heavy chain, he bashed one of its knees. The monster tried to grab him, but Asa's candlestick came down with a crack across the clutching hand. The demon howled piteously. Halfdan's medallion took a chunk from its flank; the demon staggered sideways.

Retrieving the candlestick he had thrown, Halfdan hurled it again. The fetus's left knee cracked and the demon toppled. Floundering desperately, it tried to rise, knocking a statue over in the process.

Halfdan and Asa swept in to right and left. The chamber echoed with the thump of their weapons bludgeoning home. Silver gleamed as it rose and fell.

After breaking the demon's arms, the Kragehul moved in at its head. Wide blue eyes rolling in their sockets, lids twitching open and shut, the demon twisted and shuddered as its skull was battered in.

Finally, with a long hiss, it went still. Its glow blinked out. The room filled with darkness once more.

But the gloom was short-lived; candlelight flared anew and warmth banished cold. Halfdan and Asa stared down at the spot where the sending had sprawled. No trace of it remained.

The crash of a battering ram started up behind the door. The heavy panels quivered with each stroke.

Ignoring the sounds, the Kragehul went to Zorachus. Lying on his back he smiled up at them, face pale.

"The demon's dead, I take it," he said. "Something about silver?"

"Candlesticks," Asa answered.

"And my medallion," Halfdan added smugly. "Came in handy after all. How do you feel?"

"Exhausted," Zorachus said.

At that moment, the door burst off its hinges in a shower of shattered jamb, and several green-robed men dashed in and assumed sorcerous stances, looking very fierce and stern.

"Porchos's wizards," Halfdan informed Zorachus.

"Awe-inspiring," the Sharajnaghi said.

Seeing the danger was over, the wizards dropped stance. Guards poured in. Sharthas pushed his way to the front of the brown-mailed throng.

"What happened, My Lord?" he demanded as he came up.

"We were playing midwife," Zorachus said.

chapter

14

THE SHARAJNAGHI ASKED to be taken to his own room, having decided it was safe as any other. On the way, he told Sharthas about the theft of the rings; the steward hurried off to dispatch a messenger to Porchos.

As the group entered the chamber, Zorachus saw the sullen redness of the sky outside. *The whole Western Quarter must be burning,* he thought. Anxiety filled him. It was imperative to get back in fighting kemper.

He had some food brought and it refreshed him somewhat, though he was still deathly tired. For several hours he kept himself awake by sheer force of will, long enough for a fraction of his power to return, enough for a healing spell. Then he made everyone leave except Halfdan and Asa, who promised to keep very quiet. Tightening his concentration, he lowered himself into a trance. Luckily it did not need to last very long; his wounds had been well tended, and there was no trace of infection.

Midway through the following morning he reassumed consciousness. He had Porchos's wizards dismissed and sent them off with the news that he had recovered; he also ordered more food. The Kragehul ate with him, but afterwards he sent them out and changed.

The chamber's thick stuffiness quickly drove him out to the balcony, though it was little better there. For a moment he viewed the smoke columns rising in the west; then he passed through the wrought-iron gate to the adjoining balcony and got his first look at Asa's tomato garden, which the mason had built the afternoon before.

"A passable job," Asa said.

"But will you be able to grow wax tadpoles in it?" Zorachus asked.

She laughed.

It was a small enclosure in the middle of the balcony, ringed by knee-high walls of mortared stone, rich brown loam coming up almost to the rim. Several rows of long sticks stood in the soil.

"When are you going to plant the seeds?" Zorachus asked.

"Right now," Asa replied. "Want to watch?"

"Of course."

She went over by Halfdan who was sitting on the rim, his face the very picture of boredom, a trowel and water can lying beside him. Asa picked them up, giving him a playful nudge with her elbow. He grumbled, and crossed his arms over his chest. Coming back to Zorachus, she produced a small sack of seeds and started to work.

"Zorachus," Halfdan said, "Why do you pretend you're so interested in this piddling little garden?"

"I like plants," Zorachus returned, watching Asa. "I very much approve of gardening."

"Do you like those plants in the park out there? All those flowers that look like they're made of human skin?"

Zorachus shook his head. "I can't stand them," he said. "But the reason I can't is that they're perversions of the real thing. Do you follow me?"

Halfdan thought a bit. "No."

"All right," Zorachus said. "Back in Qanar-Sharaj, the home of my order, there's a great dome. To be sure, it's nowhere near as big or spectacular as some of the domes in Khymir. But we hold our most solemn rites there and it's a very holy place; and one of the holiest things about it is a sea of plants that covers the inside walls."

"You worship these plants?"

"No, but we see their Maker's hand in them. They're living images of His thought, words which He's spoken. And inasmuch as anything is His word, it's holy."

"Words which He's spoken," Asa said. "I like that. I'm not sure what it means, but I like it."

"Who is this Maker?" Halfdan asked. "Which god is he?"

"The One who made all the others," Zorachus answered. "If they exist."

Halfdan boomed a laugh. "He made Gorm and Ygg, the All-Father?"

"He's the origin of everything. What does it say in your own tales about the gods? Did they make themselves? Or were they made by something else?" Zorachus was guessing here, but he knew what pagan cosmologies were like in general.

"They were born when the ice was licked away by the Mother of Cows." Halfdan answered stoutly.

"But they didn't make themselves?"

Halfdan's brow clouded. "No."

"Do you really want to say that these beings you worship were brought into existence by ice and cow spittle?"

"You're not looking at it the right way," Halfdan snapped. "When you put it like that, it sounds disgusting."

"All right. Maybe the spittle had nothing to do with it. Maybe it was because the cow's *tongue* was touching the ice. Even so, this bespeaks a pretty humble beginning for the gods."

"Damn it all, Zorachus, there was *magic* at work! Don't you see that?"

"Very plainly," the Sharajnaghi said. "But where did the magic come from?"

"The cow and the ice."

"But where did they come from?"

"The Mist."

"And where did the Mist come from?"

"The Great Void."

"And the magic must also have come from the Void?"

Halfdan pondered the question, "Yes."

"But can something come from nothing? Can a void be truly empty, truly a void, and yet contain magic? Or mist?"

"It doesn't sound too likely," Halfdan admitted.

"It doesn't sound too likely to me, either," Zorachus said. "I'd want to say that the magic and the Mist, if indeed your tales about these matters are true, couldn't have had nothing as their source. They might have come out of the Void, but *something* must have *brought* them out."

"And this something is the god you worship?" Asa asked.

"Yes."

"But why say this something's a god at all? Why couldn't it just be . . . well, a source?"

"Consider what it's the source of," Zorachus said. "Among other things, the gods and men get their wisdom from it. In causing them to exist, it causes their wisdom to exist. But it simply won't do to say that wisdom comes from something which is itself not wise. That's the same as saying that sense comes from nonsense. But once we admit that wisdom must be begotten by wisdom, then we must also admit that this source must be a person, a thinking being—in this case, a god. For only a thinking being can be wise."

"What about wise sayings?" Asa asked.

Zorachus laughed. He had been sloppy about his terms, but he had not expected her to catch him. She was very sharp.

"Well, they *contain* wisdom," he said. "In that sense, they're wise. Their wisdom lies in being the truth. But a god's, or a man's, lies in *knowing* it."

Asa flashed him a smile. "Ah," she said, considering this.

"But anyway, Zorachus," Halfdan said, "what does all this jabber about this source-god of yours have to do with why you don't like the trees down in the park? Or why you think it's so worthwhile to watch a woman planting tomatoes?"

"Ultimately, it has everything to do with it," Zorachus replied. "If my God is the source of all wisdom, magic, and life, then something that rejects Him rejects those things as well. It turns towards nothingness, becomes perverted. And the things it controls become perverted in their turn.

"Because they're tended by holy men who've given themselves to God, the plants at Qanar-Sharaj are creations properly used, images of God's thought fostered as signposts to point the mind to Him. But Khymir isn't like Qanar-Sharaj. The gardeners here are twisted. So, as a result, are the gardens. The Khymirians could never stand the sight of the real universe, so they've remade this little corner of it into something they could feel comfortable with—an image of themselves. The plants here are reflections of minds that have turned away from God, from existence. They're signposts pointing towards the nothingness that's the one true love, the final goal, of the people here. And nothingness is death.

"So now, perhaps, you understand why I'm impressed with Asa's gardening. She's acting from wholesome desires, and they come from God, even in people who don't realize they know Him. She's trying to give His universe a foothold in Khymir. It's a marvelous thing."

"I'm also trying to grow tomatoes," Asa said.

Halfdan was silent. Zorachus had lost him early in his reply, and the Kragehul had gone back to mulling what the Sharajnaghi had said about the gods.

"You're not angry with me, are you?" Zorachus asked him.

"You're a blasphemer, that's what you are," the Kragehul

said. "Making fun of the Mother of Cows, trying to make Ygg
and Gorm seem unimportant. . . ."

"I wasn't trying to make them seem unimportant. I was
merely trying to point out their relationship to my God—if
indeed they exist."

But Halfdan was not satisfied. "What you were trying to
point out is that they're not as important as him. And that's
blasphemy."

"Well, perhaps I'm mistaken," Zorachus replied. "But as
far as I can tell, I'm correct. And inasmuch as we think we see
the truth, the truth must be preferred."

Halfdan mulled the words. "I suppose."

"And you must admit, if the God I'm talking about really
exists, I'm doing you a favor in pointing Him out. You can't
fault a man for goodwill."

Halfdan softened at that, "I wasn't faulting you for your
goodwill," he said, almost apologetically. "I was faulting you
for your blasphemy."

"I understand. No offense taken."

"All right."

"You're a deep fellow, Zorachus," Asa said.

Halfdan laughed. "Luckily, he's got more going for him
than depth."

Zorachus laughed, too. "I don't know what I'd do without
you two . . ." He paused. "Actually, yes I do."

"And what's that, deep fellow?" Halfdan asked with a
smirk at Asa. Digging, she did not notice it.

"I'd go out of my mind," Zorachus replied.

"Out of your mind?" Halfdan asked. "What are you talking
about?"

"The reason I decided to make friends with you."

"You didn't want a bodyguard?"

"I didn't say that. But I needed—I still need—more than
that."

Asa looked up from her work. Suspicion glinted in her
eyes and Halfdan's.

"I needed people I could *talk* to," Zorachus said quickly.
"People who weren't Khymirians. Or infected by Khymir."

"So you could trust them?" Asa asked.

"So I could *like* them. So they could distract me—from
Khymir. This stinking quagmire could drag me right under."

"Only if you let it," Halfdan said. "Asa and I have been

here three years. We've resisted it all the time."

"That's true," Zorachus said. "But you had each other."

"You think the Khymirians would seduce you if you were by yourself?" Asa asked.

"No," he answered flatly. "But they might succeed in enraging me, prodding me into a bloodbath."

"And what would be wrong with that?" Halfdan demanded. "How else do you expect to take over and change things?"

"They're human beings."

"They're pigs in human form," Halfdan shot back. "And pigs should be butchered."

Zorachus shook his head. "They're badly hurt. Self-mangled. But they're still human."

"I'll be damned," Halfdan laughed.

"So would I," Zorachus said.

"That's crazy. You couldn't kill enough of them to suit me."

"I know how you feel," Zorachus said. "But God's my judge, not you. And killing human beings is a grievous thing. Even if they are Khymirians."

A slow grin crept over Halfdan's face. "You're having me on. If you were so worried about killing them, you wouldn't have come here at all. You've probably slaughtered several thousand already—though not by your own hand."

Zorachus nodded wearily; the sick pain in his face told Halfdan he was not joking. "I'm covered with blood, I know it," the Sharajnaghi said. "But there would've been more on my hands if I hadn't come. Your people's blood."

"What are you saying?" Halfdan asked.

"I was sent by my order to stop Kletus's invasion."

"You don't want to take over the city?"

"No."

Astonished, Halfdan was stopped dead by the reply. Every bit as surprised, Asa paused in her work and took up the questioning:

"You're putting yourself through all this for *other people?* Not yourself?"

"I came only to thwart the Black Priests," Zorachus answered. "I've no intention of setting myself up in their place."

This took a while to sink in.

"The better I get to know you," Asa said slowly, "the stranger you seem."

"But should we believe him about this?" Halfdan asked.

She sighed resignedly. "Might as well."

He grunted in agreement, then chuckled. "Such high purposes you have, Zorachus."

Zorachus made no reply.

"I'd think, though," Halfdan went on, "that they'd make you a lot less queasy about killing Khymirians. After all, it has to be done."

"That doesn't mean I have to like it," Zorachus said.

"A man does his work better when he likes it. Hate's a powerful weapon."

"One that God forbids me to use."

Halfdan snorted. *"Him* again. One very strange god, by the sound of it. But that's just the kind you'd be worshipping, isn't it?"

"He *is* the only one of His kind. And, as I'm his follower, I must obey His commands. That's why I'm so afraid of becoming enraged."

"Well, I suppose it makes sense," Halfdan said. "If your god's truly against it."

"If your god exists," Asa added.

"And certainly the idea that I'd snap shouldn't be too hard for you to understand," Zorachus continued.

Asa wiped her brow and got back to work. "Not at all," she said. "As a matter of fact, one of my favorite stories is about two men enraged by the Khymirians. They kill *hundreds* of them." The last sentence was awash with pure delight.

Halfdan spat. "I'll never know why you like that tale."

"Even though *hundreds* of Khymirians get killed?" Zorachus asked.

"That part's all right. But it's a vile story, nonetheless."

"It's nothing of the sort," Asa assured Zorachus. "And the end is beautiful."

"It's a stupid ending," Halfdan rumbled. "I would've slaughtered the bitch."

By this time, Zorachus's curiosity was whetted. "I'm going to have to hear this story."

Asa looked up. "Now?"

"If you wouldn't mind. Would it keep you from your work?"

"No."

Halfdan muttered a curse. "If you're going to tell it. I'm going inside."

"Zorachus wants to hear it," Asa replied, as if that were the only justification necessary.

"Well, keep your voice down. I don't want to have to go out of earshot; another demon might come looking for this deep fellow here."

He strode off; she continued to work. Zorachus admired her swift hands as she troweled and planted and watered. She began:

"In a Kragehul village near Khymir, lived a man named Rane and a woman named Astrid. They were tall and handsome and in love, so much in love that they were the laughing-stock of the village; so much that they didn't care.

"But, on the day of their marriage, their happiness was shattered. Khymirian raiders attacked the town, seizing the young and strong, putting the rest to the sword. Rane fought mightily, but was finally overcome and knocked senseless. Astrid was captured at his side.

"They were taken to Khymir and sold into the household of a Kadjafi merchant. He hated Khymir almost as much as he needed her; longing for his homeland, he planned to stay only so long as it took to set up his trading ventures. His name was Haroul.

"Astrid caught his eye. After a time, he fell in love with her. But he wasn't a man to take a woman from her mate, even if he owned her. He never told her how he felt, but to get closer to her he made friends with Rane—and came to love him as a brother. He placed him in his bodyguard. The three of them were rarely apart and strode through the mazy streets together.

"Haroul's dealings in Khymir dragged on and on. He was bargaining with the Guild and they grew stubborn, then hostile. Finally, a war broke out between them.

"At first, Haroul got the worst of it. But then the Priesthood began to give him secret support, including a wizard who warded off all sorcerous attacks. The war became a standoff.

"Realizing they couldn't destroy Haroul directly, the Guildsmen hit on a plan. They knew of his attachment to Rane and Astrid and his hatred of Khymirian ways. And so, they slipped two agents into his house. One was a beautiful young man whose mission was to seduce Rane; the other was for Astrid, a lovely woman, practically her mirror image. The Guildsmen wanted Haroul to see the people he loved become Khymirians, hoping it would break him.

"The man set to work on Rane and caught a dagger in the ribs before getting too far. But the woman, after several weeks, managed to worm her way into Astrid's bed.

"Rane discovered them and slashed off the woman's head. Terrified, Astrid wrapped a sheet about her and fled from the house. She was caught soon after by Guild soldiers, who took her through the nighted streets to their headquarters.

"Mind aflame, Rane went to tell Haroul what he'd discovered. Haroul was stunned and horrified; then wrath filled him.

"A messenger arrived from the Priests, saying they'd learned that two Guild agents had joined the household and that one was a Kragehul woman assigned to seduce Astrid. Haroul called out his retainers, fifty fierce-eyed Kadjafim, and he and Rane armed themselves; together with the priestly wizard, they marched to the Guild headquarters. They wiped out a troop of Guild soldiers at the gate, but before they could get inside, Guild wizards appeared on the balcony with Astrid, shouting to Haroul that they'd kill her if he and his men didn't lay down their arms.

"But the priest sent a demon to attack the man holding Astrid, and freed her; lifting her with magic, he brought her swiftly from the balcony. The wizards laid counterspells on her, trying to bring her back, but the Priest was too strong for them and set her down on the street, where Rane and Haroul put her under guard. Then they led the attack through the doors, which the Priest had blasted open seconds before.

"There was a great slaughter in the house. The blood of Guild wizards and soldiers ran like mountain streams down the stairways. Haroul was mortally wounded, Rane badly slashed across the chest. Even so, they broke into the chamber where the chief merchants had fled and glutted their hatred to the fullest. The room looked like a butcher's shambles when they left.

"Slowly, they made their way down to the street, followed by the few retainers that remained and the limping Priest. Astrid's guards thrust her forward. Filled with remorse, she wailed and begged Rane's forgiveness. But he looked on her with a face like a stone mask and drew his sword.

"But before he could strike, Haroul shrieked and rushed at her, waving his blade; determined to kill her himself, Rane moved to stop him and knocked the sword from his hand. Haroul crumpled to the pavement, dead.

"Weeping, Astrid reached out to Rane. He lifted his brand,

which was clotted with the Guildsmen's blood. She bowed her head, waiting for the blow. His sword sang down—and stopped an inch from her neck. He could not kill her. He loved her too much. Casting the blade to the cobbles, he knelt beside her, forgiving her with all his heart. Her tears became tears of joy as he clutched her to him. And the next morning, with the Priest's aid, they left Khymir, never to return."

Asa rose from her planting, stretched gracefully to get the kinks out of her back, and sat down on the garden wall. "I got the tale from old Gudrun, who lived outside our village in a tumbledown shack. I think I must have been her only friend. Everyone else stayed away from her, saying she was a witch who told bad fortunes and then made them come true. They used to call her Gudrun Death Horse. She was always kind to me, though. I stole off to her house many times, and she told me many stories. But none stuck in my mind like that one. I was shocked when I learned the Guild was still thriving; I thought it had been completely destroyed."

"Why do you like the story so much?" Zorachus asked.

"I'm not really sure. But it's probably the ending. It's wonderful. To think he'd forgive her like that. . . ." She smiled.

"Sometimes, hearing you and Halfdan talk, I didn't think your hearts had much place for forgiveness."

"I don't know about Halfdan. He always said he would've killed Astrid if he'd been in Rane's place. But I'm not so hard-minded. I could've forgiven her. After all, women are so. . . ."

"What?"

"Beautiful."

He understood her far too well. It was only natural that women should awaken desire, especially in one who had never tasted their love. Their beauty promised so much; Asa's promised so much. Gazing at her face, he felt a keen pang of longing.

If only you hadn't taken the vows, he told himself, *Halfdan would have quite a battle on his hands.*

He caught himself.

But you have taken the vows. And Asa is Halfdan's. They're one flesh.

"Zorachus?" Asa asked. "Is something the matter?"

He looked away from her.

You love her, don't you, fool?

"Zorachus?" Asa pressed.

You've fallen in love with another man's wife. You, a Shar-ajnaghi Master. Shame flooded through him.

"I'm going back to my room," he said. "I'm still feeling a bit dizzy."

"Should I get Halfdan?" she asked.

Zorachus shook his head. "I'd like to be alone," he said, and returned to his chamber.

As he lay down on the bed, he noticed his reflection in a mirror close by. His face was red and sweaty. His cheeks and forehead looked like raw meat.

"Pig," he grunted, but did not turn away. Staring steadily at himself, he sat up; a morbid impulse pushed him over to the glass. His face was even more repulsive close up. Distended pores oozed perspiration; one of his nostrils had begun to run. He wiped his nose, saw another stream trail down. For the first time in his life, he felt a surge of disgust at the very idea of flesh. He was a soul encased in muck, and the muck was smothering him.

"A Sharajnagha Master," he jeered. But all he could see in the mirror was a Khymirian, the son of Mancdaman Zan-charthus. He had been spawned in Khymir. Was it his destiny to let this city claim him? Was allowing himself to fall in love with another man's wife merely the first step, his chief danger not overreaction to the Khymirians, but that he would become like them? The more he stared at his reflection, the more it seemed to be gloating at him, eyes filled with wicked amusement.

Like it has a life of its own, he thought.

Smiling, it nodded.

What in—

As he stood paralyzed, its hand shot toward its belt snatching the hilt of a dagger he was not wearing; licking through the surface of the mirror, the blade flashed at the Sharajnaghi.

Reflexes took over; he dodged, knocking down the mirror with a kick. Glass splintered, and there was a scream. A pool of blood widened around each mirror shard.

The door banged open and the wardens charged through, brandishing swords and silver candlesticks. Seconds later, Asa rushed in from the balcony, followed shortly by Halfdan.

"My reflection just tried to stab me," Zorachus said,

twitching a nervous grin. He had never heard of such a thing
before, but he had no doubt that the attack had been conjured
in Banipal Khezach. He turned to one of the guards. "Find
Sharthas. Tell him I want every mirror in this place removed. I
don't want to see my face in this house again."

chapter

15

NEAR SUNSET, A message arrived from Porchos saying the rings were recovered and summoning Zorachus to a Guild war council.

"When do we leave?" Asa asked.

"We?" Halfdan demanded. "That fight in the square wasn't enough for you?"

"No."

"You're not coming this time," Zorachus told her firmly. "Kletus might send another demon. You'll be safer here."

"But I'm not going to stay—"

"Oh yes you are."

"Well then," Asa seethed, "shall I take it out on Halfdan when you get back?"

"Halfdan has nothing to do with this."

"That's right, Asa," Halfdan smirked.

"And don't tell me how you'll kill yourself if we don't come back," Zorachus went on. "If we're killed out there, you'll probably die too. But you might die in an attack even if we didn't."

"That's telling her," Halfdan said.

"You're going to be very sorry, Halfdan," Asa said.

"He'd be sorrier watching you ripped to pieces," Zorachus answered.

"But . . ."

"You're not coming, and that's final."

She stamped her foot and crossed her arms on her chest. "I saved your life last night. And when I hit that redclad in the eye with—"

"Think of this as me returning the favor."

"If you're so worried about me, why didn't you leave me behind the other day?"

Zorachus wanted to answer: *Because I didn't know I loved*

you then. But what he said was: "We should have, but we let
you bully us."

"I bullied the two of you?"

"Give it up, Asa," Halfdan said.

She turned her back on them, simmering.

An hour later, Zorachus and Halfdan rode from the palace
escorted by thirty retainers on foot, many bearing torches. The
darkening streets were nearly deserted; windows were heavily
shuttered. The air smelled of smoke and rotting flesh. Bodies
of priestly sympathizers hung heels up from balconies and
walls. Ravens cawed and flapped in the stinking dusk; horn
blasts and hoofbeats sounded in the distance, and muffled
thunder growled.

The company reached Porchos's house. Screams echoed
dimly from inside—_prisoner being tortured_, Zorachus
thought. He looked along the top of the outer wall. Torchlight
glistened on the severed heads impaled there, their skin already cooked slimy by the heat, even though they were barely
a day old.

He was swiftly taken to Porchos's soundproof sanctum. All
the Chief Guildsmen were there. Terse greetings were ex-
changed and Porchos handed Zorachus's ring-sack to him.

"Dr. Aliphar apologizes for his slave," the merchant said.
"The culprit was properly punished. Did you see the heads on
the wall? His was the one stuck above the gate—right over
the keystone."

Smiling in polite appreciation, Zorachus looked into the
pouch. The rings flamed. He pulled the drawstring and hung
the pouch around his neck.

"I suppose we'd better get down to business," Porchos
said. "If you'll all come to the table please. . . ."

On it was spread a great parchment map of Khymir. A red
line divided the city roughly in half. Wooden blocks of various
sizes marked key positions.

"The black blocks are enemy strongholds," Maranchthus
explained. "Green is for Guild. As should be obvious, the
Priesthood has near-complete control in the north and west
quarters. We control the rest." He pointed to a green block just
south of the red line. "That's your house, Lord Mancdaman."
He pointed to a black mass directly across the line, by far the
largest block on the map. "That's Banipal Khezach."

"We've been considering whether you should stay in your

palace," Porchos told Zorachus. "It is, after all, so close to the Tower. You might take up with me. We'd leave your house well-garrisoned, of course."

"You'd have all the sorcerous protection you could want," Maranchthus added.

"Let me think," Zorachus said. He guessed their concern for his safety was genuine enough, but also that they were trying to increase his dependence on them, to deprive him of his own troops, his own stronghold. Once the Priesthood was finished, and his usefulness ended, they would want him to be an easy target. He knew he could always move out of the palace and still insist on having his own household. But such a demand, by making it obvious that he had discovered their secret intention, would only heighten their anxiety, make them more desperate. He could not afford that. He did not want their wizards casting death spells against him the moment the Priesthood collapsed. There was no telling how long it would take him to flee Khymir.

"Well?" Porchos asked presently.

"I think I'd better stay at the palace," Zorachus announced. "It wouldn't look well if I moved out."

"Your safety's more important than show," Maranchthus said.

"It's not just a matter of show," Zorachus replied. "It would be wise to keep a mage of my rank at the palace simply for combat purposes. You don't have any other mages of my rank, do you?" He assumed that they had had observers at the duel.

"No," Porchos said. Suddenly he looked at Zorachus side-long. "Why didn't you kill Zarathonzar when he was stunned?"

The question caught the Sharajnaghi off guard. He knew the truth would simply not be believed; he scrambled for an answer they *would* accept, one that would ease their suspicion of treachery.

"It's rather hard to explain," he began.

"Try anyway," Porchos answered.

"You've heard of the Influences?"

Porchos and the others nodded.

"Well, the Powers that presided over my birth forbid me to kill on certain days. . . ."

"Why?"

"That's what's hard to explain. It always seemed like an

arbitrary injunction to me. But the Powers are known for their inscrutabil—"

"What about all those redclads you blasted?" Maranchthus broke in.

"*I* didn't blast them," Zorachus returned. "The demons in my rings did. When I'm endangered, they intervene—even to the point of manipulating my body so they can take proper aim. But Zarathonzar wasn't endangering me—not once I'd stunned him."

"What about when you cut him in half?"

"It was an accident. I was only trying to remove him from this plane. He broke my concentration, caused the portal to snap shut prematurely."

Maranchthus said no more, apparently convinced. But Porchos was not.

"Why didn't you kill him?" he pressed.

He's no fool, Zorachus told himself. He shrugged and smiled. "For mercy's sake," he said. After all, the Guildsmen *had* to stick with him.

"You expect us to believe that?" Porchos demanded.

"It's the truth."

The Guildsman snapped: "Then we don't want the truth."

"I didn't think you would. Let's just say I didn't because of—a quirk."

"That quirk nearly buried us all," an obese Guildsman grated, sweat running from his chin like drool. "What if he'd won?"

"He didn't. That's all that matters."

Porchos seethed. "Why didn't you kill him? I insist on the truth!"

"I don't have to answer to you," Zorachus answered.

The calmness of his voice unnerved them. "What kind of game are you playing?" Porchos cried, face livid.

Zorachus smiled. "I don't play games. The real world's much more interesting. Do you gentlemen have anything more to say?"

There was a long silence. Then Maranchthus answered thickly:

"We want you to draft another denunciation. A very wild-eyed one. It doesn't have to make any sense. We simply just want to get people's blood up."

"Very well," Zorachus said.

"We have some other work for you, too. You're free to turn it down, of course. . . ."

"What is it?"

"As you can see from the map, there are still some enemy strongholds left in our territory. But only one of them," he pointed to a large black block, "is a real threat: the Southside Armory. It's vital that we take it soon."

"Very soon," Porchos said.

"Why?" Zorachus asked.

"We control the city gate and we've got the harbor ramp blocked up," Porchos replied. "But the enemy has the harbor itself, and as far as we can tell there are over a thousand troops down there—marines, raiders, sailors. They can only enter the city one way—through the lift in the armory. If they reached the armory and broke out, they could overrun a large part of the Foreign Quarter."

"Now, we have several agents inside the armory, and one of them's a wizard; he's been sending out messages through his familiars. He and his comrades have been stirring up quite a hornet's nest, lighting fires, damaging the lift, sabotaging efforts to repair it. But, unfortunately, the Priests also have wizards inside, so it won't be long before they discover our men and get the lift working.

"By tomorrow morning we'll be able to muster three hundred troops for an assault on the armory; but we'll need a wizard to breach the doors. A very powerful wizard."

"I see," Zorachus said. "What are you going to do with the prisoners you take?"

"We might not take any. The men in the armory probably have a very good idea of what will happen to them if they surrender. But if we *do* take any alive, they'll make splendid object lessons."

"You couldn't sell them as slaves?" Zorachus asked. "Exchange them for men held by the Priests?"

"We don't need slaves. And if the Priests took any of our men alive there probably isn't enough left of them to exchange. But that's beside the point. Will you aid us?"

"On one condition: Priests' men who surrender will be turned over to me."

For a moment the merchants looked stunned; then their eyes blazed. He had expected their anger; he knew they thought he was trying to gain recruits. But he could not allow the prisoners to be used as "object lessons." Not if he opened the armory and thus had a direct hand in their capture.

"What will you do with them?" Porchos burst out.

"Probably sell them," Zorachus answered. Actually, he did not know what he would do. Sharajnaghim were prohibited from trading, or even holding, slaves.

"What do you want to sell them for?" Maranchthus snarled. "You don't need the money. What's this strange aversion to spilling blood?"

"Do you accept my terms?" Zorachus asked, wondering if a suitable prison for the captives could be bought.

Porchos and Maranchthus stepped back from the table. The other merchants did likewise, clustering around them. Whispering, the group moved into a corner, hissing like a knot of vipers. After several minutes they came back again, looking flustered.

"We accept," Porchos gritted, glaring.

"Now," Zorachus said, "about that denunciation. . . ."

It took several hours to grind out the first draft. He tried to give them what they wanted, a simple torrent of vitriol. In the end, he got the vituperation down pat, but all of it was very closely reasoned. Whether that would add to or subtract from its effect, he could only guess.

He wrote a second draft and signed it, learned when and where tomorrow's attack would be mustered, and took his leave. Gathering his escort, he started back to his palace. Torches flaring, the column wound northward through the night streets.

"I forgot to ask you," Halfdan said, riding beside the Sharajnaghi, "What did you think of Asa's story?"

"I liked it well enough. It reminded me of the three of us. . . ."

"What do you mean by that?" Halfdan asked sharply.

"The good part. The three of them against Khymir."

"That's all right," Halfdan said, relaxing. "I suppose we *are* alike that way. But that only makes it more horrible."

"Rane forgives her. I don't think that's horrible."

Halfdan spat. "She should've been killed."

"Isn't someone entitled to one moment of weakness?"

"It all depends."

"On what?"

"What was done during that moment. Some sins rot people

away, damage them beyond cure. . . . Would you have forgiven her?"

"I think so."

"Would you forgive yourself if you made love to a man?"

Zorachus hesitated. "I'd like to think so . . ."

Halfdan pounced: "But you wouldn't, would you? You'd always smell the rot."

"Yes."

"Why be harder on yourself than on someone else?"

"Because I wouldn't know why they did it," Zorachus said. "I wouldn't have the slightest idea of how much they were damaged. It would be different with one of my own sins. Tell me, Halfdan: would you kill Asa if she betrayed you that way?"

The Kragehul's face went grim as a basalt mask. "I'd kill her if she betrayed me in any way," he said. Zorachus felt a sick pang. "If she betrayed me with a woman, killing her would be the *least* I'd do."

Then the stone mask broke. Halfdan laughed. "Luckily, there's no chance of that. We do go on about the strangest things." He goaded his mount with his heels. "Ygg blast this grade!"

The street slanted steeply, the winding bed of a ravine of leaning facades. Blackwall Hill, up which it climbed, was a long ridge running east to west. It was one of the few rises in Khymir. It was well-known as a horse killer and man killer, but, if one was bound from Porchos's house to the Mancdaman Palace, there was no quick way round it. The retainers staggered and puffed, dragging their mailed bodies up the slope as shadowy stone faces grinned down at their efforts from facades on either side. Black moths, drawn by the torches fluttered about the troops like spots before the eyes of a drunken man.

The column reached a short, level stretch, where Zorachus ordered a brief respite; then the climb resumed. They skirted a sluggish tide of black sludge flowing from the door of a house with the words *Priests' pigs* splattered over it in white paint, and entered a stinking tunnel formed by arching roofs; gloom thickened about their bobbing torches. Utterly undisturbed by the presence of so many humans, a battalion of black rats marched unhurriedly from one garbage-floored alley to another, each bearing a bit of sharpened bone in its jaws. Zorachus and his men eyed them respectfully; there were more than a few murmurs of relief when the rodents were left behind. The column moved deeper and deeper into the tunnel.

Suddenly, a shutter banged open on the right, the sound reverberating like thunder between the crazily tilting facades; retainers swore, drawing steel and silver, and Zorachus snatched for his ring-sack.

An old crone stood at the window, silhouetted by a green glow, face lit by the retainers' torches, gnarled hands gripping the sill like bird's claws.

"What do you want?" Zorachus cried, reining his mount around.

She said nothing, but a hooded figure appeared behind her and bellowed: "Go to *sleep!*" At first, Zorachus did not know if the command was for him or her; then a cord went round her neck, there was a muffled crack as her neck snapped, and she was flung savagely backwards. Both figures vanished, but presently a hand rose behind the wall, grabbed the shutter and closed it.

"Come on!" Zorachus cried to his men. The ascent continued. Yard by yard, the air, already foul, worsened drastically; a stench strong enough to be tasted filled the upper reaches of the tunnel. Its source proved to be a dead redclad, hanging head-down from the arch at the tunnel's end. The corpse had not been there when the company went south.

Hands over their noses, the lead retainers trudged past, coughing. Then came Halfdan and Zorachus.

The chain holding the body broke. With a sound like a melon smashed by a hammer, the redclad struck the pavement head-first beside Zorachus's horse. The beast shied and the retainers downhill halted, shrinking back from the corpse. Zorachus watched the body, half expecting it to get up. But the only hint of movement was the squirm of maggots that had burst from the broken skull.

"He won't hurt us," the Sharajnaghi cried.

The men below hesitated and whispered to each other, but finally started forward.

"So many omens," Halfdan said quietly as he and the Sharajnaghi goaded their horses up the grade.

Zorachus did not answer.

Ahead, the way ran straight; the hilltop could be seen, not far now, the walls of the street-canyon standing out dimly against the paler darkness of the sky, which was seared now and again by far-off lightning. Eager to end the climb, the

company moved more quickly. Mailed tramping and the clop
of hooves echoed hollowly.

Glancing along one side of the street, Zorachus noticed
another strung-up corpse—a naked man. Attached by one
heel to a balcony hanging far out over the cobbles, the body
was strangely contorted, spine impossibly curved, limbs
bowed jointlessly, one leg tied literally in a knot. *Broken on
the wheel,* Zorachus thought to himself.

A feeble breeze swept down from the crown of the hill, the
first wind of any sort he had felt in Khymir. The corpse
swayed back and forth, much more than the Sharajnaghi
would have expected in such a mild current.

His gaze followed the dead face as it swung. The mouth
was flung open in a silent howl, dark insects flying in and out.
Glazed, bugging from their sockets, the eyes stared sight-
lessly—

—then slitted in a knowing leer. Two tongues erupted from
the gaping mouth. Morkûlg's aura struck Zorachus like a blow
in the face.

"God save us," the Sharajnaghi breathed.

Still hanging rigidly upside down, the corpse detached itself from the balcony, rose, and vanished in the gloom. Some
retainers saw it shoot skyward; oaths rang out.

"What's wrong?" Halfdan demanded.

Before Zorachus could answer, crimson light flooded over
them; house-huge, tongues twitching, Morkûlg rose over the
hillcrest like a bloodstained moon.

"An illusion?" Halfdan cried.

Zorachus's rings glittered as he slipped them on. "No, but
it's not real either. Not yet—"

Their mounts snorted and kicked; Halfdan's reared, spilling
him. Wind knocked out by the fall, he floundered on the cobbles. Moments later, Zorachus also went down. Both horses
clattered off frantically. So did the retainers. Zorachus and
Halfdan were nearly trampled.

"Stand your ground!" the Sharajnaghi roared, leaping to his
feet, thigh and forearm smarting where he had taken the
ground. The retainers ignored him.

He rushed over to Halfdan. "Can you get up?"

Halfdan only gasped. Zorachus thought of carrying him,
but looked crestward first.

Morkûlg's lower tongue was lengthening, tip uncurling; a
glowing greenish-yellow bundle rolled out, hurtling down the

slant. There was nothing illusory about it.

Zorachus planted himself in front of Halfdan, blue light-ning snaking from his rings and slamming the bundle to a smoking standstill.

The phosphorescent mass remained motionless for a mo-ment. Then it snapped upright, standing on end; a cyclonic blur, it unwound.

Zorachus launched two more bolts. They passed between the now parted halves of the bundle—a nude woman and a lamia, long dead, skin hanging in tatters from their bones, charred holes showing where the first bolts had struck them. Shrieking like fugitives from a madhouse in hell, they swept downwards, hands reaching out talonlike.

The demon-rings flamed. The woman kept coming till she dropped in two pieces. It took three blasts to hammer the lamia apart.

But neither monstrosity was finished. The pieces shud-dered, crawled, and flopped down the slant. Shrieks poured from the decayed throats.

Zorachus turned to Halfdan. The Kragehul was trying to rise. Zorachus moved to get a shoulder under him but heard the fragments scrabbling close—God almighty, how could dead meat move so fast? He spun, demon thunderbolts flaring from his fists, blowing the pieces into even smaller bits. Barely slowing the charnel onslaught, he succeeded mainly in multiplying the fragments squirming to the attack. Patches of moldy skin humped toward him over the cobbles. Sinews wound side to side like snakes. Severed below the wrist, knocked skyward by the shock from a crackling strike, the lamia's left hand flipped through the air, scuttling up his trousers like a giant spider. He grabbed it, wrenched it loose, and hurled it away. Another dead hand locked onto his boot; the top of the woman's body, now only a head, shoulder, and arm, reeled itself forward, grinning jaws clacking. Zorachus blew the worm-eaten face to steaming bits, but the hand still held, skeletal fingers knifing through his boot leather. Unable to yank it free, he sent a demon-bolt ripping across its back and it exploded. Somehow, a finger spun up into his beard, wriggling. He plucked it away before it could pierce him. A tiny chunk of decay wormed into his mouth; nearly retching, he spat it out and staggered back, suddenly aware of Halfdan at his side.

"Can you run?" the Sharajnaghi croaked.

Halfdan gulped air, bringing his heel down on a strip of corruption that squirmed too close. Ragged claw marks showed on his hands

"I'll try," he said. "But look! The carrion's stopped moving!"

It was true; yet Morkûlg the Mask still hung above the hillcrest, his red light washing the street in blood, and Zorachus saw he had fully materialized. The *real* attack would begin now. The time for games was over.

The Mask's sideward tongue lashed out and down, vanishing behind the houses on the left. The other lunged down the street, a sinuous, gleaming tentacle. Zorachus blew on his rings and burned several holes in it. It flinched back, wavered, came on again. He and Halfdan turned and fled.

Before they had gone too far, the first tongue gushed out of an alley ahead and came questing up the hill at them. No escape that way.

People were shouting from balconies on either side of them; doors opened and curious, red-limned faces looked out. Zorachus hurtled through the nearest entrance, dodging a teenage girl; Halfdan bowled her over and they pounded down a taperlit corridor.

Behind them, a tongue swept in over the threshold, crushing the girl, flooding the hallway, a tide of dark, glistening muscle. The passage reverberated with rumbling thunder.

They dodged into a side passage; Halfdan kept running, but Zorachus stopped and turned, assuming a stance. He loosed as many cataract strikes as he could, force-letting. Then, as the rumbling in the hall set his lungs vibrating and his teeth chattering, he mouthed a spell. The Influences were with him; a portal opened in the main hallway. It was not big enough for the whole tongue to slide inside, but even so the careening mass was neatly cored, the hollowed sleeve shooting past the junction. Outside, a throat like a pipe organ winded a cry that shook the foundations of Khymir.

Zorachus snapped the portal shut. Trailing a swath of black ichor, the sleeve retreated, its thunder fading swiftly.

He heard a crash above him, more rumbling, and footbeats thudding in back of him. He spun to see Halfdan racing towards him. Beyond the Kragehul, the second tongue rolled down a flight of stairs like a cascade of oil, smashing two children trying to flee before it. It roared towards Halfdan, rapidly outstripping him. The Kragehul hurled himself out of

its path, launched his huge body at an adjoining door, battering it down, scrambled through as a chorus of shrieks sounded
within. The tongue slid swiftly, inexorably towards Zorachus.

Remaining where he was, he opened another, larger portal
practically at his feet. The tongue passed inside, yard after
yard vanishing into thin air. Zorachus retreated into the main
hallway and closed the portal, severing the tongue. Like a
giant, wounded worm, the black-spouting stump shot backward along the hall. The floor and walls shook with agonized
roars from outside; dust rained from the ceiling.

Halfdan burst from his refuge with a nude dwarf clutching
his neck, kissing his face. He reached back and flipped the
creature into the opposite wall with bone-breaking force, then
ran up to Zorachus.

"What did you do?" he asked breathlessly.

"Shut a portal on the tongue."

"Can you open one for us?"

"We'd be killed. The Influences aren't right."

"You and your magic," Halfdan growled. "Let's try and
find a back way out of here."

They ran down the main corridor, paying no attention to
the fearful people peering out at them from half-open doorways. Halfdan panted: "What do you think he'll try next—"

There came a beating, as of many small wings. Zorachus
cried out, pointing to a stairwell ahead. A cloud of black billowed down, a swarm of miniature demons.

It engulfed Zorachus and Halfdan. Tiny fangs and claws
raked them. Bubbling with blood, piping voices chittered obscenities in their lacerated ears. Trying to keep their faces and
throats covered, the two were swiftly driven back.

Zorachus fell, not far from the front door. Halfdan tripped
over him, shrieking. Battling to ignore pain and distraction,
the Sharajnaghi started a spell, lost the thread after a white-hot
spurt of agony, started again. Talons peeled skin back from his
wounds, scraped bone-deep through his flesh; his whole body
quivered in torment. But somehow he finished.

A loud buzzing swept the hall. The demons stopped ripping at him. Lowering his bleeding hands, he looked up—and
laughed.

Scores of hornets, each bigger than a man's thumb and
haloed with a golden aura, swarmed among the swirling pinions, diving in and out, planting sting after sting. Soon the
floor was littered with the batlike sendings. The tiny bodies

swelled amazingly as the venom did its work; then they vanished.

The surviving demons swirled out through the door, hornets humming in pursuit. Zorachus crawled to the threshold, chanced a look outside. The black wings sped towards Morkûlg, silhouetted by his blood-red light. The Mask's eyes were wide open like black tunnel mouths. The foremost demons reached shelter inside; the rest were cut off as the huge lids closed. The hornets made short work of them, before starting in on Morkûlg himself. His mutilated tongues lashed vainly to fend them away; great domes, aggregates of a hundred stings or more, bulged from his stricken flesh.

He roared, eyes opening once more to reveal pools of eddying yellow light. Hurling himself to his feet, Zorachus rushed back from the threshold.

Outside, two flaming beams flared from Morkûlg's eyes, converging on the house. The doorway erupted in a blast of blue and crimson fire. Incandescent stone crumbled, flew in molten showers.

Scorched and deafened, Zorachus and Halfdan raced once more down the main hallway. Behind them, the front of the house collapsed under fresh salvos.

Choking on clouds of dust, bumping into panicked people, they pelted along the quaking corridor. At last they emerged, with several others, in a blind, high-walled courtyard.

Almost at once, red light bathed the enclosure and black fluid splattered out of the sky. They looked up.

Morkûlg hovered above them, parallel to the ground, wounded tongues dangling. The hornets still swarmed about him and had taken a horrendous toll; his features were wildly bloated, the mushrooming welts beginning to burst, puffing purple vapor. His eyes were swollen shut, but one twitched open, a mere slit. Yellow fire seethed between the bulging lids, ready to strike downward. . . .

The welt-vapor ignited with a heavy *whoom*.

Morkûlg rocked as flame exploded across his face; eyelids vanished, blasted away, baring blazing sockets. Howling, he shot skyward, twin tongues whipping like burning snakes; up he sped till he was tiny with distance, shattering at last in a saffron fireball that disappeared almost as soon as it blossomed.

"You're a marvel," Halfdan panted beside Zorachus.

"I'm *lucky,*" the Sharajnaghi gasped. "I didn't know the

welts would burst and burn that way. . .Distracting Morkûlg was the best I hoped for. And anyway, the hornets did the *real* work."

Halfdan and the other people drew back as the insects buzzed near Zorachus, circling around him, waiting to be returned to their plane. Warned by some alien foreknowledge, they had barely escaped incineration when Morkûlg caught fire. Zorachus thanked them mentally and dismissed them.

"Come on, Halfdan," he said. "Let's see if we can find our men."

chapter

16

As it turned out, the retainers were also looking for Zorachus. He and Halfdan met them shortly after emerging from the partially ruined house. Watching from down near the tunnel mouth, the soldiers had seen Morkûlg's destruction and were anxious to get back into Zorachus's good graces. He was not feeling particularly vengeful now that it was all over—especially when he considered that they would have been no use whatsoever, except, perhaps, against the dead woman and the lamia. He had simply not known what form Morkûlg's attacks would take when he ordered the troops to hold their ground.

The column took shape once more, reaching the Mancda-man palace a half-hour later. Shartas tended Halfdan's wounds; Zorachus went to his room and lowered himself into a healing trance.

Two hours before dawn, the Sharajnaghi rose. A bleary eyed Halfdan greeted him in the hall, one arm around Asa's nightrobed waist; Zorachus felt a twinge of jealousy but stifled it.

Halfdan gave Asa a kiss, and she dragged herself back to bed without the slightest protest that she had not been allowed to join them.

The two men went downstairs, mustered forty fresh troops, and set out through the still-dark streets. Eventually, they came to the bonfire-lit barracks yard where Porchos and Maranchthus waited with three hundred brown-mailed soldiers and six Guild wizards. Both Guildsmen were mounted and armored.

"I see you're not wearing a bodyguard," Zorachus said to Porchos.

"They're no help against arrows," Porchos replied.

"Or anything else, I'll wager," Maranchthus muttered.

The company departed.

Night was already fading. Even though the city was still steeped in the shadow of the eastern mountains, the sky was pale blue by the time the armory came in view.

Round-walled, squat, and black, the armory stood hublike in the center of a circular plaza. All the streets joining the circle were barricaded with cobbles, Guild troops manning the rude walls, sharpening swords and spear points on stones, adjusting straps on helmets and shields. Figures stirred in the windows of the houses fronting the plaza—Guild archers.

The attack was to be launched from a huge house opposite the armory's northern side; the assault force entered through a back way. Porchos and Maranchthus deployed the troops, then took up positions with Zorachus and the wizards in a large room with one iron-grilled window. Through it, the massive gates of the armory's loophole-flanked main entrance could be seen.

"Are there warding spells on those doors?" Zorachus asked.

Porchos nodded. "Our mages will counter them."

"Have your troops been told of last night's agreement?"

"Yes."

"Very good," Zorachus took the demon-rings out. Porchos signaled to the wizards. Forming a circle, they bowed their heads and began to drone the counterspells.

Zorachus eyed the armory doors. He guessed they were locked by a great central bolt, or perhaps several of them, and decided his best strategy would be to loose maximum strikes all along the crack between the valves. Halfdan stood behind him with a water bag, ready to douse the rings.

The counterspells were consummated. Blue light flashed from the doors and bits of stone cracked off the lintel; cobbles leaped up from the street in spurts of dust. Zorachus raised his hands, positioning the rings before openings in the window grille, readying himself to strike. . . .

A postern creaked open in one of the armory doors and a darkly spattered white flag pushed through the crevice.

"What kind of trick—" Porchos began.

"It might not be a trick at all," Zorachus replied. "Remember your promise. Let's hear what they have to say."

Porchos hesitated, then took up the trumpet he wore on his baldric and sounded the Guild cease-fire. An armored figure staggered through the postern, waving the flag and pushing back his helmet.

"That's one of our agents," Porchos said as the man drew nearer. The fellow stumbled, landed on his hands and knees, picked himself up and kept coming. A long rent could be seen in the mail on his chest. He passed out of sight beyond the corner of the window.

Shortly, a Guild officer entered the room with the wounded man clinging to his shoulder; laying him on a cot, the officer stepped back, and Porchos and Maranchthus hurried over, followed by Zorachus.

"The armory's yours," the agent whispered, blood trickling from the corner of his mouth. "They're all dead. . . ." His eyes rolled up and he stiffened. Porchos turned to Maranchthus, beaming.

"All dead," Maranchthus said, grinning back at him.

"Lieutenant," Porchos said to the officer, "send someone over to check."

The officer nodded and left.

"What do you think happened over there?" Zorachus asked Porchos.

Porchos laughed. "Can't you guess?"

Zorachus said nothing, though a sickening suspicion had dawned in him.

Soon, a soldier making slowly for the armory, came into view outside, looking back over his shoulder from time to time with a face pale as whey. The closer he got to the postern, the more tremulous his steps grew; whimpering, he stopped ten feet away.

"Go on, dog!" a harsh voice cried. "Go on, or we'll shoot you ourselves!"

The scout started forward again. He paused momentarily at the threshold, then vanished inside. Several minutes passed before he reemerged and beckoned.

Porchos turned to Zorachus. "I think you should come with us," he said. "It might relieve you of some delusions."

Despite his apprehension, Zorachus nodded. He and Half-dan followed the Chief Guildsmen out into the street. A crowd of soldiers came behind.

The scout still stood near the postern, trembling but smiling. He saluted Porchos and Maranchthus as they came up.

"Coward," Maranchthus snapped and spat on him. As he started past, almost as an afterthought, the Guildsman whipped a poniard from his belt and buried it in the scout's beard. Remaining upright only long enough for Maranchthus to pluck the blade free, the scout fell forward. Zorachus and Halfdan had to step over him to enter the postern.

Before them stretched a broad corridor echoing with Porchos's and Maranchthus's laughter, puddled with blood and strewn with the bodies of the armory's defenders. Many still clutched the blades they had slaughtered themselves—or their comrades—with.

The Sharajnaghi and Kragehul paused, but Porchos beckoned, grinning smugly, and they slowly strode forward over the bodies. Dead men stared at them, some blankly, some grimacing; others, still smiling with the terrible pleasure they had taken with them into the next world, had been masturbating or having sex with each other even as they died. Many had gone far beyond mere suicide; one man had literally smashed his brains out against a wall, while another, a severed thumb clenched in his teeth, had bitten off the fingers of one hand.

"No prisoners here, Lord Mancdaman," Maranchthus called back gloatingly.

Zorachus ignored him. "But we would have spared you," he whispered to the dead; marching like an automaton, he was horrified to the core of his being.

They came out in the central hall. There, the bodies were less thick. Porchos and Maranchthus halted by the elevator shaft. Above it was a hole in the ceiling where the pulley stanchion had been ripped out. The lift itself had fallen down the shaft.

A corpse lay by the rim of the pit. Porchos turned it over with his foot.

"Another of our men," he said as Zorachus and Halfdan came up. "The wizard. He must have broken the pulley."

"And died soon after," Maranchthus said. "I'm surprised our other man lasted as long as he did."

"They must've thought he was dead. That was quite a slash in him. And besides, they had other things on their minds. Suicide requires some concentration, I expect. Even when you're enjoying it."

"I would've fought," Halfdan grated, eyeing a tangle of corpses nearby.

"Fought, Kragehul?" Porchos asked. "Why? They were about to wake from this senseless dream of a life in any case. They were trapped, mice under the cat's paw, their last hope

gone. They didn't know we had such, a soft touch among us."
He jeered at Zorachus. "And so they chose to die by their own
hands. Some thought it would be less painful. Some made it
more, and came like sleepers in heat."

"I would've fought," Halfdan repeated, puzzled and
enraged, tears of hatred welling from his eyes. He had lived
long among Khymirians, but could still be shocked by the
twisted anti-realities of their minds.

"You," Porchos replied in a voice thick with contempt,
"are a stinking barbarian dolt."

Halfdan regarded him silently. The fury seemed to leave
his eyes. He looked almost thoughtful.

"Stop staring at me, dog," Porchos spat.

Halfdan continued looking at him.

"Halfdan," Zorachus began—just as Porchos slapped the
Kragehul across the face.

Roaring, Halfdan grabbed the merchant by the throat,
holding him out at arm's length over the shaft. The Guildsman's eyes bulged out and he gripped Halfdan's wrist with
both hands. Soldiers converged, shouting, and Maranchthus
leaped in back of Halfdan, poniard in hand.

"Drop him and you're dead," he snarled. "Set him on the
rim."

Knowing Halfdan would be killed the instant Porchos was
safe, Zorachus extended his hands, rings gleaming.

"Maranchthus, get back," he said.

The merchant's eyes darted sidewards. "Have you gone
mad?"

"I don't want my bodyguard killed," Zorachus answered.
"Move back. Slowly. And tell your men to withdraw."

Maranchthus did as he was told. As he and the troops retreated warily, Zorachus said, "Halfdan, set Porchos down."

Halfdan snarled something unintelligible.

"Halfdan!" Zorachus barked.

The Kragehul obeyed. Coughing and sputtering, Porchos
collapsed on the floor. Zorachus knelt by his side, keeping his
eyes on Maranchthus and the troops.

"I apologize for my bodyguard, and for threatening Maranchthus just now," the Sharajnaghi said.

It was a few moments before Porchos replied, and when he
did he paused between words as if to inject as much concentrated venom into each one as he could: *"I . . . want . . . the
. . . Kragehul's . . . head!"*

The words rasped Zorachus's eardrums like fingernails across slate; he looked sidelong at Porchos for a few moments. The Guildsman's face was blotched with red spots and his bloodshot eyes glistened and twitched; his spittle-flecked lips were peeled back, quivering, and his teeth grinned whitely, clenched tightly together. The sight was enough to make the Sharajnaghi want to leap up and smash his twisted, bloated hideousness with both feet, to print his heels deep in the merchant's features, to feel bone snap and make blood spurt. . . . Struggling with himself, arrow scar flaring red on his cheek, he looked away from Porchos, back at Maranchthus and the soldiers. They all seemed to wear the same mask as Porchos. How easy, how splendid it would be to unleash a spate of demon-bolts, tear their heads apart, send eyes and teeth and bits of skull flying. . . . He cast his gaze floorward.

"I'll punish my servant my own way," he said.

"I want the pig's head!" Porchos shrieked, jerking upwards, spit and phlegm spraying through his teeth, spattering Zorachus's chin. The Sharajnaghi wiped the drops away with a trembling hand.

"Do you want my support?" he asked.

"You need us as much as we need you! Kill him!"

"Don't be ridiculous," Zorachus answered, rising. His hands clenched and unclenched at his sides, and light pulsed behind the knife-sharp facets of his rings; aroused by his anger and torment, the demons ached to kill. "We'll be off now. Come on, Halfdan."

They headed towards the clustered soldiers. A lane opened swiftly, obligingly; a few of them had seen what the rings could do and the rest had heard. There was no rage on their faces now, if indeed there ever had been, only fright.

The pair passed through, going out into the corpse-littered corridor beyond. Soon they heard footsteps behind and looked back. Zorachus's retainers were following; they knew who was the real power in the Guild faction, even if they had been hired by Porchos and Maranchthus.

Zorachus and Halfdan reached the street.

"Don't you ever—*ever,* damn you—slip like that again," Zorachus rumbled. "We've come too far to have you lose control and ruin everything."

Halfdan looked shamefaced and gave no reply. But the moment the words were out of his mouth, Zorachus felt grotesquely hypocritical. He had little right to criticize. He him-

self had almost snapped, begun the bloodbath that he feared
above all else. His mind still roiled with thwarted slaughter-
lust.

God, God, he thought. *How I want to kill them all. . . .*

Returning to the house opposite the armory, they went out
the back and mounted up. The retainers formed a column
about them and the company set off.

Zorachus and Halfdan were silent all the way back to the
palace. Going directly to his room, the Sharajnaghi lay down.

Sleep proved impossible. If he was not torturing himself
for coming so close to the brink, he was remembering the
heaps of self-butchered dead. He was under siege, hemmed in
by loathsome enemies and allies hardly less loathsome, afflicted by a potent temptation to usurp God's place and wreak
a Judgment Day all his own. Yet he was also unable to do
good, powerless to mitigate the savagery in which he found
himself, trapped in a city where cruelty was taken so much for
granted that his enemies would slay themselves before they
could even be offered mercy . . . He shook his head, digging
his fingers into his scalp, almost wishing that he could rip his
skull open and let all his pent-up frustrations come exploding
forth.

No, he could not sleep. He needed to pace, or better still,
take a long solitary walk—calm himself down, drain off the
pressure building inside him, pray. Pray most of all.

He stood, considering the park; but it was too dangerous,
and being surrounded by those waxen, fulsome leaves would
only intensify his mood.

He went out into the hall, telling the guards not to follow;
finding a narrow staircase, he ascended. At the top he came
out in a vaulted corridor unused for decades; a thick layer of
dust covered the floor, matted the tapestries on the walls.
Hazy sunlight seeped through slitted windows on the right.

Praying silently, he started down the passageway. Rounding a corner, then another, he came to a stretch where the dust
had recently been disturbed. Footprints showed, shiny and
black, baring the marble floor, leading from a stairwell to an
open door. Despite the turmoil inside him, his curiosity was
piqued. He went to the door and looked inside.

Seated at a small table in a small, windowless room, a
bottle, goblet, and burning candle before him. Sharthas was
cutting grooves in the tabletop with a little knife. There was
something disquieting about the scene, as if he were a ghost

repeating some meaningless action it had been performing
when its life had ended . . .

Suddenly Sharthas looked up, saw Zorachus, and shot to
his feet, mouth sagging. Zorachus was astonished by his reaction; the steward looked like he had been caught committing a
murder.

"Why aren't you working?" Zorachus demanded, partially
for lack of anything better to say, partially because Sharthas's
behavior was so suspicious.

"Actually, sir . . . Lord Mancdaman. . . ."

Zorachus went to the table. It was old and splintery, top
scarred with carved initials and dozens of Sharthas's grooves,
each of which ended in a deft, tightly cut curve.

Sharthas saw Zorachus looking at them and said, "It's a
habit of mine, a little twitch. The table was so old, I assumed
no one would mind. . . ."

"Why aren't you working?" Zorachus asked again.

"I've already fulfilled my morning rounds," Sharthas said
and gulped. "Most of them, anyway. . . . Things are well in
hand . . . I just thought I'd have a nip." He nodded toward the
bottle.

"Why did you sneak all the way up here? Feeling guilty?"

Sharthas nodded, "I feel guilty about everything."

"I see," Zorachus said, picking up the bottle, it was uncorked; he sniffed it and winced. "Couldn't you do better than
this?"

"I didn't want to take any of your good wine, and. . . ."

"Smells like pretty strong stuff."

"It is."

"Good enough," Zorachus said. He pulled up a chair and
sat. He motioned Sharthas back down. "I can use a jolt." He
took a long pull.

"If I might be so bold," Sharthas said, "is there something
the matter?"

"There is, indeed," Zorachus answered. "How long have
you been up here?"

"Ten minutes or so. I decided I needed a dose of fortitude
after Halfdan shouted at me. He was in such a foul mood,
standing at the bottom of the main stair and cursing. Did you
quarrel?"

"I was pretty sharp with him. Porchos slapped him, so
Halfdan laid hands on him. We could have both been killed.
And I almost. . . ."

"What, my Lord?"

"Never mind. Did you hear what happened to the garrison?"

Sharthas nodded. "One of the guards told me."

Zorachus took another pull. "I saw a man who'd chewed off the fingers from one of his hands. He still had a thumb hanging from his mouth. There was another who'd smashed his brains out against a wall. You'd think he would've died long before his skull opened. He must have been a very determined man. . . ." He looked at Sharthas. "There are children, insane children who mutilate themselves any way they can. You can't talk to them or reach them. They've shut themselves off from the whole universe. They're like mad animals, or worse, and all they ever seem to think about is smashing their heads against walls and gouging out their own eyes and chewing off their fingers."

There was a long pause. "Maybe they know something you don't."

"About what?"

"Themselves. Maybe they're born with a sense of justice the rest of us lack."

"I don't believe it," Zorachus answered.

"Then why do they do it?"

"I don't know."

Sharthas continued, "Of course, maybe they don't have a reason at all. Maybe they're just like the rest of us." He laughed. "People are such wretched things."

Zorachus studied the steward's seamed, weary face. "You've been in Khymir too long."

"Long enough," Sharthas agreed. "But I can't help thinking we're all Khymirians inside."

"You think I'm like that?" Zorachus asked—and immediately, almost gloatingly reminded himself of his own bloodlust, and his yearning for another man's wife. . . .

"You might be an exception," Sharthas said. "You seem to be a decent sort. But at the risk of being insubordinate. . . ."

"Go on."

"You're only human, my Lord. And you must have come to Khymir for *something*. Considering what this city has to offer . . ."

"I hate Khymir," Zorachus broke in.

"So do I," Sharthas answered. "But we both stay, don't we? We could go if we really wanted to."

Zorachus leaned forward. *"You* can go. I'll give you gold, all you can take. Leave and never look back."

Sharthas gave a watery smile. "Very generous of you. And what about my lovely black whore?"

"Leave her," Zorachus said.

"You make it sound very easy. But I want her more than anything else in the world. I have to stay to get what I want."

"You can change that," Zorachus pressed. "Force yourself to see what she's doing to you."

"I don't have to force myself. The fact that I'm her willing slave is always before me. It only deepens my conviction that I should be enslaved."

"Drivel," Zorachus snapped.

"Yes," Sharthas said meekly. "It is drivel. If I had an ounce of brains or nerve I wouldn't lend myself to the farce. I'd kill myself. But since I can't do that, I must soothe my conscience the best I can."

"By debasing yourself further?"

"By destroying myself by inches—the only suicide a coward like me would ever attempt."

"But why not try to be cured?" Zorachus asked. "Leave Khymir. Go to Thangura, to Qanar-Sharaj. The Order that raised me has many wise and holy men. They'd try to help you. . . ."

"I don't deserve help."

"What did you do to deserve annihilation?"

"The same as everyone else. I was born."

"Do you really think we're all damned from birth? That we have no free will?"

Sharthas smiled again. "Of course we do. We know exactly what we're doing, what our choices are. And in the end, we fall. Nothing makes us fall. But we always do."

"How do you know?" Zorachus demanded.

"How, my Lord? I've lived in Khymir these past twenty years. Can you tell me that such a sty could exist if human beings weren't rotten at the core?"

"Then why isn't every city like Khymir?"

"How do you know they're not? Do you really know what other people are like behind closed doors? Snot-eaters and scab-pickers, rubbing themselves on beds and reaching into their pants and thinking vile thoughts?" He paused. "How many times have you thought of stabbing your best friend?"

"I don't know what you're talking about," Zorachus said.

Even for a man in Khymir, he was sweating profusely.

"Maybe you don't, my Lord," Sharthas conceded. "Maybe you're made of steel."

"Would it make you happier to know I had such thoughts?"

"Nothing would make me happier," Sharthas replied. "Knowing you were like me would only convince me further that the world is as I see it. Knowing that you're not would only make me see how much more wretched I was."

Zorachus felt cornered. "You're talking nonsense."

"Of course. Everything is nonsense."

The Sharajnaghi realized the futility of argument. Still, the instinctive reply rose to his lips: "Even saying that everything is nonsense?"

Sharthas stood up. "There's a fly on your sleeve," he said, pointing.

Zorachus looked at his sleeve. There was no fly.

And Sharthas was gone.

chapter

17

IN THE WEEKS that followed, Zorachus was attacked eight times by sendings. He destroyed them all with small cost to himself or his followers; but he took scant comfort. He knew the Priesthood would not relent no matter how many of their demons he conquered, and there was ever a gnawing dread at the back of his mind.

During the same period, three Chief Guildsmen were killed. The first was silently flayed by a demon in his bed, the next torn to pieces by a being that materialized beside him in his armored palanquin. Shortly after the second's death, the Priesthood slipped men into Guild territory to post promises of more assassinations and offers of rewards for deeds done in the priestly cause. The Guild responded with counterthreats and counteroffers, and held a public demonstration of the deadlier sorcerous arts, in which three Guild wizards executed several dozen "traitors" in various hideous ways. Marmaros Maranchthus presided over the affair, extolling the Guild's might and ferocity.

Next morning, he was found squashed like a wad of clay into a ceiling corner of his bath chamber.

The Guild, meanwhile, had had little success with its own sendings, one reason being that Zorachus took no part in them, even though he was asked repeatedly; Sharajnaghim were not permitted to use conjured beings for any purposes other than training, immediate self-defense, or immediate protection of others. The Order's Divine Dispensation was strictly limited in regard to demons, and non-demonic entities were not to be endangered except in the direst need. But Zorachus never explained any of that to the Guildsmen, giving excuses based on the Influences. He knew they knew he was lying, but they would have thought the same if he told them the truth,

226

and taken insult as well. They were not fools. After a time they simply stopped requesting such help from him. And the failures of their wizards continued to mount.

Yet in matters other than sendings, the Guild had much success, and Zorachus, to a large degree, was responsible. He was the linchpin in several spectacular victories, actions that crushed major troop strikes from the north. And most important of all, with his speeches and public appearances and tracts, he kept the Guild cause popular. Finding it necessary to go beyond simply attacking the Priesthood (his audience already knew what the priests were like, and were easily bored) he managed, without ever explicitly describing anything of the sort, to conjure up images of a new golden age, a time of unending orgies and bloody games that would spring into existence the instant the priesthood fell. Never once did he actually lie; the Khymirians, so adept at self-deception, supplied themselves with all the falsehoods necessary. Still he loathed the charade. He was, after all, the instigator, if not the author, of so much untruth. And he had to spend so much time trying to think like a Khymirian, trying to guess what turns of phrase would best deceive a degenerate . . . whenever he finished writing a speech or pamphlet, he felt covered in slime.

But behind the walls of Mother Khymir there was little he could do that did not give him that feeling. He hated his dealings with the Guild. He hated dealing with his own household, most of whom were Khymirians or foreigners sunk in Khymirian ways; he could hardly walk from his room to the palace's front gate without seeing one obscenity after another. He tried, through Sharthas, to keep the staff in rein, but when it came to their pleasures they would not be restrained; the coupling bodies seemed like fixtures in the halls and parlors, and the air grew stale with the odor of lubricants, genitals, and sweat. Whenever he was not out on Guild errands, he kept more and more to his own chamber, with the Kragehul his only company.

They were the strongest anchor his mind possessed, but even so, he knew his friendship with them was growing ever more tainted, spoiling in the throbbing Khymirian heat. The closer he drew to them, the more he wanted Asa, the more he betrayed Halfdan in his thoughts; and he could not resist seizing every chance to more deeply fall in love. More than once, when Halfdan turned in early, Zorachus stayed up late into the night with Asa, listening to Kragehul myths, telling her of his faith and his God. Then his eyes would linger on her face and he would feel a strange mixture of exaltation and guilt; but the exaltation always deserted him when she left. Often too anguished to sleep, he told himself that his feelings were corrupt, that he should never allow himself to be alone with her, that all his furtive joy must end. But whenever he was with her he could not control his emotions; he could not refuse her if she offered to stay with him. And, though he prayed desperately for the strength to stifle his love for her, he slipped farther and farther into the honeyed web.

Eyes blank, jaw sagging, the young novice lay panting atop Sathaswentha, bearing her long muscular legs on his shoulders. Sathaswentha gazed up at him, feasting on the drained idiocy of his face. With one last deep thrust, he finished.

"Get off," she said, smiling contemptuously.

He obeyed. She sat on the edge of the bed. He stroked her back weakly. Laughing, she stood, went to a basin and washed herself. Her robes were slung over a chair nearby; rapidly she slipped them on, stepped into her shoes, and changed sex.

"Must you leave?" the acolyte asked.

"I've duties in the main chapel," Sathaswenthar replied. "Get dressed and go."

"Did you enjoy yourself?"

"After a fashion, yes."

A look of listless puzzlement cross the acolyte's face. "What do you mean?"

"That we weren't enjoying the same things."

"Ah, of course," the novice said, completely misunderstanding him. He began to rub himself slowly against the sheet, clenching and unclenching his sweat-glistening buttocks. "Would you like *me* to play the woman?"

"I'm *done* with you," Sathaswenthar said, voice keen with menace.

The novice gulped. Rising, he dressed and left hurriedly. Sathaswenthar followed him into the hallway, shutting the door and locking it. Watching the fleeing novice, he recalled what it had been like to lie with the young fool. It had been a particularly edifying experience; the man had a passion for clumsy positions, and his body was a gushing wellspring of sweat and slime. They were a most ludicrous sight in the mirror, twined knots of blood-purpled flesh, wallowing and squatting ... it would be very useful to summon up images of their lovemaking during meditations on the baseness of flesh. He would not recall the delicious sensations, of course; he would not remember how he had sunk several times to the novice's brutish level, losing all control. He would take only what was useful from the experience, refuse to admit to himself that he had taken any sensual pleasure, stifle all suspicion that his frenzied couplings had not moved him any closer to True Spirituality. Tchernobog had set His seal upon the Way of Sensuality, the affirmation of organic vileness through experience of the organic; who was he, Sathaswenthar, to question it?

Hearing footsteps behind him, Sathaswenthar turned; another novice stood before him.

"My Lord," the man said, "His Anointed Steward wishes to see you in his quarters."

Sathaswenthar nodded. The novice swept off.

Sathaswenthar went swiftly to Kletus's chambers. Lysthragon was with the High Priest.

"There you are," Kletus said as Sathaswenthar arrived. "Good news."

"About what?"

"We've established a contact in the Mancdaman palace."

Sathaswenthar clapped his hands together. "Splendid. Will you have Zorachus poisoned?"

Kletus shook his head. "He's too well protected by food-tasters."

"Stabbed?"

"That's out, too. Our man isn't suicidal. No: I think it would be better if we had Zorachus eliminate himself."

"And how can we get him to do that?" Sathaswenthar asked.

"Our agent's apparently a keen observer of human beings," Kletus began. "He's certain Zorachus is infatuated with his bodyguard's wife. Zorachus won't sleep with her, but he's passionately attached to her nonetheless."

"Why won't he sleep with her?"

"*Because* she's his bodyguard's wife. He thinks there's some kind of sacred bond between married people."

Sathaswenthar's face registered numb amazement. "What?"

"Zorachus is *insane*," Lysthragon said, distorting his face with his fingers, turning his back to Sathaswenthar. Jerking his head around, he looked over his shoulder like a demented owl. "In-sane."

"Incredible as it might seem," Kletus said, "he really does believe some of those Sharajnaghi sham teachings. But not all of them, evidently; he's still trying to usurp my power. And he must be destroyed."

"Granted," Sathaswenthar said. "But how?"

Kletus smiled. "By kidnapping the girl."

Sathaswenthar mulled it over. "We could get all sorts of concessions, I suppose, but. . . ."

"We don't want concessions," Kletus answered.

"What then? Do you really think he'd exchange himself for her?"

"I doubt that he's *that* crazy," Kletus said. "But we might let him think he could save her and escape in the bargain. Suppose her abductors left some kind of trail. And suppose it led into the lowest levels of the catacombs. Several thousand Shreeth would be able to deal with him, don't you think?"

Sathaswenthar nodded. "But why go to such effort? If he follows the trail, we could simply ambush him."

Kletus shook his head. "He's too powerful—and lucky."

Sathaswenthar shrugged. "Eventually his luck'll run out, and then it won't matter how powerful he is."

"We can't count on that."

"We could make sure he passes between two houses full of crossbowmen. How could he escape?"

"I've already made up my mind," Kletus answered.

But Sathaswenthar was unwilling to let it rest. "Why is it necessary to use the Shreeth?" he demanded.

Kletus made no answer.

"Well, if he's going down into the catacombs, surely we can try to attack him on the way."

"No."

"Lysthragon," Sathaswenthar said, "what do you think of all this?"

Lysthragon giggled and turned once more. He was chewing something; when he gulped it down and showed his teeth in a monkeylike grin, they were stained green.

"If Lord Kletus has made his mind up, what can we do?" he asked.

"Nothing," Kletus said.

Sathaswenthar scrutinized the High Priest. "What is it that you're not telling us?"

"Nothing," Kletus replied, "save that I've been—how shall I say it—inspired. And no matter how much you try to dissuade me, I'll remain convinced of my inspiration. Don't you remember when we turned on Ordog? All the times I ignored your well-thought-out plans and relied solely on my own genius? When the Voice speaks to me, I listen."

"That's all very well," Sathaswenthar said. "But surely our only goal is to see Zorachus killed. And surely we'd increase our chances if we posted men to shoot him."

"It's not necessary," Kletus answered.

"You know," Sathaswenthar said thickly, "your 'Voice' advised us to bring Zorachus back to Khymir."

"That's true," Kletus replied, unfazed. "And Zorachus did touch off this war. I must have misinterpreted. But if the war results, as I believe it will, in the final annihilation of the Guild, he'll have served my purpose well enough. My Providence is mysterious in its workings, I admit. But have faith. All will be well."

But Sathaswenthar could summon no faith. He sensed that something was badly awry and apprehension gripped him; as sometimes happened when he was under stress, he began to change rapidly from sex to sex.

Kletus watched the transformations for a few moments, knowing well what they signified.

"Fool," he growled. "Leave me."

Sathaswentha-Sathaswenthar turned and strode away, thinking a crossbowman or two might be stationed anyway.

The sunset was red as a live coal, silhouetting the western thunderclouds; threatening shadow-shapes of men and monsters reared against the last light. Slowly, the crimson glow died and the sky purpled, deepening to black, shrouding Khymir in night.

Zorachus was in Halfdan's room. Dead to the world, Asa lay on the bed; she had been drinking too much lately and had had a great deal of wine at dinner. Zorachus had helped Halfdan carry her upstairs.

"Can't say I blame her," Zorachus said, weary and slightly sick. He also had drunk too much, and felt as if he were sweating to death inside a soggy blanket like a man stricken with fever. The touch of Asa's flesh had only added to the heat.

"I know what you mean," Halfdan said. "It's getting so that all I'd like to do is sleep."

Zorachus smiled in grim sympathy. "Blot the whole world out?"

"Just this damn city. Did you see those girls in the hall-way?"

Zorachus shook his head.

"They were in one of the niches. Looked like a snake eating its own tail."

"We could have our meals up here," Zorachus suggested. "We wouldn't have to bother with the outside any more than necessary. . . ."

You sound just like Kletus, he told himself—and thrust the thought aside.

"I don't think I could stand it," Halfdan said. "Would you really like to have those food-tasters crowding about in our rooms? I'd like to think there are places in this palace that are still ours." He looked sidelong at Zorachus. "What do you think of those people, anyway?"

"They're necessary," Zorachus said.

"Even so, they give me the shivers."

"Why them in particular?"

"Haven't you ever watched them? They enjoy their work. They stand around waiting to die of poison, and they enjoy it. That look they get on their faces. . . . Gorm's hammer, I'm glad they don't go near my food or Asa's. Most of the time I can ignore them, but if they were always close by. . . ."

Zorachus shrugged. "I guess I'm not as sensitive about it as you are. I spend my time wondering when one of them is going to drop."

"That damned ritual," Halfdan went on. "First one tries the dainties. Then another tries the wine, and a third tries the meat. . . ."

"Enough," Zorachus broke in. "I'd rather not think of them at all."

"What *would* you rather think about?" There was the hint of an edge in Halfdan's voice; Zorachus wondered if he were finally feeling the strain of their perpetual company.

"Asa's garden." the Sharajnaghi replied. "I think I'll go out and see how it's doing."

Halfdan snorted. "You and those plants."

Zorachus headed for the balcony, picking up a lamp. "Care to join me?"

Halfdan said nothing. Zorachus went out by the garden. The lamplight fell on rows of green, climbing vines, the only wholesome plants he had ever seen in Khymir. He thought of the dome at Qanar-Sharaj—the sea of leaves; a telling memory of the fresh green smell pierced his hazebound mind.

He stood beside the garden for what might have been a minute or an hour. Then a loud knocking and Sharthas's muffled voice brought him back to Khymir. Off in the distance, thunder rolled.

Leaving the lamp on the garden rim, he went back into the room. Halfdan opened the door. Sharthas looked terrified.

"Lord Mancdaman!" he cried, waving his arms.

"What's the matter?" Zorachus demanded.

"There's a giant beetle in the kitchen!" the steward squawked. "It bit one of the cooks!"

Zorachus and Halfdan, followed him downstairs, trailed by the doorwardens.

Four feet long, the beetle was horned and studded, standing motionless on its jointed legs, chitin shining, antennae poised. Guards clustered by the doors, watching it. The kitchen help had cleared out.

Zorachus slipped the rings on. "Get back from those doorways, everyone!" he commanded. As if startled by his voice, the insect flinched, and began to emit a piercing whine. Then it spread its wings and whirred through the air, straight at him.

Demon-bolts crackled, and the beetle exploded. Bits of chitin and yellow blood spattered the floor and tables nearby —and vanished.

"So much for that," Zorachus said, wondering why his foes had dispatched such a useless sending.

As he started back for the stairs, several breathless retainers rushed up; a small demon had appeared in one of the armories. He went with them and killed it, but it was not long before yet another minor sending was reported.

"I think I'd better go up and stay with Asa," Halfdan told the Sharajnaghi. "Something might appear in our room."

"Go on," Zorachus said, and went to deal with the third demon. For the better part of an hour, he blasted man-sized toads, crabs, and bats all over the first floor of the palace. Guessing they were only a prelude, he expected something more dangerous would appear any moment. But it never did.

Finally, the materialization stopped. Returning the rings to their pouch, he went back up to the Kragehul's room with the doorwardens.

Fear flooded his mind as he entered, He cried out; the guards rushed in.

Halfdan lay sprawled on the floor. His eyes were closed, but he was breathing. The bed was empty. Asa was nowhere to be seen.

"Try to bring Halfdan round," Zorachus told the doorwards and went over to the bed. A trail of red drops led from it out onto the balcony, which was still faintly lit by the lamp he had left on the garden's rim. He followed the trail to the railing, which was liberally splashed; two grappling hooks clutched the marble and thin silken ropes dangled over the side. Torchlight from a window bathed the flags below. Even from the second story, red spots were visible.

He turned. Something in Asa's garden caught his eye—most of the plants had been rooted up, ripped apart. He hardly knew whether to laugh or shriek.

He went back into the room. Halfdan had regained his senses and was up on his knees, shaking his head groggily.

"Did you find Asa?" he asked Zorachus.

"She's been captured," Zorachus said. "What happened to you?"

"There was a man in here," Halfdan answered. "He shut the door behind me and I turned. He had some of Asa's jewelry, the necklaces I bought her the other day. Must've stayed behind to do some thieving. . . . When I saw him I went for my sword, but he was too fast. Caught me with a kick, right in the side of the face. . . ." The Kragehul got to his feet, wobbling.

"Can you walk?"

"I'll do more than that," Halfdan snarled. "I'll be ready to split skulls in a minute. They took my wife."

And my love, Zorachus thought, burning with the same rage. Indeed, splitting the bastards' skulls would hardly satisfy him; for a moment he saw himself wrenching his sword out of a shattered brow and licking the blood off the edge.

Enough, fool, his conscience cried.

"Come with me," he said, Halfdan and the retainers followed him over to the droplet trail. "See those red spots?"

"You think it's Asa's blood?" Halfdan asked.

"I don't think it's blood at all—color's too bright. It's a

deliberately laid trail. We're supposed to follow it."

"And we will, won't we?" Halfdan growled.

Zorachus nodded. "Of course. And whoever stole Asa knew we would. They had this all worked out. They must have an ambush set up . . ." He paused. "Asa must've been drugged at dinner. It would be hard to get at me with all those tasters and watchers, but *she* wasn't protected."

"Who could've done it?" Halfdan asked, rubbing his bruised cheek, standing more steadily every second.

"I don't know. But there's no use worrying about that now." Zorachus looked at the doorwardens. "Tell Shartas that Halfdan and I are going to get Asa back." He took his rings back out.

"Only the two of you my Lord?" one of the guards asked.

Zorachus put the rings on. "We'll move faster that way. And quieter."

"Come on," Halfdan said. "She might not have long to live."

If she's still alive at all, Zorachus thought.

They went out on the balcony, climbed over the side. As they lighted on the flags, Zorachus muttered a spell that sent a shaft of white light stabbing from his left palm, and they raced off down the stone path leading into the park, following the droplets, plunging along under the trees. Reaching the park's western exit, they found the gate flung wide, and paused.

"I wonder what happened to the guards here?" Halfdan asked.

"They're probably somewhere in the bushes," Zorachus answered, "grinning ear to ear."

He leaned out, looked right, then left along the street. It was small and empty, brooding with the wartime hush. Torches guttered in wallset sockets, and the red drops were plainly visible on the cobbles, leading south.

"I've a thought," Halfdan said. "What if they've split up? What if the ones leaving the trail don't have Asa at all?"

"That occurred to me," Zorachus said. "But what can we do?"

Halfdan laughed sardonically. "Trust them."

They slipped through the gate running as silently as possible, Zorachus holding his glowing hand under his tunic—the light was unnecessary now and would have been a potential warning to enemies. But it was still available at an instant's notice.

They passed one ominous looking alley mouth after another, wondering what darkness might conceal, hearts pounding in their throats. Silent, closed doors loomed threateningly, shadowed beneath overhanging lintels, promising to burst open any moment in a flood of attackers.

When are they going to spring the trap? Zorachus thought. *What are we blundering into?*

A dark shape lurched out of an archway; the Sharajnaghi nearly blasted it before he realized it was only an old man. Zorachus barked a nervous laugh, almost wishing that it had been an ambusher, that the suspense was over and the killing could begin. . . . Blinking stupidly, the old man sat down, crooning to himself. They dashed on. More alleyways, more doors flashed by, where would the attack come from?

Up ahead, Zorachus noticed two dark, unshuttered windows in houses opposite each other. That was strange—every other window he had seen was closed up tight.

Pulling his hand from his shirt, he beamed light into the opening on the right. A crossbowman stood there, weapon raised. Dazzled by the glare, he loosed his bolt prematurely. It sang by Zorachus's ear; the Sharajnaghi ducked reflexively and a second bolt, from the other house, barely missed his head.

As the arbalesters tried to reload, he stopped, flinging his arms out. Demon lightning flared. Bodies rocked back from the windows and smoke billowed out into the night.

Zorachus nearly raised a howl of triumph—but bottled it within.

"Let's just hope Kletus doesn't have any more ambushes planned," he said as Halfdan came up beside him. They started forward once more.

After a time the street wound to the west and narrowed, becoming a mere crevice between scabrous, dank facades. It brought them to a small square, where a slender stone booth, keystone carved into a skull, reared up from the cobbles, black doorway yawning like the mouth of a giant serpent. The droplets led into the darkness.

Zorachus went to the entrance. A strong charnel smell rose in his nostrils, borne by a warm, damp wind. He sent a beam of light down into the murk. A long stairway was revealed, plunging steeply, endlessly, its walls covered with grey mold and trickling with greenish rivulets. The steps were worn and slippery looking, clearly marked with red spots.

"I wish I'd worn my armor," Halfdan said.

"Do you have any idea where these steps lead?" Zorachus asked.

"Down to the catacombs," Halfdan said. "Porchos told you about them, remember? When you asked about Lazarak?"

"Lazarak," Zorachus said, almost under his breath, remembering the tale of a murdered general transformed into a dragon in his tomb. Despite the heat, a chill swept the Sharajnaghi.

"What in hell do those bastards have in mind?" Halfdan asked.

"Who knows? In we go."

chapter

18

SLOWLY, THEY HEADED down the steps. Footing was treacherous and they almost fell several times. Large spiders and loathsome, spiny insects scuttled out of their way. Glowing worms dropped on them from above, squealing like tiny babies if trod upon. Scaly tails jerked into holes as the men approached. At one point, Zorachus spotted a small rag doll, stained and tattered, lying on the steps below, and got close enough to see that there were several nails driven into the head; then a rat stuck its snout from a crack, snatched up the doll's leg in its mouth, and yanked the toy from sight.

The stairs plunged down and down. The air grew heavier with the smell of decay. Nodules appeared on the walls, fist-sized fungus domes, looking uncannily like small, repulsive imp faces. When brushed, they burst, green muck vomiting from their "mouths," its sour stench contesting the sweet death odor.

"Tell me, Zorachus," Halfdan said wiping a spattered hand on his trews, "did your God create these filthy quats?"

"I expect so," Zorachus replied. "But Tchernobog must've made some changes somewhere along the line."

"You've got an answer for everything, haven't you?"

"No. You just always ask the right questions."

Uncomfortable with his own glibness, Zorachus continued in his mind: *Why don't you ask who made Tchernobog? Or why God gave him the power to act contrary to His will?*

They reached the bottom, coming out in a chamber so low they could barely stand upright. The walls were pierced with many round mouths, entrances to tunnels and stairwells, and there were holes in the ceiling as well, with rotting rope ladders hanging out. A steady stream of the glowing worms poured from one of the ceiling openings, and a teeming mound of them had collected beneath.

238

Feeling the demon-ring beginning to eat into his flesh, the Sharajnaghi changed ring fingers as he and Halfdan, breaking into a jog, followed the trail into a passage on the right. The tunnel was lined with niches; tiers of moldering bodies rose to the ceiling. The linen swathing the corpses was darkly stained —even with embalming, bodies did not keep well in the heat and damp. Here and there a slime-covered skull, phosphorescent vapors drifting from its eyesockets, grinned out at Zorachus and Halfdan as they passed; pools of black ooze gleamed on the charnel shelves. The smell was horrific, as most of the corpses were fairly new—there was apparently a swift turnover among occupants of the niches. Bones, skulls, and linen wrappings littered the floor.

The droplet trail led straight ahead for several hundred yards, then veered to the left, going down another flight of steps into a great, serpentine hall. Here the dead were better preserved in niches faced with thick, all-but-unbreakable glass; the bodies often seemed quite pristine, neatly bandaged bundles with hardly a spot of fluid. The stone around some of the niches was intricately carven and there were nameplates of engraved iron. Soon individual sarcophagi began to appear, finely worked adamantine cases; the coffins became more and more fabulous, their transparent sides supported by slender metal dragons and floral work.

As the richness of the tombs increased, so did the skill of the embalmers. Soon there were no cerements to be seen; naked corpses, their flesh as pink as life, met the eye. In some instances there were even two or three bodies in a single coffin, placed in natural looking coital positions, mouths sagging with soundless moans, glass eyes rolling in simulated passion. There were also pets among the dead—monkeys, snakes, and cats, lamias and other hybrids, bizarre creatures with bits of human anatomy, usually sexual, set among parts wholly alien; often these too were coitally entwined with human corpses. In one coffin was a nude woman, perfectly preserved, legs wrapped around a human-headed crocodile.

Zorachus and Halfdan paused to rest, but continued on their way after a scant few minutes, goaded as much by the horror of their surroundings as eagerness to find Asa. They descended more levels; Zorachus, hands burning, changed ring fingers several times. Finally, in spite of the risk, he put the rings away.

They passed through a huge echoing chamber half-a-mile long, filled with cyclopean tombs warded by stone demons thirty feet high; they skirted gaping pits filled with dust and bones, where the ancient, anonymous poor mingled; they stumbled through the rubble of a partially ruined chapel dedicated to a grisly maggot-god—a gigantic figure of the worm deity arched over the crumbling altar, blind face gnawing a stone infant. Smaller maggots had been carved all along the length of the statue, tunneling in and out.

After three hours, deep beneath the streets of Khymir, the Sharajnaghi and Kragehul reached the brink of a vertical shaft five feet wide. A series of rungs, splotched with red and set close together, led down the side of the shaft. Zorachus stabbed a beam of light into the gloom below. There were tunnel mouths at odd intervals beside the rungs, but he could not see the bottom of the shaft.

They started down. Small and hard to grasp, the holds made for a nerveracking descent—they did not seem designed for human hands.

Hundreds of yards into the shaft, Zorachus and Halfdan alighted in a tunnel to rest, flexing their fingers—then took to the rungs once more.

Soon they came to a hole wider than the others; the red drops led over its threshold. This tunnel was thickly coated with mold, and yard-long curtains of nitrate hung from its ceiling; the occupants of its niches had rotted away completely. Heaps of broken stone marked numerous cave-ins, and there were many cracks in the floor and walls, some tiny, some a foot wide. The size of the cracks increased the farther in Zorachus and Halfdan pressed, and the rubble piles grew larger, one finally blocking the passage; there the trail turned to the left, down an adjoining passage. At first glance, this tunnel looked likewise obstructed a short distance ahead, but the trail led up over the rubble, toward the hole in the ceiling left by the collapse. Climbing up and over the scree, they followed the droplets to an open doorway, through which came a slowly pulsating, yellow light, and an intermittent roar.

"What do you think's making that sound?" Halfdan asked quietly.

"Sounds like a sleeping . . ." Zorachus stopped dead, realizing what he was about to say.

Halfdan gave an uneasy laugh. "Doesn't it, now?"

They reached the doorway and there they halted, filled with dread.

The floor before them sagged in a vast depression, a crater walled with cinders and crushed rock. At the bottom slept a titanic, golden-scaled dragon, neck curled to one side. Its head was flanked with curving horns; wrinkled leathery pinions were folded across its back. Roaring yellow flame jetted from its nose as it breathed, and there were many small fires about it, bubbling fumaroles of molten rock.

"Lazarak of the Golden Mail," Halfdan said in hushed tones.

Zorachus nodded, awestruck by the dragon's size. Lazarak was the largest creature he had ever seen. The serpent Zathlan had been longer, perhaps, but nowhere near as massive. The Sharajnaghi asked:

"Didn't Porchos say that Lazarak tries to smash his way out when he wakes?"

"Yes," Halfdan answered, "That must be where all this rubble came from."

"I see now why all those surrounding tunnels collapsed."

"Let's hope we don't wake him."

"Let's *pray.*"

"Should I pray to *my* gods?"

"If you think it will work, by all means."

Zorachus eyed the trail. It led out over the sloping debris, well lit by the dragon fires. He started to put his luminous hand into his shirt, realized he would probably need it for balance, and revoked the light spell. He and Halfdan went out onto the rubble, following the droplets around the rim of the depression. They moved slowly, planting their feet with extreme caution, trying to disturb the stones and cinders as little as possible.

Lazarak slept on.

After forty-five minutes, they neared a half-crumbled doorway, towards which the trail pointed. Halfdan pulled ahead of Zorachus, gaining the opening first. Fifteen feet behind, the Sharajnaghi sped up unconsciously, recklessness creeping into his movements.

Stones shifted; the scree gave way beneath him. In a rattling shower of rock fragments and pulverized slag, he rolled down the slope at breakneck speed, dust billowing about him.

Bruised and bleeding, he came to a half-buried halt barely five feet from one of Lazarak's outstretched front claws. The

Sharajnaghi lay completely motionless, wondering if those excruciating aches were from broken bones. His dizzy gaze was riveted on Lazarak's face.

To his horror, the horned head began to turn and a great, red eye cracked open. But exactly at that moment, a fresh slide of small stones came rattling down over Zorachus's head and shoulders, burying him completely.

He did not breathe, not even knowing if he could. He held his breath until his mind reeled—then exhaled slowly. The stones were loose, and there was air tasting of soot and slate.

He remained under the debris for several minutes, then gradually lifted his head. The stones falling off seemed to make all the noise in the world, but Lazarak, slumbering once more, took no notice. He had only stirred in his sleep; it took more than a minor slide to rouse him.

Zorachus raised himself on one elbow and felt for the ring pouch. It was still around his neck. He looked back up the slant. Halfdan was near the doorway, peering down at him.

Working his way out of the stones, the Sharajnaghi limped back by Lazarak's tail, as far away from the dragon's hooded eye as possible, before starting up the slope.

The loose tumulus all but denied him purchase; gaining even a few yards was frustrating and exhausting labor, and it sometimes seemed he slid back two for every three he climbed. But, fixing his mind on Asa, he clawed numbly upwards, forcing himself to the top. There he stood a while, working his bruised arms.

Across the chamber, Halfdan beckoned impatiently, Zorachus started circling back toward him.

Slowly his movements grew clumsier and clumsier. His battered muscles were cramping, and he almost slipped twice. Stride by agonizing stride, he dragged himself along the rim of the crater, collapsing at last on the door's threshold. Halfdan pulled him in.

"How badly are you hurt?" Halfdan said.

"Nothing serious, I think," Zorachus said. "I've got to rest a bit. . . ." Setting his back against the tunnel wall, he closed his eyes.

Instantly, Halfdan was on him, shaking him violently.

"Stay awake," the Kragehul snarled. "We've got to find Asa."

Zorachus nodded dazedly. Halfdan yanked him to his feet.

"Can you walk?" the Kragehul demanded.

Zorachus nodded again.

"Light your hand back up and we'll be off."

Zorachus complied, and they started down the tunnel, jumping cracks, climbing piles of rubble. Summoning hidden reserves of strength, Zorachus pushed his body mercilessly. *We've got to find Asa*, he told himself again and again. Eventually, the aches went numb and the cramps worked themselves out. He took a grim satisfaction in the machinelike rise and fall of his legs. Impatient, Halfdan began to trot; Zorachus kept pace.

The trail took many twists and turns, in and out of dozens of tunnels, descending steadily into regions where niches had never been carved into the stone, leading at last to the bank of a slow, dark river. A final splotch of red had been placed on the left side of the passage mouth, the downstream side.

Zorachus leaned out over the water, searching the tunnel's walls with his hand-beam. There were no ledges to follow. Pulling out his sword, he knelt, thrusting it down into the warm water. His arm went in to the elbow before the blade point connected with a hard bottom.

"It's not too deep," he said pulling the sword out. Looking back at Halfdan, he wiped it on his trousers and resheathed it. "Not by the edge at least. They probably carried her."

"I don't think so," Halfdan replied, pointing to an eyebolt in the wall set back several feet from the bank. "I'd wager they had a boat tied up here."

"But *we'll* have to wade," Zorachus said and climbed over the side, Halfdan following. They headed downstream, the current's warmth a great relief to Zorachus's battered legs.

He and Halfdan slogged forward for what might have been an hour, eventually reaching a large, runneled grotto. Several mouths opened on it; the nearest, a crawlspace, was well above the waterline and fronted by a tongue of sloping, greyish rock. On the stony projection, a small boat was drawn up.

They made over to the craft. It was empty. And no droplet trail led away from it.

"Maybe they ran out of dye," Zorachus said.

"Maybe they didn't come down in the boat at all." Suddenly Halfdan cocked his head to one side. "Did you hear anything?"

"No," Zorachus answered, beaming light over the entrance of the crawlspace.

"Something like splashing?"

Zorachus shook his head, face dimly grey-lit by the reflection from the stone. "If they didn't come down in the boat," he said slowly, "if they let it drift down with the current, and left by another route, then who pulled the boat out of the wa—"

"*Shhh!*" Halfdan hissed. "Listen!"

Zorachus listened. This time he heard it, faint but distinct, coming from one of the tunnel mouths. He took the rings out again and put them on.

"*Shreeth*," Halfdan said.

"The creatures that live under the catacombs," the Sharajnaghi said. "Are they dangerous?"

"Deadly," Halfdan answered. "They keep to themselves, but when someone intrudes. . . ."

"Now I understand," Zorachus said. "We were lured down here to be killed by them. And they have Asa."

The splashing came steadily closer.

"In we go," Zorachus said, dropping to his belly and entering the crawlspace.

"What if they come in after us?" Halfdan demanded.

"It depends on how big they are." Zorachus replied, scrabbling along the stony floor. "Are they man-sized?"

"Smaller, I think."

"Then they'll catch up to us pretty quickly—*if* they follow. They might not know we're here."

They managed to get a good way into the tunnel as the splashing grew steadily louder and louder behind them.

They're making straight for this passage, Zorachus thought. *Any second now they'll be inside—*

The sound of scuttling bodies and scratching claws swept up the tunnel.

"Here they come!" Halfdan cried.

"Lie flat!" Zorachus answered. "As flat as you can!"

Halfdan pressed himself against the floor. Zorachus backed up and twisted his head round, stabbing the light-shaft through the narrow space between Halfdan's back and the ceiling. Milky eyes gleamed and blinked in the beam, and misshapen blue-green hands shot up, warding half-glimpsed faces; but the Shreeth still scuttled forward.

Zorachus loosed a carefully aimed demon-bolt. There were shrieks like the wrenching of rusty gates, and a burst of yellow smoke, stinking like scorched pork, billowed over Half-dan.

"You burned my back!" Halfdan cried, starting up, coughing

"Keep down!" Zorachus snapped, wishing he'd had the foresight to let Halfdan go first.

Halfdan obeyed and Zorachus loosed another bolt, but there were no more shrieks, no noises of any kind; the smoke blocked his vision. Were all the Shreeth dead? Or were the survivors merely lying low?

"Come on," he said, eyes watering at the reek. They hauled themselves forward. There was no sound of pursuit.

A red-lit opening appeared in the distance. As they crawled toward it, the passage tightened; soon they felt the squeeze. Only by the most violent exertions could they progress, and Halfdan's burned back was badly scraped. At one point, it took them a minute to get six feet.

Mercifully, the tunnel widened a bit after that and they made better progress for a time. But as they neared the exit the passage tightened again. Writhing and struggling, they inched forward.

Worming through the opening, Zorachus found himself on a narrow stone bridge. It spanned a vast chasm whose walls were limned in lurid crimson; he looked over the side, a hot powerful draft sweeping his face. Five hundred feet below snaked a river of molten lava, glowing fiercely, shimmering under heat convections.

"I hear something," Halfdan said, still in the tunnel. "I think they're dragging the bodies back. . . ."

Zorachus turned. The Kragehul's head and arms emerged, but he came no further, chest and back pressed tightly against the stone.

"I'm stuck," he said. "Help me."

Zorachus grabbed his wrist. They strained and struggled for several vain minutes, then stopped to rest.

Behind Halfdan, the dragging noises continued, growing steadily more distant. The men resumed their efforts after a time but made no progress. They paused again.

The dragging stopped. Slithering sounds began. The Shreeth were coming. Fast.

Once more Halfdan and Zorachus took up the struggle, battling feverishly against the stone vise. Halfdan scraped for-

ward an inch, then two. He began to scream at the pain from
his burns. Zorachus's fingers dug powerfully into his flesh.

The Shreeth came closer and closer. Halfdan squeezed forward another half-inch, stuck fast again. He pushed with his
feet, squirmed, and fought.

"Can you use the rings?" he gritted, tears of pain and exer-
tion rolling from his eyes, face drenched with sweat. "They're
right behind me."

"There's not enough space!" Zorachus answered, pulling
with all his might. "Come on! Push!"

Halfdan kicked and strained. Zorachus's nails bit through
his skin, drawing blood. The Sharajnaghi's teeth shone white.
The slitherings and scrapings were loud now, so loud. . . .

Halfdan slipped free. Zorachus dragged him forward.

A three-fingered claw shot through the opening, grabbing
Halfdan's left ankle with tremendous power. He set his right
foot against the wall, bracing himself.

Letting one of Halfdan's arms go, Zorachus sent a demon-
bolt crackling over the Kragehul's legs, into the darkness of
the passage. The claw opened. He let Halfdan scramble past
him, loosed more bolts. Screams from the crawlspace, then
silence.

Rising, he blew on the rings, switched them to different
fingers, and headed across the bridge with Halfdan. A shadowy tunnel mouth opened on the far side, about four feet
high. As they entered, Zorachus called a halt, looking back at
the crawlspace.

Several smoking bundles, the dead Shreeth, came rolling
out through the opening and tumbled over the sides of the
bridge.

"There's so little room in that tunnel," Zorachus said.
"There could have only been one of them pushing those
bodies, maybe two . . . those things must be *strong*."

"They're strong all right," Halfdan agreed. "When that
claw grabbed me it felt like my leg was being pulled from its
socket."

Suddenly they saw a dozen or so stunted figures crawl onto
the span, rise, and come pelting across.

Zorachus stepped back out onto the bridge, assuming a
Dragon Stance. Cataract strikes knocked the Shreeth off the
span in twos and threes. More rusty-gate shrieks; black against
the molten glare. The dwarfish bodies hurtled down, catching

fire as the heat increased, striking the lava in orange spatters.

He watched the far side for a few more minutes. No more Shreeth appeared. Hunching over, he went back into the tunnel. He and Halfdan pressed on.

The floor sloped downward steadily, and the passage curved to the right, like a descending corkscrew. The curve tightened; small steps appeared. The heat intensified and the air grew stifling, developing a bitter tang. The walls began to glow with a sulphurous phosphorescence—cool light, but it seemed to add to the heat nonetheless. Zorachus extinguished his hand-beam.

They reached the bottom of the stairs. There, a cruel dilemma faced them; three dark crawlways opened in the stone. After five minutes, the decision fell to Halfdan. He paused, and then they wriggled into the left-hand hole. The squeeze was not too tight and they made good progress, coming out in a round-arched chamber tall enough for them to sit upright. There they rested, eyeing the way out—a wormhole that pierced the ceiling at a slant.

"Do you think we'll find her?" Halfdan asked.

"I don't have the slightest idea," Zorachus answered. "And even if we do, that's no guarantee we'll get out of this. It'll be a long climb back. And Kletus must've been pretty sure the Shreeth would finish us."

They sat a while in silence.

"What if she's dead?" Halfdan asked.

"No point even thinking about it."

"Oh no? What if she's dead, but *we* get out of here alive? What then?"

"What are you talking about? Revenge?"

"Yes. Will you help me? With your magic we might break into Banipal Khezach. . . ."

"No," Zorachus said.

"Why not?"

"A Sharajnaghi can't kill for revenge."

"Who gives a damn about your crazy scruples! She's my wife. I won't let her sleep unavenged."

"Halfdan, Halfdan," Zorachus said. "There's nothing I'd like better than ripping Kletus's eyes out with my own nails for what he's done to us already. But. . . ." He paused, imagining the High Priest with his sockets emptied, head jerking back and forth, blood rushing down his cheeks . . . the Sharajnaghi twitched an involuntary smile before choking off the sheer pleasure of the thought.

"But what?" Halfdan demanded.

"For all we know, she's still alive," Zorachus said wearily.

"Does that mean you'll help me if she's dead?"

"I didn't say that," Zorachus answered.

But what will my answer be when I find out? he wondered. Another silence. He felt the cramps returning.

"Let's go," he said. "I'll be stone stiff in a minute."

He looked up into the hole.

Blinking back at him was a flat, scaly face with round white eyes, its fanged grin six inches wide, impossibly manic, backswept lips lined with deep wrinkles. Before he could move, the lips fell like a moist sack over his head, tightening under his chin, they yanked his whole body up off the floor, drawing his face toward the glowing teeth. Between the fangs, a stinking crevice yawned, and his nose was almost inside when the jaws snapped convulsively shut and the slimy teeth slid harmlessly over his skin. The lips went slack and he tumbled back to the floor, gasping for breath. A silver dagger hilt jutting from its temple, the Shreeth's head nodded limply through the hole.

"Thanks," Zorachus told Halfdan, shuddering.

The Kragehul grunted something, reached up and pulled the dagger out. Green in the yellow light, blood streamed forth, and the lolling head swung horribly to and fro, distended lipsack swaying.

"Just to make sure," Zorachus said, and stuck his hand up over the corpse to fire a demon-bolt along the tunnel.

Instantly, a scaly grip locked on his wrist, jerking him up into the hole. Lacking the space to pull him past its dead cohort, the creature began to twist his arm, apparently trying to wring it off.

He loosed a bolt. Flying stone and flame stung his hand as the Shreeth let him go. Turning his fist dead-on into the tunnel, he launched a second bolt. Shrieks mingled with the echoes of the ring blast and a broad runnel of ichor sought a path beside the first Shreeth's body. Cooling the ring in the rilling gore, he switched it to another finger, shouting: "Back to the stairs!"

They crawled from the chamber. Coming out in the stairwell, they stood pondering their next move.

Stone rasped on stone. "There!" Halfdan cried, pointing. Two doors, which had been perfectly concealed in the stairwell's irregular walls, were grinding open above.

Zorachus's first thought was that he and Halfdan should retreat into one of the wormholes behind them; but they were too narrow for quick escape.

"Up the steps!" he cried, drawing his sword. Their only chance was to get *above* the Shreeth, gain the advantage of position.

"What if there's a whole hive of them up there?" Halfdan demanded.

"Come on!" Zorachus answered, but it was already too late, the Shreeth were boiling from the openings, brandishing their left hands, which were drastically elongated with fingers fused into single clawed clubs of bone. They poured down the steps like a flood.

Zorachus blasted the first five to steaming rags and others tripped over the mangled dead, but the cascade of tumbling bodies forced the humans back from the steps; retreating towards the crawlspaces, they set their backs to the wall. Club-hands flailed at them, some embedded with iron studs or spikes; sweeping his sword two-handed, Halfdan batted strokes aside and sliced through arms, sent heads flying from shoulders. Zorachus blasted with the rings, lashed out with kicks, and drove his sword through chests and faces.

For a brief, savage span they held out, but the odds against them were too great. A club-hand glanced off Halfdan's skull, and he fell. Zorachus jumped astride him, fighting furiously, but moments later the sword was knocked from his hand. He cleared a space before him with demon-bolts, flinging corpses backward. Then a Shreeth rushed up from the side and struck him down. Head ringing, the Sharajnaghi tried to rise, but they swarmed over him, hit him twice more, and began binding his limbs. He was dimly conscious of them removing his sword belt, and bursts of dull pain penetrated his hazebound mind as the creatures plucked the rings from his scorched fingers; some kind of fetid covering went over his head, and he was lifted up and borne off.

chapter

19

THE JOURNEY LASTED some time. His mind cleared, but his muscles tightened into excruciating knots—the Shreeth held him almost completely rigid and he could not flex his limbs.

The Shreeth halted in an intensely hot place, even more stifling than the stairwell. Some kind of assembly was in progress; Shreeth voices, all shrill whines and snarls and clicks, echoed back and forth. Underlying all was a steady rumble intermixed with hollow bubbling and rushing sounds.

The parley went on for what seemed an hour, at least, during which Zorachus's captors continued holding him rock still. It seemed they were incapable of fatigue.

If only they'd put me down, he thought—bound as he was, he could have assumed a position for force-letting. But as long as they kept him immobile, force-letting was impossible, and the Influences precluded any spells that could have been used without it.

Eventually, the Shreeth fell silent, and those holding him started forward again. He heard their feet clanging, as if on metal; once across the resonant surface, they went a short distance and turned, set him down at last, and retreated.

A second group clanged out, deposited something behind him—Halfdan, he guessed by the grunt—and withdrew; a third group laid another object in front of him. Some kind of complex activity followed, accompanied by shrill chanting; Zorachus was certain it was a ritual. When it ended, there was a sound like something sliding from a sack, and a thudding impact.

"Bastards!" came Asa's voice.

His heart leaped.

The covering was yanked from his head. She lay before him, bound head to foot. Her face was bruised, her upper lip swollen, her hair filthy and lank, but the mere sight of her seemed to justify all the fear and agony he had endured since setting out. Even if he died in the next few minutes, he had reached her side. She smiled ruefully at him.

The Shreeth withdrew—more clanging, then a ringing grate of metal on rock.

Asa raised herself, looking over him. "Halfdan too," she said, and sank back down. "You're a pair of idiots, but I'm glad to see you."

"A pair of idiots," Halfdan said groggily behind the Sharajnaghi. "That's a fine thing to say."

"When did you come round?" Zorachus asked Asa.

"Before Kletus's men reached the catacombs. They told me they were leaving a trail for you." She laughed. "You know, they ran into a Guild patrol seconds later. But they weren't dressed like priests' men and managed to lie their way out of it. They said I was a spy, that they were bringing me to Porchos. If only I hadn't been gagged . . ."

"When did they take it off?"

"They didn't. It was those little monsters. They saw I was beginning to choke on it. It's a pity they don't understand Khymirian. I came up with some first-rate curses."

"But they left you tied?"

She nodded.

"How did they drag you through the crawlspace? I would've thought you'd be scraped to pieces."

"They put me in a thick, hide bag. The outside of it was waxed, I think. They spilled me out of it just before they took the hoods off you and Half—"

"A pair of idiots," her husband broke in, nudging Zorachus. "After all we've been through, the first thing she does is call us a pair of idiots."

She snapped something at him in Kragehul and a vicious argument ensued, the two of them snarling back and forth over Zorachus.

Ignoring them, he flexed his limbs, fighting his cramps. Gradually, the knots of pain loosened somewhat.

He sat up slowly, looking about. They were on a small circular island of rock. To the right, separated from the island by a twenty-foot gulf, was a huge, yellow-glowing cave hollowed from the side of a redlit cliff face. A metallic gangway lay by the edge of the cliff, obviously what the Shreeth had used going to and from the island. Some fifty feet beyond the gangway was a great crowd of prostrate Shreeth, chanting in low, rasping voices, brows pressed against the rock.

To the left stretched a vast lake of molten lava; Zorachus guessed it was at least a hundred yards below the surface on which he sat. The lava seethed in spots, sending up incandescent geysers, but was covered with a shiny black crust elsewhere. The molten lake was hemmed by sheer precipices, and islands of black stone reared up from the liquid rock. One of these, directly in the middle, was carved into a frowning stone face hundreds of feet tall. It was grim and angular, with heavy hooded eyes.

Zorachus lay back down, wormed his way around the rim of the island. It proved to be the crown of a smooth-sided pillar of rock. Crimson and saffron fires swirled three hundred feet below.

He rested. Next to him lay his sword, sheathed; the demon-rings had been placed on the scabbard. Halfdan's sword and dagger, also sheathed, were nearby. A ritual circle of metallic powder had been drawn about the weapons.

He looked back at the Shreeth. They were still prostrate, still chanting.

"Why did they put us out here?" Halfdan asked. He and Asa had settled their differences and were sitting up now. Asa gazed wistfully at him, tears in her eyes. A bitter pang of jealousy stung Zorachus.

"We're sacrifices," the Sharajnaghi answered, looking away from them. "That's why they took us alive. That idol in the lava must be their god. They laid us and our weapons here as an offering."

"But what are they going to *do* with us?" Halfdan asked. "Just let us starve, or stifle to death?"

"It's getting hard for me to breathe," Asa put in. "With the heat and these ropes. . . ."

"Think you can last a bit longer?" Zorachus asked.

"What do you have in mind?"

"Getting us untied, at least."

Working himself into position for force-letting, he tightened his concentration, generated two shields from his palms, dissolved them, repeated the process a dozen times. At last he drained off enough force to conjure and muttered a formula; two dark, ratlike creatures with tiny pale human hands materialized beside him, wearing jeweled necklaces and gold belts. Standing on their hind legs, they eyed him attentively, sniffing the air.

"Hot," one said, in White Quarossian.

"I know," Zorachus replied in the same tongue. "Free me and my friends."

They started in on his bonds with hands and teeth; thongs popped and slackened. Finishing in less than a minute, the creatures turned to Halfdan, then Asa.

And all the while Zorachus watched the Shreeth, wondering when they would look up.

The rodents completed their work. He thanked them and returned them to their own dimension.

"What now?" Halfdan asked.

"Pretend you're still tied," Zorachus answered. "If our luck holds, I'll—

One of the Shreeth, larger than the rest and wearing a spiny bone headdress, rose and came forward from the prostrate throng; going over to a platform on the right where a gong hung from a triangular frame, it mounted the steps, took up a hammer, and struck the gong three crashing blows. The notes rang out across the burning lake, and the black stone walls gave them hollowly, ominously, back again. Returning the hammer, the Shreeth went down from the platform and resumed its place among the others.

"I didn't like the sound of that," Halfdan said. "Almost as if it was summoning something."

"We'd best be off," Zorachus said.

"How?"

The Sharajnaghi did not answer, but rose to his feet and assumed a Griffin Stance. Binding the gangway, he lifted it gently, turned it around, and set it down over the gap between pillar and cliff edge. Halfdan and Asa started to get up, but he motioned them back down and uttered a spell.

In a flare of yellow glory, a squadron of golden hornets appeared above him and he dispatched them across the gap; a shining storm, they descended on the Shreeth, furiously planting sting after sting.

But the Shreeth made no effort to flee or resist. Barely flinching, keeping their faces pressed against the stone, they continued their prayers. Zorachus was impressed and pleased with their devotion, confident the hornets' venom would work even on the pious.

"Arm yourselves," he told Halfdan and Asa, going to the weapons. He slipped his rings on unburnt fingers, took up his sword belt and girt it on. Halfdan got his brand and Asa snatched up the dagger.

"Let's go," Zorachus said, and they started out onto the bridge.

A thunderous cry sounded behind, shaking the pillar, loosing streamers of rock dust from the arched ceiling. They looked back.

Two patches of bubbles had broken the black crust before the idol, and from them rose a pair of immense stone hands, lava sloughing from the blunt fingers. The idol's vast, slumberous eyes opened, revealing slits of cobalt-blue fire. It had taken a long time to wake.

Dashing over the gangway, its intended victims could hear the colossus slogging forward through the lake; ahead, the Shreeth were finally rising, wobbling, sting-swollen troll shapes, batting vainly at the darting hornets. Sting welts spurting dark vapor, the creatures stumbled toward the fugitives.

Zorachus and the Kragehul made for a luminous tunnel mouth in the right side of the cave. The Sharajnaghi blasted several of the foremost Shreeth, who burst into flame as they catapulted back against their vapor-streaming fellows. Body after body flared, fire running hungrily from limb to limb.

Zorachus banished the hornets. Threading a gauntlet of blazing figures, he and his companions pelted into the tunnel.

Outside, the stone giant roared again as they disappeared and sent a smoking hand crashing into the temple-cave, crushing dying Shreeth; a huge forefinger jabbed into the tunnel, just short of the fleeing humans. Then, with a boneshaking rumble, it withdrew.

The trio raced on. The phosphorescent tunnel narrowed and forked; from the lefthand passage came shrill cries and pounding footbeats—distant, but coming closer. A trail of green blood led from the other. Halfdan grinned at Zorachus.

"We wounded a lot of them back at the stairwell," the Kragehul said, "and they marked the route back for us!"

"Gracious little maggots," Zorachus said. "I only wish we'd bled them more—" he stopped, amazed by the malice he felt for the creatures. It was not as if they were human beings, Black Priests, or Guildsmen. . . .

God, what is happening to me?

He dashed into the tunnel, leading the way. They sped in and out of a labyrinth of yellow-lit corridors. At one junction they met six Shreeth and hacked them down, trampling them underfoot; but the monsters' shrieks brought cries from behind, and soon the clamor of pursuit grew.

"How far back do you think they are?" Asa panted to Zorachus.

"Hard to tell with the echoes," he answered. "But they must be pretty close."

"And gaining," Halfdan said.

They tried to go faster, and for a time seemed to be out-distancing the Shreeth; but Asa could not keep pace for long. Zorachus called a halt.

"We could find a better place for a stand..." Halfdan began.

Zorachus cut his protest short. "This'll do." His words were barely audible with the approaching din; when he resummoned the hornets, the spell was completely drowned out.

A crowd of Shreeth surged into view around a bend, and the hornets streaked to meet them. Stings drove through scaly hides, but with suicidal zeal the Shreeth continued their head-long rush, crying in pain, slapping at the elusive attackers.

Zorachus and the Kragehul moved back and the Shreeth slowed and staggered, bandy legs giving out. One after another they toppled, yet still they wriggled and scrabbled after the humans. Banishing the hornets, Zorachus sent a single demon-bolt into the crawlers. They burned like a river of oil.

The fugitives pressed on, the passage shrinking about them; after a time they had to walk hunched over.

"We'll be on our bellies in a minute or two," Halfdan said.

"I don't think so," Zorachus said. "They *carried* us the whole distance." As if to prove his point, the tunnel came shortly to a flat, dead end.

"The blood trail leads right up to the stone," he said, running his hands around the edge of the barrier. "I think this is one of the doors that gives on the stairwell."

"But how do we open it?" Halfdan asked.

Zorachus tripped a switch and the barrier grated outward. Going through, he found himself on the steps, as expected. Halfdan and Asa came out beside him.

They rested for a time, alert for the slightest sound. But save for the rush of their breath, the silence was complete.

"Up we go," Zorachus said at last, flexing his fingers after returning the rings to their pouch. "We might make it yet."

They ascended. As they passed the point where the yellow phosphorescence faded, Zorachus kindled the glow in his hand once more. They climbed steadily till steps became ramp; legs aching, lungs burning, they rested again. But their breath was only half caught when the low rumble of thudding feet came echoing from below.

"Gorm's hammer," Halfdan said looking at Zorachus. "Can you summon the hornets again?"

"A Sharajnaghi can only call them three times," Zorachus answered. "But even if privilege still remained, I don't have enough power. Sheer physical exhaustion. Let's get to the bridge. I might be able to blast it away behind us."

They resumed the ascent. Reaching the span, they crossed over. Asa slipped into the crawlspace and Halfdan struggled after; but he had less difficulty going in than he had coming out. Knowing the whole bridge might collapse under the shock from the demon-bolts, Zorachus yearned to follow. But he had to face the span to launch them, and backing into the hole was impossible.

Sheathing his sword, he took out his rings again and slipped them on, fingers quivering with pain at their touch. He hurled bolt after bolt at the center of the bridge and the span shook, sparks and flakes of stone flying from its surface. Yet after ten seconds of pounding, it was still intact. Nostrils filled with the odor of his own seared flesh, he glanced over at the far doorway, listening as the pursuit came closer. Crouching, he turned, shouting into the crawlspace:

"It didn't work! I'll hold them as long as I can!"

"We'll wait by the water!" came Halfdan's reply.

Zorachus switched ring fingers gingerly, rose, and turned. The Shreeth were screaming now, sharp cries above the footbeats. By the sound of it, there were thousands of the dwarfish monsters.

Assuming a Dragon Stance, Zorachus stood and waited, fully expecting to die. His most telling magic was denied him; his native power was too sapped by fatigue. And while he might still loose bolts, or whip his body into a frenzy of sword work, he knew it would not be enough. He prayed.

The din grew. One by one, the Shreeth rushed out across the bridge.

"Good-bye, Asa," he said, and started in with cataract bolts. Twin torrents of crimson power exploding against its chest, the first Shreeth spun round, the second slamming into it; limbs tangled, they tottered sideways. Zorachus gave them a second blast, flinging them over the side in a scintillant burst of shattered energy. Force flooding from his palms, he hammered the next twelve into the gulf in quick succession—none got farther than the middle of the bridge. But he exhausted his cataract strikes in the process, and the other Shreeth, unfazed, gained ground before he switched stances and lashed out with yellow stun beams. More Shreeth pitched into the abyss. The instant they came in range, the bolts converged, smashing them off their feet. But the rest never wavered. And soon the stun bolts too were exhausted.

Dropping stance altogether, Zorachus extended his fists, rings gleaming. Demon-bolts flew, splashing the chasm walls in their blue glare. Shreeth twisted, jerked, exploded; heads tumbled forward as bodies were ripped out from under them. It was butchery pure and simple, and to Zorachus's relief he took no pleasure in it, hoping against hope that the creatures would learn the lesson, turn, and run.

But they kept pouring across the span, a shrieking file of inhuman suicides.

The heat from the rings grew too great. Zorachus spat and blew on the righthand one, reached for his sword. With a terrific effort he forced his seared fingers to lock around the hilt and swept the blade free.

A Shreeth charged in and he lopped off its club-hand and kicked the screeching horror in the chest. Rocking backward, it was hurled out of the way by the creature behind, which then caught Zorachus's point square in the eye; lips going slack, mouth sagging over its chin as though its face were melting, it quivered hideously on the end of his blade, then slumped in a heap as he ripped the sword free. A third Shreeth leaped over the crumpled form; parrying a club stroke, Zorachus grabbed the creature in midair by the wattled neck and cast it sideways into the void. A fourth came flying at him and he ducked under its blow, slashing it across the belly and sending it spinning over the edge.

There was a lull in the onslaught after that, and he stood panting, watching a second line pelt toward him, wondering if he should use the rings again. . . .

Suddenly, the one he had stabbed in the eye jumped up in front of him, club-hand raised. Zorachus's hands came up and two demon-bolts took it just below the neck in a tremendous flash of light; when the flare faded, he saw the Shreeth's corpse still on its feet, huge gouge blasted out between the shoulders, the head and much of the chest completely gone. Kicking the body from the bridge, he turned the rings on the approaching file. But it was only moments before the heat forced him to relent, and it was cut and thrust once more.

His sword sang home again and again. His victims whirled head over heels toward the lava, catching fire like moths above a flame, splashing in the molten stone. Pushing himself to the limit and beyond, he fought numbly, mechanically, reflexes totally in control; hardly realizing what he was doing, he began to advance. One after another, the Shreeth raced to meet him—and were slaughtered.

He reached the center of the bridge, steel tearing through a scaly throat. Blood spraying from the wound, the Shreeth dropped from sight. Zorachus moved to meet the next—

And halted. The bridge was empty ahead, clear all the way to the door. And the door was silent.

"Glory to God in the highest," he mumbled.

His head whirled. Whatever had sustained him during the fight was gone now, and he felt for the first time the full pain of his burns and dizzying fatigue.

He turned and took several steps, swaying, almost falling over the side. Gulping, he sank to his knees. Without wiping his sword, he resheathed it, and put the rings back in their pouch. Slowly, he crawled back to the wormhole. He stopped and sat with his back to the opening, feeling he could go no further, trying to watch the far doorway. His eyelids felt leaden. He allowed them to close—

And woke with a start several minutes later. Halfdan's voice echoed down the tunnel behind him:

"Zorachus!"

The Sharajnaghi turned around, too weary to be angry with himself for dozing off.

"I'm here," he cried. "I killed them all . . . I think."

"Are you wounded?"

"No. Just tired."

"Can you make it?"

Zorachus nodded.

"Can you make it?" Halfdan repeated, more urgently.

"Yes!" Zorachus yelled irritably. Crawling into the hole, he managed to get several yards before falling asleep again.

The next thing he knew, someone was tugging at his wrists. He opened his eyes. His palm was still glowing, and in its light he saw Asa staring at him, face written with consternation.

"Are you all right?" she asked.

"You're lovely," he said. "It was all worth it."

"Are you all right?"

"I will be when I've gotten some more sleep." He closed his eyes again. She tugged at him once more.

"Watch the fingers!" he yelped. "Where's Halfdan?"

"Back by the water. He sent me because I'm small enough to back up. Let's go."

Zorachus squirmed sluggishly forward.

An hour later, they emerged from the tunnel. Mouth parched, the Sharajnaghi dragged like a lizard down to the water and gulped his fill. Crawling back from the edge, he turned over and looked up at Halfdan, who was sitting on the gunwale of the boat.

"Have you seen any of *them?*" he asked.

Halfdan shook his head. "Haven't heard anything, either. What happened back there?"

"I must have killed a hundred of them. Most of it was sword work. Not that I didn't use my rings. They almost ruined my hands—especially my sword hand. We'll have to find a place where I can enter a healing trance or I won't be able to climb those handholds in the shaft."

"Couldn't you float yourself up?" Asa asked. "With magic?"

"My powers will be nearly nonexistent for a while. The Influences are about to shift against me, and I'm drained enough as it is. I don't think I've ever been so exhausted. I'll be lucky if I can manage the trance."

"Do you think you can wade upstream?" Halfdan asked.

"I expect so," Zorachus said. "But I'll fall apart afterwards."

"That'll be all right. Kletus's men felt the landing was safe. I suppose the Shreeth don't come much farther than this backwater."

"I hope you're right," Zorachus said rising.

They set out. Once again, the warm water was a balm to aching muscles; even against the current, Zorachus got on fairly well. But toward the end he grew dizzy again, and the Kragehul had to support him. Reaching the landing, they climbed up and went a few hundred yards into the tunnel before halting. Zorachus lay down and extinguished the handbeam. He was a long time lowering himself into his trance.

chapter

20

AFTER TWO HOURS the Sharajnaghi reassumed perception. Restoring the light, he wiped his ooze-covered fingers on his already filthy clothes. The burns were gone.

Halfdan eyed Zorachus's fingers. "That healing magic of yours never fails to amaze me. You'll have to teach it to me someday."

"It took me four years to learn it," Zorachus replied.

"Ah, well," Halfdan said sadly. "I don't suppose we'll still know each other in four years." He paused. "It's a shame. You're a splendid fellow—in your own strange way."

"Thank you," Zorachus replied. "But who knows when we'll part company?" he laughed. "The war might drag on forever."

"That's not too likely," Halfdan said seriously. "If things go on as they are, everyone in Khymir'll be dead by next spring."

"I was only joking."

Halfdan blinked.

"Will you go back south when the war's done?" Asa asked Zorachus.

He nodded. "To Qanar-Sharaj," he said dully.

"You don't sound too happy about it."

"I am, believe me," he answered. But no poignant memories of home reached him now; he felt only frustration at being unable to tell her how much he dreaded leaving her. He had endured so much for her sake. . . .

"Where will you and Halfdan go?" he asked, shifting the subject away from himself.

"To Siglafstad."

"Siglafstad?"

"My uncle Siglaf's holding," Asa explained.

"Quite a place," Halfdan said. "Perhaps you could visit it after you leave Khymir. You could probably take one of Siglaf's ships south. He's always sending them to the Kadjafi countries on trade ventures."

Zorachus got to his feet. "I'll consider it, But in the meantime let's get going."

They set off along the red droplet trail.

"At first I thought the dye was your blood," Halfdan told Asa.

"That's what they wanted you to think," she said. "They had huge skin bottles of the stuff. One of them, a big black man, did nothing but carry it. There were two other blacks, even bigger than the first, carrying me. They took turns."

"Did you make it hard on them?" Zorachus asked.

"I tried. But I was trussed up tight and they were about the strongest men I've ever seen."

Climbing ramps and stairs, they came to corridors where the stone was cracked and rubble littered the floors; it was not long before they found themselves on the threshold of Lazarak's chamber.

"One last hurdle," Zorachus said nodding toward the slumbering monster, revoking the light spell as they headed out onto the dragon-lit debris, practically at a crawl.

"Watch yourself," Halfdan whispered to Asa. "The rubble's loose, so plant your feet carefully. One misstep and down you go to His Lordship there."

They crept forward, yard by yard. And, for the time being, the tumulus held firm beneath them. Small stones and cinders bounced down the slope, but mercifully, nothing larger. Lazarak slept on.

Whenever possible, Zorachus stole glances at the monster below, half out of suspense, half from wonder; in his own way, Lazarak was beautiful, a marvel of shining golden scales, his saurian face perfectly serene, almost regal. It was hard to imagine that the dragon was capable of rampages that had hollowed a cavern hundreds of yards wide and unguessably high. He marveled to think of Lazarak's vengeance-lust—

And suddenly found himself sympathizing with it. He knew well how one might go to fantastic lengths to strike back at Khymir—under the right circumstances, nothing might seem insane. The dragon's plight was so similar to his own; like Lazarak, he had been terribly provoked, and he also was trapped, prevented from consummating the vengeance he de-

sired, not by stone walls, but by conscience. He was pinioned
by the law, the curse God had written in his heart; his deepest
impulses were being repressed, his freedom smothered, his
nature violated. It was only human to want to return evil for
evil, pay it back ten, twenty, a hundredfold—especially when
exacting such retribution was well within his power. He had
the capacity to inflict horrors on his enemies that even they
could scarcely imagine. What would he not be capable of if he
unleashed his full fury? He smiled, relishing the possibilities.
How glorious it would be to show Kletus what it truly meant
to trifle with Mancdaman Zorachus, to visit all the torments of
hell on the High Priest, to fall on him like the wrath of
God. . . .

A large flat stone tilted beneath him, and he nearly lost his
footing. Breathing hard, he stopped for a few moments. He
had not been paying attention. His mind had been rambling,
filling itself with demonic nonsense, gnawed one moment by
resentment against heaven, titillated the next by fantasies of
becoming heaven's scourge . . . his close call had been a warning sign, he was sure of it. And it was not lost on him.

"Thank you, my lord," he said under his breath. "Forgive
me. And give me strength, I beg you." Bending his mind to
the task at hand, he continued on.

Gradually, they worked their way around the curve. More
than once the slope shifted slightly beneath them, seeming to
foreshadow some greater treachery, and they paused, hearts in
their throats; but always the rubble settled back into fragile
stability. Lazarak's dreams went undisturbed; scales rasping
monotonously against the debris as he breathed, he never
stirred, flames gushing and receding from his snout, reflected
fire gleaming sun-bright on his burnished horns.

The trio slowly moved ahead. The doorway was still tiny
with distance, but they were closing the gap, if only at a slug's
pace. Two hundred yards and they would be safe—

Halfdan slipped.

Digging toes and hands into the cinders and rock fragments, he caught himself almost instantly, but the damage was
already done. Bits of debris bounced and slithered down the
slope, dislodging bigger pieces, and soon the slide began in
earnest—a rattling wave of stone and powdered slag, churning towards Lazarak, obscuring several of the molten pools,
covering the dragon's foreclaw and much of his snout.

Zorachus and the Kragehul remained rooted in place, eyes

riveted on the monster. Dragon fire quickly melted through the stones blocking his nostrils; bit by bit the slide slackened. He did not move.

Halfdan stood up cautiously. Once the slide ended, the trio started forward once more.

"Thought I'd really done it for a moment there," Halfdan whispered. *Another close one*, Zorachus thought. *How much more of this can I—*

Red light flared on the fringe of sight; he looked down at Lazarak. The dragon's great right eye was open now, bright crimson, slit pupils like a cat's. He had had his fill of sleep.

"Oh my God," Zorachus breathed.

Lazarak lifted his head, stones and dust raining from his snout. The monster's teeth grinned wickedly, and he turned his head this way and that, eyes filled with a malice more scorching than any sane mind could spawn. Raising himself on his forelegs, spiked maw opening wide, he emitted a geyserlike hiss, then a tremendous raw combination of bellow and shriek. Stone shattered at the cry; deafened, Zorachus and the Kragehul rushed forward over the rubble, casting all caution aside. Behind them, boulders cracked off from the cave wall ground down into the depression, each starting its own stone-slide.

Lazarak did not see the humans; his terrible eyes were blind. He had only one purpose, the one which had consumed him for a hundred years and more: to resume his war against the prisoning stone.

Bellowing once more, muscles playing and knotting beneath his shimmering armor, he rose on his immense hindlegs, spreading his wings. Surging with fiery maggots, a huge rent smoked in his chest, unhealed, unhealable, a wellspring of endless pain, a perpetual reminder of how he had been betrayed. Wings beating with a force that scattered rocks like dust motes, he craned his head round, his wrath erupting in a hurricane of flame, melting a vast stretch of wall. Then, pinions thudding, tail whipping, he leaped aloft, hurtling up and up, smashing at last against the ceiling; flame billowed and blossomed across the scarred vault, and he shot downward in an incandescent shower of sparks and molten rock. Checking his descent, he swept upward once more, this time at a slant, thundering into a wall, ripping and goring and pummelling the stone, blasting out his cry of fury, raging at the barriers that defied him.

* * *

Zorachus and the Kragehul raced for the exit, the debris beneath them quivering like a living thing, settling and shifting, a fog of dust puffing up between the stone.

Asa fell. Halfdan grabbed her arm as he passed, dragging her forward over the rubble. An instant later, a fifty-foot swath of the tumulus they had just crossed gave way. Halfdan paused and Asa rose, robe torn, stained with blood.

Not realizing she had fallen, Zorachus had pulled far ahead of them, but suddenly the scree shifted under him and he rolled with it fifteen yards. Somehow he managed to get to his feet, wobbling. A second slide poured down toward him and he dashed out of its way, then scrambled up a patch of rocky grade stable enough to give him purchase and rejoined the Kragehul near the door.

Splashes of molten stone had fallen by the exit, partially blocking it with jagged, still smoking detritus. Zorachus and Asa dived through; looking up for a split second, Halfdan saw a cloud of splintered rock hurtling down. He was not close enough to lunge through the door, so he pivoted, sprinting to the right as the cascade crashed down before the door, burying it beneath a mound ten feet high.

He looked up once more. The dragon circled overhead, battering the walls and striking the ceiling. Stone fell all around the Kragehul as the slopes slithered downward; the tumulus before the doorway began to collapse. He went toward it, saw the lintel come into view. Soon a gap two feet wide had opened between lintel and rubble. He got down on all fours and tried to crawl through, but a plummetting rock gashed his arm and he halted; the rubble gave way with greater speed, and he slid backward five feet. The shifting slowed; scrabbling up he slipped through the opening. Moments later it was buried again, and a gust of flame, dust and stone fragments followed him over the debris on the far side.

Zorachus helped him to his feet. The Sharajnaghi's hand was glowing once more, and when the light showed Halfdan's arm, Asa cried out; ears still numb from the dragon's roars, Halfdan did not hear. Neither, of course, did Asa—for an appalling second she thought she was dumb as well as deaf.

Hurriedly they descended the scree into the tunnel beneath, the entrance of which had been widened by Lazarak's ongoing earthquake; pelted by stones falling from the ceiling, showered by dust, they leaped over cracks and plunged past crumbling walls, section after section of the tunnel sagging and collapsing behind them.

They sped on. The droplet trail was dust-covered much of the way, but where the patina was less deep, the red soaked through just enough for them to find their way.

After a time they reached places where the tremors were muffled, and the tunnels showed no signs of collapse; panting, they stopped to rest. All had gotten blows on the head and shoulders, and their blood flowed freely. But the worst wound was Halfdan's gash. Tearing a strip from her robe, Asa bandaged the wound as well as she could, and after a time the blood flow stopped.

They pushed on to the shaft and began the climb. Every few levels, Halfdan's bandage worked loose, the blood starting afresh each time; again and again they slipped into the nearest tunnel mouth to retighten the rag.

Coming to the top of the shaft, they continued upward through the catacombs, plodding finally to the foot of the last staircase. Far above shone a tiny rectangle of sunlight; after a long pause, gathering up their strength, they began the daunting trudge toward it. The climb proved one of the greatest torments they had yet endured, for Halfdan was by that time very weak and had to be supported and pulled, even dragged. But eventually the charnel smell lessened and the light from above grew and they emerged at last, blinking and stumbling, barely able to hear their own blissful cries.

chapter

21

OULCHAR LYSTHRAGON LOVED puerile cruelty. Nothing pleased him better than dealing out little doses of idiot malice. This is not to say he did not appreciate viciousness on the grand scale; but the lack of intimacy, and the risks that were sometimes involved, rendered such cruelty unsuitable to him as pure entertainment. He much preferred inserting himself like a poisoned sliver into situations that held no hint of danger, irritating those who surrounded him with perfect imbecilities, and remaining immune (so he thought) simply because of the silliness of his manner. Indeed, most people, including himself, never realized how destructive he could be. His victims often ignored him for a mere clown—even as the subliminal current of his nonsequiturs filtered into their minds. When he encountered the right sort of person, he could awaken every insanity lying dormant in their minds without speaking to them (or more properly, *at* them) for more than five minutes. For them, meeting him was the start of a plunge into nonsense from which they would never recover; a plunge which he himself had taken, for he was just such a personality, and had long ago withered in the stench of his own decomposition.

Today he sat in his little chamber at a little table. On his right was a pail half-filled with dead toads, on his left a covered pail containing live ones. Before him was a small circle, carved into the tabletop, and a foot beyond that was a yard-square bed of nails.

He took a live toad out, covered its eyes with tape, and set it down in the circle. Grinning his wide, wizened grin, he waited a few seconds, then tapped the toad's hindquarters, triggering a leap forward onto the nails. Once the creature stopped struggling, he lifted it off the impaling points and dropped it in the pail on the right.

There was a knock at the door and he went to answer it; a

novice told him he was wanted in Kletus's garden, where the
High Priest and Sathaswentha awaited him.

"I see," Lysthragon said, and pointed back to the pails.
"My toads are in those. I want you to keep an eye on them.
Especially the dead ones."

The novice, a new recruit, knew little of Lysthragon and he
cracked a smile, thinking it a joke. "I must be off, my Lord,"
he said.

Instantly Lysthragon snatched one of his hands and bit his
thumb, teeth shearing to the bone. The victim tried to wrench
his hand away, but Lysthragon held it fast, and the shrieking
novice only tore his flesh further.

"Please, my Lord!" he cried. "Let me—"

Lysthragon drove a small fist twice into the fellow's groin
before releasing the maimed digit, and the novice fell on his
knees, grimacing with pain.

"Do as I say," Lysthragon hissed, shoving his blood-
painted mouth next to the novice's ear, "or I'll eat your face."

The novice nodded.

Paying him no further heed, Lysthragon went to Kletus's
garden. Inside, he found the High Priest's fungoid replicas
filled with wallowing life, a pumping, clasping, pale-pink sea,
stretching to infinity in the mirrors. Kletus himself seemed to
be paying no attention to them, but stood talking to Sathaswentha and Thulusu. Of the three, only Thulusu looked
unruffled, his huge body completely at ease, helmet under one
arm, steel hand resting on his belt. Sathaswentha trembled as
if with ague, and darkish blotches of stubble flared and disappeared on her cheeks. Kletus was sweating profusely, eating
chunk after chunk of meat, voice half-strangled.

Lysthragon pointed to the replicas as he came up. "Pink
worms," he said.

"Some people bite their nails," Kletus replied. "Moving
those bodies is my little nervous habit. At least it's original."

"Zorachus is alive," Sathaswentha said.

Lysthragon grinned at Kletus, infantile face creasing into a
mass of wrinkles. "What happened to your precious Shreeth?"

Finishing his meat wallet, Kletus took out another. "I don't
know," he answered. "Our agent said he went down into their
tunnels. . . ."

"And fought his way back out," Sathaswentha said. "I
hope he never decides to pay us a visit."

"Why not?" Kletus asked. "Powerful as he is, he could never stand against our united strength."

"Powerful as he is, the Shreeth should have killed him," Sathaswentha shot back. "Your Voice played you false. Admit it!"

"Fools!" Kletus snarled, bits of meat dropping from his mouth. "Perhaps *you'd* like to take command?"

"I'd be satisfied if you were simply more willing to listen to advice from now on."

Kletus said nothing, simmering. Lysthragon moved closer to him.

"You can ask for our opinions anytime," the midget said, pushing Kletus's sleeve up. "Our tongues are always at your disposal." Very delicately, he licked the High Priest's arm.

Temper badly frayed by the news about Zorachus, Kletus growled, hurled his meat wallet down, grabbed Lysthragon by the hair and lifted him squealing off the ground; turning, he hurled him among the churning replicas.

After being buffeted for a few moments, Lysthragon rose and, keeping his eyes full on Kletus, spat on the replicas before him.

Kletus roared and assumed a stance; knowing he was no match for the High Priest, Lysthragon screeched. But before Kletus could launch his bolts, Thulusu came between him and his prey.

"I hear the Guild laughing already," the black said.

Kletus's arms dropped to his sides.

"Very prudent," Sathaswentha said.

Kletus gave her a basilisk-like stare. "Keep this in mind," he grated. "If it weren't for me, Zorachus would have your guts for garters."

"Think so?" Sathaswentha asked. "If he wanted them, he could probably take them—even if you forbade it."

"Nothing can defy my will," Kletus answered.

"Then we've nothing to worry about," Sathaswentha said, mock-cheerfully. "The Shreeth killed Zorachus."

By now, Lysthragon had threaded a path through the replicas. He was no longer grinning. The soft, child's face had returned, puffed and petulant. He had not expected Kletus to react so strongly, even to the spitting; although he did not realize it, he had already passed the point where he could gauge the danger in a given situation. He had seen Kletus's agitation. He had known his actions would badly aggravate him; indeed, that was the point. But it had not occurred to him that Kletus would lash out. Details were becoming independent in Lysthragon's mind; his ability to recognize contexts was decaying. The idiocies he had fostered for use on others had not only crept into the center of his being, they were hastening his terminal dissolution even now, and he had neither the will nor the inclination to oppose them.

"Lord Kletus rules everything," he said. "He willed me to lick his arm. He simply *had* to have my spittle." he giggled. "Spittle is *everything*. Spittle and piss."

Kletus battled to control himself. "I'll tolerate this," he said. "I could kill you both, but I'll let it go—for now."

"And then what?" Sathaswentha asked. "Will your Voice tell you the proper time to strike? Will you trust it then? It might not be telling you the truth. It's lied before."

"Spittle and *piss,*" Lysthragon said, circling Kletus, plucking at his robes. "We should all be High Priest."

"You need our support," Sathaswentha told Kletus. "Agreed, you might be able to kill us. And you could probably survive the loss of two wizards of our class. But what if our factions turned on you, as I assure you they would? Our followers don't love you my Lord. They love you less than they love us, which is saying much. No, I'd think you'd want to preserve their loyalty. Especially now that your Voice isn't working anymore."

"Blasphemer," Kletus growled.

Sathaswentha smirked. "Blasphemy, eh? What blasphemy is there in simply telling the truth? I recognized your plan as a fool's dream the minute I heard it."

"Spittle and piss," Lysthragon said, plucking at Kletus again. "We should all be High Priest. You should listen to me, Kletus. You should think hard about every little thing I say."

"I'm Grand Master of this Order," Kletus rumbled. "I will lead. *I alone*. My voice is infallible."

"Then why is Zorachus still alive?" Sathaswentha asked.

A chorus of hissing voices, which seemed to come from everywhere at once, answered her: "Because *I* willed it so."

The temperature plummeted; they looked wildly about. In the mirrors they saw the reflections of Kletus's replicas rising slowly to their feet, eyes rolled back, even as the replicas themselves remained writhing on the floor.

"*I* am Kletus's voice," the reflections said, plumes of chill vapor puffing from their mouths, smoking forth from the surfaces of the mirrors. "*I* am his inspiration, his genius. *I am Tchernobog.*"

Despite his terror, Kletus smiled. His vindication had come.

Tchernobog continued: "*I* nurtured Kletus, gave him his vocation, granted him the High Priesthood when the time was right. *I* told him to bring Zorachus back to Khymir, for Zorachus was the catalyst to ignite the war against the Guild; the Guild has to fall before the invasion of Muspellheim can begin. And Zorachus has to fall before the Guild will be broken—by listening to me and luring Zorachus down into the depths, Kletus brought him almost to the edge. Having saved the girl, having gone through so much for her, Zorachus has come ever more deeply under her spell—which is now the linchpin of his mind. Remove it, and he will be destroyed."

Stuttering with cold and fear, Kletus asked: "H-how can we do it, m-my Lord?"

And Tchernobog answered.

Kletus's smile became a nervous grin. "M-my Lord and my God," he said. "As easily as that. . . . ?"

"Have faith," Tchernobog replied. "All will be well."

The reflections of the replicas sank down once more, and dry heat filled the room. Kletus regained his composure almost immediately; triumph glittering in his eyes, he looked at Lysthragon and Sathaswentha. They had moved closer to one another, trembling.

"Shall we all be High Priest?" he asked.

Sathaswentha was silent. Lysthragon loosed a jittery giggle.

"Lysthragon," Kletus began, "you said before that I willed you to lick my arm. Well, now I'm willing you to lick my foot."

Lysthragon's mind was not so badly decayed that he would disobey the Chosen of Tchernobog. He even took a certain pleasure in complying. After all, it was insane to enjoy it.

The gash in Halfdan's arm festered and he grew feverish. Sharthas seemed helpless, so Dr. Aliphar was brought in again. A day later, the fever broke. But Halfdan had lost much blood, and kept to his bed, sleeping for long stretches.

During that time, Zorachus tried to find out who had drugged Asa. A special interrogator, adept at throwing people off balance, was sent in by Porchos. One by one, the guards and servants were brought to Zorachus's room and questioned, and some apparent headway was made; one of the food-tasters, a young girl, got very agitated, even though she confessed to nothing. Zorachus and the interrogator decided to give her a second session, and Sharthas was sent to fetch her.

Grimacing, with a knife slash across the hand, the steward returned a short time later, saying she had attacked him after hearing the summons, then stabbed herself. Zorachus wanted to feel some sorrow at her suicide, but found he could not force it. He was too relieved that the culprit was out of the way.

Her replacement arrived two days later—a tall, handsome black woman with a voluptuous figure and straightened hair. Her name was Leahkalah, and she rapidly established herself as one of the palace's best-traveled bodies, with a marked preference for women. Zorachus found her practically unavoidable; she attended at all his meals, of course, and at times he seemed unable to leave his chamber without seeing her and her latest female paramour embracing in some niche or parlor. Even when she was not actually present, the palace was full of whispered rumors; whenever he overheard the guards or servants talking among themselves, it was always about her.

One night, as he and Asa dined alone (Halfdan was asleep upstairs), Leahkalah and another food-taster, a middle-aged-but-still-attractive blonde, having completed their duties, retired to a nearby couch and started in on each other. Zorachus was taken completely aback by the sheer brazenness of it, and wondered at first if she had been told that such behavior was forbidden around him. But then he realized his own responsibility; he had already been much more lenient with her than with the rest of the household. It was much harder to clamp down on debauchery he found genuinely erotic. More than once he had stood watching her make love, unwilling to call a halt to it until he had seen enough to guarantee the lubricity of his dreams.

And so it was now; he could not take his eyes off the two women. They were both naked and feasting hungrily on each other before he finally ordered them from the room. Gathering up her garments, Leahkalah smiled mockingly at him, then left with the blonde.

He tried to finish his meal, but found he could down nothing but wine. There was no conversation. Asa, red-faced, avoided eye contact with him every time he looked her way.

After a time they went back upstairs. She left him at his threshold and he watched her go, eyes held by the gentle sway of her hips.

Suddenly she stopped, staring at a niche on the right. He went to see what the matter was.

Leahkalah, nude and sweating, mouth sagging in a silent gasp, stood against the back of the niche. The blonde, also nude, knelt before her, one of Leahkalah's long, muscular black legs draped over her shoulder, toes tightly curled. The black woman's eyes rolled and fluttered; noticing Zorachus and Asa, she extended her pink tongue, glossing the red thickness of her upper lip.

Zorachus wrenched his eyes away. He and Asa looked at each other. Her cheeks were brightly flushed.

"Go on," he told her. "Halfdan's probably awake by now."

What might have been a flicker of guilt crossed her face; she went slowly to her room.

Zorachus looked back at Leahkalah. Her hard black eyes swept him up and down in lewd inspection. Her lithe, sinewy hands were tangled in the blonde's sweat-lank hair, her palms pressed against the woman's scalp; then the black's left hand rose; she grasped her own nipple between thumb and forefinger and softly rolled it.

"Be off with—" Zorachus's command faltered as a long moan broke from Leahkalah's lips; her whole body shuddered, and all at once she pulled the blonde's face back from between her legs, slid down the wall, and wrapped her arms around her, kissing her repeatedly.

Zorachus turned and entered his room. Closing the door, he leaned up against it.

His body screamed for release; self-accusation racked his mind. For several minutes he swung wildly between thoughts of ordering the two women into his room and, more alarming still, thoughts of self-mutilation. He tried to push it all out of his head, but only succeeded in remembering that final glimpse of Asa's face, that flicker of guilt. The turmoil inside him intensified till he thought his skull would crack. What had she felt, staring at the lovers in the niche? Had she too been aroused? One loathsome corner of his soul was thrilled by the idea; a new image, deliciously poisonous, entered his mind— Asa kneeling before Leahkalah, thrusting her face greedily forward, glutting herself on the black woman's flesh. *God,* he thought, *to have them both. . . .*

"Stop it," he said, pressing his hands against the sides of his head; for an instant he seemed to feel his temples expanding, as if his skull were about to burst. Sharthas's words came back to him: *We're all Khymirians inside.* Never did the phrase seem so potent. He knew he could not trust himself. And the shame in Asa's expression proved beyond all doubt that she was every bit as much a pig.

Proved? came reason's voice. *Beyond all doubt?* But the protest was so thin, so tinny, like a hateful insect buzzing in his ear; he was sliding deep into the trough and mere logic would not check the descent. Asa was such a part of him now; how could she not be infected, when he was so diseased?

"Stop it," he said again, this time in a feeble whisper, rocking his head from side to side, pulse hammering, stomach filled with nervous heat. He sensed he was going mad, but that only increased his self-loathing. He could control his mind no better than he controlled his lust. He was a Sharajnaghi Adept of the Seventh Level, but his blood was winning out over all his training. The veneer of the *Comahi Irakhoum* was being stripped away from him, and layer after layer of hidden perversity were being revealed. It was no longer enough for him to covet another man's wife—now he wanted her with another woman, grew inflamed at the very thought of them embracing, kissing, suckling on each other . . . his imagination raced. The squirming possibilities seemed endless; there were so many ways to savor the poison, to smother himself in honeyed damnation, to go giggling and smiling like Tchernaar into the putrescent dark, the endless death of the spirit he so richly deserved. . . .

The heat in his stomach surged and exploded. It was only with a ferocious effort of will that he choked back the vomit, tendons standing out like cables on his neck, the veins of his temples bulging. His bones seemed to vibrate inside his flesh.

He staggered out into the middle of the floor, thought of the mirror that had been removed, looked over at the spot where it had stood. If only the glass had still been there—he wanted desperately to smash some image of himself, purge the rage and frustration he felt. But he realized that even that would not have satisfied him; he was seized by an urge to slam his face against something, flatten his features into pulp. Going to the wall before him, he stood quaking in front of it for a time, fighting the need to snap his face forward even as he summoned the will to do it, aching to feel the punishment. The spark came; "Pig," he grunted to himself, and butted his face into the stone, the impact exploding against his brow and nose. White-hot pain flared inside his skull and blood trickled from his nostrils. "Pig," he said again, and smashed his face against the wall once more, then tottered back and fell to his knees, shaking his head.

Gradually, the pain subsided. The turmoil in his mind eased—somewhat.

He rose. Self-loathing still gripped him, but now that he had punished himself he could allow reason and his faith in Asa to reassert themselves—if only just barely. He forced himself to acknowledge that he had no right to impute his corruption to others. To fill his soul with venom against Asa, against his love, was monstrous.

"You've no right even to judge a Khymirian," he whispered. *Pity.*

Wiping the blood from his nose, he went out onto the balcony and tried to pray.

But concentration proved impossible. The night was close and sticky, and he kept hearing snatches of obscene conversation—about Leahkalah—from below; ever since Asa's abduction, guards had been stationed beneath the balconies.

Prayer dying on his lips, he decided it might be best to seek the less-frequented parts of the palace and walk himself out of his deadly state of mind.

He went back into the room and noticed that blood had dripped onto his grey Sharajnaghi tunic; not wanting to alarm his doorwards, he got a cloth, held it under his nose until the blood stopped flowing, then washed his face and hands at a basin and changed into a fresh garment. Going outside, he forbade the guards to follow him and set off along the corridor, heading resolutely away from the niche where he had seen Leahkalah and the blonde.

Watching her sleeping husband, Asa sat beside her bed, assailed by the close heat, acutely aware of the way her sweat-soaked clothes clung to her breasts and belly and thighs. She wished he were awake and well. She wanted to talk to him, to feel his arms around her, to be distracted from herself. She would welcome his love.

But she would not wake him. He had not made love to her

since the night before she was abducted, but she would manage. Smiling, she studied his face. She loved it dearly, and never more so than when he was asleep—it always reminded her of the first time she had laid eyes on him, one warm summer's day in her father's field where he had decided to take a nap; she had practically tripped over him. His face had been different then—no scars, no broken nose. But even then it was not beautiful. She supposed he might be downright ugly now, in an endearing sort of way. Strange that she could love his face when there were other things far more beautiful, and beauty promised so much.

She thought about his body. It was powerful and broad-shouldered, without a trace of fat; its strength was delightfully terrifying, and there was nothing she loved better than bearing its weight. But there was nothing beautiful about it. It was made for work, combat, and love, and fulfilled its tasks admirably. Yet there was nothing about it that existed for its own sake, worthy all by itself.

That was the difference between men and women, or so she told herself. Marvelous as they were, men needed women to give them meaning, to give them beauty. She had never understood why so many of her female friends back in her village found male bodies so exciting; it was being sought after by men that had always aroused her, knowing and feeling she was beautiful, that she was the treasure, the thing worth having.

But it was not only men who yearned for beauty. Even before she was brought to Khymir, she had thought of other women. Gudrun's story had awakened the desire in her when she was twelve years old, and even though she accepted the prohibitions her people placed on such love, that had never quenched her longings. She was always on guard against them, but sometimes it was hard to shunt them aside. Sometimes she would see things, like Leahkalah and the blonde . . . even now, her curiosity was up. Leahkalah's face and body were so handsome. Asa wondered if making love to her would be as splendid as she suspected.

Yet she entertained no real thought of putting those suspicions to the test. She had every intention of keeping faith with Halfdan, remaining true to her people's code.

Still, she was troubled. The sweat stains spread; she felt her nipples hardening beneath the sodden fabric, and she had to keep her legs closed to stop the perspiration from running

down between her thighs. She licked salty beads from her
upper lip; her smooth flesh felt good beneath her tongue.

I wonder what Leahkalah's sweat tastes like? she thought
—and immediately banished the question from her mind. Bit
by bit, the heat seemed to increase, milking more and more
sweat from her body. Completely soaked now, her clothes
were molded to her like a second skin. She almost wished the
mirror were still in the room. What did she need anyone for if
she had a mirror?

Instantly she recoiled from the thought.

*You should just lie down beside your husband and go to
sleep.*

But she was not tired enough. Perhaps she needed a walk,
a good stretch of the legs in parts of the palace where there
was little chance of passing coupling bodies.

Kissing Halfdan, she went outside, telling her newly ap-
pointed doorwards to remain behind. On an impulse, she
looked at the niche; it was empty. Bare feet making no sound,
she headed off, pulling a taper from its socket and carrying it
with her, anticipating dark corridors.

She rounded a corner—and stopped. Several yards ahead,
a life-size female nude carved in ebony, stood beside the
righthand wall; Leahkalah's, fully clad, was gazing raptly at
it. Noticing Asa out of the corner of her eye, she turned her
head. Silently they stood staring at each other. Then a slow
smile spread across Leahkalah's lips.

Hand glowing, Zorachus made his way about the upper
stories. For nearly an hour he strode along the dusty passages, going up and down flights of stairs, praying on and off,
growing steadily calmer.

He came to the room where he had talked with Sharthas.
He had passed it several times before, but now the door was
open a crack, and candlelight seeped through.

"Sharthas?" he called.

"Lord Mancdaman?" came the steward's voice within.

Zorachus entered. Sharthas sat at the table, head down, the
same wine bottle before him, empty now. Zorachus sat next to
him. The steward did not look up.

"Finished for the night?" Zorachus asked.

"I think so, my Lord," the steward replied.

"You're not sure?"

Sharthas shrugged. "Maybe I simply wanted to be alone."

"You'd rather I left?"

"Certainly not, my Lord. But I'm surprised you're willing to talk to me again, now that it's just the two of us. I thought I upset you the last time."

"Yes," Zorachus replied, and suddenly realized how strange it was that he had put himself in the same situation. He did not really want to talk to anyone, let alone Sharthas. On what obscure impulse had he acted? Was some of his self-hatred still riding him? This would be punishment—of a sort.

"I apologize," Sharthas said. "I'm such a bother when I get on those streaks. Nobody should have to put up with such talk."

Zorachus said nothing. Sharthas looked up at last, apparently trying to read the Sharajnaghi's face.

"That look in your eyes. . . ." The steward's voice trailed off.

"What does it say to you?"

"That you despise me."

"I don't," Zorachus answered, truthfully enough. "I try not to despise anyone." *Not even myself,* he thought. "Tell me: do you see that look in everyone's eyes?"

"When they look at me. So much of the time, people don't even want to see me. I don't blame them."

"I'm sure you don't. But let's not talk about how much you hate yourself."

"All right, my Lord."

"The new girl's very popular," Zorachus said, "What's her name? Leahkalah?" Almost immediately, he regretted saying anything about it; he did not want to be reminded of that scene in the niche, or his scabrous fantasies. It was almost as if a voice had whispered in his ear, prompting him to speak.

"Leahkalah," Sharthas said, nodding. "She's already queen of the household. Of the serving women, at least. None of them can refuse her. Such a lovely black whore." A tear spilled from his eye. "Sound familiar?"

"I'm surprised she's a food-taster. With her looks, I would've thought she could do better."

Sharthas took out his knife, playing with it. "Food-tasters are a special sort. The professionals, at any rate. She doesn't care if she dies."

"She told you that?"

"Several times. But even if she hadn't, it's written all over her face." Sharthas started in with his blade, making grooves in the table, ending each stroke with that deft flip of the wrist. He had carved hundreds of little furrows since Zorachus's last visit.

"The knife reminds me," Zorachus said. "How's that cut of yours doing?"

"I just took the bandage off a few hours ago," Sharthas said. "I'm coming along nicely." To prove his point he raised his hand.

Zorachus reacted with mute shock—the stitch-seamed cut was shaped almost exactly like the grooves in the table. The flourish at the end was unmistakable.

"My Lord?" Sharthas asked.

Standing, Zorachus backed away from him, watching him closely.

"*You* cut yourself, didn't you?" the Sharajnaghi asked.

"What?"

"On the hand. Those grooves gave you away."

Sharthas's eyes darted to the tabletop, then back to Zorachus; they widened in terror.

Zorachus went on: "*You* killed the girl, and cut yourself to make it look like—"

Sharthas hurled the knife. Zorachus dodged, heard it rebound from the wall behind him. Clattering to the floor, it bounced against his boot.

Sharthas reached into his robes, pulled out another. Zorachus scooped up the blade on the floor and threw it underhand, striking Sharthas in the chest. The steward looked down at the hilt, shaking his head slowly, sadly. He dropped the second knife.

Zorachus went back by him. "How long have you been working for Kletus?" he asked.

"Ever since Chatonha found out I was your steward," Sharthas gasped. "She's . . . she's one of his agents. I couldn't resist her. . . ." He lifted his head. "Beware, my Lord . . ."

"Of what?"

"She's in this house. Worked her way in with the Guild, took out her pretty nosering. *Leahkalah is Chatonha.*"

Zorachus thundered an oath.

Sharthas coughed. "They want her to seduce Asa. . . . To throw you off balance . . ."

Zorachus bolted for the door.

"Wait," Sharthas wailed.

Zorachus turned.

"Forgive me," the steward begged.

Zorachus said nothing.

Sharthas's eyes closed. He slumped sideways from the chair.

Zorachus dashed into the hall and around to the stairs that came out by his room. The sick warmth had welled up in his stomach once again, and he launched into a desperate prayer as he hurtled down the steps, begging that his worst fears might not be realized. Coming to the Kragehul's room, he asked the doorwards if Asa was inside; one pointed off along the hall.

"She left a while ago, my Lord," the man explained. "Told us not to follow her."

"Have you seen Leahkalah?"

"She went the same way a bit earlier. What's wrong, my Lord?"

Giving no answer, Zorachus was off, charging down the corridor. He heard the guards coming after him but waved them back.

Rounding the corner, he slowed as the ebony statue came in view. The sight infuriated him; he wanted to hurl himself at it, eager to topple it, to smash it against the floor.

But before he could spring, he noticed a partially open doorway nearby and heard a moan from inside; he went softly to the door, slipping inside. Going down a short corridor, he reached the threshold of a small room lit by a single taper. The glow bathed a large bed; Chatonha and Asa lay on the covers, nude and glistening with sweat, the black woman's face cradled between Asa's thighs. Asa moaned again, mouth slack, eyes closed, hips rocking gently.

Horrified and aroused, Zorachus stepped into the room. Asa heard him and opened her eyes. They were glazed and empty—it was a moment or two before she saw him. Then they filled with shock and her body tightened.

Chatonha raised herself on one elbow; the sight of the Sharajnaghi seemed to amuse her. Sitting up, she beckoned with one hand, stroking Asa with the other.

Zorachus took another step, loins and blood burning, the foundations of his mind crumbling. He made slowly for the bed, noticing that Asa's hips were undulating again, even though her face was still frozen with dismay.

He reached the bed, trembling. Chatonha rose, grasped his shoulders softly. Her mouth sought his, tongue probing, saliva warm and glutinous and salty.

He had never been with a woman. Was that how their mouths tasted?

Or was that Asa? Slime from the woman he loved?

His mind ripped free from the rutting fever, erupting with a lust far more potent. The arrow scar on his cheek flared red.

He jerked his face back from Chatonha's kiss, and his hands swept up, sinking into her throat. She gasped, but there was no fear in her eyes; a self-satisfied smile spread across her face, contemptuous, even triumphant. Through the haze of madness he recalled what Sharthas had said: *She doesn't care if she dies.* But that only fanned Zorachus's already white-hot fury, and as his face began to mirror the change within, twitching muscle by ridged muscle into a mask of mind-bending malevolence, her expression melted from smug superiority to pure terror, and he remembered *with relish* that the mere sight of devils was said to be one of the chief torments of the damned.

She started to fight, but her muscles were already drained by approaching death and there was little strength in her kicks and punches; when she tried to claw his face, it seemed like a mere caress. Her eyes bulged, and her tongue protruded, writhing slowly, wetly, like a transfixed slug, laughing low in his throat, he forced his hands against her lower jaw, driving her teeth upward. Her mouth snicked shut, and her tongue slid over his hands, dropping to the floor.

"Enjoying it, slut?" he grinned, hands sinking ever deeper into her flesh. "Is it good?" Cartilage gave, crunching beneath his palms, and all at once her throat seemed much smaller; face blackened to purple, white eyes all but bursting from their sockets, she died.

He hurled the body aside, staring at Asa. She had not stirred, but now his murderous glare was more than enough to shatter her paralysis; leaping from the bed, she dashed past him from the room.

He made no attempt to follow but turned to Chatonha's corpse; picking it up by the left arm, he slammed it against the nearest wall, pinning it to the stone with a cabled fist. Drilling his blows home with a devastating combination of unbridled ferocity and perfect technique, he rained punches on the black flesh, and the room was filled with the explosions of his breath and the snap of broken bones; blood spattered his face again and again, and his throat was worn raw with shrieks.

Finally he let her slide to the floor and turned, rumbling. The doorwards stood clustered in the corridor, swords drawn.

"Get out!" he roared.

They did not move. He took several steps towards them, hands and face running with blood, eyes burning like live coals.

"*Get out!*" he roared again.

They moved back, terrified, retreating through the door. Paying them no more heed, he turned once more; going to the bed, he flipped it over onto Chatonha's corpse, shattered the frame with snap-kicks, hammered the spars into chips and kindling. Then he took out the rings and slipped them on, and as his shrieks and roars turned into gusting mad laughter, he began launching bolts, blasting the mattress, setting it aflame, knocking chunks out of the window casement, firing demon lightning through the ceiling. Broken stone rained around him, striking his head and shoulders. His scalp was torn, his ring fingers scorched, but he felt no pain, his rage absolute, the raving dictator of his mind.

Asa ran back towards her room, bumping into the doorwards who were rushing even then to see what the shrieking was all about. She told them Zorachus had gone insane and had torn her clothes off trying to rape her. They raced past, and she ran to her door, hurling it open. Snatching up a robe, she put it on and dashed to the bed, shaking Halfdan violently.

"I'm awake," he mumbled at last.

She tugged on his arm as hard as she could. "Come on," she cried. "He'll kill us both!"

"Who?"

"Zorachus! He tried to. . . ." She stopped short, realizing her husband would certainly attack him if he thought Zorachus had attempted to rape her.

"Tried to what?"

She tugged on his arm. "Come on!"

"Is that him screaming?"

She nodded quickly.

"Did he hurt you?"

"No."

"Then what happened?"

"I don't know!"

Halfdan stood up and stumbled over to his sword belt and clothes, dressed himself, and girt on his sword. Asa grabbed his arm again, pulling him frantically toward the door.

"Let go," he snapped, and yanked free, pushing ahead of her into the corridor. He heard Zorachus's rings crackling now, and booming, crazed laughter. He staggered down the hall, Asa at his heels, grabbing at him repeatedly. Finally, his groggy mind awash with fear and vexation, he turned and slapped her across the face. She sank down whimpering.

He turned a corner. The laughter and crackling were coming from a red-lit doorway ahead of him. Intermittently, to the sound of the demon strikes, brilliant blue-white flashes blotted out the fire glow. The guards clustered by the threshold, looking in.

The laughter and flashing stopped. As Halfdan joined the guards, Zorachus emerged from the doorway, face twisted with wrath and webbed with blood, the rings flaming viciously on his smoking fingers. Almost as if they were being pushed back by a tangible wall of hatred, the men before him retreated.

"Zorachus!" Halfdan cried. "What's wrong?"

Zorachus shrieked at him hoarsely. Halfdan tried to stand his ground, even though he felt his mind withering in the glare from the Sharajnaghi's mad-dragon eyes; he checked his retreat for an instant, but no longer. He and the guards drew back and back. The doorwards turned and ran when they passed the corner, rushing down a stair, and their terror infected other guards even then rushing to the top. Halfdan, meanwhile, screwed up his will and halted beside Asa; face wet with tears, she was still on her knees where he had left her.

"While there's still time, Halfdan. . . ." she began.

"We stay here," he answered, drawing his sword.

Zorachus came into view, stopping several feet from them. His eyes were riveted on Asa and he raised his hands; immediately Halfdan put himself between her and the rings.

"What happened, Zorachus?" he demanded, battling to keep his nerve.

Zorachus lowered his hands. "Leave this house," he grated. "Go now. Take as much gold from the storeroom as you please. But go."

"I'm not leaving till you tell me what happened."

A freezing smile bared Zorachus's teeth. "Leave now, or I swear to God I'll kill you both."

Halfdan's resolve snapped. Without another word, he hauled Asa up and led her away.

Zorachus watched them; just before they reached the stairs, Asa gave him a last, tormented, backward glance. In answer, he loosed a ringing howl and dropped on all fours weeping, huge frame racked with sobs.

His soul was laid waste, a ruin. She had betrayed him, betrayed Halfdan, betrayed everything. She too was a Khymirian inside, lusting after her own image, embracing sterility for a twitch in the genitals. The loving wife and gardener were mere fronts for her worm-eaten passions.

Poor Halfdan! Poor stupid, trusting Halfdan. He had no idea what he had wed, joined his flesh to; and Asa was not going to tell him. The irony was perfect and hideous. Halfdan Skarp-Hedinsson, hating all things Khymirian, unknowingly married to one. . . .

A darker thought occurred to Zorachus, a more-perfect irony. Was Halfdan like Asa? Like Porchos, like Lysthragon and Kletus, like the whole filthy brood? The Sharajnaghi hardly knew what crawled inside the Kragehul's mind. Was the Halfdan he knew only a facade? With a shock he found himself unable to think otherwise. With that willful clarity that always characterized his best insights, he saw that he would never again be able to trust a human soul. Least of all his own.

He had been aroused as never before by that scene on the bed. He had ached to join those naked bodies, and had given in, if only for a moment. He had kissed Chatonha, savored the taste of Asa on her tongue. And where it would have been bad enough to go further with that, his ultimate reaction had been far worse. For the first time, the blood-lusting demon that he had feared for so long had been released. He had enjoyed strangling Chatonha; he had enjoyed pounding her dead face into pulp. He knew that if she were alive again, he could slowly tear her limb from limb and exult in every second of it. His intellect and moral sense were appalled, but his bloodlust was not dimmed—killing Chatonha had not purged but increased it. It wanted more blood, and he would not deny it. Those who had driven him to this pass would pay. He would take sweet vengeance for what had been done to Asa, for what had been done to his own soul, even if he were damned for it; vengeance for forcing him to take vengeance. He was perfectly aware that his only sane alternative was to leave Khymir. But he would not leave until Banipal Khezach was a shambles of slaughter, and Kletus and his accomplices were dead.

Slowly he stood, unfolding his massive, deadly limbs.

chapter

22

THUNDER BOOMED ACROSS the rooftops of Mother Khymir and the thick atmosphere vibrated. There was nothing strange in that; even so, the city's people waited tensely for each new hammer stroke. A pall of fear, fear of something unknown and terrible, had descended upon them. Lovers felt it in the midst of their coupling and drew more tightly together, hoping that somehow the mere pressure of flesh upon flesh could bring salvation, knowing it would not. Prisoners in cells buried deep beneath the city streets felt it and huddled in rat-infested corners, the sane ones silent, the insane shrieking at the top of their lungs. Addicts and drunkards sensed it even in the midst of their stupors and their skin rose in gooseflesh, and they pissed themselves unknowingly. The shadow of a vast, dark hand had deepened over Khymir; somewhere in the cold black heavens, in an alien plane where goodness and the laws of logic themselves were denied to the point of annihilation, the King of Devils reveled in the knowledge that the master stroke he had so long prepared was set in motion at last.

In full armor, Mancdaman Zorachus strode down the pillar-lined avenue towards Banipal Khezach, sword in hand. With all his heart and will he impelled himself forward, perfectly in control, without illusions about the task at hand.

He was full of power. He could feel it. Hate and rage had spurred a ferocious generation of power and the Influences were with him to an incredible degree. So many spells were open to him, some without force-letting—he had already used one such formula back at the palace, summoning a demon of the Twenty-Seventh Plane. Trafficking with such an entity was strictly forbidden to Sharajnaghim, but he had needed information and had gotten it the only way he could. . . .

A squad of marines rode in through the pillars ahead carry-

ing torches, red light flaring on their helms, spears, and black
scale-mail. Reining up their mounts, they paused, talking in
the middle of the road, unaware at first of Zorachus's approach. But shortly one noticed him and cried out, and the
others wheeled to look.

"Halt!" their captain shouted.

Zorachus paid him no heed.

Lowering their spears they started towards him at a trot.

He stopped at last; raising the sword, he uttered a spell. His
blade glowed sickly yellow-green and a beam shot from its
tip, splitting into several tangents. Screams rang out as they
struck; wrapped in pulsing bilious light, the first marines
dropped their spears and torches, rocking in the saddle, flesh
sloughing from their skulls. As they disintegrated their mounts
went wild, bolting, and the other marines spurred and fled.
Hooves clattered away through the night.

Zorachus continued forward, lowering his blade. It occurred to him that he should already be begging God's forgiveness for using the decay spell. Sharajnaghim learned it
only to devise countermeasures; it was banned even as a last
resort. But that was nothing to him now.

Shouts up ahead—the redclads at the tower's entrance had
seen the green flares and heard the shrieks and were calling to
the riders. As Zorachus came into the glow from the wall-set
torches, two guards were even then rushing to investigate,
blades drawn. They swore when they saw him; he raised his
sword once more, repeated the spell. The bolt licked out,
forking, and they staggered and collapsed in fetid heaps.

Seeing that, their comrades retreated, rushing in through a
postern in the lefthand valve, closing it behind them. Horns
brayed from the windows on either side of the gate and crossbowmen appeared at the openings, silhouetted against the
lights within, priming their weapons.

Sprinting for the great doors, Zorachus reached them before the arbalesters could loose. He pressed his back against
the knobbed steel, out of eye (and crossbow) shot from the
window, safe for the moment.

Slinging sweat from his eyes, he cried a powerful conjur-
ing spell. Black smoke gushed up from the roadway. Out of it,
a squat, humanoid form, barely four feet tall, faceless and
heavily armored, materialized on the roadway. Quarrels
bounced off it harmlessly.

Zorachus gave a mental command and the demon streaked

to the postern, pounding its maul like fists against the steel.
Within seconds the postern gave way and crossbow bolts
hummed through the gap, shattering on the squat monstrosity,
which now stood motionless, awaiting Zorachus's next order.
Receiving it, the demon sprang through the entrance. Zorachus heard weapons clanging against the demon's armor, a
barrage of shrieks, ripping and wrenching sounds—then silence.

He went to the postern and entered. Inside, the ashen light
of the bas-reliefs bathed a floor littered with dismembered
bodies. Apparently, no redclads had escaped. Even the stairways leading to the windows were choked with mangled dead.
Standing statue-like near Zorachus, the demon was covered
with ruby gore.

The hall echoed with approaching shouts and footbeats. A
crowd of acolytes and redclads was rushing towards him; he
dispatched the demon to deal with them. It did not take long.

Zorachus ran up the corridor and down the side passage
where Kletus's lift was located, sending the demon on ahead
to take care of the guards at the lift door. The demon vanished
as Zorachus arrived—the spell that had conjured it was short-
lived and unrepeatable.

Zorachus entered, thinking the lift demon's name, which
he had learned from the being he had summoned back at the
palace; the car rose. Cutting his thumb with his sword, he
wrote the name on the wall in blood, When the car halted, he
added the Black Malgronese word for "stay," to hold the lift in
place and bar Kletus's quarters to all reinforcements for an
hour at least.

He stepped out in the corridor that led to the sorcery-proof
chamber. Two guards shouted at the far end, clapping hands
to hilts.

Rings blasting, he rushed forward. With bone-splintering
force the redclads hurtled back against the walls on either side
of the door, then slid floorward, mail-scales rasping down the
stone blocks.

He reached the threshold, looked in. Ten redclads rushed
up onto the floor's low crown and halted. Thulusu was among
them, steel hand gleaming.

"Come in, Lord Mancdaman," the huge black called, voice
echoing hollowly.

Zorachus grabbed a longsword from one of the corpses and
entered the room slowly, holding the great brand high in his

left hand, the shortsword low in his right.

"At last you've decided to pay us a visit," Thulusu continued almost cheerfully, thoughts of betraying Kletus already filtering through his mind, all his doubts about Zorachus now dispelled; only a man driven by pure bloodlust would hurl himself alone against the full might of Banipal Khezach. . . .

Zorachus walked silently up the slant.

"I think, however, before you come any further, that you should stop and parley—"

Zorachus had come close enough for the black to see the implacable glint in his eyes; all thought of treason left the redclad captain.

"At him!" he cried, and they all swarmed down, drawing their swords, steel flashing bitterly.

Zorachus roared in answer—the sound alone, a deafening promise of annihilation, almost pounding them to a standstill.

Charging up on the left, he avoided the bulk of them, but two still blocked his path; veering toward the outermost, he ducked a stroke whistling at his head and lunged with his shortsword, punching the point through red scale-mail, driving six inches of steel into the man's chest.

The other redclad rushed in, but before his blow could fall Zorachus slashed his hands off with the longsword. The redclad's glaive clanged to the floor, hands still locked around the hilt. The man screamed and rolled down the slant.

Thulusu and another redclad sped to take his place. Zorachus's shortsword was still buried in the man he had stabbed; whirling the corpse around, he hurled it off the point, into their path, and all three tumbled down toward the door.

He ran crabwise to the top. A redclad pelted up at him, sword held high. Zorachus jerked back from the descending stroke, felt its wind on his cheek. His opponent lifted his brand once more; Zorachus shoved his longsword into the hollow of the redclad's throat and the man toppled backward like a falling tree.

A redclad charged up on the left and dealt Zorachus a glancing blow on the helmet. The Sharajnaghi answered by slamming his shortsword into the redclad's side, feeling savage satisfaction as his arm vibrated with the shock of hilt against scale-mail. He tugged; air hissed from the punctured lung, following the blade from the wound. Blood frothed in the hole, a crimson lather of it sliding down the redclad's body as he collapsed, face almost comical with amazement.

Footbeats clattered behind Zorachus from the right. Looping the longsword so that it pointed backward, he dropped to one knee. Two brands hissed inches above his head; driving the longsword into the man behind, he twisted around and sent his other weapon chugging thirstily into the redclad on the right. Disengaging both blades, he leaped up, bounded over the stroke of a redclad before him, and clove the man's head.

He now stood alone on the bulge. A redclad waited off to the left, watching him tensely. Thulusu was over by the door. A third man, standing close to the black, began a dash from the room.

Thulusu's steel whirled. Screeching through the neck guard of the fellow's helmet, it sheared off his head just above the jaw. The black pointed to his remaining man.

"I'll give you the same if you run!" he bellowed.

Zorachus laughed. "You won't get the chance!" he cried. "You're both *mine!*"

"Come on!" Thulusu cried, and both redclads hammered up the slant.

Zorachus paid no attention to Thulusu, but wheeling, sped toward the other man. The redclad proved faster than he expected. Zorachus parried with his longsword, but his single-handed grip was no match for that two-handed sweep, and the curving hilt was wrenched from his grasp and the blade bounced across the floor. He lunged with the shortsword; the redclad parried and the Sharajnaghi's weapon shattered, jagged shards flying.

He almost opted for his pommel-mace then and there, but heard Thulusu hard upon him and dashed to the right toward a fallen sword, both redclads following. He nearly reached the hilt, but slipped on a patch of blood-spattered floor, rolling down the slant five feet past the brand. Battling to his knees, Zorachus reversed his grip on the shortsword's hilt, springing the pommel catch. Thulusu's lackey was nearest him, closing in, sword gleaming. Zorachus hurled himself to the side of the descending blade and swung his arm; shooting out on its chain, the pommel wrapped around the redclad's leg just under the knee. Zorachus pulled and the man went down, fingers flying open as he struck the floor, sword bouncing from his grasp. Zorachus dropped the hilt shard and grabbed up the longsword with both hands, just as Thulusu launched a terrific stroke at his head. Zorachus managed to parry, even though the impact knocked him on his side. Thulusu recovered and slashed downward. Zorachus rolled away. The sword bit the floor in a puff of sparks and powdered stone.

The Sharajnaghi leaped to his feet. He and Thulusu traded a half-dozen clanging blows. Zorachus took a shallow cut across the chin, bashed a dent in Thulusu's helm. Thulusu flashed a white grimace, blood streaming down his face, red on ebony.

The other redclad, having freed his leg and snatched a fallen brand, stormed into the fight. Zorachus retreated, setting his back to the wall. Longsword whirling in a flashing triple-butterfly stroke, he defended himself flawlessly, watching for an opening.

Thulusu's man faltered, pausing in mid-return. Zorachus charged forward on the man's free side, slashing him across the chest, cleaving heart and lungs. Mail plates flying, the man spun to the floor trailing a bright crimson spiral.

Thulusu leaped over the corpse. Zorachus turned to face him. Grunting as their blades connected, spittle bursting from their lips, they jolted back and forth, the chamber ringing like a stricken bell about them. Thulusu gashed Zorachus's arm; Zorachus replied with a stroke that reft the hem of Thulusu's scale-mail, ripping his left thigh. That was the deeper wound; soon Thulusu's trouser leg was shiny with blood, and his movements, still swift, grew clumsy. The sliced limb sagging beneath him. After one savage parry, he staggered and nearly fell, leaving his right shoulder wide open as he fought for balance. . . .

Zorachus's sword sang down, shearing mail, severing the black's right arm. Still holding his blade with his remaining hand, Thulusu stumbled backwards, mouth flung open in an ear-splitting roar. The roar gave way to a string of garbled oaths; Zorachus thought Thulusu was cursing him, but the black's anger was at himself. He had had all the time in the world to switch allegiance, and now. . . .

Zorachus followed. Thulusu raised his brand for a last stroke; Zorachus chopped his remaining arm off, and laughing wildly, completed the terrible Cohort Ravener drill—slicing off Thulusu's goggling head, shearing his torso through the shortribs, severing his legs between hip and knee.

Zorachus grabbed up the head by one of the helmet horns. Still conscious, Thulusu stared at him, mouth working; it looked strangely as if he were almost trying to apologize.

Spitting full into his eyes, Zorachus laughed and hurled the
head against a wall.

He went to the entrance of Kletus's chambers. Before him,
the vast banquet hall was empty. It occurred to him that he
might have time to discard his armor—now that he was past
the sorcery-proof chamber there was less need for it, and
while it was useful against force-bolts, the presence of so
much iron could interfere disastrously with the casting of
higher-level spells. But the Influences were so strongly in his
favor that he guessed he should risk leaving it on.

"Kletus!" he cried.

Echoes ran and faded.

"Kletus!"

He strode forward.

"Kletus!"

At that, the High Priest emerged unhurriedly from a doorway on the far side, left shield up, and came some distance
out onto the floor before stopping.

"Fool!" he cried. "I'm here. But not alone."

He signaled. Sathaswenthar and Lysthragon appeared,
right shields raised, and planted themselves on either side of
him.

"You're in *my* universe, Zorachus!" Kletus roared. "You're
one of my fancies, my whims. And I've grown tired of you."

Zorachus said nothing. He halted, flinging the sword away.

Each priest assumed a different stance. Entering a Dragon
Stance, Zorachus started to mutter a prayer—then caught
himself.

Kletus shouted. Multihued fire burst from his free hand.
Lysthragon and Sathaswenthar joined in instantly; pillars and
ceiling flashed with reflected color. Strike after strike hurtled
against Zorachus's defenses. Purple spirals and keening yellow rectangles exploded on his shield in puffs of flame.
Venomous, green snakelike bolts coiled on impact, shattered
in emerald splinters.

He felt his foremost shield weakening; soon it winked out.
The Priests doubled the intensity of their strikes. Knowing he
must reduce the odds, Zorachus launched several bolts, just
enough to drain his repellent forces, and uttered a spell.

The floor under Lysthragon revolved suddenly. But he
reacted with astounding speed, trying to whirl back into position. Zorachus launched a demon-bolt; most of it was de-

flected by the Priest's shield, the rest burning a trench across his shoulders, setting his hair and robes ablaze. Shrieking, he dived to the floor, rolling to extinguish his robes and slapping at his burning locks.

A fresh spate of strikes from the other priests kept Zorachus from finishing him; reforming his first shield, he tried the revolving spell against Kletus, but the High Priest second-guessed him and had already started a counter spell. He spun halfway around before stopping, protecting himself with his shield. Even so, his bolts were momentarily cut off.

Zorachus turned his attention to Sathaswenthar, dropping both shields. One of the priest's serpent-bolts struck him full in the chest, knocking him back several paces. But most of the brunt was absorbed by his mail and padding, and he snapped back into stance, lashing out with the most potent strikes at his command—twin bluish beams shattered Sathaswenthar's shield as though it were the thinnest glass. The priest catapulted to the floor; dazed and groaning, he began switching uncontrollably back and forth between his male and female forms.

By that time Kletus had recovered, but Zorachus had already recalled his left-hand shield, and so staved off the High Priest's onslaught, further confusing him by switching to a Griffin Stance. Dividing his concentration between defense and a binding spell, Zorachus stretched out his right hand, pointing at Sathaswentha-Sathaswenthar, lifting the protean body off the floor. He spread his middle and fourth fingers; a crimson fissure burst open in the creature's face, splitting it from crown to chin, and the black robes ripped below; torrents of blood splashed the variegated floor. Wrenched apart, Sathaswentha and Sathaswenthar, two dripping human flanks, hung quivering in midair. Zorachus hurled them both at Kletus, bowling him sideways.

There came a wild giggling from behind the High Priest; Lysthragon rushed up protected by a single shield, grey smoke curling from his shoulders, hair burnt away. He snatched at his purse, lowered his shield for an instant, and hurled the pouch at Zorachus. Its mouth widened, a ravenous black cavity, an ever-expanding window into nothingness.

Zorachus muttered a quick formula. The hole was almost upon him when a huge, crimson-glowing mouth, round and fanged, yawned above it, plunged swiftly, and swallowed the smaller hole. The red jaws closed, vanishing in the process.

Lysthragon screeched hideously, looking for all the world like a scorched, mad baby stamping the floor. Riddled by insanities of his own devising, pierced through with searing pain, dismayed by the loss of the purse, his mind snapped; as if Zorachus were a doting parent who might be cowed by a tantrum, the midget plunged forward, pouring out mispronounced obscenities.

The red mouth opened above him. Seeing its reflection on the floor, he tried to dodge; descending, it followed, engulfed him shield and all. His screams echoed hollowly for an instant inside the invisible throat; then the jaws closed, and the cries were cut off. Zorachus wondered if the Priest was happy to be reunited with his purse.

The mouth blossomed redly once more, and Zorachus turned it on Kletus, who was even then struggling to his feet, one shield up, shaking his head, still untangling himself from the ruin of his androgynous lackey. The High Priest saw the crimson maw sweep in and conjured a yard-long scorpion; as the mouth descended, the scorpion shuttled up his body, crawling into the red-lit shaft, sting flicking. The mouth jerked upward, trailing a long agonized hiss. The jaws snapped shut for the final time.

Zorachus and Kletus assumed their original stances and the fight roared on. Bolt after bolt keened through the air, exploded on shields or rebounded wildly. Struck veneer cracked and shattered, spitting splinters of jade. Light globes vanished in flurries of glass shards. The floor quaked and dust poured from the ceiling. Shields buckled; new ones rose. Counterspell followed spell, and the wizards bellowed and shrieked, dodging violently, avoiding green and blue-lit portals that yawned to receive them. Demons appeared and joined furious battle; soon whole companies of them were brought into play, clashing phalanxes of talons, whips, and lances. Chitinous claws ripped armor and fragments of studded plate whirled and flew; slathering fangs tore rubbery flesh. Noisome vapors, yellow and purple and green, swirled above the struggling bodies. Zorachus's rings flamed, bolts converging on winged monsters and splitting them open in mushrooming blasts. The hall reverberated with shrieks and rattling cries, the sound of struck armor, and the hammer of scaled feet on stone. Demon swordsmen towered over the chaos, mailed in rime that was harder than steel, hacking at each other with adamantine blades, slashing off limbs in spatters of frigid steam. The wizards fought as none before, the Influences with them both, freeing unguessed depths of power; the more they battled, the more strength they seemed to have. Zorachus's fury spurred him on to greater and greater feats; Kletus met every challenge, counterattacking with impossible force and skill, knowing he was invincible, the Chosen of Tchernobog, certain Zorachus would be destroyed. . . .

But it could not go on forever, and finally the turning point came.

Kletus began to weaken. Zorachus's monstrous legions closed in, ripping through their opponents in a storm of blood and riven armor.

Kletus moved back. His last demons went down. Even before they blinked back to their own planes, Zorachus's horrors trampled them underfoot, crunching shells and bone. Kletus's universe was in its death throes. His mind reeled with fear and despair. He knew now that Tchernobog had lied to him; Zorachus could not possibly lose. But Kletus also knew that he was the only thing in the universe, and now even he was slipping away, victim to one of his own dreams. It was all quite insane.

Vain bolts crackled from his hands. There was still defiance amid his terror. A few of the onrushing monsters were pummeled back. A few more plummeted into the portals he opened. The rest crested over him, a seething, bounding wave. . . .

Zorachus banished them with a gesture.

Kletus stood gaping for an instant, blinking stupidly, and before he could restore his shields Zorachus had the immense gratification of blasting him in the stomach with two demonbolts. They would have ripped a normal man apart, but Kletus's belly only showed two small, smoking holes. He staggered, but kept his feet.

Zorachus blasted him again. Kletus toppled backward, oily flames licking from the new wounds, sputtering out as he struck the floor.

Zorachus went up beside him. Pink spittle bursting on his lips, the High Priest tried to form the words of a spell, but his only sound was a thick gargling.

Zorachus started a formula. At the sound of it, Kletus shook his head in horrified disbelief.

Zorachus finished. "Wondering where I learned it?" he

asked. "A demon told me. The same one who told you, as a matter of fact."

Kletus was still gargling, frantically now.

"Counterspell?" Zorachus asked. "Too late. Time to pay for all that gluttony." To avoid showing the effects of his excesses, Kletus had magically compacted his fat into hard square knots, like muscle; the same spell had enabled him to bear the horrific burden.

Zorachus had revoked it.

Kletus pressed his face with his hands, as if he were trying to hold his cheeks in place; defying his efforts, they bulged up through his fingers, pushing his palms back, swelling monstrously.

"Your universe is all mine now," Zorachus said hurriedly, while Kletus could still hear. Then he stepped back.

Bones crackling under the tons of fat, Kletus's whole body was billowing. His robes split; his arms were forced out almost at right angles to his torso. A thickening roll of lard thrust his chin up and back, and his cheeks sagged over his eyes. A puddle of distended, close-cropped scalp widened behind his head. His skin grew steadily more translucent, revealing the pale curds within. It began to burst, snapping back in wrinkled folds, drawing fine webs of blood across the fat. . . .

The white mountain's growth continued unabated for perhaps a minute, then slowed and stopped. Kletus had become a vast glistening mass, splayed obscenely over the floor, without a trace of limbs or head, or any indication it had once been a human being.

At first, Zorachus had watched the metamorphosis with heady exultation. But as it progressed he began to feel the first stirrings of revulsion. It was more than mere horror at the transformation, although that was part of it; he had time to think now, to realize what he had done. The orgy of slaughter was over, his enemies slain; the lust for vengeance that had spurred him on, flinging back his conscience, was sated. Conscience was reasserting itself. By the time Kletus's corpse had swelled to its hideous limit, Zorachus's revulsion had deepened into cold, guilty nausea. The glistening abortion on the floor was his work. Once it had been a man. Now it was a diabolic jest at flesh.

He turned, took several aimless strides. His eyes fell on the halves of Sathaswenthar, male and female. Those bloody flanks had also been human. So had Lysthragon and Thulusu and Chatonha, all the guards and acolytes. He guessed he had butchered well over a hundred people. And while he did not doubt that they deserved death, and hell even more, he also knew it was not his place to take their lives—not when his sole motive was revenge. He was a murderer, steeped in the blood of his fellow men.

You'd be damned now if you'd been killed in the fighting, he told himself; seeing the pit he had so narrowly skirted, he was seized by a kind of spiritual vertigo, which intensified horrendously as he realized he had not skirted the pit at all, that he had hurled himself and not yet checked the plunge, not yet repented. Worse yet was the knowledge that repentance might not be possible; most souls were damned long before their bodies gave out, at the instant they were so mutilated by sin that willing not to sin became impossible. Death for them merely meant the removal of physical distractions, the entry into unalloyed spiritual torment. He knew he might already be in hell, irrevocably. Had he crossed the boundary? He remembered his terrible insight back at the palace, his realization that men were universally, totally corrupt. His whole personality was nothing more than a thin crust over a mire of total depravity. And if that were true, how could he repent?

He dropped to his knees, begging God to show him he was wrong. He prayed madly, ferociously, for succor; but a voice whispered that there was something inside him that would reject any aid he received. He tried to ignore the voice, to remind himself that God could still touch him. *But only if He chose to do so*, the voice insisted. *And when did he ever reward murder with salvation?*

Despair choked off supplication. Without God's help, how could he renounce the trap he had created for himself? He had enjoyed killing Kletus and the others too much. He would never be able to feel remorse for that. He might be shaken by fear, guilt, and nausea, rocked to the core—but not by remorse. The memory of his infernal rapture still thrilled him, singing in the marrow of his bones. Trying to disgust himself by imagining the gruesome details of his revenge, he succeeded only in increasing his relish. Nor was it any use telling himself that Kletus's death and transformation were the very stuff of Tchernobog's mirth; it only strengthened his certainty that Tchernobog was right about human flesh. Seizing on the horror, heresy, and blasphemy of that certainty only made him hate Kletus more; Kletus had convinced him in the first place, exposed the maggots inside Asa, brought the Sharajnaghi's own evil to full fruition. Kletus deserved death. It was proven by the very fact that he had goaded Zorachus to kill him. . . .

Zorachus rose trembling. He could not repent. With frightful, willful, insane clarity he knew he would never be ble to. How could he forgive Kletus for damning him?

Shrieks scraped up through his throat, formed themselves into words, obscene blasphemies. He cursed God for causing it all, even as he told himself that God was not responsible; even though he believed in total depravity, he still could not reject his own guilt, his own responsibility. He knew that blaming God was blasphemy, that he was only maiming his soul further by blaspheming, whereupon he screeched out more blasphemies at the being that allowed him such license.

Stripped raw, his throat began to spray blood into his mouth. He crumpled back to his knees. Through tear-blurred eyes he saw a dagger lying next to Sathaswenthar's female flank. For a moment his mind was all but blotted out by an urge to commit suicide; scrambling like a mad animal, he rushed to the dagger on all fours and drew the blade. With quaking hand he poised it before his heart—

Then let it drop. Suicide was useless. It would only fling him sooner into the realm of pure torment.

Pure torment—his terror increased tenfold as he considered it, a damned soul's only fear. It was better to remain in the body, to numb the soul with its own destruction, numb it completely before all distraction ceased. . . .

That was it, then. *Spiritual* suicide. The swift self-immolation of the will.

He heard whispering and footsteps and looked up. A group of guards and priests was coming towards him; the holding spell in the demon-lift had decayed some minutes before.

He stood. They stopped, but after a few seconds a redclad stepped out from the rest and cried in a trembling voice:

"You've killed them all?"

Drying his tears on his sleeve, swallowing blood and phlegm, Zorachus said: "Yes."

The whispering ceased; an awed hush fell over the group and they kneeled, the guards laying their swords on the floor, hilts towards him.

He strode forward. Reaching the first guard's sword, he bent and picked it up. A frigid calm had descended over his mind. He knew what he must do.

"Rise, all of you," he said.

They obeyed. He signaled to one of the priests.

"My Lord?" the priest asked, coming forward.

"What do you know of the High Priest's duties?"

"Little. But there are books. Shall we fetch them?"

Zorachus nodded. "Be quick about it."

The priests hurried off. Zorachus hefted the sword in his hand, looking at the man it belonged to. The redclad was staring at him with terror and something like adoration.

For no reason whatsoever, Zorachus split the man's head to the chin.

Here ends the first part of the history of the Fall of Manc-daman Zorachus.

The second part is called The Nightmare of God, *and tells of the revelation of Tchernobog's true design, Zorachus's crimes as High Priest, and the perils and exploits of Halfdan, Asa, and Raschid Kestrel in the war which follows.*